CROWNING
OF
MARS

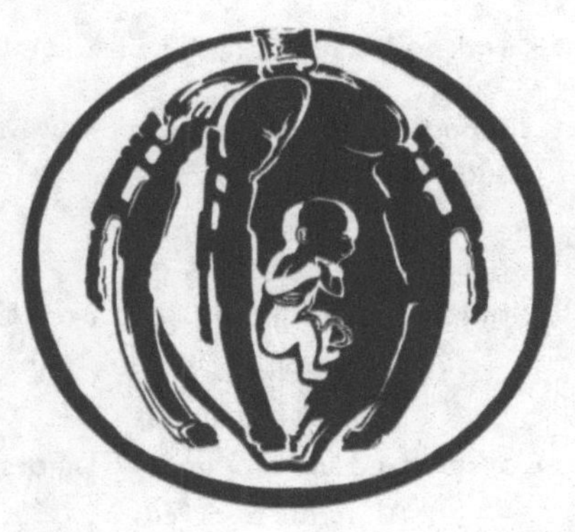

CL FORS

CL Fors

Epitome Press Publishing, Lancaster, CA
An Epitome Press Book
Paperback Edition
Cover Image and Design by CL Fors
All rights reserved.

Copyright © 2016 CL Fors

ISBN: 978-1-943212-31-6

Printed in the United States of America

DEDICATION

Dedicated to everyone who has lost loved ones to the Sars-Cov-2 virus and those who have had their lives cut short by the 2020 pandemic..

ACKNOWLEDGMENTS

In the acknowledgments for my first two books, I mentioned many of the people who influenced my early life, but my third novel wouldn't have made it into the light of day if not for the magnificent people who continue to love and support me. Jason P. Crawford, Angelique Gunnels, Aaron Fors, Alexis Fors, AnnElena Fors, Hannah Fors, Jentina Grey, Jillian Wahlquist; thank you for supporting and encouraging my writing..

TRUST

"Then, trust is something you just don't do….with anyone?" Abby tucked a lock of dripping wet, auburn hair behind one ear, scrunching her forehead in concentration as she struggled to comprehend, and crossing her arms in front of her in rhythmic strokes to keep herself afloat.

Genesis's lips curled in a smirk and she shook her head. "That's not what I said." She ducked under the water resurfacing a few feet farther out, wiping the green-tinged water from her face as she emerged. "What I said was to remain wary. Trust is not the same as blind faith."

"Like mother would have me do." The girl glanced back towards the red domes of the colony in the distance, resentment shining in the dark, mahogany eyes that dominated her pale, freckled face.

Genesis broke into a laugh. "Only, with *her*, you can be certain. She has likely told you to remain skeptical of anything *I* tell you at the very least."

Abby looked away, crimson-brown eyes giving away the validity of her friend's assumption.

Genesis waved a hand as if to dismiss the young girl's chagrin.

"As you should."

Abby cocked her head, a touch of confusion making her blink. "I should be skeptical of you?"

"Are you listening or not?" Genesis raised a brow, allowing herself to bob upward as the back of a wave reached her. "Trust each person to perform within their capacity and to act and react within their mental and emotional constraints."

Abby nodded as the full message became clear, eyes widening before she brought her reaction inward leaving her expression a canvas of neutrality.

Genesis rolled onto her back to float, exposing her bare breasts, algae speckled and chilled, to the warm rays of the sun. "I trust your mother to be on her guard when it comes to our interactions and to assume the worst of my motivations."

"But—" Abby blurted the interruption before she could stop herself and was rewarded with a glare.

"I trust you to keep most of what I say to yourself lest she end our interactions. I also trust that you'll use your intellect and your innate cunning to test what I tell you until you can prove it to yourself."

Abby remained silent, a faint blush burning in her cheeks.

"I also trust that you are learning from these 'lessons' because you and I are alike, you see that, and you thirst for my secrets."

Abby's brows pulled together and she scowled, conflicting thoughts and emotions clamoring for expression. She ducked under the waves, allowing the cold water to envelop her, folding over her shoulders, forehead, scalp, with probing, icy fingers. Focusing on the sensations of the water stinging with cold just as it soothed and caressed, she imagined it cooled her mind, a wall of ice forming inside of her skull to contain the flapping wings of child-like questions, of too many answers too quickly given, a sheet of ice molding across her cheeks, forehead, to befuddle anyone who looked and cloud her looking-glass eyes. She held her breath, opening her eyes to stare through the green water towards the bottom far below. It wasn't visible here, not with the amount of algae that still colored it and left a thin film on her skin each time she emerged. *How long can I stay under? Genesis won't pull me up. Not like mother. Mother would panic.* She stared through the murky water, eyes alert for a shadowy shape, perhaps a pod of them like the last time they'd gone so far out. *Genesis will just watch. What of Richard?* Thoughts of her sibling's caretaker brought a myriad of questions proliferating in her mind, like bacteria propagating under warm conditions, questions she wasn't ready to give voice to.

The burning in her lungs increased, intensified until it became a throbbing that consumed her thoughts and drove her to the surface.

She burst through the water just as a wave was coming in, forcing her to take a quick breath and allow it to pull her under. She went limp, waiting for the release and acknowledging the faint surge of adrenaline that accompanied the realization that there were large rocks in the near vicinity that would cut deep if the sea should choose to toss her into them.

The wave subsided, releasing her to surface again, this time with enough chance to regain her breath and prepare for the next one. The first sound she heard as she emerged from the water was Genesis's laughter. It had a ringing quality at times that sounded almost joyful, as if amusement was what she lived for. *Maybe she does.* The thought was without judgement, a pure observation in a steadied mind.

Abby grinned over at her companion. "Guess… I'd better be more wary of the waves."

Genesis smiled back in approval, the laughter having tapered off, leaving behind a glow to her yellow-gold eyes and a flush to tawny cheeks. "Better still, don't underestimate your allies or your enemies."

Abby laughed then. "Everything is a lesson."

Genesis grew serious, her face losing all signs of the previous mirth. "Always, Abby. I am the only one who can apprentice you. I take that seriously."

The girl bit her lip, rubbing it between her teeth as a wolf-cub might a scrap of meat. "But what—what if I don't want to learn your trade—or I'm no good at it?"

Genesis sighed. "I don't have one, Abby, or more accurately, I could have any." She turned in the water beginning the long swim back with smooth forward strokes. There was no need to look back, Abby would follow. "But if you want that freedom…you need to learn what I can teach you."

The shore was far off, the swim back easier with the aid of the waves pushing them as if struggling with each shove to evict them from the Martian sea in favor of the new life taking hold there.

Donovan stood waiting for their return, red sand clinging to his feet and ankles, an anxious grin pulling at the corners of his long mouth, over-large in a narrow face. "Did you see them again?"

Abby's eyes widened and she froze. Mind filling with a dense fog that numbed her, burying the link from thought to tongue. After what felt like several long minutes, stretched and distorted like Dali's melting clocks, she shook her head, pulling streams of rat-tail seaweed from the long tangles of hair that was twisted and clinging around her narrow shoulders and waist. It was something to focus on instead of Donovan and her sudden lack of speech.

Genesis glanced from Abby to Donovan, catching the girl's tharn expression and Donovan's expectant waiting, patient but still with an undercurrent of hurt. She cleared her throat and lit her own eyes with a charming smile. "Not this time."

Abby frowned, a faint downward tilt of lips that barely touched her eyes, resembling more lack of concern than disappointment as Genesis continued, speaking the words she would have said herself.

"We thought so for a moment, when we first went out."

Genesis turned the girl by the shoulders to face her back towards her but with her face away from Donovan as well, aiding in the removal of the clinging strands of sea-life as she chattered on. "Perhaps they were feeling shy, Donovan. Or they're waiting for you to come and visit them." She gave a conciliatory smile, making him blush.

"What, me? I don't swim. Watch them from the cliffs, yes…but I don't go in."

"Why not have a ship fashioned then?"

The planetologist frowned, shoving both hands into his pockets. "We could. We could at that. Just for observation, of course."

"I know you don't want to intrude on them, but this isn't Earth…" She gave a reassuring smile, leaning in just enough to garner a reluctant twitch of lips to match her own. "And if anyone ever harmed them trying to get close, there would be repercussions."

Donovan snorted, the smile turning into a smirk. "Ha! They'd regret it before I could take action. Half tame or not, these aren't the guppies of the sea that fell to mass slaughter on Earth. I've made sure of it."

Abby watched the exchange, eyes flitting between the two adults as she dried herself with a towel leaving behind a smear of green, before pulling on a lightweight blue dress. *A few smiles and choice words and they roll over like Earth dogs.* She watched a moment longer, until it was clear that Genesis had begun the process of disengaging from conversation that seemed to take so very long and, to Abby, was still pointless. Turning to leave she put the briny wind at her back breaking into a trot, her wraith-thin frame leaving behind the barest trace of footprints in the sand with only thirty-percent Earth's gravity to press it down.

✧✧✧

Theresa was where she usually could be found. Back to the door, face to the screen, guiding the construction and deconstruction of color-coded gene sequences with the turn, twist, brush of her hands, manipulating the images as if they were physical entities on the desk before her. Her mahogany eyes lacked the spark of excitement Abby was accustomed to, and her motions were perfunctory.

"And you say I need to work on task-switching." Abby smirked when her mother turned, a startled expression calling to Abby's mind the pictures of Earth creatures she had been studying since before she could remember, that were, as Theresa insisted, a part of their heritage. Only a prey animal could give that look, like the wide-eyed Gerenuk, long-necked and small framed as she and her mother were; such a delicate creature should be Martian. Would be soon enough, if it continued to thrive in the Martian wild as expected. *Not really Gerenuks though with all of the other DNA mixed in.—As we're not entirely humans either.*

The construction of DNA on the screen caught her eye and she stepped up next to her mother, reaching out a hand and giving it a spin, shock widening her own eyes as she turned to Theresa. "This is a predator species and not human? What are you working on?"

Theresa smiled, brushing a still damp tendril of her daughter's hair back from her face. "That was a quick read. I thought you weren't interested in genetics." She faced back to the image, turning it herself and pointing to the label. "This is Donovan's, really. He just wanted me to have a look at it as well, give it a few tweaks. Neither canid nor feline, but a mixture of the two. And a few surprises thrown in as well."

Abby's words flew out ahead of her in her enthusiasm. "When will we have them? Soon? The Gerenuks and the Arcanue are well-established enough aren't they? I see them on every hike, and plenty of ratbits. Practically step on then when I'm running off trail."

"They aren't called ratbits…Euchoreutes Naso Martis. It's an oversized Jerboa," Theresa laughed, eyes shining with pride and excitement of her own. "But soon I think, after testing, he'll start the first generation of these predators and a few others filling specific niches. You should go and ask him if you want to know more specifically, really."

Abby frowned. "You know I don't—well, yeah. I should." She shrugged, giving a half-hearted smile, that was dim in comparison to her previous exuberance and overshadowed by the closed off glint to her eyes like surface light struggling to reach the heavy body of a ship entombed under miles of ocean. *Sometime. When I can without my mouth sealing up and my brain turning to mush. Not when you want me to or when she wants me to.* She turned towards the small bedroom that adjoined their main room.

Theresa frowned, catching the look of hurt hidden under so many layers of avoidance in Abby's eyes. "Sorry. It's just—"

She pushed aside the construction of Feylupe DNA and opened up another.

"You say you're more interested in what Genesis does but the base skill—communication—is painful for you. How does that work?"

Abby stopped, cheeks reddening and eyes flashing. "And are you good at everything you take interest in?"

Theresa paused to consider the question. "Um…well, mostly, yes."

"Like music and singing? You don't sing duets with Kendra on stage, you sing in our room without audience."

Abby's blush of embarrassment spread to Theresa's cheeks. "Okay. Fair enough. But I know it's not my strength. I don't fancy myself a singer and start arranging public showings."

A heavy sigh escaped the girl's lips. "This isn't about my interests, it's about Genesis. If you worry about my aptitude for human relations, why not ask her if I have potential?" The child's chest heaved, vehemence showing in every feature, as her feathered brows pulled down around eyes flashing with distress.

Theresa turned to face her daughter, taking in the agitation in her posture that had seeped into the soft voice, usually so calm and dispassionate. "I'm sorry, Abby. No, I don't have to ask her because you will excel at whatever interest you pursue. I just have concerns about you apprenticing with Genesis. I wonder if she is pushing you to focus on something that is a struggle for you. But we've discussed my concerns and I need to leave it at that."

She stepped closer, reaching out one hand to brush the girl's cheek, still rounder with youth but so much more lean than even just a few months ago. "You may be younger than when I apprenticed, but that was a different time and place, a different girl. Eleven is old enough, and human relations is valuable if it interests you."

Abby's smile was reluctant, the corners of her mouth twitching up before her eyes started to thaw bit by bit. "Okay."

"Maybe I'm just jealous…"

"Oh sure, I take you swimming all the time with me."

"*You* take me?" Theresa put on a perplexed frown.

"Yes, I have to hide your lab coat, so that makes me the one taking us." Abby raised a brow, still grinning and continued on the path she had started to her room. "I need to get this algae off before I'm stuck this way. You said I'd be once, you know—"

The Voice of the security AI cut in, its tone conversational. "Deimos is here to see you. Should I let him in?"

Theresa answered without looking away from the new strand of DNA rotating before her, instead tapping it in several places to split the strand into segments. "Let him in."

The door slid open with a hiss, and Abby waited, arms folded across her sides and face expressionless, as a boy, smaller and visibly younger by a few years walked through. He glanced behind him as if checking for the presence of anyone following and scanned the room to see who was there.

"You swam with my mother, yes?"

Abby nodded, admiring the pale golden eyes and full lips. *What had she said? She breeds true…* His skin was close in color to his eyes with more of a sandy hue and his hair, black like Genesis's but curly while hers was straight. "I left her speaking with Donovan. Finishing up."

The smile on his face faltered, leaving behind a disappointed scowl. "She'll come and get me then. Can I stay and help till then, Theresa?

Abby's mother gave a slow nod without breaking her concentration. I'm inserting gene packets into this sequence to heighten certain traits in the animal.

"Packets…" Deimos leaned in to examine the DNA being constructed eyes alight with curiosity.

"Yes, it's a technique I learned on Earth. DNA taken from a number of sources is combined in advance to make what we call a traits packet. We keep them on file, hundreds of them and then they can be inserted into whatever Genetic code we are working on to introduce desired traits." Theresa pulled up the previous gene strand. "You see this one here?"

Abby moved closer, shower forgotten for the moment as she narrowed her eyes at the floating DNA sequence. Deimos stared as well, nodding in affirmation.

"This is a packet used to instill a social trait into the animal. This is Donovan's Feylupe and he wants it to have a strong pack instinct like an Earth wolf. Instead of manipulating the DNA from ground zero we insert the packet."

Abby cocked her head, licking her lips as pieces fell into place in her mind. "Doesn't that give you less control of the outcome though?"

Theresa smiled in her direction. "Yes and no. Many of these packets I created myself and others were passed on to me by other genetic engineers in the AUC program on Earth." She shrugged. "The small amount of control I sacrifice is worth the decrease in time required to reinvent the wheel as it were." The smile grew into a smirk. "Not interested, huh?"

Abby smiled back. "Interested in learning—not doing."

Deimos reached out a tentative hand to rotate the strand of the Feylupe. "We need to just trade mothers for a week, Abby."

Abby shook her head, laughing as she turned back towards her room, the anticipated luxury of hot water calling her back to her previous path. "Sure, you go ahead and convince my mother and I'll convince yours."

The lights were dim, a chill breeze, salty from blowing in across the sea, sent eddies of cooler air into the warm interior of Genesis's room. Red dominated, red-ochre stone, blond-hued satin bedding on the firm pallet recessed into the wall, crimson drapes that drifted. The only other color that appeared in significant amount gave sharp contrast to the powerful display of dominance; the waving green of lettuces, hanging berries just ripening from deep green to a dark magenta, and other edibles all growing from wall mounted hydroponic chambers placed in concentric circles on the wall.

Genesis reached out to pluck a small handful of the riper berries offered up by the nearest plant, dropping them one by one into her mouth and crushing them against her tongue. The movement was performed in casual distraction as she stared at the large viewing screen that dominated the curve of wall behind her stone desk, still she savored them, licking the juice from her lips with a faint smile. The small figure on the screen before her laughed, raising both brows in delight as his face lit up with the fire of excitement, new knowledge—*acquisition.*

She laughed with him, falling back to the repetitive task of brushing the tangles and clinging strands of rat-tail seaweed from her long ebony hair. Pride glowed in the golden eyes that matched the boy-child's as she watched him interact with such comfort and ease, blending in without effort. Even David had ceased to worry, letting go of the concerns—*well-founded*—that she would ruin the child somehow. *Perhaps I would have. No, that isn't accurate. Never, me.*

The memories flooded her as they often did when she unlocked the closely guarded door that held them, tucked away like laundry folded in tight, neat bundles in military fashion. Tucked away as if forgotten along with so many other things best kept buried. Only this set of memories was still important, still shifting and altering itself in a screen of shimmering color-change as it worked to fit into the bigger picture that made up her self-image.

The troubling undercurrent of those times rose up with the same strength as when she lived it, the long months of metamorphosis and instability, the nightmares that came with growing frequency until they dominated her experience waking and sleeping, and then the breaking point. She shivered, flinching back from the precipice over which the story lurked like Martian whales schooling in deep night waters.

She sat back, staring into the mirror that filled the other half of the viewing screen, and a memory stared back. Her eyes were haunted, dark with shadows and bruised lids, leaking tears that came with no purpose, and flowed with each wave of terror that coursed through her like many thousand tiny hands with daggers for fingertips, stabbing the inner walls of her veins and arteries and setting her nerves afire. Her memories' own hand flew to cover the swollen bulge of her lower abdomen, hand pressing hard as if to stop the flutterings within. *Just stop moving.* Another flurry of motion made her flinch, such light flittings of movement and yet they could not be ignored or even tolerated. Another wave of nausea was coming, not like in the early months, but the sort that came from motion sickness combined with the creeping, itching feeling of something—*someone*—tap-tap-tapping inside without cease.

And there it was again—that flash—was it memory? Nightmare, or flashback—just an image but so vivid, teeth, fangs really, tearing into that rounded flesh, translucent and swollen, and snapping at what hid within, lapping it up and swallowing with bloodied teeth and grinning tongue, savoring the salty wetness of it. Just an image, a split second that sent her senses reeling and left her breathless and doubled over with both hands over belly and head hanging between knees as the disorientation subsided slowly.

They were whispering in the other room, barely audible concerns exchanged and breaking through her internal struggle for stability.

"I'm beyond being worried now, Carla…she is handling this."

There was a shuffle of feet, a pause. "You don't need to tell me that. She's hiding like a hibernating animal, she's suffering—but I can't help if she won't let me. I can't—won't force help on her. She needs to ask for it."

The sigh that followed was louder than the words had been. "She's not gonna do that though, is she?"

Another pause.

"I don't know…stopped seeing Theresa again, won't see me to talk either. She's only letting us monitor with her implant so we know the child is well and kicking."

Genesis winced, clenching both fists and pressing them against her forehead as she broke into sweat, beads of moisture dusting her skin in a shimmering layer that brought on a shiver. *Snap out of it!*

She squeezed her eyes shut, listening to that sharp inner voice. The one that held such strength and authority, the one with poison glands full to bursting that now dripped into the pockets of uncertainty inside her instead of being reserved for others outside of her own struggling mind. *They speak of you like an invalid, a failure…*It moved again, that fluttering, squirming thing, rolling over itself and brushing against her insides as if it had several limbs instead of just four.

Genesis's hands pressed against the flesh that it moved beneath, fingers clenching there, nails biting skin. The movements ceased as if *he* had become aware of what transpired outside of the watery living-coccoon that housed him.

She took a breath, inhaling the stillness that calmed and soothed despite the raw, stinging, pain beneath her palms. Her hands were wet, and sticky as was her skin. Confusion knitted her black winged brows and she looked down, spreading her hands in front of her to reveal the source of pain in her abdomen. There was blood there, blood and four shallow scrapes the width of her tapered fingernails as if some wild animal had attempted to disembowel her without enough reach to cut deep and spill the steaming contents of her abdominal cavity onto the red-earthen floors.

Her mouth fell open, eyes staring between wounded flesh and bloodied hands. Standing with movements that were too abrupt to convey the usual self-assured gait she pulled on her silken robe and strode into the next room from which the whispers had come.

Carla looked up, eyes soft with concern as she took her in. Genesis stopped, burning shame lighting her eyes and cutting her movements short as she looked from one concerned face to the other. David's dark eyes were conflicted, swimming with worry, fear, bravado—all commingled together as he struggled not to be the open book that he was. A spark of irritation ignited in her breast at the sight of his uncertainty, his fear of angering her.

There wasn't much that she could grab hold of to keep mental equilibrium, but this was enough. Placing a smooth smile onto her full lips, she pulled aside the edge of her robe to reveal the bleeding wounds beneath. David startled, reaching for her, a look of horror claiming his full expression. To their right, Carla gasped. It was a small sound, as if only a portion of the alarm she felt had escaped into the room before she closed her lips tight around it.

Genesis placed a hand on David's cheek, hand tingling at the intimate contact with his close-cropped beard. "Shhhhhh…this is a good thing. It's what I needed."

He tried to break in, dismay clouding his eyes as he blurted the beginning of an incoherent rebuttal.

She raised a brow. "You need to trust me. I'm going to speak with Theresa, and…" She glanced over at the youthful old woman, smooth skin and silver braids in sharp contrast to each other, who stood witnessing their exchange of words. "And Carla…If you have the time now?" The certainty in her voice wavered just enough to lend an air of vulnerability to her request.

The midwife nodded, patting David on the shoulder before turning towards the door. "I do and I will, right now even. We'll pull Theresa away from whatever busies her for the rest of the day—she'll be excited to see you again from all the worrying and bitching she's been engaging in on your account."

Genesis laughed, keeping it quiet and low to mask the edge of hysteria that had crept in of late on silent sharp-toed feet. She followed close behind, giving a quick wave to David as the door closed behind them.

Genesis looked up at the glowing screen that held the child that so resembled her with skin the warm brown of wheat fields at dusk and eyes a golden yellow that mirrored her own. He pulled her back to the present with his flashing grin and features that resembled her own to such a high degree that it inspired twinges of cognitive dissonance. It was so long ago and still she remembered it like it had only been a handful of days.

Deimos laughed in delight, gesturing to the spinning double helix that he and Theresa manipulated with their hands, pointing and discussing the genetic make-up of the creature it represented. Grasping the virtual representation of a gene sequence beginning with the universal genetic signal for a gene sequence to begin, TATA, he separated and enlarged it, squinting to focus as he read the sequence.

"This one is sex-linked, isn't it?!…" His eyes widened as the realization dawned.

Theresa's smirk was filled with approval. "Well, yes. And dominant as well. We gave it a bit of a push to increase heritability."

Genesis raised a brow. *He blends so well—no sign of Abby's reticence, but too open…like David.*

She dropped the brush, forgotten in one hand, into a drawer of her desk and with swift, fluid movements pulled on the one piece red jumpsuit that she favored for socializing.

Theresa's Lab—Pre Martian Adaptation

"We're not going to do this the way we did it before." Genesis's voice held no force of conviction, no intensity of emotion. It was a means of delivering simple fact.

If her eyes had been closed and she hadn't known her so long, Theresa might have mistaken it for one of the simulated voices used by security AI in the colony. The scientist's eyes flicked down to take in Genesis's hands holding the robe she wore closed around her. The nails were stained, smeared with dried rust from the wounds she had opened up in the skin of her taut, rounded belly.

Theresa frowned, working to keep her voice and expressions calm. "Okay, what do you mean in particular. I had no intention of using the sedative I used before. The effects on the unborn may be subtle but we don't want to adversely affect his developing brain. It wouldn't do anything so grand as to give him flippers but could alter the developing neural matrix and neurotransmitter receptivity—"

Genesis lifted a hand. "I'm well aware of the effects of sedatives on a developing fetus. What I meant was the actual procedure. You won't be climbing into my head and moving things around to suit your picture of a functional mind. Not this time."

Carla shifted her legs on the smooth, warm floor, switching which leg was leading in her butterfly stretch, eyes wide and receptive, pulling in just a bit at the corners as she took in the conversation. Theresa stood and walked to her desk, removing equipment from drawers and arranging them on the surface before her, channeling nervous energy into her motions.

Carla cocked her head to the side, the humor in her eyes safely contained. "Is this going to end with your racks tangled like two mule deer in mating season?"

Theresa flicked an irritated glance at Carla before focusing the full force of her scowl on Genesis. "If you don't consent to my help then why are you here?" Theresa seemed calm enough, but the irritation was there along with confusion. The relief she had felt when she got Carla's message that Genesis was asking for help was already beginning to dissipate in the face of reality.

"I'm here because you and Carla have what I need—the equipment, the knowledge." Genesis walked over to the equipment set out on the table and lifted the helmet up to examine between both hands. She brushed a finger over the power sensor, flinching when it lit up, trails of blue racing across the translucent surface. "How many of these do you have?"

Theresa bit back a sharp reply, closing her eyes and clenching her fingers lest she snatch the helmet back. She wet her lips and reached out with slow, precise movements.

"I don't like my equipment handled—randomly, without permission or purpose. Or turned on without good cause." She placed the equipment in question back on the table ignoring Genesis's smirk, as well as the obvious amusement that played in her yellow cat eyes.

Genesis shrugged. "I guess you wouldn't…"

"I have five of them. More than enough. But I don't see why you ask—"

Genesis just stared, the smirk having faded into a weariness and something akin to the expression a person might wear on a tossing sea when they have yet to gain their sea-legs. She placed a hand on the table, in an attempt to look casual, hiding the queasy expression too late.

Theresa removed another helmet from a cabinet recessed into the stone wall, accessing it by way of retinal scan and voice recognition. She placed the device on the table and turned to retrieve another. Her eyes were shining with excitement when she faced Genesis again. "Unless you intend to allow more than one person access to your top-security mind today—that's what you have in mind, isn't it?" Her thoughts were racing, excitement lighting them afire as the possibilities played on the electrified landscape of her scientist's brain. "But there's only myself and Carla here. Who else did you have in mind?"

Genesis lifted a helmet and placed it on her own head before Theresa could protest again. "Not someone else, myself. As I said. You won't be going into my mind and doing as you see fit. You'll have a chaperone this time."

Theresa's features twisted in confusion. She stared at Genesis, searching for any sign of jest or psychosis. The woman's brow was sweaty, darkness ringing her eyes as if sleep had not come to her since the pregnancy began, but she looked serious and certainly more stable than she had been when she dug nails into the flesh of her own abdomen like a wild animal. "Okaaaay…I really don't think you can maintain functional presence of mind while under the influence of the device. How do you expect to be in receptive and active brain states simultaneously? Because I just don't think—
"

Genesis was already reclining on a workbench. She raised a brow at Theresa. "It will work. Trust me. Now, can we start before this thing wakes up and begins clawing at my insides again?"

Carla shrugged and reached for a helmet, placing it on as she had seen Genesis do a moment before.

NEW ADDITIONS

The glowing holographic schematic filled the space in front of Neil, scaled down to his own height so that he could see and manipulate the 3D blueprint easily.

The Pinnacle resembled an old Earth cruise ship stretched to an elegant, pointed prow with a wide berth. Here represented in its original form with glowing blue, the additions, repairs, and alterations superimposed in red.

Neil brought his attention to the prow, dominated by a large viewing window through which passengers could experience the starry backdrop of space. The original window, outlined in blue, was heavily overlayed in red where changes were made. It was smaller now and reinforced by stronger multilayered transparent surfaces, framed on either side with physical and electromagnetic shields.

The view of a terraformed Mars through those same windows on their first approach appeared in his mind's eye. It was luminous against the void of space, black and muddy greens along with the iconic rusty orange of history books and the swirling white of cloud cover.

A deep ache bloomed to life at the memory and the answering smile and shake of head was wistful. *Nothing to be done for it though. Longing for dead times and ghosts.*

Stretching out both hands, Neil rotated the ship, altering a setting to zoom in on the large central areas previously reserved for boarding passengers. The rear of the ship met with a wide ring with spokes like a wheel to contain the solar sails.

"Make a final count of artillery storage and launch systems…" He spoke the command under his breath counting on the VR headset to pick it up.

A soft moan came from the darker side of the room where Kendra and the children slept. Neil glanced over to where she was curled up around little Jasrie. The quality of her breathing had changed, and this was the third such moan in the last half hour since he left the bed to work.

A soft smile pulled at the corners of his mouth before he turned back to the schematic. Kendra didn't like him to say it out loud but he knew it would be soon. *Maybe tonight.*

The numbers appeared superimposed over the schematic. It was twice what the ship boasted before repairs and remodeling since the attack. *Since the attack…*

Neil's jaw clenched and he sucked in a breath, letting it out slowly. *Can't afford to lose more sleep tonight.*

But the slow burn of buried embers was still there, anger that had long since become a part of his internal landscape, remained to flavor his thoughts, a subtle undercurrent that fueled the repair and outfitting of a ship they may otherwise have no use for. *Aside from defense…retaliation. Swift retribution, Trina would have called it.* But Trina was long gone, nine years buried after retrieval from the ruined hull of the Pinnacle where she made her stand.

The anger threatened to bubble over and take the forefront but Neil bit it back, closing out the schematic with a swipe of his hand across the hologram before returning to the bed. Kendra was moaning again and the sound held more intensity, sweat beaded on her brow. Still she slept, now disentangled from Jasrie and the boys on their large, multitiered sleeping space.

Neil lifted the oldest boy, Nile, onto the upper bunk, and lay down in the free spot, close enough to reach Kendra should she call out.

Thoughts whirled behind his closed eyelids and he pushed them aside one by one. The ship was ready, as was he, and Kendra would birth soon. Then the countdown would start until he could take the Pinnacle out from the geosynchronous station above Mars where she waited.

There's that singing again. Those large black birds must be at the window again calling for Jasrie to feed them scraps… Maybe jus' singing for you, baby boy… so come on now. A smile lit up her damp, flushed face, rivulets of sweat beading on her forehead and trickling down her cheeks in cool streams. Kendra let her head rest on her shoulder, taking slow even breaths and allowing all but her legs to go limp. Her arms were stretched around Neil's neck, allowing her to hang there in a low-squat on the nest of towels they had made on their bed. The room was quiet, not the sort of quiet one would find in a tomb where steps echo, but the sort that is full of small restful sounds, the breath of four sleeping children, heartbeats and fitful movements as a leg is thrown one way and small arms the other— the sounds of living.

The feeling came again, she knew it so well that she felt it coming on from the first sensations, a warmth that built from the caress of sunshine to the heaviness of quilted blankets left on too long as the day wore long and hot. The intensity built—heat, and a heaviness that spread throughout her womb, pulling upward. A deep moan escaped her as she pulled her lips back to reveal ivory teeth bared but not clenched. She opened her eyes as it grew stronger, filling her senses until the pulling wasn't a part of her but was her. She felt the child move down, her passage expanding around the head that turned and moved lower in response to the pressure from above.

"Ahhhhh…Come on now, yes, baby, come through now." Her words were a low croon, some whispered, some growled with tenderness. Kendra swayed her hips and tipped her ribcage forward as the contraction peaked, the last words coming out guttural and strong.

The heat subsided, slowly releasing the tension of strong uterine muscles. She went still, resting again, with shaking breaths as her awareness shifted. Her thighs shook, trembling as she broke out in a full-body sweat. She opened her eyes, blue and wide as her breath took over, fast and urgent, and she stared around the room, seeking an anchor.

Neil leaned in closer, his lips finding hers, a kiss that was warm with desire, appreciation, affirmation. Her lips clung to his, hot and trembling.

"Coming now, isn't he?"

Kendra grimaced at his words, covering his mouth with her fingertips. "Hush up, then."

She kissed him again, longer this time, lips and tongue delving into his mouth, savoring his warm breath. The kiss ended in a cry as Kendra arched her back, pulling against his neck until the muscles in her arms were taut, back arched as she came up onto her knees. Her abdomen tightened and lifted shining with moisture even in the dim pink lighting that served as a nightlight for the children. She didn't fight the force that came through her, propelling the child downward with such speed that a small corner of herself witnessed the happening with alarm. Still she didn't pull back from it. There was nowhere to escape to, the only path was through the fire, her whole body flushed with heat, and she tipped her head back, even as her uterus pulled her ribcage forward and heaved, tightening and releasing again and again.

Kendra pulled in a breath; she had been withholding it, and opened her eyes wide, flicking them down as she reached one hand between her thighs to feel the small round head, wet and rumpled with dark, curling hair, the scrunched face, that was turned towards her left thigh. Her fingers traced nub of nose and full lips, creased forehead, sticky with layers of vernix.

The heat returned, building faster this time from warmth to inferno, the pressure of the child's body as it turned, rotating shoulders lending an urgency to the sensations that came now. The strong muscle that was her uterus bunched up around what remained inside and heaved. Shoulders emerged, stretching the softened ring of tissue that had transformed from tightly locked gateway to open portal.

Kendra let out a sob, not of grief but triumph, victory, and welcoming as her newest child came forth with a gush of amniotic fluid, legs kicking and arms flailing outward in a startle as she lifted the babe to her chest, cradling the boy-child between herself and the father of her children.

"That's it baby boy…" She stroked the damp curls that grew long and soft, slick against his scalp, and lowered herself onto the ground, turning to press her back against Neil and lean back.

The pale nutmeg-brown infant opened dark grey eyes, and coughed, small gurgling cries expanding his strong lungs as the valves in his heart closed to begin the switch from fetal circulation to that of an air breathing infant.

Kendra tipped her head back to grin at Neil and was met by that look she had come to expect. Four babies and he still cried. Still stared down at her as if she had just birthed his whole world.

"That was perfect, Babe." He shook his head, damp eyes shining with wonderment.

Kendra leaned back against him, sighing, content. She glanced over at the far side of the large pallet, rumpled covers and a tumble of children, still asleep and as yet unaware of the new edition. One set of eyes, a grey-blue with flecks of green and orange stared back from deep-brown cheeks that still held the softness of toddlerhood, Dusky pink lips pulled into a wide grin that revealed fine, straight milk teeth. "We've got a baby again, don't we Mama?"

The girl, tall and mostly arms and legs scrambled over, careful not to jostle sleeping siblings, she leaned over to stare into the baby's round grey eyes.

Kendra grinned at her only girl child, and beckoned her closer.

Jasrie climbed over a mountain of extra covers and onto the free side of her father's lap to lean her face against Kendra's arm and reach a chubby hand to stroke the new addition's small back.

Kendra placed a hand on the girl's head, ruffling the tightly coiled, soft, brown hair that was several shades darker than the honey-brown of her own. "You gonna be a good big sister aren't you, baby girl?"

Jasrie nodded, following the cord with curious eyes. "You have the p'centa yet, mama?"

Kendra shook her head. "Gonna get up in a minute and see if it comes, baby. You're my best little midwife, aren't you?"

Jasrie bounced in her spot, a prideful smile lighting up her eyes. "Um-hm. I'm the best one."

Kendra turned her face up to Neil. "You hold this son of yours and call Emily an I'll see about the placenta. Cuz I'm getting hungry now and the sun looks like it's gonna be peeking around soon enough."

A trilling sound came through the partially open window, as if to agree with Kendra. The bird's song had an echo-like quality that came and went with the deeper notes of it's song, that seemed to echo the tones of the summer wind and on the high notes the sharp operatic quality of a talented soprano.

"Singing for you, baby boy. My Askia Neil."

Emily smiled down at the tiny infant, mottled pink and purple tones to the light brown skin still wet with clinging vernix and amniotic fluid. He was a good size for Mars, just over five pounds. *Lungs still sound a bit wet though.*

She held the one inch diameter sensor over the back of the babe's curled fist, nodding at the numbers that appeared and then placing the blanket back over the partially exposed infant and his mother. Looking up from the measurements and assessments she found Kendra's eyes on hers. A smile passed between them tears in both sets of eyes, and Emily nodded before glancing over to include the Captain. "Completely perfect. Just like he looks. And his lungs are sounding better by the minute, don't you think, Kendra?"

"Mm hmm. If he doesn't clear the rest in a minute I'll tip him over again." She touched the small babe's nose with a fingertip, pride shining in her eyes. "Best take care of it, Askia, or I'll have Daddy dangle y' by those toes." Kendra didn't look away from the tiny rounded face, pert nose and swollen eyes that were now open and staring back at her.

Neil chuckled, placing one large hand against the back of his third son's head with a gentleness that matched the tenderness in his gaze. "Dangle by his toes? You'd have my ass if I dangled a child of yours."

Kendra looked up at her Captain, the affection spilling over into a sigh of deep satisfaction. "You know me ..." She turned back to the child laying across her chest. "Perfect and perfectly last."

Emily laughed. "What, no number five? You did say that after Jasrie as well…"

Kendra nodded, fingertips stroking the soft contours of the tiny new face. "I did and I meant it." She spoke in a high lilting tone, leaning in as if speaking to the babe instead of her fellow midwife. "And then little Askia Neil showed up in my dreams and I had to bring him through."

A little laugh escaped Emily's lips and she averted her eyes for just a moment, smile shaking on her face as if it might peel off but holding its place through some effort on her part. "Dream babies. I can't count how many I'd have if all the ones in my dreams were real."

Kendra reached out a hand and placed it over Emily's, giving it a squeeze. There weren't any words for what passed between them.

Emily drew a breath and with it pulled herself back into the present and into Kendra's moment instead of her own. "I'll go message Gran that all was perfect as always for your births. Welcomed and settled before I even arrived—How do you feel? Bleeding?"

Kendra leaned back against the back of the bed, nestling into the mound of cushions that supported her forming a nest around the three of them. Her voice was sleepy. "Naw, just a little when the afterpains come…" She sucked in a breath, wincing as a stronger after contraction took hold. "No gushing. I'm good…You look at the placenta for me? I'm gonna just let myself sleep a bit."

Askia had found the nipple, and was falling asleep firmly attached, cheek and chin moving in the age-old rhythm of suckling at the breast with long pauses in between as he drifted into dream, lip corners twitching up in dream-smile.

Emily smiled, standing to leave them. Two hours had passed since Askia came rushing his way into the world before the sun was even close to rising, and it looked like both of them were fine to leave. "Can I give you your tea to sip?"

"Mmm Hmm…I'd love some afterbirth tea, cinnamon, Red Martian unicorn berry…" She didn't even open her eyes to answer, as close as she was to sleep.

Emily handed the steaming mug to Neil. "See if she wants a few sips before she nods off."

He took the mug, settling in closer to his wife and infant son, with a salute. "Will do."

"And call me for anything."

Satisfied that they were settled in, Emily left, one last glance at the new colony member. He'd be golden all over like most of his siblings, with that faint cinnamon undertone that Kendra had, hair and eyes included. Except for Jasrie, the only girl of the bunch, like a miniature copy of Kendra but with a deep brown skin-tone like rich soil from the gardens David cultivated and blue-green eyes flecked with orange. *I'll bet Jasrie was squealing when she first saw that baby…just a baby herself, really.*

An image popped up unbidden finding its way to the forefront of her thoughts, as vivid as it had been in the dream. A dark-haired child, narrow of frame and delicate of feature with rose petal lips and a shy smile, freckles… a little boy to tuck his small hand into her own.

In the dream he had tugged her into the Martian desert, begging her to tread lightly with a small, pointed finger across his lips. There were secrets he wanted to show her in the wilderness.

Weaving in and out of the spiny cycads and stepping over patches of lichen brush, he ran ahead to the warm red sand, the patterns of the wind marking the soaring dunes like waves on the sea.

Emily's heart beat faster; she was frightened by the speed at which he moved, the heights he climbed to scurry over the top of black-lichen encrusted boulders. Another emotion warred with the first, stilling her voice before she could caution him or call him back. This child didn't need her fears. He was strong and he had a confidence that filled her with pride.

The child disappeared over the rise of the first dune where the sun was rising. It blinded her a moment, red and golden light coming through the arched window in the empty hall.

The memory dissipated, and with it the child. *Just a dream child…*

Emily shook her head, brows creasing in annoyance. The dream, wiped from her memory by the sudden awakening when

Kendra called this morning, may as well have stayed buried. *No need to dwell on it.*

She blinked, raising a hand to block the harsh light of the sunrise as she continued towards her own room. *Kendra and her dream babies…a sweet thought.* The child's face filled in her mind's eye. *For some, anyway.* She pulled out her handheld to message Carla and found a message from the colony's midwife already waiting.

"Is the littlest of Kendra's brood in arms?"

Emily cocked her head, staring at the words as if there was some magic hidden within them. "Reply."

"Safe and sound, and in arms well before she even called me in. When are you going to teach me that trick, Gran?"

"That's how she likes it, our Kendra. If I'd have stayed home staring at her and watching like I was waiting for bread to rise, she'd have pushed me out the door."

Emily leaned in for the security scan at her door. "You did know…"

"Did, do. Every time. My old womb gets restless and achy, my back starts twinging and I feel it in my hips. If a good hike doesn't work it out I know we have one on the way."

"Huh." She spoke aloud without recording, listening to the faint echo of her voice in the empty room. "Maybe when I've been doing this as long as she has." *Or if I'd ever experienced it myself.*

The thought was a dangerous one, the sort that led to melancholy, to visits into the garden where they were buried under the aspen, grown tall and thick as the children beneath their roots should have been by now.

Her room AI's reply startled her from silent reverie. "Welcome home Emily, and good morning. Would you like the window tint decreased or the lights turned up?"

Her laughing reply was incredulous. "No, I'm going back to sleep. Leave it all off." Passing the entryway into Carla's office and turning into her own room, she tucked the bag of midwifery supplies under her desk next to Jonathan's antique leather bag of

3D print repair tools. The urge struck for her to take them out, to remove them from their entombment one by one, perhaps use them to complete one of the projects that awaited her attention once she was conscious again and capable of work.

It would have to wait; comforting as the ritual was, now was not the time, nor the mood. She stripped down, climbing into the bed and welcoming the fatigue that would fill the lonely corners of her mind where names and faces echoed and reverberated like haunts in a cemetery. Eyes heavy with sleep, she kicked the moccasins off and tucked her feet under the covers, pulling the thin quilt up over her shoulders and bunching it under her chin where the dark sunset purple of the fabric contrasted with the fire orange of her hair. Sleep so close but a moment before hovered just out of reach as a list of tasks for the day began to write itself in her head.

Her new apprentice would be in later, to be trained on some of the nuances of repairing the personal printing units installed in each room in the colony, and then they would travel to the new colony site to see the larger printing drones in action. And then there were several mothers that she planned to check up on. With Carla out and Kendra newly birthed they would all fall to her. She started to doze, sliding in and out of the layers of sleep, errant thoughts intruding and pulling her back to consciousness less and less frequently.

Donovan was expecting her to lunch with him up on the cliffs. A small smile crept onto her face, replacing some of the shadows of fatigue as fleeting images became more vivid and metamorphosed into dream. Dream Donovan pulled at his black braid, a shy smile, a gesture of hand, Arcanue pawed the dirt, scrabbling up into the steeper climbs, startling the Martian cliff rooks that were nesting in the rocky overhangs above the water. *So beautiful up here…the ocean thrashing below on the rocks…*

She tumbled into dream, finding herself chasing after a sand rat with a small hand nestled in hers, pulling her along.

Carla shook her head, a rain of coarse silver waves falling across her bare shoulders. *'Course I always know...* She dropped the handheld onto the nest of woven fabrics, the electronic device clashing with the simplicity of the surroundings. Straight lines of sharp-edged silver with glowing screen contrasting against the soft hand-crafted flaws in deep reds, oranges, and greens of the Martian plant and soil derived pigments of Carla's textiles.

The midwife stood, allowing the blankets to fall away, as she reached into the basket of dried herbs and weaving supplies that sat at the base of the pallet tucked into a depression in the floor of the cave. From it she retrieved a ceramic flask and tipped it back, drinking the contents as she walked towards the small fire that burned several feet away. She shivered, a draft from the tunnels that wound deeper into the mountain finding her bare skin before the fire could warm her. Squatting down before it, she tossed in three more bricks of fuel, a combination of Arcanue dung and lichen grass, tightly packed into the shape of a small log.

The flames licked upward, welcoming the offering, and inviting her fingers in as well. The old woman smiled, allowing the warmth to fill her chilled hands before pulling them back to a safe distance. The firelight glowed on her freckled, sun-blotched skin, still mostly smooth and firm against lean muscles despite the century she lived on Earth and the just over a decade since they'd settled on Mars. *Still needed here, though...Em and Kendra could take up my space...pass on the legacy, help the colony stay the course.* Her still nimble fingers took up the task of braiding the waves of silvery hair that curtained her, lest a draft send it into the flames. Carla, felt a twinge of unease at the thought and looked inward. *They're not ready though...still learning the ways. Or Em, wouldn't have to ask how I feel 'em comin'.* There were too many bits and pieces of knowledge merging to make the picture, so clear she felt it in her own bones, so intimately linked to it that the rush of hormones flooded her as it did the mother herself, the rocky, ovoid moons speeding around Mars, the winds, and the tide—not strong like it was on Earth but she still felt it, the feel of the woman's early signs, not yet clear on their own but, when grounded in years of experience and knowledge, she couldn't not know. Even up here in the West mountains she felt it.

But that isn't all of it, is it now?...

Carla shifted her thoughts outward. *Some change coming...feels as certain as the coming of a child—only less...* Carla pushed, recalling the off expressions, the undercurrent of cold water under a sun warmed surface, reaching for some greater idea of what she felt coming on. *Too many little pieces from too many people to put together. It'll come though.*

Time to go back for now. Em would have to fill the gap all on her own if not and that wasn't fair just yet. Dropping the loose braid behind one shoulder, she rose from the floor with brisk steps over to the wall that held her garments in the wide crevices that seemed to have been fashioned just for such a purpose. *Don't want her thinking she can't take her own time while she's young.*

The birth was well over, but some checking in was in order. Carla grabbed the belt that held the water flask and pemmican, as well as her handheld as she hiked.

No, it wouldn't do to leave her the whole responsibility of being *with woman* in such a large colony. Not if she was to ever consider giving in to her own future. The one she'd come here for and had ripped away.

Lifting a large bowl, printed to resemble wood grain like those carved on Earth when the forests were cleared, she poured a stream of red sand over the small but well-fed fire. She stared into the coals as the flames were smothered out and closed her eyes, allowing the smoke to reach her before she turned away to dress in the one-piece climbing suit and weighted garments that had clothed her on the way up into the West mountains.

The howling of the autumn winds grew louder as she neared the end of the tunnel leading out to the sheer cliff that would begin her climb down. The sound was still low and almost distant so early in the season, but far below, the cloud of red-brown dust that accompanied it each year obscured the domes of the colony from view.

Kneeling down at the edge of the precipice, Carla grabbed the rough rock ledge with both hands and lowered herself down to hang until her toes found the ledge below. Pulling herself to the side, she reached down again. Her hands and bare feet knew the path down by rote, her muscles strong enough to make the climb with quick, sure movements, only breaking into a light sweat by the time she reached the lower, more gradual portion of the climb.

Carla dropped the last ten feet, landing amidst a patch of young palm-like cycads, not much taller than the ferns that grew under the aspens near the base of the mountain. Her sudden presence startled the pollinating beetles that crawled along the tops of the plants, sending them into a buzzing cloud of blue and green iridescence above her head.

The midwife grinned, brushing a wayward arthropod from her hair, before taking up a fast jog back to the colony, the winds strong enough to give the feeling of near flight as she leapt from one outcropping to the next. She startled a lone Arkanue from a nearby ledge, exhilaration flaring up in her heart and lighting her veins afire as she raced the buck. The glossy red and black coat of the oversized Martian goat species shone in the sunlight, his nostrils flaring, eyes wide and frightened from the sudden chase until he veered off to the north and further into the mountains and the midwife continued South-east.

"Maybe…maybe I don't feel comfortable yet. There are so many bits and pieces to put together. Like a thousand pieces scattered and spiraling around my head each time I try…At least I think that's it. Sometimes I just freeze up and I can't." Abby's eyes were wide and swimming with doubt. "Some of it fits into place but the rest…wshhhh! And it's like a wall of cotton in my brain and I can't push words past my heart pounding." She gestured with both hands as if creating a whirlwind around her head and then shrugged. "Is this what it really looks like?" She gestured around her at the narrow hallway that was so much taller and brighter than the red stone halls of the Martian colony.

The surface of the walls seemed a melted conglomeration of colors, textures, and even words that drew her attention, and the overhead lights were bright, a glaring near daylight gleam that was almost as distracting as the walls.

"Near enough." Bram, a head taller than her but narrow of frame, nodded and turned the corridor to lead her deeper into the complex. The hall branched into two more, one leading into several more bedrooms and ending in a stairwell that led into the gym. "You've seen most of it before now, but I have something I want to show you…"

Stopping at the next room, he waited for the greeting and the click of the electronic lock and then glanced over at Abby with a half smile. "It's an old building we're in now, so some areas don't have sliding doors."

"Welcome back, Bram. Will your guest be entering with you?"

"Yes, indeed, or neither would I…" He pushed a hand through the thick messy brown hair that was many shades lighter than Abby's own and with less red in it.

"Of course, carry on then."

Abby laughed, following her brother through the door that clicked and then swung open before them. The room was dark until they entered, the same glaring white lights flickering on as they crossed the room, and in the middle of it was a large platform on which the thing sat.

She cocked her head, reaching out to brush her fingers along the smooth silicone contours of the egg shaped structure. "I've seen these in Donovan's lab. We grow animals in them and mother has schematics for something similar she's working on."

Bram grinned. "Sure, but this is one of the ones that you were in…and the rest of us." He leaned forward, staring into the empty AUC chamber that one of the hundred had grown and developed in from blastocyst to full term progeny. "I found it in the storage room of Richard's lab, collecting dust."

Abby pulled at the narrow opening at the bottom, the flexible silicone opening stretching around her hand like the mouth of a large pink caterpillar. "And you came out here." She twisted her hand, pushing it in farther, and touching the inner surface before removing her hand to stare at it before reaching for the top of the chamber and pressing at the surface until she found a seal.

"And I came out here…" She glanced over at him. "Mother told me about it. She broke the seal and wrapped me in the RPU attaching it to herself, sealing it so I'd keep growing." She grew solemn, and then met his curious gaze with eyes that had darkened and grown still and unreadable. "She has scars there from it." With the brush of her hand she drew the scars onto her own chest in a large circle just below her collarbones.

Bram's expression was one of quiet awe. "And then she took you with her."

Abby nodded, allowing the tapered waves of auburn hair, darker than her mahogany brown eyes to fall forward in a comforting curtain that threw a shadow over her eyes as well as the sides of her face. "I wish she could have brought you too—don't you?"

He thought for several long moments, allowing the silence between them to draw out as if she were waiting on a reply to a message from Earth instead of using the VR Comm for dream talk. After a time, he looked up, his expression one of quiet satisfaction. "No. Because then I wouldn't have seen Earth; this way I'll have—perspective."

Abby sighed, accepting the answer and turning to walk from the room. "At least I've seen it through your eyes, and you've seen Mars—sort of." She gave a half-hearted smile. "Two more years and you'll see it for yourself. The Pinnacle is repaired now, nearly."

Bram started to answer but was cut off by a louder more expressive voice entering the conversation. A tall, robust boy of the same age with black coffee ringlets and green eyes resolved into being next to Bram, the image becoming more solid as he moved. He nudged Bram in the shoulder and tossed a wink and a smirk at Abby. "You two didn't even invite me!"

"You were sleeping, Gavin, as usual." Abby arched a brow in good imitation of Genesis's signature expression.

Gavin caught sight of the AUC chamber between the two children and broke into a grin, eyes lighting up with mischief. "Showing her the baby box…mutant maker, creature cooker?" He broke into wild laughter at Abby's look of shock, despite her quick recovery to a more neutral expression.

"Mutant? Hardly…if you call us that then it isn't just us. Everyone and everything else on Mars as well, now they've had their DNA altered to reproduce on Mars."

Gavin shrugged. "Doesn't change facts."

Abby looked askance at him, a slight smile playing across her lips. "Facts? Most sources of information are limited and biased and any 'information' not science based is subjective…even science is mutable, as we gain more knowledge—as are we." She flashed a grin at both brothers. "I like mutant-maker best, I think—"

Gavin stepped over to the AUC, placing both hands on the

translucent glass-like tubing that curved along the sides like four slender leaf-like sepals surrounding a rosebud. He stared inside without looking away and spoke in a subdued voice. "Can you imagine, growing in there where you can see out, until one day it drains of all fluid and forces you out through the bottom? Cold air, rough hands—from one prison to the next." He pinched the bridge of his nose as if stifling a sneeze mirroring a motion from his physical self outside of the VR comm.

Abby stared, unable to discern whether he was serious or there was another punchline coming. She listened as he described what they had all experienced, and took a step closer to the AUC.

The light dimmed and took on a pinkish quality, the heavy whirring thrum of fans and the rush of fluid coursing through large pipes overhead filled the room. Inside the AUC dim grey eyes opened looking back from a tiny face, translucent skin mapped with snaking red capillaries.

She blinked, forcing the image back to where it must have come from, Gavin's mind—or maybe hers.

The sound faded into the background and the white lighting that filled the room a moment before, returned. Abby scowled. "Stop it, Gavin. You know a little warning would be better if you want to change scenery.

"Don't you remember it, though." His expression was earnest and he stared without flinching away, compelling her with his eyes.

She stared back, expression blank and unreadable and shook her head in a slow back and forth motion. "No, I don't." As if to punctuate the statement within her own mind she felt something gripping the back of her neck, her ankles, a slick plastic surface wrapping her as she struggled against the vise-like grip. The fighting exhausted her and then she slept, waking to the face she knew staring down at her in a different light, no longer dim and pink but instead faintly bluish and brighter.

Abby turned away from the AUC and Gavin's penetrating stare to address Bram. "Oh hey, where is Aurelia? She didn't answer the comm call, neither did Santana."

Gavin grew less serious, answering before Bram could. "She's out in the city catching rats." He leaned in closer to whisper. "Something to cuddle at night I think."

Bram shook his head, sandy brown waves falling into his eyes. "She's studying them, you know. Prefers the real thing to the sim programs."

Abby nodded, thankful for the change of subject. "Oh, sure...I've seen her rats. She needed more?"

The boys shrugged almost in unison and Bram winced at Gavin's cavalier expression and at the throbbing ache that was building along pressure points in jaw, neck, and forehead. "Some of them don't last very long is all."

"Oh."

Bram scratched the back of his neck pressing his fingers into the point where skull met cervical vertebrae, leaving the hand there to provide counter pressure to the headache that was building. "Yeah. There are quite a lot of them, at least."

Abby turned to leave the room, stepping through the door and walking down the hall. "At least there's that." She turned back to face them with a sudden grin. "You showed me this so let let me show you more of Mars, I'll shift the setting for us and..."

Gavin pushed past her and rolled his eyes. "If that's all that's going on here I have other things to do. Gelsimmium wants me to dust her shelves while she's away on her pre-apprenticeship expedition. Only difference between that and Mars is the color of the dust."

Abby's eyes grew wide with hurt before she narrowed them and put on a small smile. "Suit yourself Gavin. You'll have plenty of time to get used to Mars once you get here.

He grit his teeth around his words and flashed an expression she couldn't place. Was he angry at her? Mocking her? It didn't matter, she was right.

"Sure, Abby. That's right. We'll all have a lot to adjust to soon." He pulled off his VR headset, exiting the conversation without warning.

Bram was rubbing a hand across his forehead, with a grimace of embarrassment. "Sorry about that, I mean, I'm not Gavin but, yeah. Sorry."

She shrugged. "What's with him lately?"

"Dunno…He's moody, snapping at everyone, and no one seems to want to put up with his shit like we used to."

"It's okay, but…maybe ask him. You're closer what with me being so many million miles away and all that—33.9 million, in case you wondered."

Bram nodded, and smiled at her joke. "I definitely needed to know that."

"You're welcome. And Bram—love you, you know."

"Love you too, sis." He gave her a quick salute from military history before signing off.

Abby pulled off her VR headset and stretched. An hour had passed in what seemed like a few minutes of conversation, thanks to the time delays between Earth and Mars. The sun was lower and the evening winds were kicking up with a hollow howling sound. Restlessness pulled at her and she jumped onto the bed alcove to look out the window. This side of the dome overlooked the dunes.

Theresa wouldn't notice if shelf quietly, the sand would still be warm against her feet from the heat of the sun. Worry crossed her features, shadowing her eyes. Gavin didn't know what he was talking about. They were all going to love Mars, and how much would that matter anyway. She and Mother were here.

The wind met her outside, and the sand was warm, the wind strong enough to whip her dark auburn-red hair around her and still her whirling thoughts for now.

Light and shadow alternated, flickering and scattering in a hurried, trembling dance with the wind outside. Aspen leaves, thick and green and bearing the scars of a long summer brushed the tinted window glass, the light scraping sound noticeable only if one listened past the heavy moan of late summer winds that grew louder with each passing day. A smile played on Emily's lips, the sunlight making a warm pink glow through the curtain of closed eyelids threaded through with the meandering trails of tiny arteries. She toyed with the idea of opening her eyes, stretching and readjusting her position in the bed. The languid feeling in her limbs called to mind mornings, back on Earth, the sort when youth still allowed a measure of forgetfulness and the urgency to accomplish hadn't been so strong. The last few layers of sleep faded as she regained full lucidity and her cornflower blue eyes opened wide.

She sat up, brushing aside any more rest for the day along with the covers. She glanced over at the window, the source of the mesmerizing sunlit leaf patterns that had played across her face moments before. If the sun was coming in this window it was well past mid-day and she had overshot her plans to lunch with Donovan. Her lips pulled down in a frown, brows creasing as the list of worries and anxious considerations settled back onto her head and shoulders like a weighted mantle on a higher gravity planet than Mars.

Reaching over onto the pallet, Emily grasped her handheld in both hands, and activated the screen by voice. "Messages please."

The handheld's AI answered in a smooth androgynous voice. "You have seven messages. Would you like them read aloud, or played for your convenience or would you like a list that you may archive select messages for later consumption?"

Emily shrugged her shoulders and stood to dress for the wind, collecting a heavy, hooded cloak from the closet with attached face scarf. "Did Donovan leave a message?"

"He left two. Would you like them played?"

"Yes, please." The smile was genuine, but held an edge of apprehension, an instability that left a tremble at the corners of her lips.

The voice of the AI was replaced by the stumbling tenor of the planetologist, his words starting and stopping, tumbling over each other and then breaking off for short pauses as if a number of trains of thought competed for space on his tongue. "You were at a birth…I was told, well I asked, rather, when you didn't answer. Funny, I asked the Captain to ask Kendra and then of course, was able to congratulate him on their latest…addition." A short laugh erupted before he continued. Emily's smile rested more comfortably on her face and the tension in her shoulders eased as she listened to his casual message. "You hear the wind I expect, through the message and your walls. I'm up on the hill for lunch as planned and you're likely sleeping. I'll be here come evening as well if you want a rain check then."

The message ended followed by the second one barely audible through the background of wind that he must have forgotten to cancel out in his excitement. Even still when he stopped speaking she could hear what he was calling her attention to in the background. It was singing, some high pitched and keening, some lower and melodic, almost mirroring the tones of the wind. The whales were at the cliffs today and singing for him then. Emily's smile broadened and she tucked her handheld into a pocket concealed in a fold of her sepia robe and wrapped the scarf across her face before stepping out into the central garden.

The horizon was red with the gathering dust of the windy season, a haze of burnt umber sand that mixed with the clouds when they came in and exaggerated the royal purple and magenta hues of the Martian sunsets.

She set out across the garden, glancing past the stocky dark-leafed Martian-stripe tomatoes to the West mountains where Carla likely was. *Up in some cave, most likely. Or clinging to some narrow precipice despite the heavy winds. Her refuge.*

She shook her head. Nothing kept Grandmother when the mountains called.

Instead of hopping the far wall as Carla did, Emily passed through the gate, cringing at the faint screech of sand clogged hinges.

The ache that built in her calves as she topped the first rise made it clear that a gradual incline is an incline nonetheless. She picked up speed, transitioning to a loping jog as the incline increased, dodging the spiny pine green cycads that populated the slope even hiding in the crimson and green ferns that had proliferated under the copses of aspens.

The sun was lower than the hilltop now, silhouetting the figure that knelt at the top, a black cutout of a man against the deep blue sky with a glowing halo around his figure. He stood, lifting a smaller form of a child up above his head and tossing her. Emily could hear them now, their laughter, muffled words on the wind.

She stopped, heart in her throat for just a moment before her eyes softened and she smiled. The smile held as she approached the pair, out of breath from her swift progression up the steep rise.

Donovan turned, grinning, his features now visible, no longer a nondescript silhouette. "You made it. See Ali, you've won the bet now." He smiled down at the girl who sat cross legged in the lichen-grass. Dark eyes beamed up at him from the lightly-tanned face that seemed imbued with the warm light of the lowering sun. Alicole stood, wrapping slender arms around Emily in an exuberant embrace.

Emily smiled back, seeing the girl and the babe she had witnessed emerging from her mother's birth passage seven short years ago. The delicate nose and dark grey eyes, now black, that seemed to have an upward tilt to their corners. The fine black hair that now came down in lightly curling wisps beside her cheeks, the shy smile that was Donovan's.

Donovan, stepped forward reaching down to offer Emily a hand up the final rise of the cliff. "I'm glad you came." He caught her eyes with his own warm brown ones and she smiled, holding the visual embrace just long enough to bring a blush to her cheeks before she looked away.

Emily turned her attention to Donovan's daughter where she sat at their feet. "Are you staying with us for hilltop supper and whale-watching tonight?" The girl shook her head, lips pulling into a joyful smirk that sparked with her own happy secret.

"Little Coli is going hiking with her mothers for star gazing this evening, the old trail I think."

Emily nodded and then turned her smile back to Alicole who had pulled herself up from the ground and was brushing the red-brown dirt from her hiking clothes. The child's brows knit and she shook her head. "No, papa, We are going higher than that! Mama Lissa convinced Mama Kira that I am a better climber than even the Arkanue on the cliffs."

He laughed, shaking his head and letting the laughter flow around them in the cooling evening air. The wind had picked up again and was trying to push them away from the cliffs, perhaps back to the domed colony complex instead where they could find refuge from its cold blasts.

Alicole's eyes widened, her head whipping around in the direction of the colony. "But we can only go high up if I'm not late!" Without further explanation Coli jumped into Donovan's arms and squeezed him hard, and then turned and ran down the hill along the well-trodden dirt trail, arms and legs pinwheeling with the momentum.

Emily stared after her, hands coming up to squeeze her upper arms and pin them to her chest. The smile on her lips was genuine but covered layers of hollow, gray, aching like sunlight illuminating the thawed puddle on the surface of a lake, still frozen solid from a hard winter. A thin, reedy, song came on the wind then, traveling through the layers of deep water over the edge of the cliff and entering her thoughts.

She turned, striding to the edge and looking down at the dark-pine-green water below, almost black where the overhanging cliff shadowed and formed a cave that extended to the ocean floor, the spawning cave.

Several more watery voices joined in, each with their own range of notes, their own song. Pale shapes passed in and out of view under the water, faster than creatures of such a size should move.

"They're here to mate, you know, returning to the cave they started in…" Donovan was closer now, kneeling down and watching over the edge with rapt attention, just a few feet from where she stood. She sat next to him, leaning her back against his side and following his gaze as the wind pushed her hair back from her forehead.

Several pale shapes emerged from the water, long dappled gray beaks emerging first and pointing up to the cliffs as they opened to reveal rows of smooth, ivory teeth. Another sound, like rounds of high-pitched laughter emerged as they greeted each other, shining wet bodies caressing as they rubbed sides and nuzzled faces. The nearest to the cliffs rolled on the surface, long narrow fins paddling the water and then spreading as if offering an embrace, the movement revealed an underbelly that was at first glance a gleaming white but on closer inspection opalesced like a pale abalone shell in the sunlight.

Emily, held her breath, eyes misting. "They are perfection…but…" She hesitated.

Donovan flicked his gaze over, breaking away from the display, concern pulled at his features. "What?"

She continued. "I just wonder…you've made them all. Sent them out on their own…is it hard for you?" Her voice trailed off with the question as she leaned just a bit further, staring at the playful creatures below. "Like a father, maybe? I've seen you stare long and hard at the population numbers of the Arcanue, the ratbits…and these ones. And I can tell it's not the numbers you are seeing when you do it."

A surprised laugh escaped Donovan's lips and he turned, startled and faintly blushing. The first words came out in a stumbling rush. "That's, well…well yes it's a, a thing, yes. You always do this, Emily." He smiled, shaking his head as he followed her gaze and then leaned closer to draw her attention by pointing. "You see the one there with the darker dappling on the sides? That's Pacifica. And the two that just came up in the shadow there, Atlantis and Meridian…I don't just see the numbers, no."

Emily leaned over, resting her cheek against his as she looked where he directed. "Like letting Alicole roam the countryside without you, isn't it?"

Donovan winced. "There's nothing to worry about."

She laughed, the sound warm and familiar. "But you do, don't you."

He shrugged, climbing back to his knees and pulling her up to join him. "Sure, yes, but you know that route just leads to madness…" He glanced at his silent handheld and held it up with a wry smile. "Counting the minutes until her mothers register that she is with them and it pings my device here, checking and double checking the genetic make-up of each new ratbit even after they've been raised and released…Come on." He gestured towards the flatter portion of the hilltop further back from the edge. A thin outdoor blanket covered the patch of dry lichen-grass that grew there mirroring the hanging variety that grew from the young aspens, dangling down to brush their shoulders as they sat.

Donovan pulled a large flask of liquid and two glasses from a brown woven bag that was resting at the base of a tree. "Juice or spice brew with our sandwiches? I have both." His grin was bright in the dimming light of the oncoming sunset, an orange and mauve glow tinting his black hair and the side of his jaw.

Emily sat down, pulling her knees in and wrapping her arms around them and leaning her cheek there. "Sandwiches then? Is it Gran's bread?"

"Yes, well—no. It's Carla's recipe but rendered by myself and Alicole, who insisted she learn it and make our sandwiches for this evening."

Emily raised her brows and smiled. "And?"

"And it's…pretty good. Just a bit dense, but the flavor is just right. Faintly sour, tangy rather, nutty, salted just right…Emily?"

She had fallen to tracing with her fingers in the reddish sand and looked up startled, blue eyes wide and flickering with shadows.

Donovan sat next to her, resting the sandwich he had retrieved on his lap, as he brushed the hair from her face with one gentle gesture. "You okay?"

Emily blinked, pulling in a deep, shaky breath, finding her dropped smile and dusting it off. "Still tired from getting up for the birth I think and it just seems…I was having those dreams again, and you know I love talking about Alicole and the others—"

"Oh." Donovan frowned. "I'm sorry, Emily. A birth and then this, me rambling on about Ali and the animals. I should have thought of it."

"It isn't just that, though. Tomorrow's the anniversary."

"It is, isn't it." He pushed a hand through his hair, fingers catching on the spirals of wind tangled hair. "I remembered the last one and the next is—"

"Please, don't. It's a lot to remember. How many days of the year does a normal person want to spend in mourning? You don't—you don't have to remember them all with me."

He stared back at her, eyes serious. "Yes I do, Emily. I want to, but… Are you going to—Can I just ask you this?"

She caught her breath and held it nodding, hoping that the withheld breath might cushion the inevitable blow.

"It's been nine years, nine years with you helping and all the others having as many as they want. No more issues, so why not you Emily? Why don't you have yours?"

The only children I'm meant to have are dead ones… The old thought spoke before she could catch it and refute the refrain with logic, with sensibility. Her jaw was tight when she looked at him. "It's just been too long, Donovan. I've missed the chance to have my own."

"No,… that isn't it. I don't believe it. Even Carla still could, you know—." He reached out, hand hesitant as he touched her cheek. "What is it really—Emily, you tell me things, usually—some things. We're friends and well, sometimes more, I think."

Emily flinched, shame crossing her features like a living shadow. "We are, more than friends. I just…"

He shook his head. "No, it's okay. You don't have to quantify it or anything for me, until you want to at least."

Emily laughed, the sound small and bitter in the wind that was picking up to a gale, toppling the sealed jug of Martian Vineberry juice and knocking the top layers from their sandwiches. A mournful croon from the white Whalefins filled the wind that shoved their backs into the powdery white aspen bark of the trees behind them.

She reached with frantic hands, gathering bread and lettuces before they tumbled into the red sand from the edge of the picnic blanket. "That isn't fair though. Just because I'm in extended mourning doesn't mean you should be waiting around without any returns."

Donovan rescued the toppled juice jug and remaining sandwich parts, the two of them moving in concert as they packaged their supper back into his satchel for retreat. Once completed the task left them standing facing each other, heavy winds whipping their hair into a blur of red and black around solemn faces. "Hey, I'm not a victim here. I'm your friend." A half smirk found its way to his lips. "A close friend?"

She smiled back. "Yeah."

"Okay, then. Anything else we can work on when and if we want. My return is having good dinner company and a friend who will listen to all of the gene pairs I'm considering for a new species while I get giddy about it and go into the kind of detail that most people tune out…So, isn't my part to ask why you haven't gone for the one thing you came to Mars for?"

She turned, gesturing for him to follow as she bounded down the hill, feet finding the handholds by muscle memory as she followed the well-worn path.

She waited for him to catch up before answering, her eyes were calmer now but swimming with spinning thoughts. "I don't know yet. It WAS what I wanted and then when Jon died—I got confused. Did I still want it? I started helping Carla with all of the babies coming, and I just couldn't picture raising his children without him there."

"Wouldn't he have wanted you to? Expected it? I mean, we all have our genetic samples on file for exactly that reason, don't we?"

"But we didn't want it that way." It was a simple statement, the sort that ended an argument with its finality.

Donovan placed a hand on her shoulder as they reached the bottom of the steep decline. "And what about your dreams? What does Carla have to say about them. Psychologists say dreams are—"

She shook her head. "I don't tell Gran about my dreams unless I'm looking for a push. And I'm not."

"Oh." The wind was less intense at the base of the cliff but still urged them back towards the colony where the thick Soil composite walls and warm hallways waited to enfold them in safety. *That and the children, safely buried in the garden beneath my aspen, their tiny forms turned to soil, composted into their base components by water, microbes and Martian red worms…taken up by the roots of the aspen.* All four of them waiting for a daily visit. *Mother to the dead.*

She shook her head to knock the thought free and leave it out in the wind driven red sand. A smile replacing the furrowed brow and slash of tight lips as they reached the garden wall, and it opened with a welcoming chime.

"Did you enjoy your supper?" The Garden AI's voice sounded a bit like Trina's had, second in command on the Pinnacle and lost years ago. *Neil must have asked for that—early on when the pain was still fresh—salt in the wounds for his mistake.* The scowl tried to return and she pushed it back with a sigh then glanced over at Donovan as they stepped back into the colony boundaries.

The hand that held Emily's wavered as she grasped it, there one moment and gone the next leaving her staring wide-eyed into the sandstorm all around.

A small laugh caused her to look down. The laughing face was there again. The small hand with such short dimpled fingers was wrapped in her own. The eyes were strange though, shifting—brown one moment and then grey, pointed almond shapes and at the next glance wider and round.

Emily kneeled down, taking both hands before they could dissipate again. She traced the round cheek with her hand and pushed wisps of black hair from the child's eyes.

"Are you mine then?"

The child frowned and then shrugged as she turned to free a hand and point across the nearest dune. "I no know." The child's voice was high, words formed clumsily.

She pointed again, tugging with such little force on Emily's hand.

"What's in'a sand?" Letting go of Emily's hand the child, nearly a baby still, gave an exaggerated shrug, raising both palms above shoulder height. Her eyes lit up with excitement. "Let's go see them."

She turned and ran then, short rounded legs carrying her faster across the sand than was possible.

Emily ran after, fear forcing her to push herself to dry-mouthed exhaustion. She crested the dune and stared at the jumbled landscape. The child was gone and in her stead was a sand- field filled with remains, humans, arcanue, and others, bones bleaching white under the hot sun, flesh withering and being stripped away by beetles and scavenging ratbits.

The Aspens that must have been the one's from the garden were canted at impossible angles, their roots discourged from the dark soil that resembled chunks of clotted blood more than humus. Emily stared at those naked roots in horror. They appeared to be writhing, pushing forth small rotting bundles that Emily recognized with dawning horror.

The child was gone and these were all that remained. *The only children I'm meant to have are dead ones…*

Emily recoiled from the sight before her, rapid blinking as if to unsee. *No, no, that's a lie.* Her heart raced, and she turned to run.

The quality of illumination shifted, and the strong, heady scent of lavender permeated her dream.

There were fields of it surrounding her, for what must be miles in each direction. Row after row of dusty green bushes with tall waving stalks topped with tufts of pale purple. They were in full bloom, and a metallic hum signaled the arrival of pollinators, minute, metallic constructs that shimmered in the sunlight.

Emily sighed as the scene set off a sense memory from long past, not from Earth but from the VR sleep-aide's induced reality. The neural pathway was so well worn that it pulled her out of nightmare again and again.

A smile of realization slid onto her lips as a degree of awareness grew, supplanting several layers of dream. Deeper sleep would return once her heart rate and brainwaves signaled it was safe to allow free-dreaming again, but for now she walked down the rows of lavender, brushing her fingertips over the soft blossoms.

# SLOW BURN

EARTH—WGC EUR-ASIA EPIDEMIOLOGY HEADQUARTERS

Ivanna reached up to catch the incoming box of coveted tissue tossed from the neighboring workstation and snatched out an accidental handful to catch the violent series of sneezes. It could be held back no longer.

"Better watch that. Decontamination is right over there waiting for you."

Ivanna lifted watery, red eyes to glare at her colleague. "Allergies, it's allergies. Just like yours, and every-damn-body else this month." She lifted the tissue to catch another sneeze and a series of coughs before tossing the box back.

Xavi chuckled and extracted a tissue for the same purpose, unfolding and refolding it into a complicated origami pocket while scrunching his nose and waiting for the itch to morph into the inevitable. "Yes, well. Our supervisor believes you. She didn't even come in today herself." He leaned closer to whisper. "Hives she said, but I think she wanted to pass the quarterly write-up off on us."

The briefing write-up was already open on their shared screen and half finished. Ivanna shook her head with a smile and focused on the data left to input before they could collect signatures and send the briefing up the WGC chain of command. Almost finished. The last heading, **Emerging Threats,** was already in place. She entered the next three bullet points and then paused between **Widespread Allergic Disease to include Atopic Dermatitis, Anaphylaxis, seasonal Allergic Rhinitis, and Allergic Asthma** and **Isolated Outbreaks: Ebola Virus Tai Forest Strain, Pneumonic Plague—Y-Pestis—X, Coronavirus-24**. The itching on her soft pallet was growing intolerable with every passing moment. Maybe she forgot to take the little white pill that was her seasonal salvation before coming in this morning. Maybe it just wasn't working, or it wasn't allergies.

She shoved the blunt muscle of her tongue against the rough of her mouth, fighting against the itch, all the while wishing that her tongue was barbed and rough like a cat's instead of smooth and meaty like the useless toad of a tongue humans had to cope with. *No claws, no fangs or armor and a stubby toad tongue. How pathetic.*

The tissue, maybe, would blunt her nails just enough. She wrapped one finger in tissue and reached into the high arch of her soft palate gently scraping with the now damp tissue as a barrier. It, dried her mouth out and stuck, coming apart, and the itch only intensified; now it was so sharp that her eyes were stinging and burning and her nose running onto the back of her hand.

"Ivanna…" Xavi was staring, and he looked concerned.

Fuck the tissue! Fucking itching!! She scraped the roof of her mouth in a sudden frenzy and felt a layer of the soft, wet, skin over harder tissue beneath give way. She tasted blood and withdrew her hand, sputtering and coughing as she tried to remove the clinging bits of sodden tissue that were now red with saliva-diluted blood.

Her colleague was still staring, and her cheeks were hot and reddened with shame. It was *her* fucking mouth…why did she feel that shakiness in her knees and the heavy lump in her gut, the burning ears that signaled she was embarrassed like a kid caught defacing property or maybe herself…*Cut my own mouth…bleeding.*

She passed a hand across her lips and was grateful to see the wetness there was mostly spit and not blood. She tried to shrug and paste on a smile as she stepped away from the workspace. "Scratched myself…um, gonna just, go get cleaned up. Wanna finish the briefing and send it? Just the last couple bullet points and supporting attachments to add…"

Xavi cleared his throat trying to look anywhere but her face and seemed grateful for the excuse to turn attention to the briefing enlarged on the screen. "Uhhh, yup. I can do that. You um, you okay?"

"Mm-hm. Just scraped my mouth yesterday on an apple and sneezing reopened it." The lie slid out with ease and it sounded okay. *If you don't consider that he just saw me scrape my mouth like a rabid animal. Sure. Right.*

She cleared her throat again and found she'd run out of socially appropriate words to pile on top of and bury the awkwardness she was feeling, and instead of digging for more, turned abruptly and left.

The bathroom was next to the patio and she could hear the sounds of summer even through the thick, hail-resistant glass dome that surrounded it, a keening screech of insects singing to potential mates that just made her think of pollen, the carefully planted, nurtured and cultivated trees in the garden and elsewhere bursting with blossoms and spreading the gametes in the air. The itching in her throat and eyes intensified at the thought and she detoured to a refreshment station a few yards to the left of the bathroom.

One very specific command to the AI-controlled refreshment station and she was soon several soothing gulps into a pina colada flavored Icee and the itching was reduced already to a faint tickle. Even the bleeding scrape on the roof of her mouth that throbbed and tasted of iron a moment before was numbed away.

Ivanna leaned back against the wall and slid down before

taking another gulp and holding the sweet, blended ice against the roof of her mouth until it melted.

Across the way, through the glass windows, the trilling mating calls blurred into a high-pitched ring that Ivanna tuned out even as she watched the flit of many wings from tree-top to treetop. **Plagues of locusts, cockroach, cicadas, and ticks...** The last bullet point came to mind again. Crops were safe in vertical farming complexes, but roaches especially were well known vectors for infectious disease. That was the point of the briefing, after all: to stay prepared. She sighed and stood up from the cool tile. *Could'a fallen asleep there—allergy brain fog, but work calls. Better double check Xavi or he'll forget an attachment like the last time and the time before that.* Ivanna's handheld buzzed in her pocket. The first few times she didn't notice over the sway of her hips, the impact of her heels on the tiles as she hurried back to her workstation, but it was insistent. The message was displayed on the screen, from Xavi. Their supervisor wouldn't be in tomorrow either, it seemed. She was in the hospital.

She scanned into the office and met Xavi's equally startled gaze. "Hey..." She held up her handheld and he did the same. "So why...?"

His voice had a bit of a shake to it, and he swallowed as if there was something in his throat that he wanted to keep from coming up. "Dunno, but we're both called in to the medical wing for tests. Contact tracing and all that."

Ivanna nodded. She tried to compose her features and fight down the twinge of alarm that tied itself to the faint tickle in the back of her throat. Hives weren't contagious, and neither was allergic rhinitis.

Greg rubbed at the pale white scar on the underside of his

forearm. It was jagged but had faded into a subtle ghost over the past eleven years. It was a bad break. He traced the line again and then swiped at the rolling bead of sweat that followed his hairline downward to the edge of his jaw. He caught it with the edge of his hand before it could dive off.

The skin at the base of his jawline was still tender, but the swelling had gone five days ago. He was fully treated, healed up, clean bill of health. They caught it fast as always, now, thanks to past experience—no more complacency, overcrowding; poverty and whatever edge any ambitious microbe had over them was bridged by nanocytes to monitor and diagnose invading organisms quicker than the immune system on its own.

Pneumonic plague was still nothing to mess around with; it knocked a healthy person out fast. Greg got up from the daybed he had spent the last five days recovering on. The room spun, greyed out like television static, and he could hear a sharp ringing in his ears. It filled his senses and he flailed out to catch himself, knowing the fall was inevitable. *Anemic…I'm probably still anemic, like the ones who were in recovery when I came down with it.*

But the fall didn't come.

The wall was there against his hand when his hearing returned. A broadcast was playing on his screen, advising voluntary self-quarantine for anyone experiencing flu symptoms, and the paternal voice seemed to drone on and loop back on itself, repeating key points like an old-timer who'd refused longevity treatments, preferring to go out while telling the same stories again and again.

The room faded in from dappled grey fog and he could see the broadcast now. There were what he assumed to be hotspots on a map, looking like last winter, though then it was the latest Coronavirus strain making its rounds. The seasonal vaccine sent that one packing. This would be the same, but with containment and antibiotics.

Greg kept a hand on the wall, and he moved more slowly this time, heading for the kitchen and cold water. His mouth tasted stale and dried out. The water set him to shaking and forced the realization that his flat was cold, his thermostat reset to some ridiculous arctic blast while he was still feeling feverish. *Where was that medical paperwork? Five days was enough to not feel like this…I'm missing too much work. Theresa was gonna worry, or think I'm shoving the work off on her.*

"I don't work with Theresa anymore." The words spoken aloud were sobering and he sat down hard on the white kitchen tiles. He whispered it again to himself, forehead crumpling as hot tears filled his eyes. "I don't…and I can't even tell her."

Knees splayed and feet planted on the tile, he leaned forward in push-back-the-nausea pose, with his head between his knees. But he wasn't nauseous, was he? Shaking, light-headed, and his ears felt hot. She was still there, in his head, a memory that had resurfaced and stuck there in the cobwebs and confusion. Theresa, when she unbuttoned her lab coat and the front of her shirt and stood there in front of him, smiling. Theresa, when she'd lifted up onto her toes and kissed him. Only this time, she didn't wait for a response for several painful moments and then run out. This time he grabbed her upper arms and pulled her in for another kiss, hands roving inside that open shirt, grasping, squeezing, and she didn't stop him.

Droplets of sweat were trailing down his face again, and the room, cold a moment before, felt like a sauna, heat building around him…or maybe it came from inside, building up in his gut and spreading into his loins where he could sense the blood pulsing, stiffening him to the point of pain. Greg groaned in discomfort, embarrassment, and curled himself into a ball on the cold tile. Eleven years she'd been gone from Earth, longer if you count the years avoiding each other before she left. Why remember now? His breaths came in rapid gasps and he lost track. The room was somehow unfamiliar and, while he was aware that he was lying on a floor, he couldn't place how long he'd *been* lying on that floor or how much longer he might stay there.

The broadcast continued with a bullet point list of recommendations for seeking testing and care at the sign of first symptoms, and Greg felt a wave of relief wash over him because he'd had early treatment and was nearly better. Weak, maybe, a little shaky, but lying on the cold tile he felt more hopeful than he had in years.

EARTH-REPRODUCTIVE COUNCIL HEADQUARTERS

Ania's hand over hers pressed Tasha's into the firm full moon of her rounded abdomen, holding it there as they both waited, foreheads pressed together as they exchanged grins. Their smiles were genuine, but their eyes were tired, the skin beneath them dusky with fatigue and their lips and eyelids pale and waxy.

Tasha's smile wavered, shadows in her sepia-colored eyes flickering as she tried to hide them away. Her own belly was smooth again, the cesarean access panel a tightly sealed seam of pliable silver silicone. How many weeks was it since it was stretched to full capacity, just like her own skin around it, gathering ragged pink stretch marks to accommodate the latest passenger? But she was empty now. For a moment she could picture herself opened up in her mind's eye, the inner layer exposed, revealing the bleeding endometrium of her vacated uterus. Lochia still flowed, that's how recent it had been. She flinched away from the painful imagery. Ania didn't notice. The thump a moment later was hard enough to move their hands and force a startled laugh from both pairs of lips. Tasha lifted her hand and pulled Ania in for a tight squeeze, and Melody crowded in to feel as well. Elise stood back with knit brows. The smile on her lips was half formed; no doubt she meant it as a full smile but ran out of energy part-way through.

"See that? She's doing better in there than we are out here." They turned to include the most senior of the surrogates in the moment.

"Come feel, Elise. They can kick together." Ania came closer and pressed her belly against Elise's, leaning her head on the older woman's shoulder to whisper. "Hey, you okay?"

"Sure, just tired still. Eight months is a shit time to get that sick."

Ania nodded and closed her eyes. "No arguments here."

Tasha heard the exchange and watched Melody join the group snuggle in the hall, but her attention was elsewhere. Her message inbox was full, a welcome distraction. It had been, what... seven days quarantine? No phone. Pneumonic flu, they said, and she wasn't even feeling that bad until a couple hours before they collected them all up for testing, treatment, quarantine. The rest was a blur.

She scrolled down the messages. Most were from Daniel. Her heartbeat kicked up and she felt a thrill run south and fill her belly with heat. *At least that's still working.*

The last message was the one that mattered. Tasha grinned as she read it, a blush spreading down her cheeks onto the pale skin of her throat where her pulse quickened again. It was hot in here, or maybe her fever was coming back. She typed a quick reply, glancing over at her fellow surrogates, where they were still cooing over their full bellies.

"You want me now or later? Clean bill of health. I'll be in my suite waiting if you really missed me as much as all that."

Footsteps meant Melody was looking over her shoulder again. She tucked her handheld into a pocket and felt the buzz of a quick reply. It was the smirk that gave her away.

"Is that your Daniel then? Don't you think rest like the medbot ordered is more important than—"

Tasha cut her off as Ania and Elise joined them, each taking up a position flanking Tasha and Melody as they turned the corner towards the Surrogacy Complex.

"I think I'm feeling better and have had enough rest. And that my messages are not your business." She softened the chastisement with a teasing tone. It wasn't Melody's business any more than two thirds of what she talked about was, but her gossip was harmless.

"Alright, alright…I just think if you're the only one having any fun we should at least enjoy it vicariously. But fine, be stingy."

Tasha shook her head at Melody and the other two who were laughing along. "You want to come and watch then?"

"No."

"No."

Melody arched a brow. "Maybe…and why not? We do everything else together."

They all burst into laughter. Tasha reached for Melody and kissed her on the cheek before stopping in front of her door. She felt lighter than she had for a long time. "Love you, girls." They waved and blew kisses back as they continued to their own suites.

The door slid open after a scan and she stepped inside. It was warm and dark, and soon Daniel would be there to celebrate their recovery. She closed her eyes in the dim, letting her thoughts drift, and watched the color show of shapes and figures playing on the back of her eyelids. She let herself doze. She was tired, suddenly, and hot all over. Daniel would scan himself in and wake her. He had authorization.

Tasha sucked in a breath as the cough abated and mumbled an apology.

Sweat beads coalesced on her brow, trembling and sliding

down forehead and jawline before pattering onto the pale blue sheets of the bed. Tasha stared as they soaked into the fabric, iridescence fading and color shifting. Was it the sunset through the window-glass, or was it red? Blood-red droplets seeping in and bleeding together into faces laughing? She blinked, lifting one hand from the mattress and leaving only the other to support the force of Daniel's flesh pressing into hers in rhythmic thrusts.

Scrubbing a hand across her eyes, Tasha refocused. The faces laughed back from the bloody sheet, or was it the red-gold gleam of refracted sunlight?

Her face contorted in dismay and she clenched her eyes shut against what she saw there. She sucked in a breath and opened her eyes afraid of what she would see. The sheets were clean, damp with their sweat but that was all. *It's just the light, Tasha—the light and I'm tired is all...*

She rocked her hips back to meet his, directing him deeper, a high-pitched wail escaping her lips with each thrust against her cervix. Relaxing the walls of her yoni, she welcomed him deeper still that she might retreat into the sensations in her nether regions. She arched her back, shifted the point where their bodies joined to rub against the pulsing core of her pleasure as if positioning to scratch an itch that could not be satisfied.

The intensity built, sharpening until she could no longer relax into it, and she reached back to grab Daniel's hip before sliding away and pushing him down onto the bed with a smile of apology. She sighed, eyes still closed, and mumbled into his ear.

"Little change of pace..."

She slid one thigh over him, hands stroking his exposed member against her own warm wetness before guiding him inside.

"That's better then, isn't it?" Daniel's abdominal muscles bunched up, chest tightening against her palms as he leaned up, hot breath against her ear. "So good, Tasha..." he moaned as she leaned forward, hips still tilting against his as they moved in unison towards the same point of pleasure on the near horizon.

Daniel's head fell back against the pillow and he smiled, a deep moan escaping as Tasha rocked and swayed against him, pressing her nails into his chest for leverage. There were lights sparking in the dark beneath her eyelids, like ghost lights left by staring at a bright light. Only these held shapes that were less random: bent over figures…entangled, clenching hands grasping…

She squeezed her eyes tighter.

"You feel that?" Her voice was hurried, interspersed with breaths. "Should be right this time…"

"Mmmmm…It's always right, Tasha…open your eyes, I want to see you cum!" She opened her eyes, lids flying open to leave the ghost lights behind in the darkness. Anything better than those dim amorphous shapes that filled her belly with dread, a shame-filled dread that somehow brought the peak of pleasure building there faster instead of frightening it off.

Her hands were on his face, caressing the smooth planes of his jaw and cheekbones, as vision returned from the greyed-out blur of tightly clenched lids.

But it wasn't there. Not as it should have been, not Daniel's. She closed her eyes and opened them again but the horror in front of her remained. She lowered shaking hands to his skin and instead of smooth, finely sculpted bone structure, the tissues were deformed, marred, wet and sticky.

The eyes were sunken as if buried in deep folds of melting tissue.

"Daniel?!" Her voice broke, locking up in her throat as she began to panic.

The withered face moaned, its mouth a dark cavern of twisted growths, pulled open in a scream now as Tasha lashed out and dug deeper for the eyes that should have been there. Her hands clenched around the bleeding face, nails digging in. She couldn't find them, and the panic rose, panic and revulsion as the well-loved face pulled apart in her hands like strings of warm, sticky taffy.

She slammed her eyes shut against the images and then opened them. *It would be gone, wouldn't it? Like before?*

It wasn't sunset through the window glass. It was blood. Daniel's blood on his face and her hands.

Tasha screamed, scrambling off of the body that could not be Daniel and closed her eyes until the shaking started. There was something cold and hard behind her, vertical, the side of a wall, a desk…it didn't matter. The ghost lights were still there beneath her eyelids, melting and reforming, moving to the rapid beat of her pulse. But they were better than the bloody sunset and the melted man on the bed. He thrashed there, bucking and flailing as he screamed, engorged member pointing up at the ceiling still like a flag waving surrender. He was saying something, but she couldn't decipher the words, couldn't focus in.

Her breath came in shallow pants, another cough forcing itself between clenched teeth. The rhythmic pulsing between her thighs had not ceased but instead built-in intensity. Tasha moaned, something more of a whimper that was raw with unsatisfied need. One hand moved down her belly, slick with sweat and blood, as if it knew better than Tasha what was needed. She was still wet with their shared passion, her tissues engorged and throbbing for release. Her fingers worked there, massaging, squeezing, sliding inside, with a clumsy urgency that left her stinging and raw, tears sliding down her cheeks from eyes squeezed closed like locked doors.

There were screams, still, from the bed, and the sharp, metallic screech of an alarm, but her moaning and the thrum of her rapid pulse in her ears drowned them out.

CACOPHONY

Cacophony…The word echoed in Aurelia's head, bouncing in the chaos of sounds as answer to them. Water dripped and trickled down the algae-covered walls in the dimly-lit cavern, and the scurryings and scratchings of many small bodies all combined to form a complicated din. Every sound wave, no matter how diffuse, registered on her ears and was catalogued, filed away. Her blue-green eyes, wide in her narrow face and framed by short unruly wisps of sandy blond hair, darted from one landmark to the next as she moved through the dark space. A sudden droplet of cold water from somewhere high above splashed onto her forehead and she scrubbed it away, wincing as her sleeve brushed eyelids tender and itching. The pervasive smell of mildew was making the itching hard to ignore.

Aurelia passed under a toppled colonnade and the last streams of light from the first floor of the decaying building were strangled out by shadow. Propped between a half-column and the slippery, debris-littered ground rested a marble placard three times the girl's size, the text worn but still legible. *Theatre Comedie Royale.* She tilted her head, pausing beneath the sign, one hand reaching up to caress the cold stone. It was damp, like everything else here, and slick with the growth of molds and algae. Images of how it must have looked flooded her mind, the room filling with a warm light and illuminating the lush red carpet that moldered in scraps and piles against the stone and cement floors and walls. The columns, bleached in her mind's eye, took on a rich polished gleam of fresh alabaster, the grime of centuries wiped away. She could almost hear the creaks and groans as the structure took on its original shape, columns pieced back together and ceiling beams risen from the splintering wreckage, the stage she had passed on the first floor shining and ready to play host to actors of the long past, those from a time when the arts were called from somewhere deep within instead of being programmed into one's genetics and pushed from the cradle to the grave. *But wasn't it the same? If it was a part of one's make-up, did the source matter?*

The scratching, scrambling, high-pitched squeaking grew louder as she progressed, placing her steps with care and crouching low to avoid brushing against the detritus that lined the walls and hung from above. The great swathes of rotting tapestry drip drip dripped, collecting minerals and hardening as they rotted like stalactites in a cave.

The final turn was ahead. She remembered the way, and despite the darkness her eyes caught and held even the faint illumination, shining in the dark and aiding her. The cage was devoid of movement and empty at first glance, but as she approached, Aurelia saw the blood. The trap door was closed, so nothing else could have gotten inside. Scenarios played out rapid-speed in her mind as she struggled to process what didn't make sense. The bodies of the rats within were shredded and wet with blood, some with their entrails spilled out next to their lifeless forms, stiffened and frozen in time. They were piled up against one translucent wall, the bait on the other side untouched.

The girl crouched down, closer, mumbling under her breath. "Too many in the cage at once, maybe, or a sound, high-pitched enough to make them frenzied, too many males…"

She scowled, flicking on the light that was embedded in the

wrists of her jumpsuit and then widened her eyes and leaned in, blinking rapid-fire to take still images and video of the box and its contents from several angles. She paused then, cocking her head and focusing in on the sound that she had been hearing the whole time but not fully processing. *Thought it was the trapped ones, I guess.*

Rising to her feet with one smooth motion, she turned from the cage and jogged deeper into the dilapidated building. The staircase was just ahead, as was the main source of the sound, louder and sharper in quality as she approached, perhaps a million voices raised in combat.

She pulled herself up short several yards before reaching the wide staircase and dropped to the ground, the damp wood creaking and groaning under even her light weight as she crawled to the edge. The floorboards were cracked and splintered here, broken off to form a deep chasm that led into the lower basements of the once-proud structure. There, in the pitch darkness, the sound reached a disturbing crescendo.

Aurelia leaned over the edge and stared into the pit that she had found months ago during her first foray into the abandoned theater on the far edge of the long-deserted city. The rats nested down below in the basements; it was the largest nest she had found yet, or at least the largest within her reach. The rats were still there, evidenced by the deafening sound and the stench that forced her to cover the lower half of her face with her sleeve.

They were there and she could see them, squirming and writhing, muscular bodies bunched up and then lashing out again and again with fang and claw. It was as if the whole colony had formed one giant mass of rat flesh that had no other desire but to devour itself. The rats tore into each other and struggled, not to flee, but to dig in and sink teeth into the nearest body that presented itself...but there was something else. Once latched on with tooth and claw, they writhed against one another, going through the motions of mating whether they were positioned to do so or not.

Aurelia's head jerked up and her stomach turned, a bolt of white-hot fear twisting in her gut and spreading into her nerves. There was no indication that they would attack her; in fact, if they were going to take notice, they should have already smelled her, but the fact remained that this was not normal rat behavior. *I better tell Richard.*

Scooting across the weakened portion of the floor and back towards the hall that would lead her away from the rat nest, she made every effort to be silent, sweat beading in the creases of her scowling forehead and tickling the sensitive skin above her lip.

Once past the turn, she broke into a bounding run, dodging crumbling boulders of plaster and stone, taking care to avoid the piles of moldering upholstery lest she slip and find herself face down in decay. *And draw attention my way…* The thought pushed her feet towards the growing light that filtered down through the broken, high-vaulted ceiling and reached the first floor but no further. Perhaps he knew she'd snuck out already and was waiting for her. *But he doesn't know about the rats or he'd have told me. I think.*

Stepping out through the arched doorway and taking the steps several at a time, she stood in the middle of the empty street. In the distance she could see the reclamation drones moving in and out of a skyscraper, taking it down one material at a time, one drone removing window glass and melting it down for reuse, another collecting metals. She waited, allowing her breathing to settle back into an even rhythm and the electric current of fear to subside in the sunshine that helped to blur out the scenes from the theatre basement.

With just a glance back at the building, she pulled out her handheld, hesitated, and then sent a message form and ordered a call.

The VR Comm link was spotty, fading out, shifting back in with full clarity but in a different setting. It was like trying to Comm a small child without the mental focus to hold the imagery in place.

Colors were too bright, incongruent details flashing into focus. A red lamp without a shade glared in Richard's eyes right next to Aesa, shining on her glossy black hair and tinting her eyes the same red of the round bulb. He stared at it for a long moment before returning to her face.

"Maybe if you slow down and explain a bit, we can figure this out." Aesa grabbed a fistful of her own hair and pulled it over her face, growling in what seemed like intense frustration.

Richard strode over to her and grasped her hands, gently shaking her hair loose and lowering them before letting go. "You said they've tied your hands. Keeping secrets."

She nodded.

"That you're scared of what's happening. What exactly would that be?" Aesa looked up at him, eyes that flickered with fear the moment before going soft. She reached up, grasped the back of his neck and pulled his face down to hers, nipping his bottom lip between her teeth and then tipping her head back with sudden laughter. It poured out of her like water gushing from the mouth of a fountain, with no sign of slowing.

Richard grew still, very still, and grabbed her face between both hands. "Aesa, focus. Please, are you sick?"

"Only, only if… I'm sick for you, Richard…" The laughter continued, breaking up her words.

Now it was his turn to growl in frustration. "What are you afraid of? Why the comm today?"

Aesa's laughter tapered off and her eyes cleared.

"Diadonna…she's playing the Martian Colony…probably planning another attack." The laughter was coming back in sudden hiccups and bursts, but her eyes were bright with fear. "I'm quarantined, sick again…she's been—poisoning me because I told her I disagree."

Richard's eyes were cold and the room around them dimmed. The red lamp was gone, replaced by sterile white lights that resembled those in the medical wing of the WGC. Still, the room wasn't solid; the windows shifted location from one blink to the next and furniture was equally impermanent. "No. Diadonna and I have an understanding about Mars. It's common knowledge; that's why I supported her election. If she was threatening the colonies, I'd have heard it from them already."

Aesa was sitting at a newly-present metal desk, with a four-legged stool that spun 90 degrees back and forth in a swaying motion. There was a wine glass in her hand, and she held it out towards him. "If you trust her so much, then why not drink from the glass she gave me?"

Richard's face smoothed over as realization dawned. Aesa was sick, but it was a sickness of the mind. "It's blood, you know, I can taste it. The salt of it…making me drink my own blood until it kills me."

Richard cleared his throat and glanced at the message from Aurelia that appeared in his line of sight in the comm. "Aesa, I'll see if I can help. Just, rest for now…I need to see a girl about a rat, and then I'll get back to you."

Aesa was staring into her red wine in her glass when he broke the comm. *Or blood, I suppose; it's her construct, after all.*

He felt a twinge of regret for her sudden and steep decline. Hopefully treatment would be effective…there were options. VR therapy, medications. The psychologists assigned to the WGC were among the best.

He pocketed his handheld and VR headset and made his way down the hall, footsteps echoing in the silent corridor as he crossed the large complex hurrying. Aurelia's message told him nothing except that she'd snuck out again, but the call coming in was enough to cause alarm.

That wasn't normal for Richard: twitchiness, irrational jumping to conclusions. Logical progression from one possible outcome to the most likely, yes, but not paranoia. *Aesa's mental landscape rubbing off on me. Maybe I'll check her file, talk to Diadonna…* He stopped to answer the call, and then, seeing it was only a voice comm, kept walking. He could walk and talk. These children would have tied him up in skillful knots and taken over the WGC long ago otherwise. He was smirking at his own humor when Aurelia's voice came through. No tears, or obvious distress, but he knew her. Aurelia was scared.

"Are you bringing one back?" His voice was smooth, gentleness and patience competing as the primary characteristic.

Aurelia took a breath, "You needn't be angry, Richard. It was for my research…but no, sadly, I do not have one." She could hear him think; the pause was so obvious as he gathered his thoughts and collected any wayward emotions. She was glad she had only opened up a voice comm and couldn't see his eyes just then, that hazel green that could be equally kind and terrifying, depending on what she had done most recently and whether it was in direct contradiction to his rules or just a small bend in them.

"Aurelia, I won't waste my energy on anger, here. You are reading into my concern because you are aware that your actions were, yet again, reckless." He paused. "No samples then? Nothing to test in the lab?"

She turned back towards the building, gray-black and pitted from acid rain and more than one fire years ago. "I can easily go back in and get the bodies, my cage. But I thought, to ask you before touching it…" She felt the stinging itch in the corner of her eyes that was a constant companion the past week, along with a persistent itching on the roof of her mouth. She scrubbed it with her tongue and blinked her eyes, hoping that would help, painfully aware that she shouldn't scratch it, shouldn't touch her face until she was decontaminated.

She heard the sigh of withheld breath released. "Good. Come back then."

Aurelia glanced back at the shadowed entrance to the Theatre. "With or without the samples?"

"Without. We'll send a drone in to retrieve it. Come back now and report to the decontamination center on the East wing of the WGC. They handle more than the west building."

She cleared her throat, wishing that tickle would go away. "Okay, but…um, Richard?"

"Yes, Aurelia?" Her voice shook a little now, just enough for him to wince on the other end of the comm. "I'm just sorry, if I messed up. I'm sorry."

"I know. Just come back now."

SUSPICIONS

Theresa traced the contours of Richard's fingers with her own, stroking from tip to base and then following the faint web between each finger to the next. They were wider than her own but still tapered, giving the appearance of dexterity and competence.

A white scar, fine but jagged, ran from one index finger to where it joined the thumb. Theresa paused in her tracing and glanced up to find Richard's gaze distracted, distant.

"What's this one from?"

He rubbed his thumb across the scar, a distant smile curling his lips. "Erlenmeyer flask. I was fitting it with a stopper for vacuum filtration. The lab was old, equipment older, and it broke under pressure."

He pushed one strand of chestnut brown hair from her forehead, falling silent as he stared at the VR simulated highlights there.

"Richard?"

"Hm?"

"Your thoughts aren't here. You need to get back? VR Comm with distance canceling does take up more time…"

Richard tightened his brow, pressing his lips together as if smothering some unwise words between them before answering.

"Normally I'd argue that VR Comm with you was worth the loss of sleep—it is late on Earth, the children are sleeping now, but…"

Theresa cocked her head, sitting up from where she rested against his chest. "But not this time?"

"I'm neglecting responsibilities that I need to catch up on—"

He stood up, pulling her with him.

"Several of the children are out on preparatory apprenticeship expeditions, and the ones back here are prone to…misadventure. I've several figurative fires to put out and messes to clean up."

"As you told me—" Richard nodded, hair a mix of dark brown and white falling forward with the motion. "But it's their first trip away from the complex without me—away from my guidance and testing their independence."

"Can't you still comm with them?" Theresa tried on what she imagined was a comforting smile, succeeding with something half-nervous, half-amused.

Richard shook his head and laughed. "I have good reason to worry, you know…they are your children, and their propensity to find or fall into—unexpected circumstance, is uncanny. Including Aurelia…"

Theresa's smile turned into dry laughter. "Wouldn't you say, especially Aurelia? She and Gavin, between the two we could almost equal the number of 'unexpected events' from all of the others."

Richard began buttoning his shirt. His signal to leave the VR Comm.

Theresa stepped back, wrapping her arms around herself to avoid showing the unease that ending a comm always brought. "And what is she into now? Let her rats loose down the WGC's halls again?"

A wry smile matched the sudden spark of dark amusement that touched his eyes and he hesitated before finding his reply. "Not quite but—close enough. And I must return to cleaning up after her. Don't bother trying to comm with her —I'm told that her headache today is such that she couldn't possibly."

The last button completed, Richard leaned forward, pulling Theresa's VR form against his own and pressing lips to hers. Theresa returned the kiss, warm and promising less distraction at the next meeting. A deep sigh escaped as he pulled away, catching her eyes with his own chestnut and green ones and offering a smile.

"Be good."

The connection broke and Theresa found herself staring at her own reflection in the VR Comm headset.

She pulled it off and squeezed her eyes shut to begin clearing the ache of overstimulation that was a part of VR recovery, flexing her fingers and stretching her neck to speed the return of coordination and trust in her body's movements.

Theresa pressed her fingers against her lips. Those kisses always closely resembled the one from Earth—the only one. It was worth repeating, but after nearly eleven years had taken on a stale quality that resembled a dream stuck on loop—the sort that left her aching for the next scene of real-life to break free of the replay.

Huh, he didn't say what Aurelia was into, really…something with her rats again.

Theresa pictured the tiny pink-toed feet skittering across a lab counter, running along the piping in the old AUC lab of the reproductive council. They tried to keep them out, but some slipped through the covered vents and the sound deterrents, perhaps through some unknown entrance. And there they would be, illuminated by her computer screen as they held her last stick of cinnamon gum between tiny hands, gnawing at the wrapper until both wrapper and gum were devoured.

Theresa smiled, imagining Aurelia surrounded by such creatures as the girl had shown her in VR Comm once. Aurelia's eyes brightened so when she spoke of the rats. It was hard to be critical of them.

She stood to finish stretching, then turned towards the small arched window facing east. Aurelia's pointed nose, crinkling for emphasis as she gesticulated towards her many cages, still hovered in her mind's eye, and was joined by Bram, Gavin, Irena, Gelsemium, Caspian…so many. The faint nausea leftover from VR began to fade, replaced by an empty hollow. *Of course he needed to leave to tend to them. And she couldn't.*

Theresa cleared her throat and adjusted the pins that held stray hairs of her bun in place. Her lab coat wasn't in need of adjustment. She gave it the customary tug nonetheless, then turned to her laboratory screen and the public security cameras to find Abby.

Theresa allowed the foam full of hissing bubbles to envelop her feet, clenching her jaw against the cold as it rose up to ankles and then calves.

It pulled at her legs as it receded, but with such a gradual ebb that she could easily resist. Theresa wrapped her hands around her arms, rubbing at the mottled and goosebump-roughened skin there.

Abby danced closer, enjoying the slow receding of foamy water, hazarding a glance out into the bay where the waves were impressive. The next incoming wave would be slow to approach, due to the low gravity, but it would be high enough to see the colony domes from a new angle if she kept her head above water.

She quirked a brow at her mother, expression otherwise impassive. "We could have waited until later in the day when it warms, if you're too cold."

Theresa pulled in a breath and shook herself as if to still the shivers. "Or we could just get in and we'll feel warmer, yes?"

Abby grinned. "That's what I was thinking, but I didn't think you would."

"Then I've given you the wrong impression." Theresa ran, kicking up foam and sand as she made for deeper water. Abby followed, catching up as they reached the shift in color from pale olive green to a darker forest green that indicated depth. The large waves here were rolling still, not the ones that would break over them and pull them under.

"Better?"

Theresa's laugh was genuine, if shaky. "No, still cold if that's what you mean. But definitely worth it."

Abby sighed, rolling onto her back to float. "You couldn't swim on Earth, could you?" It was stated as fact with just enough incredulity to give evidence to Abby's time on Mars, having never experienced Earth.

"Um, yes, I couldn't swim like this. The oceans were off limits. There were pools though, indoors, simulated waves...not the same."

"It's good we're on Mars then."

Theresa saw the AUC lab as it appeared in memory: Abby in the Capsule-like AUC unit and then sealed against her chest in the RPU, brow creasing as she imagined the alternate choices, staying when Richard asked, or never removing Abby from her AUC. Her voice was low with the weight of those thoughts. "Yes. It is. They'd have likely taken you from me otherwise...and better never to see Earth, never get attached if it's not your home. And it isn't."

Abby frowned. "Do you think the others will miss it...? Will they settle in to Mars like we have?"

Theresa tread water, staring out at the oncoming wave. "They'll...under or over this one?"

Abby turned in the same direction, following Theresa's gaze. "Under." And she dove then, swimming farther out as the wave lifted her with it. Theresa dove a moment after. The water under the wave was colder but it no longer chilled her, instead giving the time underwater a dream-like quality.

They rose together at the tail-end of the wave, laughing and out of breath as they came down from it into the level swell of ocean.

"They'll have your…help…but it will be harder than being born here, and harder than choosing it like our original colonists did."

Abby nodded. "What if some of them don't want to come?"

Theresa turned back towards the beach, beginning the swim back and expecting Abby to follow. "They'll come because Richard says they must, and hopefully because we're here. Mars is the future for us, Abby. Not Earth."

Abby's questions stopped as they swam back and stepped out from the water, wading until they reached the crimson sand that clung to their wet ankles. The girl stood toying with strings of rat-tail seaweed, deep in thought.

Theresa frowned at her sudden silence and the unsettled feeling she was picking up from her daughter, when just before they'd been enjoying the waves and each other's company. "Abby, you spoke with some of them not long ago…was Aurelia into some trouble with her rats?"

Abby remained silent, thinking, and Theresa waited until it appeared that she wouldn't answer.

"Abby?"

"She was not on the VR Comm when I invited them. She was out collecting more rats, apparently." She pressed her lips together and frowned, thinking. "She often goes without telling Richard, I believe. That could be all it was, right?"

Theresa's brows creased, but she nodded. "Yes, I think so. It sounded like something like that."

Melissa stared ahead of her. The message that flashed on the screen was a scramble of letters and numbers that refused to come together and make sense as she fought back the sting of eyestrain and the mental fog of overwhelm.

She blinked twice and then closed her eyes for a long moment as she pulled her focus back from the many thoughts that crowded their way into her mind, vying for attention—*three hours until the meeting with Genesis, Neil's baby came, summer winds are coming on now— heavy ones not far off—then early winter storms…*

She opened her eyes again, reading the message before her.

Mars Council Lead Melissa Espinosa,

The World Governing Council has transferred leadership to myself, Diadonna Cantor, this First day of August, 2324.

As my first order of business with regards to the Martian Colony, I would like to extend my deepest regrets and long overdue condolences for the altercation between Earth and Mars and the resulting losses that occurred. While the files on Martian colonization research were closed out and archived years ago, I am making it my priority to ascertain the answers to yours and Captain Neil's questions; in particular, the possibility of falsified research. I have not been privy to any of that information up to this point, but I will not let the issue stand. I will instead search out the truth of the matter.

It is my hope that in the name of Earth and Mars we can cultivate not only a firm truce but cooperation for the good of humankind.

Warmest Regards,

Diadonna Cantor

Diadonna Cantor

Pushing back from the desk with a forceful shove, Melissa stood and scowled at her handheld. "Nine years and you want an accord?! Nine years of threats and silence…Two terms are enough. Not a fucking wonder Neil was done." She spit the words under her breath, rolling her eyes when the voice recognition on her handheld keyed on with a gleam of blue light.

"Is that the message you would like to send?" The voice was an understated androgynous simulation that had replaced the cheerful, sunshiny AI that she had preferred before the pressure had amped up halfway through her first term.

"Gods, no!"

"Alright. Do you have one composed to send, or would you like one of your prewritten messages to be chosen by my topic matching program?"

Melissa sighed, pushing back the short wisps of fine brown hair that tickled her forehead. A sweat had broken out on the light-beige skin that tanned under Earth sun but was sallow from too much time indoors and too many meals skipped.

"No. I've got this one. Record and transcribe:

"Ms. Cantor, My sincere congratulations on your recent promotion. May you find the position of power and the accompanying pressure suits your sunny disposition. Your message has been received and, while, your sentiments are quite welcome, I hope you'll understand that I must answer with caution. Nine years have passed since we were attacked, essentially without giving cause and without receiving warning, and we still look up to find loved ones missing."

She pursed her lips, pausing to collect her thoughts once more and banish the echo of a quirky smile and youthful brown eyes that came into mental focus unbidden.

"Your offer of information is accepted, of course, and we will remain in communication, as we have attempted to do for the past nine years. Whether an accord will arise or not, I cannot see at this time. And so, in that spirit, I consent to move forward towards that end so long as you maintain full transparency and are true to your promised goals.

Martian Council Lead,
Melissa Espinosa

Melissa Espinosa"

Melissa let out a deep sigh as the message sent. A VR Comm interaction would likely be in order in the near future. But not until she and the Captain conferred.

Voice comm would suffice for now.

"Connect to Captain Neil."

The answering voice was a whisper accompanied by the sound of shifting blankets, the breathing sounds of deep slumber, and finally the slide of a door, after which Neil cleared his throat and adjusted volume.

"Didn't want to wake anyone. What's up, Governor?"

"A Diadonna Cantor, foremost of the candidates on Earth—as per Genesis's intelligence--has taken the WGC ruling seat, and she wants an accord between us. She sends her apologies—"

A choked laugh came through from Neil's end. "And did you tell her where she could shove her apologies and her accord—"

Melissa smiled. "No, I told her we would cautiously consider interaction and accept the information she is promising…But what I want to hear from you is how close your Pinnacle is to ready — for a return trip to our mother-planet. And are you ready to follow through?"

Neil's voice took on a sharper tone, resolve tightening his vocal cords, "You know I am."

Melissa nodded to the empty room. "Okay Neil, g'night."

The incoming message chime sounded just as she closed the comm with Captain Neil and she winced. It was late, and the last message was more than enough to process.

She opened it, of course she opened it, and confusion creased her forehead, irritation sparking in her eyes as she read the first line under the heading.

Mars Council Lead Melissa Espinosa, Why would you call me a liar?! Twisting my heartfelt sentiments, doubting my promises…it almost seems as if you don't want peace with Earth. Perhaps what's boiling up here started in your little head. Head of the Justice Department before you took Council lead and you think I wouldn't suspect —

The message cut off there as if sent, with no closing statement or official signature block. Melissa's heart was beating hard and fast in her own ears and she felt a rising heat that was some confusing mix of anger and alarm. *Could they know Neil was repairing the Pinnacle—that he planned to fly it there fully armed?*

The next message chime startled her even more than the last now that she had adrenaline coursing through her bloodstream. She didn't want to read any more messages; she wanted to type a nasty reply, something threatening, something to turn the tables and make the woman on the other end of the last message feel how she felt. The Pinnacle couldn't make its return flight to Earth soon enough. But if there was anything she knew about being in a leadership role it was to never type while angry, or petty, or prideful, never reply without a cool head, period.

She pulled in a deep breath and opened the message, face twisting in confusion and disbelief.

Mars Council Lead Melissa Espinosa,

I am embarrassed to admit my aide has suffered a mental breakdown and is responsible for the previous message. Her decline has been sudden and alarming, or else this could not have happened. She is now on medical leave. Please, arrange a VR Comm with me at your first convenience so we can smooth this over. My desire for an accord stands and I hope we can pretend the previous message from my aide was never sent.

My Sincerest Apologies,
Diadonna Cantor

Diadonna Cantor

Melissa dropped her handheld on the surface of her desk as if burned by it and stared at it there, half expecting another chime before she could shut-down all notifications for the night. There were no more sounds from it, no more chimes, and let out her breath. She'd reread them all in the morning when her head was clear, forward them to Neil as well. *Sleep had damn well better come fast.*

QUARANTINE

Aurelia's thin, pale, fingers twisted in her hair, fine like singed corn silk, without most of the pigment her sibling's hair came with but still not truly blonde. It wasn't hers, really. Preplanned, programmed, chosen simply for an artificial construct of variety, not in her mother's or father's genetics but instead extracted and added in for some purpose she could guess at but never confirm. Like the rats in her many cages, bred for the purpose of experiment instead of the joy of it. But she enjoyed the rats, didn't she? The rough feel of their whiplike tails as she stroked them against her cheeks, their oil drop eyes staring into her own with minute hands resting on the bridge of her nose, and silken fur beneath her fingertips.

Her fingers stuck together, bound by spirals of tightly spun hair strands. She took a breath, realizing that she had been withholding it, and released her fingers to begin twisting them again, trying a number of times to bind them up to still their shivers. But her hair was too short to fully serve the purpose. She let out a shaky breath again and opened her eyes, glancing at the screens on the opposite wall from where she leaned back against the metal surface.

The humming had stopped a moment before, end-effectors of

the robotic arms that surrounded her withdrawing and going still, blood, sweat, skin and throat swabs taken.

Aurelia's eyes flitted from one data panel to the next, searching for the information she awaited. There were too many lights and too many streams of data neither processed nor translated.

The data froze in place, lights shifting from green to red. Aurelia's eyes widened as the voice came from above, confirming her suspicions. "Signs of unfamiliar pathogen detected within nasal passages and skin surfaces. Infection status: pending. Decontamination and 48-hour quarantine required." The medical bot paused as if considering the next words carefully. "I'm so sorry for the inconvenience and distress this will cause you."

Aurelia sighed, breath fogging the wall, before she sat up and folded her arms, awaiting the next step. The room was cold, but decontamination would be worse.

At least the next part.

The spray from the ceiling was colder than ice water and had a lingering sting to it that would make the hot shower that followed less than comfortable, like the feel of peppermint oils applied to the skin and then held under scalding hot water. And the strong soaps they used made her eyes feel dry and ache. And then the UV lamps.

There would be multiple rounds of decontamination, depending on how much of a show of it they were going to make. They knew as well as she did that if it was going to take hold, then decontamination would do nothing at this point.

She closed her eyes and welcomed the hot water. In her mind's eye, the outer layers of her skin cracked and sloughed off under the driving rain that came down like so many minute nails shot from the shower head.

Her thoughts wandered again such that the heat of the shower became a secondary sensation. She was underground with the rats again, hearing their sharp squeals and the scritch-scratching as their oblong bodies started to spasm throughout the labyrinth of tunnels in the walls, then went still. The only sound was her hitching breath as the same took hold of her, twisting and shaking her body as she fell to the damp floor, kicking and flailing until she stilled like the rats.

The water had stopped now and she was staring before her, eyes hollow as the chasm in her belly that left her feeling all hollowed out. Aurelia swallowed, imagining an itchy, roughness in her throat that made the sides of her esophagus stick and rub and bring on a cough. She flinched against a crawling sensation at the back of her neck and scratched it violently, leaving reddened streaks that broke the skin in one or two places. Get out of your head. It's too soon for any symptoms. *Only a child would waste energy fearing one outcome of many possible. And I'm not THAT sort of child.*

She slowed her breathing and opened and closed her eyes several times as if to reset her whole perspective.

The walls were grey, metallic, and there were numerous panels, screens, and openings for the robotic arms that served to decontaminate her in lieu of any human that could be contaminated themselves. There were many steps left in the process and, as this was not her first time in decontamination, she knew them all by heart. Aurelia smiled at the predictability of the treatments and began the countdown in her mind. 172,800 seconds until the next round of tests, if she made it that far.

Richard's viewing screen was in active research mode, tipped on its back to form a glowing tabletop that was currently projecting the holographic representations of the WGC capitol on one half of the screen and reclamation block 63B of the ruins on the other. The crumbling theater was represented in an outline of blue light, the rat colony below it represented in red, red that dimmed and winked out like lights in an apartment high rise going out at curfew, isolated sparks disappearing one at a time around the outskirts and then small clusters fading, larger pools of light dimming and flickering. The voice call on his headset went through, but his eyes and hands continued to track the data on the screen.

"Diadonna, question…"

The voice on the other end of the call sounded amused, curious. "Yes?"

"Why is the East Wing medical center full of quarantine patients, and why does Aesa think you mean to threaten Mars again?"

Diadonna laughed but she no longer sounded amused. "I'm going to go ahead and humor you…the medical wing is full because we had an outbreak of pneumonic plague cases in the Reproductive Council branch, among the surrogates. We caught it early, haven't lost a single one, but you know how it spreads—quite a few came down with it." She paused before continuing, waiting for some response but filling the empty air when none came. "But what do Aesa's accusations have to do with your first question? You aren't prone to believing conspiracy theories."

Richard raised a brow but she couldn't see it. "The connection is that Aesa claimed to be in quarantine because you were trying to silence her, among other things."

Diadonna's patience cracked, and Richard could hear the anger in her voice now. "Aesa was not in quarantine—well, not since recovering from our little outbreak. She was back out until last night, when she almost sabotaged our progress with Mars with an ill-timed message to Melissa Espinosa. She has—lost her grasp on reality."

Richard listened, eyes narrowed. There was a subtle shift in Diadonna's tone as she lowered her voice. She wasn't lying.

"Why, Richard, would I threaten Mars, when my whole platform for election was to repair our relationship, rebuild so we could open up more colonies?"

"You wouldn't. Thank you. One last question."

"Yes?" Her voice had a strained break in it that was always there when she was pushing herself too hard, like rope slowly tearing under a heavy load.

"Any idea where the outbreak started?" "No. Check with epidemiology if you want more on that. But it's contained now."

"Sure, thanks, Diadonna." *Pneumonic plague, then, maybe—except that doesn't fit what Aurelia got into…ripping each other to pieces, higher mating urge…*Richard pulled off the headset and stared at the screen, his focus unwavering again as he took in the visual data, expression impassive and eyes unblinking. Another cluster of red light faded into darkness and he cocked his head to the side.

The other half of the screen that was a real-time aerial map of the whole city and the outskirts held the same pattern, buildings and other inanimate features in blue, rats in red, humans in orange and yellow. The rat population in the outskirts was high, especially in the old tunnels beneath the city that once served to transport sewage and water. It was also for mass transit. All of these functions were above ground now: water collected, cleaned, and recirculated, waste composted, transit accomplished by way of magnetic rails, and on-demand electric drone vehicles. There was no need to tunnel beneath the city and weaken its structural integrity, nor provide breeding grounds for the rats and cockroaches that were largely unaffected by the changing climate. And yet many of these old outposts of human society long past remained, left behind to collect the swollen colonies of Earth's wildlife.

Thoughts welled up, racing on multiple tracks in his mind, where in another's they might have collided half formed, too many competing to make it where they were headed, or instead one pushing another out in order to fit. *An epizootic, sudden, and spreading like fire in a wind-tunnel. She was exposed to it, then. We'll know quickly how weak they are…and how strong we are. Aurelia —*

And they kept coming, each thought accompanied by several side considerations and actions to take in response.

He opened recent files sent to the WGC council using his official clearance. The Epidemiology briefing for the quarter had no mention of this epizootic, but there were some others. The plague outbreaks were mentioned, an uptick in environmental allergens, Ebola. The document was long and detailed. Locust swarms, some headed here and expected to block out the sky for a full day; the cicadas that were widespread now, a favorite snack for the rats. He could hear them through the windows, singing to each other, if you could call that ear-ringing buzz a song.

There were several more paragraphs, one dedicated to the latest coronavirus strain and the timeline for this year's vaccine. The next paragraph was the same, covering influenza updates.

If it wasn't mentioned here, that meant there was a good chance that Epidemiology headquarters didn't know, that it was that new, or localized here. For now.

He spoke to the AI, words coming rapid-fire, grateful that it could keep up. "Compose urgent communication for the Epidemiology Headquarters and include the live data I've compiled on the localized rat epizootic. Send with urgent heading and request follow-up information."

"Composing now; would you like to include a personal message?" "No, no. Just extrapolate pleasantries using my previous patterns. This is urgent…and forward a copy to Diadonna, please."

"Message sent and forwarded!" Richard nodded to the empty room and pushed a hand through his hair. He closed out the program, silencing his handheld and pocketing it in his lab coat. A spark of excitement flared up in his mind, coupled with an equally powerful thrum of urgency propelling the thoughts faster. There was time yet to see where this would lead. *Diadonna thinks her outbreaks are contained—but what about this one?* His shoes clicked on the tiles at the same speed as his thoughts as he crossed the room and headed to the East Quarantine Center.

The green leaves of twisting, interwoven Ficus branches pointed limply towards the floor, casting shadows against the walls from all four corners of the Surrogate Center's recreation room. They were dying, dropping their yellow bodies onto the short, cropped mud brown carpets. Even still, a leaf-litter carpet had not formed, couldn't in the face of the many blinking Mousebots that perused the room, small and unobtrusive as they kept the space tidy through silent vacuum and manual pick-up by scooping arms for larger pieces of trash.

They went largely unnoticed, even by the many pairs of damp, red-rimmed eyes that stared through them, seeing shadows and dark thoughts instead of the room that held them.

Ania's hands crossed and uncrossed over the moon-like swell of her abdomen, fingers interlacing to lock in the nervous energy that was evident in darting eyes and shifting posture even as she sat reclining under the weight of her advanced pregnancy.

Her wide brown eyes, framed by black lash, flicked over to the nearest of her companions, opening further as if the alarm within them pushed against her eyelids with splayed legs, forcing them open to let the fear out through their twin portals.

"Tasha was stressing out, though. She wasn't ready to go again so soon after handing off the last. Maybe that's what pushed her over—"

The larger woman to her left, short of stature but with pregnancy better hidden beneath the padding on her abdomen, nodded as she spoke. The look in her squinted hazel eyes didn't change despite her seeming agreement; they held a hollowed-out expression that belied her posture of solid nonchalance. "She was stressing. Saw the counselor every day all the way up till it happened—once she was out of quarantine for that flu we had — but I hear she was going b'cause she had to and wasn't talking."

Another voice joined, husky and low, though whether from evidence of long hours crying or the natural quality of her voice only the other surrogates knew. Perhaps both. "But Daniel? She liked him, said she'd keep on with him until they made her switch with the next conception…if they did even."

Elise continued nodding, soft arms and milk-swollen breasts swaying with the vigorous motion this time. "She did like him." Her eyes narrowed a bit more. "I liked him. We matched up once." A deep sigh blew from between her lips; it was heavy with some emotion, something that carried with it the ache of abandoned possessions, left to go cold and gather dust, shared laughter left to fade into receding memory.

The silence drew out between them, filling with dropped thoughts like the everglades with discarded plastics. One of them would motion as if to speak, and then the words would dry up somewhere between intention and voice box.

Melody's ragged voice spoke again, somehow gathering up all of the unspoken ghosts of thought and pressing them together for presentation like a tailor sewing rags into whole cloth.

"How they found them, though…covered in each other's blood, her raving and clawing at—at herself." She shivered, flicking haunted grey eyes over the others to gauge their silent reactions before she pulled more of the sodden swamp of thoughts out for them to examine. Elise nodded more slowly now, as if the effort it took grew weightier with each word uttered. Ania was crying again, silent tears that slid down and stung; she wiped at them with such violence.

"I heard she was in a coma, had some kind of seizure, and back in quarantine."

Ania spoke up then, words lashing out like thorned vines wielded whip-like. "How could you hear it?! They haven't been in since we all got out again. Not a single person. Just the med bots to test us as usual!" Her eyes flared with white hot rage, one fist clenching at her side and the other pressing against the swollen mound of her belly as if to shield the inhabitant beneath.

Melody flinched but then continued, with lowered voice and no small amount of venom. "Like usual? No, they came earlier and they tested longer, not just the usual things…and how could I know? Because my handler came just after it happened, and she likes to talk. And she hasn't been back, to me or any of you, yes?"

None of the women moved or nodded now. None shook their heads or spoke to refute it. Elise covered a dry cough with her arm but refused to flinch away from the wide-eyed stares.

Ania uttered a guttural shout, standing to pace, hands raking through coal-black hair pulling as if to remove it by the roots.

Melody's low voice continued undaunted. "She had something, I bet you, and they tested us for it—and they haven't come back in, have they?" Melody wiped a hand across her fevered brow, staring at the glistening sweat there with an anxious gleam in her eyes, staring close as if she might see some definitive sign of illness, some proof to their fears if she looked long enough and hard enough.

Ania rushed towards her, slapping the sweat damp hand away from Melody's face before leaning her own in to take its place.

"Stop it! Just stop it! You're scaring everyone with your damn stories—you don't know any more than the rest of us. We all got treated, and we're fine. Tasha lost her shit because she stopped talking to the therapist."

Melody shoved her with both hands, and the couch arm caught her by the back of her knees, sending the heavily pregnant woman sprawling across it.

Elise uncrossed her well-padded arms and offered one to Ania so that she could right herself. The scowl that darkened her face with storm clouds was deep and craggy with anger.

"What are you doing? You don't make it physical, either of you; enough, then!" She grabbed both of their wrists to hold them apart, somehow unaware that she was breaking her own rules.

The daylight-simulating lights dimmed, as if to flicker off, only to be replaced by a red flashing glare and the alto tones of the alert system. All eyes turned to the ceiling for answers as if the change in lighting could somewhere clue them in to the nature of the alert.

The Surrogate Complex's AI answered the unspoken question in their widened eyes. "Full quarantine has gone into effect. You are each to report to the medical wing for immediate treatment and quarantine. It is in yours and the progeny's best interests that you receive immediate treatment." The voice went silent, but the lights continued to flicker red.

"Treatment for what?! We're in recovery!"

The surrogates' eyes were wide, pupils dilated. The red lights of the quarantine announcement shone in their glassy surfaces and gleamed off of Ania's steadily trailing tears.

She was the first to stand and walk towards the exit to the recreation room, still trembling with rage, her eyes flicking daggers back at Melody. The door would lead to a hall, a hall that wound around the complex and ultimately ended with the medical wing.

RISING FEVER

Richard stared through the thick glass into the high clouds, black and tumbling closer. His fingers tap-tapped against the icy surface, creating an intricate rhythm as he surveyed the horizon. Most of what he could see was in shadow, the ring of mountains in the distance dwarfed by the mega-storm approaching. It was going to shake the high towers of the reproductive council for certain, and the WGC as well, when it reached them, but that was just a small fraction of what was coming. *Storms we can handle—at least until infrastructure fails…..and will it? Is this the one that'll finish it?*

He pushed a hand through chestnut brown hair, threaded with more silver than his mature but un-aging face could justify, with jaw and forehead powerful from decades of androgen exposure but lacking the signs of age-induced infirmity.

Turning his back to the storm he licked his lips, a smile forming as he faced the other man in the room. "And you called me here for?" He spiraled his hand mid-air as if to draw out the other man's response. "Eleven years without setting foot in the council headquarters makes this quite a momentous occasion, don't you think? Where are the crystal goblets and ancient wines?" The words were steeped in heavy sarcasm, like a black tea left forgotten too long.

The responding slow clap made him raise a brow. The high-backed office chair turned on smooth ball bearings and stopped to face him. Morton Steiner clapped one last time, thick fingers enhancing the sound in the acoustically superior board room. His heavy frame filled the chair, broad shoulders emerging on either side as if he had perhaps chosen the wrong seat. His eyes were sharp with bitterness and…something else, something raw and reminiscent of a newly caged animal, not caged long enough to be hungry but with the growing knowledge that he soon would be gut-gnawing, ribs showing through taut skin—*starving*. "You can cut the shit, Richard. We set our dice and took a roll, and you came up on top. Drop it now and let's talk."

Richard moved to the edge of the round oaken table, placing both hands on the smooth surface as he leaned there, the gesture casual, belying the look in his eyes. "What you did was above and beyond any sort of groundwork we may have set before that." A fire flared in his pupils, burning with the intensity of a forge set to smelt the steel within. "No one does what you did with me and comes back from it. Period. I'm here, well, simply to make certain you are aware of that fact before it catches up with you." He tilted his head. "Or have you forgotten how detailed and long-lasting my memory is for slights?"

Morton raised both brows for emphasis and his hands as if to clap, pausing them just before they came together. "Do you need another round of applause for that little soliloquy? It wasn't personal. How's that? *Wasn't* personal. If you had done your job right, then it wouldn't have gone down that way—But that's not what I brought you here for, damnit!"

"Not personal? You ordered the termination of MY project. One that we made agreements about from the infancy of the thing." Richard's eyes went cold, unreadable, his face expressionless as he nodded. "What are we here to discuss if not your 'impersonal betrayal?'" The rats winking out like lights in the dark scratched at the back of his mind, and he saw Aurelia's feverish face in quarantine, counting under her breath. *Does he know?*

"Something more pressing. And, well, we don't have to get shit-faced and kiss on each other to see eye to eye on this one."

Richard opened his mouth to speak, irritation clear in the deep green and hazel eyes that glared from below dark brows.

Morton's fist hit the table, causing an involuntary startle not in Richard but himself instead. The caged animal look returned, but with more intensity. It looked ready to scrabble its way up the arm of the next handler that came close enough, leaving blood and rabies in its wake. "Just shut up now—please. We have an issue coming up that—" Morton's self-assured voice wavered, and Richard stared, stone-faced, as he continued, all argument silenced. *He already knows…for how long?*

"There's something hitting the surrogates hard. It's taken 2/3 of them, and we thought that was it. Actually thought they were all in recovery for a hot minute."

Richard licked his lips. "Thought? You're talking about the plague outbreak Diadonna had contained?"

Morton rubbed his face with both hands, leaving just those crazed eyes visible. "Yeah. They relapsed twice—fast, then third time's a charm, the big one." He mimicked an explosion with lips and hands.

"Now it's popping up in other places, outside of the Reproductive Council."

"Are you sure it's the plague—Yersinia Pestis, that you're dealing with? It's easily treatable with antibiotics."

"Yeah, yeah…that's what it is. But it's killing them. Antibiotics clear it but it comes right back—epidemiology identified it. And the way it kills is the same. Autopsies confirmed it too." Steiner cracked his neck and massaged the muscles at the base of his skull with one hand, his eyes widening and lips moving without words for a moment before he continued. "There is one thing, though. Some of them are going crazy from it…violent." A shiver that was half spasm ran through him. The room wasn't cold, but he rubbed his bare arms.

Richard's full attention was on the Head of the Reproductive Council, eyes narrowed in concentration despite his otherwise calm demeanor. *It's too fast to have come from Aurelia—started sooner or elsewhere then, or it's just a worse plague outbreak than Diadonna thought.* The urge to leave, to return to his lab, gripped Richard. "Other places? How far? And is it possible it's another strain, maybe altered by the Councils? A research accident?"

"No. Not unless it's changed so much that the lab isn't recognizing it yet." He hesitated before answering the last question, scrubbing a hand across the sweat that glistened on the sides of his ruddy neck. "They have cases confirmed in all outposts, all continents. We have the first deaths, though."

"Cases like yours? Persistent relapse, resistance to antibiotic treatment, violent outbursts? Or just the pneumonic plague outbreaks that Epidemiology was already tracking?"

"You tell me, Richard…"

"Fine. You were right." He strode around the table and towards the antique, heavy double doors that served as the only non-mechanized exit in the building.

"About?—Wait, You're leaving?" His look was incredulous, eyes filling with alarm.

Richard pulled open the double doors, continuing to speak without decreasing pace. "Send it to my lab. Not the real thing, of course—your researchers can package up the data. I'll have it sorted for you in a week or—" He slowed then, laughing as he threw a glance back at the head of the reproductive council. "Or you'll be dead."

EARTH—WGC EUR-ASIA EPIDEMIOLOGY HEADQUARTERS

The distance across the lab seemed so much more cramped and claustrophobic with the lights dimmed for power conservation. The open plan workspaces, separated off on three or four sides depending on the containment level, were all dark except for her own. The normally well-lit spaces in-between, empty now, seemed to absorb and cancel out any light that made it there, as if even the shadows were feeling this heaviness.

She broke the glassy-eyed stare that she was locked in and fought for focus, grasping for some motivation, some rope to pull herself in a tangible direction. She turned her eyes back to her own workstation, searching—and found the faces of her colleagues there.

The largest screen in the room was bright and required her attention. As empty as the physical lab was, the people that made up epidemiology were all present there on the screen divided up in their own sections, quarantined. Some were hooked up to personal medbots for treatment of more advanced symptoms. Dr. Carson was skeletal—he was always thin, but his neck looked swollen, inflated more on one side than the other and painted with fading bruises. His eyes were bright with fever and caffeine, but he was animated, focused and alert. She felt a dulled wave of shame. It was distant, like an oncoming wave that looked large enough to pull her under but never got within reach. She observed it but didn't touch it. She observed her observation of it as well and felt a laugh building up but couldn't stop it. *None of this is funny. I'm not even sick like some of them; why can't I focus? Maybe I* am *sick. Am I muted?*

She was still muted.

The full course of antibiotics was finished today. In fact, she'd popped the last pill this morning while attending the cremation service for Alexis Duchain, preeminent research scientist and department supervisor for the WGC's Epidemiology task force. *Quite a credential to go into the incinerator.* Ivanna flinched at the callousness of the thought and the vivid mental image of the flames taking Alexis's body, the reflections on the glass between them that gave the illusion that Alexis was moving, shaking in another seizure as she burned. She had glanced over at Xavi. His eyes were red, and not from allergies this time; those pills were working too, it seemed. Her own itching was gone, replaced by a dry ache. She didn't feel sick at all. Never had, really. They caught it so early after Alexis died, seizing up and hitting her head like she had.

She rubbed her eyes and pressed the heels of her hands against them before focusing back on the screen. There was a heaviness in her hands and in her head that felt like fog or cotton batting.

It felt like dreaming.

Maybe it was the death. She wasn't crying like Xavi, but that didn't mean she didn't care. Alexis was good to work for. That little tap that she did when she approached Ivanna's desk, not to rush her but a greeting of sorts, and then she would wait until Ivanna looked up and dive in to a detailed account of the latest project. Ivanna saw her shaking on the hospital bed, in the fire, only this time Alexis turned and looked at her with hollow eyes, reached for her.

Xavi was on the screen, third window in the top row, enlarged because he was speaking, instead of the workspace next to her. Ivanna looked at the death toll and her mouth fell open, a lance of fear hitting her. Didn't make sense.

She unmuted the speakers and herself, rubbing a hand across her eyes. They were speaking too quickly, words that she knew the meaning of rushed through her mind before she could grab them and make solid connections.

"It looks like a different strain of Y. Pestis—"

"Responsible for the black death, it's taking hold in the lungs as well as the lymph nodes, pneumonic plague."

"No, the strain is the same as previous outbreaks—"

"No, no, no…we may not have found a difference but it *is* acting different and we need to look at why—"

"We are and we will, Doctor. But the symptom picture is not consistent, and I think you are conflating separate outbreaks. It's a bad year for this."

"Yes, we knew that going into it, and we're overdue for a pandemic based on all prevailing…"

They were arguing now, losing focus. Alexis would be mediating this, redirecting them to the research, smoothing over bruised egos.

Xavi was ignoring it, dictating the background information into their database. "…historically with a fatality rate of 100% for this pneumonic variety, but in modern times a rate of 30 to 60 % fatality with early administration of antibiotics. This new strain Y. Pestis X appears to resist available antibiotic treatment, resulting in fatal relapse and, through as yet unexplored mechanisms, is causing psychiatric symptoms. Based on data from our North American headquarters showing a concurrent epizootic in the rat population, the most likely vectors for human infection are flea and rat as was seen with historical pandemics—"

"But that isn't confirmed yet, is it? You have my data from WGC North America—the epizootic rate, the live samples. Have we compared strains?"

A Dr. Brant, screen six bottom row, was addressing Xavi directly. His eyes looked clear, focused, and there were no medibot monitors or IVs connected to him that she could see.

Xavi cleared his throat, flinching from the direct attention. "Um, well, we had delays. I'll send what we have, but yes, the strains for human infection here and in two other locations, including your own, match your rats at the North America Headquarters."

She was staring again, and time had passed. How much time? Twenty-three of the forty-eight screens were now empty, muted, or logged off. Xavi was still dictating but had muted himself, and the doctor that was questioning him earlier was nowhere to be seen. There was a throbbing headache building at the base of her skull and she massaged there with one hand. It was dark out now.

She lifted the cup of iced coffee, now melted, and took a gulp, grimacing at the watered down, stale taste of it that coated her tongue. It splashed onto the desk.

Shit…Her hands were shaking and she felt queasy, scared. Opening a private chat, she leaned in as if to avoid anyone else hearing, but the lab was empty and her connection to the main forum muted. "Xavi…hey, I…I think I feel sick."

He paused and turned to look at her in the chat, wetting his lips with a nervous pass of his tongue. "'Sick how? You finish the full course?"

"Yeah I did. It doesn't feel like that. It's ah, headache, brain fog…I think I just lost like an hour staring at this screen…and I don't know, I don't remember it."

Xavi looked relieved. "Sounds like dehydration and stress. We've been on this for hours. That's why a bunch of them have logged off for a couple hours…Go hook up to your medibot to be sure, get an IV, get checked out. And sleep."

"I don't think it's sleep." She was fidgeting, eyes wide, attention shifting around the empty room, there were people in the shadows, ducked down and watching. It wasn't a fear or a possibility in her head, it was a certainty. She frowned at Xavi and then back at the curled-up shape under the desk next to her own. It was rocking against the floor, a man unclothed; that grew clearer as she approached.

"Ivanna…What's the verdict? You calling it a night?…Ivanna…" Xavi's voice was distant, muffled, not like the sounds in the room with her, ragged breath, the slide of skin on skin.

He had a hand between his thighs, grasping, moaning. Ivanna's cheeks flushed with embarrassment as she realized what was happening here in the dark empty laboratory.

She was alone except for the man under the desk. *I should call security in…He's breaking quarantine…* Her hand didn't move towards her handheld in her pocket. She didn't open her mouth to engage security using the AI system for the laboratory.

She stepped closer, pressing her lips together. He turned, saw her, didn't stop his movements. She knew that face; it was somewhere buried in the cottony fog in her head. His eyes were shining in the dark, inviting her to watch. And she did. *The room felt so much warmer, an incinerator suddenly. Like the one that took Alexis this morning…burnt her up still moving.*

She put a hand to her own forehead, slid it down the front of her shirt where her breath heaved in her ribcage, the sound of it ragged in her own ears. The heat wasn't in the room. It was underneath her own skin, burning her up as she crawled under the desk.

Greg pressed the tips of his long fingers into the tender swellings under his jaw and watched in the mirror in morbid fascination. The tissues were turgid and discolored, like a deep bruise, hot to the touch and outer edges red with inflammation. These weren't the only ones; there were several more. He raised a shirtless arm, revealing the same swellings to the mirror in front of his naked body. These ones were even larger and rivaled by the uneven masses sprouting from the sparsely-haired area along his inner thighs.

When had they come back? While he was on the kitchen tile…? He wasn't sure how long he had been lying there, fading in and out, or when he'd stripped down, clothes a crumpled mass in front of the food processing unit, but the thought brought up memory flashes that made him blush with shame. His fever dreams were full of Theresa—in ways that never happened during their brief interlude. The clothes were still damp from his sweat, beginning to dry and crust over in places.

He lifted a shaking hand to his damp forehead and felt the heat baking off before he touched skin. There was something he was going to do, somewhere Richard told him to go, but his thoughts kept trailing away without him, down one path or another every time he thought he knew what direction he'd been heading.

He looked down at the crumpled, soiled clothing on the bathroom counter as if they were abandoned monoliths dedicated to some angry god, left behind and now devoid of meaning. A sequence of moments passed, each one bleeding into the next as Greg examined himself in the mirror, the pile of clothes, the darkening sky through the far windows that gave a coveted view of the abandoned outskirts on the far borders of the city.

He was shivering all over, so hot and still he shivered. *"Come in to the treatment center. I'll meet you. If you haven't relapsed yet, you will."* A message on his handheld scrolled across the screen, grabbing his attention and jarring his memory long enough for him to put on his pants. He couldn't close them all the way without pain from the swelling, so he just pulled on his shirt without tucking it. That's right… He was going in for treatment. This was a relapse, then, and not just a lingering weakness from before.

A sudden spike of fear pierced the complacent fog in his head, and he picked up the handheld as another message registered, silently—sounds were too sharp for the growing pain in his skull. *"Arranging transport for myself and Phase Four. Come in and I'll get you on it."*

That seemed important, seemed like something he should care

about, but instead it circled around his mind, a string of dry words carrying indecipherable portent.

He shook his head to clear it, to stop the replay, and a sharp stab of pain shot through the muscles in the back of his neck. He grasped his skull between his hands and sucked in one breath after another, panting as he waited for the pain and the ringing in his ears to subside so he could go—somewhere.

But his attention caught his reflection in the far window, and he stepped towards it. Watery, bloodshot eyes widened as he edged closer. It wasn't clear until he got close-something about his reflection-and as it came into focus before him, as his eyes and foggy brain deciphered the information, his mouth fell open in a grimace.

The hands that held his head were squeezed too tight and, instead of leaving pressure marks, they stuck into the skin beneath them, into the skin and the rubbery, pliable tissues underneath that stretched as he pulled. A small amount of clear liquid dribbled out from each depression as he explored them with tentative fingers, and he lapped at it from the corner of his lips. It was both salty and sweet and he was—so thirsty suddenly. *I'm burning up from fever; of course I'm thirsty.*

The strangeness of what he was seeing occurred to him and he closed his eyes, counting to ten, opened them and then checked his hand for the marble. There was no marble there—that meant he wasn't dreaming. But there *was* fluid; instead of clear fluid, this was warm and red.

Greg's head was throbbing, *pounding*, really, and he couldn't turn his face away from the reflection if he wanted to. His neck wouldn't move, it was so stiff and painful. *I could run, head to where I was meeting…someone…Richard. It was Richard. And the progeny, not my progeny.* He shivered again, not from the fever but from the thought of a hundred clamoring voices, small grabbing hands and mouths echoing his name. No, not his; Richard had taken care of that, done him a favor. Hadn't he? Or had he done Richard the favor? He couldn't remember now. Theresa was there in the window-glass, her hands massaging his scalp as clear fluid leaked down the sides of his face, tickling his ears and wetting his collarbones. *"It's just the bad memories, Greg—the blood tide leaking out, so you can let it go now."* It was Theresa's voice he heard, but intimate, whispered into his ear as he imagined it might have been if he'd said yes that night. *"Remember how we'd sing it in the lab... 'Get your boards out, get your boards out. Blood tide's rollin' in. There're bodies in the surf, and smoke on the wind. Oo-Whoa-o-o—'"*

He was going somewhere but he couldn't remember where. It didn't seem so urgent with Theresa here, and it could wait until he got some pills for this bitch of a headache. Sweat dripped in his eyes and he rubbed the back of a hand across his face. It brushed against several deep scratches on his forehead that ran from scalp to cheek and were still seeping blood—but he didn't feel it. He felt better than he had in a while—aside from the headache. There was no reason to hurry off anywhere, except maybe out to the garden rooftop for fresh air.

Another message scrolled across his handheld on the counter as he entered his code into the automated medication dispensary next to the food processor. *"Greg...? It's been six hours since I sent the last message and no answer. Hope you're headed in. I'll check the rosters but I can't come looking."*

He swallowed the pills with several gulps of water; they were large and stuck to the sides of his swollen esophagus, but they didn't scrape like he expected. He really was feeling better.

The urge to get out sped his sluggish movements, directed his steps to the elevator and the large glass-domed rooftop on the top floor. The passage of time was fluid, strange, and he couldn't seem to track it. He stared at the numbers shifting as he went up, but they seemed to merge and skip, to melt, and then they weren't there at all and the elevator was still.

There were more people there than he expected when the

doors slid open, and he hesitated before stepping out into fresh night air. Large filters and fans recirculated the air from outside the garden to cool and clean it, but it was still fresher than what could be had inside the building and he gulped it down like an oxygen-starved carp dropped back in the water.

The noises of the city seemed louder tonight: the frequent passage of railcars with their dry whooping sound, an indecipherable din of distant voices and background noises melding into a clamor that seemed to vibrate with upheaval. He stood there, still, in the doorway, listening to the many sounds through the higher-pitched shriek of insect mating calls that seemed to come from all around the garden, until something or someone knocked him off his feet from behind. He barely felt the impact, pulling himself up to kneeling from the hard ground with slow and methodical movements, languid as if he were underwater.

"Hey, what ha—" The other person was speaking; he thought he recognized them out of the corner of his eye, a Mr. Glover from the floor below his, assigned to city engineering—the sort who carried his coffee along from home to respect rations instead of making use of the machines at work—but when he faced them head on, he saw who it really was.

It didn't make sense, it didn't have to, but Theresa was there on the ground next to him now, leaning over him and shoving him to the ground, pulling at his pants with forceful jerks.

"Why are you up here? Trying to get away from me again?" Her voice rose into a shout as she forced herself onto him, her own clothes already torn and hanging off, the small neatly manicured hands that he remembered from the lab sliding to encircle his throat and grab hold of his collar.

"No I —I was just, I needed some air…" He gasped the words as her hands massaged his neck, pressing down with a weight that her slight body couldn't justify.

She leaned down to his ear as she squeezed tighter,

whispering, voice low, huskier than he remembered. "Say you'll stay on the project with me, and stand up to Steiner, come to Mars and we can do this all night…" But the eyes were hers, that deep chestnut brown, the spark of intelligence so few could keep up with.

His vision was blurring out, grey static replacing her face hovering above him and he smiled, closed his eyes. When he opened them again, the face was thicker, nose longer, a grimace instead of a smile playing out on the man's features as he pushed Greg into the garden soil with his own body mass, sweat dripping from his fevered brow onto Greg's.

It was only a flash and then he saw what was really there: Theresa rocking on top of him, her cheeks flushed not with fever but passion, neatly coiled hair coming loose around her face as he'd imagined it might.

It was what he wanted to see as the fever burnt away his willpower and he blacked out on the rooftop. The other was just in his head, a painful fever dream distracting him from her, and he was grateful when he couldn't see it anymore.

AGENDAS

Martian sunlight slanted through the skylight, painting rainbows on the curve of the wall behind Donovan. The AUCs were shielded from it with large panels that controlled light in and out. Emily could see them still: Donovan's many species of progeny.

"This is the last of them in this phase. The team and I are fine-tuning each one with some outsourcing to Theresa." Donovan's face was alight with animation as he pointed at the holograms. "Five predators for this iteration filling specific roles. Two insectivores, a large pack-hunting carnivore—the feylupe, mollusk-eating fish, and this one will prey on Rattus Oryctolagus…" He returned to the first hologram, a small bird derived from a titmouse and designed to eat cycad-beetles.

"Poor ratbits…" Emily stared at the minute red and brown bird with a small blunt beak as she mused. "Donovan, what was that last one? It looked, um, familiar."

He shrugged, busying himself with detailed notes for the insectivorous bird. "You've seen all the sketches and files before. Probably…"

Emily, flicked the hologram to the side, returning to the previous one. "No, no, I haven't seen this one. I'd remember." She leaned in, staring with wide eyes at the small predator. "Beautiful and, um, terrifying."

The hologram creature was no larger than a turkey and was bipedal, bouncing upright in hologram form on three-toed feet with long sharp claws. Its wings seemed a bit small for flight, but this was a juvenile, according to the description. It could have been a bird, except that, in place of a beak, its strong jaws housed teeth like that of a crocodile. Emily shivered, pulling her lip between her teeth and furrowing her brows. "So this will eat ratbits? And what else?"

Donovan met her gaze, pressing his lips together in a way that she'd long since come to know as a sign he digging in his heels. "That's it for now, until there is more overlap of species."

Emily started to speak, twice, before following through and allowing her words to emerge. "They look dangerous—large enough to take a child…"

"Well, they aren't. Or I wouldn't make them yet. We don't have a prey animal well-established enough to take that kind of stress." He crossed his arms over his chest, expression sour, words clipped.

"Well, I guess Theresa would say something if they were going to be a problem, or the other teams." Emily shrugged and pushed the short locks of sunset-red hair behind her ears as she tried for a peace offering.

Donovan closed out the digital file and the hissing creature winked from existence. "Yeah, I'm sure they will…if there are any objections…but it, uh, stings a bit that you don't trust my word of expertise on it."

Emily started to protest and then crinkled her nose and shrugged. "You know, that's fair. If you need to be offended, I get it… but you know, having peer review and second opinions is how science works—safely. It's how we avoid getting caught up and missing things."

Donovan stared down at his hands, lifting a fingernail to his mouth as he fell back to the old habit of biting them without realizing. "If I asked Carla for a second opinion on a birth thing you were sure of, I think you'd, um, you'd be offended. At least a little…"

Emily nodded. "Yeah, maybe. But I'd swallow it because that's what we have to do if the *right* outcome is more important than *being* right."

"Fine. Sure…" Donovan pulled up the hologram again and then, with a swipe right in the space next to its snapping jaws, he pulled up a display of vital statistics. "But just look at her! Perfection pulled from the history of Earth but tailored for Mars. They'll live in small family units—packs of females with roving males. Running to hunt, but once they hit maturity, hollow bones and robust flight wings will allow them to take to the air."

Emily smiled and shook her head. "I can see why you are so enamored—but none of this is making me less worried…"

"Emily, don't you think I've considered the threat to humans with any predator I create? I can work it into their genetics to avoid us for the most part."

"Huh, okayyyy…and what about—?"

"Em, we can't avoid having predators. If we want functioning ecosystems, why not have spectacular ones—no different than lions, or Komodo dragons, crocodiles, cassowary. This is something I explain again and again and feel like I'm talking to a wall. We have to let go of some control for a fully-functioning natural habitat on Mars. Take Earth; we wiped out our predators, and until the vegetation failed and weather became too unstable, we got population explosions in all of the r-strategy species—many low-investment offspring. Why does that matter for us? They overload the ecosystem, eat themselves and us into a decline, and with populations high we get spread of diseases that can rarely, but not never, cross species. Bam…Bam… Bam! Happens fast and hard when you try to repair or build an ecosystem carelessly, or too cautiously. You don't want risk to human life?! You will end up with much higher loss at the end of the line."

Emily was nodding, arms crossed over her chest as Donovan finished. "Okay."

He cleared his throat, looking suddenly uneasy as he watched her expression. "No, I mean, you're right, Donovan. This is your area of expertise. I'm sorry."

Emily leaned in to headbutt his shoulder, and then left her cheek there. "It's fine, I'm convinced. Just, get those second opinions."

"Second, third, fourth…you realize there is built in oversight with our Mars Council, right?"

"Yeah, and then you'll give them the speech you just gave me, and they'll hand you the reins; rightly so, I guess."

Donovan laughed, the nervous sound of it belying the confidence he exuded when he spoke a moment before. He shrugged and swiped left on the hovering image.

The hologram flexed its immature, claw-tipped wings, iridescent feathers flashing as it tried out clumsy flapping motions before winking out again.

The door hissed open and Melissa straightened from the scan, a smile taking over her whole face despite the concerns that had taken up residence in the corners of her mind.

The newest of Kendra and Neil's progeny stared into the space she now occupied, eyes wide and unfocused with the fuzzy vision of the newly-born. The small round head bobbed against Neil's shoulder, then came to rest, moldable cheek pressed into the Captain's neck as the muddy grey eyes closed and opened in slow motion, finally settling on the closed position of unavoidable sleep.

Neil put a finger to his lips, continuing the shushing sound that he was already making into the newborn's ear. His voice was above a whisper, eyes beaming at the child he held in his arms instead of his guest. "You must be here to see this little prince, because I'm still on leave." Neil gave a quick wink.

Melissa rolled her eyes and strode across the room to where Kendra was semi-reclining on a daybed with their three elder children napping in a tumbled sprawl. She leaned in to kiss Kendra's cheek and smiled, removing a soft bundle from her side pocket and placing it into one of Kendra's waiting hands. "Will you tell your husband I can do my job just fine without him, and that I'm here to see the one who did all the work? Even if this is a few days late…"

Kendra snorted, shaking her head and grinning wide at the soft woven blanket as she unwrapped it. The grin shifted to a softer, more genuine smile as she passed a hand over the smooth fabric woven in threads of sunset hues with tiny, silhouetted figures dancing across it.

"It isn't just from me. It's a collaborative effort. I commissioned it from Emily, so she designed it, and Carla insisted it would be better hand-knitted than printed—so here it is."

A soft, female voice intoned loud enough for the inhabitants to hear, signaling the beginning and end of its speech with a sound that mimicked a throat clearing. "Umch-uhn…Carla has arrived for your follow-up appointment and awaits entry."

Neil's mumbled reply was just audible as he swayed his son back and forth, soothing the child into deeper sleep. "Don't leave the midwife waiting…let her in."

The door hissed once more and Carla entered, a subdued exuberance coming in with her in the scent of mountain rain and spicy, Martian lichen-grass that clung to her still-damp braids. Sweeping over to Neil, she placed a cautious hand on Askia's back, feeling the gentle rhythm of his breath as he slept. Her sharp eyes took in his color and muscle tone, the symmetry of his features, and the eye flutters of REM sleep as her palm against his back took count of breaths and heartbeat. She removed her hand slowly, allowing it to hover above the little one's back just a moment longer before placing it on Captain Neil's free shoulder.

"Not even a week on the outside and you've already gotten him settled in."

Neil nodded, an understated shrug and a smile highlighting his words. "He gets full up on milk and wants a good bounce."

Carla turned to where Kendra rested, running her hands over the gift.

"I see you have it now—took several of us to come up with but I think it turned out. It's the mural on the main garden wall, you know…Martian children running on the dunes."

Kendra pushed a long twist of soft curls out of her eyes and leaned her head on the bed. "You know I know the one. It's my favorite, or you wouldn't've used it."

Carla chuckled, sliding out of the way as Neil leaned down to place Askia on Kendra's chest. His tiny fists fell limp and open at his sides, the only sign that he might waken a sudden intake of breath at the change of location.

Carla lowered her voice to a whisper, and Melissa patted Kendra's hand before getting up to leave.

"Your milk must be in strong, then—how's your energy?"

Kendra draped the sunset blanket over Askia's back, also covering her chest and halfway down her legs.

"A bit low, I think, but Jasrie still nurses some and it's early yet."

"It is." The midwife nodded. "Rest and heal now or pay for it later. Nothing needs you to get up too soon." She glanced over at Neil, where he'd taken up a position against the far wall, watching the conversation. "He can handle the big ones, and everything else. I'm here to take up the slack with our pregnancies until you are up moving again."

Kendra gave a sleepy smile. "Till the mountains call you back up. Ain't that right?"

Carla licked her lips. "The mountains have agreed to stay silent until further notice." The two women exchanged a look.

By the door, Melissa lingered, snapping silently to get the Captain's attention. "Maybe you should check your E-mails before your leave is up, Neil."

Her voice was low and even, carrying an undercurrent like the quicker flow beneath a river's surface, and she caught his gaze and held it before stepping through the automatic door.

Kendra's breathing had evened out, her arms gently framing the progeny nestled between her breasts, her eyelashes twitching with dream before she opened them again, laughing at herself for drifting so fast.

Carla smiled. "You just sleep; I'll be around."

Kendra's eyes were already closing again as she nodded.

The midwife rose and joined Captain Neil, crossing her arms over her chest as she leaned her back against the same wall.

"What was that about? I am nothing if not master of subtext. I know when and where the seedlings are about to break soil, just can't always know which plant they'll be."

Neil stretched stiff arms and glanced down at his friend and sometimes midwife. "She wants me to check my messages." Carla snorted.

"I gathered that."

He hesitated before saying any more, then caved under the grey-blue gaze that seemed to have grown sharper as the moment drew on.

"I've just ignored some comms from Earth. Not really something I want to touch just now."

Carla's eyes widened, surprise opening her expression. "Oh. What would Earth want to discuss at this point, and what makes them think you'd want to hear it—and isn't that Melissa's responsibility now?"

Neil's expression darkened, brows tightening and pulling

together, forming a ravine between his tawny-brown eyes.

"I don't know. Haven't a damn clue and I don't really need one—Melissa says the WGC has a new leader and she wants to 'have an accord,' whatever the hell that means. Everything after that I'm leaving unopened in the inbox."

He stretched his arms out in front of him, then cracked each knuckle one at a time as if unable to hold in the nervous energy.

Carla placed a hand on Neil's shoulder, squeezing and then patting the tense muscle there.

"You know where my office is and what I'm there for, right?"

He licked his lips, eyes pulling away and finding an object on the far wall to rest on instead of holding her gaze. "I do."

"Alright then." Carla dropped her hand to her side and turned to the door. "Some things buried will compost nicely, if you turn the soil, toss in some worms, tend it…others will just rot, especially when buried deep and left there." She nodded for emphasis as the door hissed open.

"Okay then."

Genesis stood, stretched, and pulled off the VR headset. She paced her room, allowing the sparse simplicity of the space, red-ochre walls and floors, wine-colored drapes and sheets and the soft touch of climbing plants in wall sconces from David's green thumb, fall out of focus. Her thoughts were elsewhere.

Neil and Melissa's E-mails, with Earth and with each other, scrolled through her memory like the glowing databank she stored them in.

Neil still wanted revenge—Melissa seemed to be encouraging that archaic urge for some reason. Their latest Council lead was head of the justice department, her field of expertise one with a brutal history. But then wasn't now, and Melissa preached rehabilitation, exile at the most. Why not force him into Carla's office to put his fixation to rest? VR therapy was effective—startlingly effective, for her.

She sat down on the edge of her bed, stroking the silky sheets with one hand as she delved into memory. There were things there she was still piecing together, still integrating into her current self.

The snow…the wolf howls always keyed her in to the memory…it tied it all together.

The snow was falling in large flakes, more air than ice, and they melted at the lightest touch of fingertip or tongue. It was just cold enough to stick, the crumpled brown leaves of fall and persistent blades of toughened green grass peeking through the thin layer that had accumulated on the ground. Theresa stared at the familiar landscape, expecting to see wolves peering through the underbrush, sharp-toothed grins and yellow eyes glinting. She turned in a slow circle and found Carla behind her, catching snowflakes in an outstretched palm.

The older woman's smile was incredulous. "Snow?"

Theresa shrugged. "It's just a construct. Something Genesis's mind latched on to. Snow, wolves…I haven't the faintest idea why those things."

Carla squinted, deep in thought, and then spoke in a low mumble. "Ask me again after we're done today. I have some ideas. It's my second calling, after all."

The crunch of a branch on the opposite side of the small meadow heralded Genesis's arrival. She strode forward with poise and confidence, the polished movements of a dominant predator. Her smile was more a smirk as she met eyes with Carla. "I look forward to hearing your psychobabble and hypotheses on my inner workings when we're finished here—you didn't think you could whisper and dissemble when directly linked to my mind, did you?"

Carla licked her lips, cracking a smile. "I guess not. Easy to forget where we are with all this." She swept an arm outward, gesturing towards the grey sky and skeletal trees, the sharp smell of the young pines ringing the meadow. "So how do we do this?"

It was Theresa's turn to speak. "The same as before but from the inside." She glanced at Genesis to look for objections. "The last time Genesis and I did this, I wasn't hooked in but instead had a program that controlled moment by moment, interacting with Genesis. This will be more free form…messy. We'll have to find our way into Genesis's neural programming, her core belief systems, and alter them through new experience, forge new neural pathways…"

Carla was nodding, long silvery braid in one hand, while the other hand twisted the bottom into a fine rat tail around one finger. She stared at Genesis's proud figure against the backdrop of fallen snow, noting the contrast between the image projected here in the woman's mind and the real thing. Here Genesis was poised and polished, with no hint of the pregnancy that had already wrought such havoc on her. Genesis smiled under the close scrutiny even as Carla stepped closer, eyes narrowed.

The dark, bruised patches under Genesis's eyes were no longer in evidence and the rounding of cheek and shoulder, the slightly swollen abdomen, were all gone.

She didn't step away as Carla approached, tilting her head back to look into the taller woman's darkened eyes, no longer the shimmering gold but instead a dim, tarnished version of themselves. Instead, Genesis looked down at the old woman, eyes puzzled and… something else. Was she frightened…? It seemed so; the shadows darted there in her eyes as if fleeing a confrontation. The smile below them sat frozen on her lips.

Carla reached out a hand, waving it in the direction of Genesis's flat, firm belly. "What's this, then? Think you can just leave such a decision behind like extra luggage?" She turned and looked at Theresa before bringing her attention back to Genesis. "You can't, you know—oh, you can change your mind and terminate it, of course." She grasped one of Genesis's hands, turning it over in her own to showcase the sharp nail points that grew there. "Better not to do it with these, I think—but you can't just wish it away. Not like rabbits." She shook her head, allowing the frown to prevail. "The stress could kill it, or harm it at least. Not something you want to hang your coat on though."

Genesis pulled her hand back as if burned and shot a glare at the midwife. "I'm—"

Her projection faded as she struggled for words, brightening, then dimming again, and then winking out almost entirely as if her presence was controlled by a dimmer switch. Closing her eyes, she took in a quick breath and then turned her renewed attention back to Carla.

"This is only a portion of my consciousness, if you recall. It was necessary to split myself for this to work and as the— pregnancy —is the main focal point of this endeavor, I left it, so to speak, with my other half."

She raised a brow, fixing Carla with a sharp stare as if daring the old woman to question her explanation further.

The midwife stared back, nodding at thoughts she kept to herself and then turning to survey the forest.

"Well now, it would seem our first task is to find the woman of the hour." She glanced back at Genesis once more. "Or the rest of her, anyway."

The winds shifted, kicking up eddies of icy air full of snowflakes a bit too sharp and wet to conjure nostalgic scenes from a wintery Earth long past.

Theresa shifted her lab coat on her shoulders, checking the line-up of buttons to be sure she hadn't missed any. The motion was one of habit, unconscious as only a small portion of her consciousness registered the cold that came from within the subject's mind instead of the air in the lab.

Her attention was elsewhere and she stepped forward suddenly, then crouched low, brushing the powdery, white snow with two fingers, revealing some of the dark substrate below.

Carla and Genesis edged forward, peering down at what Theresa had revealed.

There was a shape there, an impression in the lower layers of snow as well as the forest floor below it. A tri-lobed ovoid shape with four smaller, near-perfect eclipses that tapered to points. An animal print.

Theresa glanced up at the two women, who watched intently, and brushed the snow aside in a circle around the print, revealing the next paw-shaped depression, and the next.

Theresa crawled forward, following the prints with a faint smile stretching her lips.

She spoke in low tones, the staccato precision of her speech more apparent as she devoted little attention to it. "Like I said before. A recurring theme—or thread if you will…wolves."

Genesis sounded bored as she followed, arms swinging at her side, eyes wandering the upper branches of pines that were now crowding around them, blocking out the sky, heavy with grey as if a weighted blanket hovered just above. "Recurring theme or not…" She wet her lips before continuing. "Paw prints in the snow are likely to lead us in circles through the underbrush after a bleeding rabbit."

Theresa paused in her search, raising both brows as she looked askance at her companion. "How many rabbits do you have running loose in your mind?"

Genesis scowled down at her but gave no immediate reply aside from the scathing glare.

Theresa stared back, then turned to the snow and the prints without further comment.

Carla let out a low chuckle. "Let's not forget our common

goal here—"

Theresa was up and running before she could consider a reply; in fact, it was quite obvious that she had either not heard or not processed Carla's attempt to soothe the conflict between herself and Genesis.

The top layers of snow were thinner here under the trees, and the prints more easily seen without the gentle excavation that was so slow and tedious.

It wasn't a full-on sprint, not here in the deep forest that surrounded them like a crowd of silent, motionless bodies, thin and tall as if stretched in the long mirror-like windows of a skyscraper. Carla ran along with her, silvery braid swishing behind her from the loping gait created by the necessity to avoid or jump over fallen branches and underbrush. Genesis refused to run but somehow did not fall behind as she followed, blank expression mirroring the snow-covered ground that spread out before them as they entered a sudden clearing.

The tracks that passed through the clearing seemed to all but disappear on the other side. Theresa circled the space again and again, crouching to clear snow and push aside ice-coated ferns. Her breaths huffed out before her in the cold air, making her presence more tangible than it should have been here.

Carla's voice was low, to avoid detection by their elusive quarry. "There's no rush here, you know. You said yourself that time will feel different, protracted…Perhaps we're missing something in our haste." Theresa sat back on her heels, staring out at the ring of trees before them. "I'm not—" She let out a huff of breath like dragon smoke. "I'm not hurrying….just focused."

Genesis laughed, the sound of it cheerful and incongruent with the mood of the other two present. She was standing behind them and to the left, leaning against a gray lodgepole pine.

Theresa ran her teeth across her bottom lip, rubbing them together. Her serious demeanor turned agitated with a speed that startled Carla.

"You sound as if you are pleased with our slow progress…as if it amuses you." She clenched her fists, pressing them down into the snow she crouched upon. "Maybe you've forgotten that you asked for our help and that's why we're here?"

Genesis's eyes narrowed, glinting like wet stones in the shadow of the tree branches that extended above her head. "No, I haven't. But I've done my part in all this." She gestured to the frozen landscape with one hand. "Here you are."

Carla crouched down next to Theresa and put a hand on her shoulder. "She did the hard part: agreeing to this and letting us come in here. Now we just have to find the way—in."

A WATCHFUL EYE

"Eight… seven, um--six, five and, four, three…" Aurelia pointed one finger at the intercom as if to cue the next act to come on stage. Her eyes were closed where she lay resting on the padded bench on her side, knees pulled up into a fetal position, giving the appearance of sleep. Only the whispered countdown gave evidence to her semi-wakeful state.

The silence was broken just as she ran out of numbers, by the same metallic flavored AI as before.

"Contamination still present. I'm terribly sorry, but your quarantine will have to be extended for another 48 hours. Closer monitoring and testing of your mucosal secretions and your blood, lymph fluid, and saliva will be taken via specialized nanocyte insertion to assess the progression of your infection."

Aurelia rolled onto her back and fetched a deep sigh. Her cheeks were flushed pink with heat and a sheen of sweat adorned her forehead, the skin there a patchwork of uneven red blotches.

"At what point will I be moved from quarantine to treatment--huh? It's kinda obvious that I'm sick…" She paused to catch her breath, pulling air in with a rasping wheeze. "Or give me back my handheld so I can talk to Richard."

The AI voice took on a paternal tone. "You would do well to

conserve your energy as your body takes on this fight. An attendant would provide nothing at this juncture, as there are as yet no known treatments for this illness aside from broad-spectrum antibiotics, which you are already receiving. Nutritive liquid containing your nanocytes and ice water are to your left in the wall unit. Below that, you will find bedding and other comfort items, as I informed you earlier. Should the antibiotics work, relapse is expected, and you'll be hooked to the medibot in your cubicle for intensive care."

An electronic whir sounded as the drawers opened, producing the aforementioned contents. The wall fountain above, producing a bottle of blue nutritive fluid.

Aurelia's eyes narrowed and her voice became petulant. "Then let me talk to Richard--just, give me my handheld or call him in here, now."

She pulled herself upright, grabbing the blue filled bottle in one hand and opening the spill-proof top with her teeth. With the other she snatched a small blanket and wrapped herself. She leaned against the wall, still shivering despite the warmth of the room and the effectiveness of the blanket. She took several gulps past the raw, feeling of her throat and paused to pull in several breaths. There was a whine in her lungs and a heavy feeling when she tried to fill them, a tightness that left her feeling thirsty for more air no matter how full they were.

The liquid was icy and soothed some of the pain. Microscopic man-made cells, nanocytes, spun in her mind's eye as she drank it down, giving off faint illumination like microscopic unicellular fireflies that would collect video footage for the cause. *What cause? Don't die—worthy cause.*

Aurelia awaited further reply from the AI—the requested handheld and a call to Richard, hopefully. She expected a refusal; instead, the lack of immediate response stretched into near silence, filled with only the sound of her labored breathing and the beat of blood in her arteries as she drifted into fitful sleep.

The security camera lent a vivid orange glow to the footage despite the lateness of the hour when it was taken. Twenty-six of the 436 rooms filled Richard's viewing screen, and in each of them figures moved. It was not the movement of evening settling-in, nor preparation for the night's sleep. The inhabitants of the quarantine rooms moved as if someone else held their strings, sending them pacing one moment, then prostrate, only to careen towards their roommates with claw-fingered hands and teeth bared until they hit the thick transparent dividers between the quarantine cells.

The blood was darker in the dim orange glow and it adorned most featured in the twenty-six rooms: blood from the cuts and bites dealt to self, or incurred during such a collision with the walls as they acted out some desperate drama in their own minds.

Richard stared, transfixed, watching as the flailing, raging shapes thrashed on the floors or beds, copulating with invisible partners with a force that would leave bruises.

This is not pneumonic plague. Not Y. Pestis as we know it.

Sixteen more of the rooms were filled as well, but in these ones the patients were strapped to medicots, some flailing with delirium but with slow, weakened movements. They were in the advanced stages of what did resemble the black death: bodies riddled with sores, extremities blackened and gangrenous. They were still breathing, but wouldn't be much longer, by the looks of it.

"Replay footage from three weeks before first episode, double speed, low sound." The earlier footage was different. These earliest patients were surrogates, some with pregnancies showing at various stages. They looked frightened but not very ill, not yet. Coughing, sweating, what looked like allergies; a fever, based on their readings in the database, but nothing extreme seemed wrong with them.

Antibiotics were given, a full course, the most effective broad-spectrum antibiotics for Y. Pestis, and they recovered.

Richard watched their movements, their behaviors looking for some clue, some missed symptom, but there was nothing that couldn't be explained by as side effects of an oncoming infection with a serious bacterium and the fallout from that. Irritability, headaches, malaise, fevers…anemia and low bp…

He mumbled to himself as he replayed their first quarantine again. "Low BP and persistent anemia…both of those made worse by advanced pregnancy…"

He advanced the footage through their first recovery and release to when they returned, terrified, tearful, bickering. The ones strapped to the medibots grew angrier, agitated, self-harming, some catatonic, some seizures followed by death, but most relapsed into a delayed but full onset of plague symptoms.

He paused the footage and turned his attention to the window of current information from their onsite epidemiology department. Within the WGC headquarters and attached Reproductive Council Center, cases were increasing: thirty-six new ones today, but deaths were slower, drawn out. Only seven more went into the incinerators.

He opened another window, security footage for another section of quarantine rooms 216 through 246. He entered the patient's genetic code identifier AUCPH3269BIO to narrow down the room he was looking for. Room 218 was displayed on the screen. Richard's expression didn't change, but he pulled in a slow breath as he assessed the girl curled into a fetal position on the bed. Her short blonde hair was plastered to her forehead, cheeks, and neck in damp tangles, by the sweat that he could see glistening in the overhead lights.

His eyes narrowed and he cracked his neck, shifting it as he grew still. *High fever, swelling lymph nodes, bruising, breathing labored. She'll fight it, then relapse…maybe she won't relapse.* His eyes darkened with anger, and he turned away, moving the footage to the far-left

corner of his screen to focus on the reports from epidemiology.
Time will tell.

LOSS OF CONTACT

Theresa frowned at the hologram for several moments, fingers tugging at the pockets of her labcoat as she took in the vital statistics of the creature that grew and developed in the simulation in front of her, from embryo, to hatchling, to fledgling, and finally taking flight as a full-grown raptor.

"So Donovan—you're planning to populate Mars with dinosaurs?" Donovan rubbed the back of his neck, worrying his bottom lip between his teeth, then stepped closer to the large hologram of a Martian Raptor; he gesticulated towards it, eyes shining with exuberance.

"This is only one, and it's a derivative species—you can see that, of course. Adapted to Mars and to interaction —rather, lack of interaction, with humans. If we leave them alone, they will leave us alone."

He shrugged, satisfied with his own reasoning.

Theresa stepped closer to the hologram, coming to stand next to Donovan without taking her eyes off of the raptor, whose iridescent feathers had grown long and capable of flight as it simulated maturity.

"There are reasons that we never recreated them on Earth, outside of fiction novels and cinematic disaster films…"

He arched a brow, cocking his head to the side. "You are referencing fiction for us to base our decisions on now?"

Theresa leaned in, stroking one of the fourteen flight feathers with an outstretched hand, causing it to shimmer and lose the illusion of solidity.

"Um, yes and no. Good fiction stems from solid scientific thinking and has a basis in proven theories. I'm just saying that when we achieved the skills to recreate mammoths, and dinosaurs, megalodons, we shied away for a number of reasons."

Donovan threw his hands up in irritation. "You need to brush up on history. They shied away because of a misguided fear of 'playing God,' and because by the time we put religion and politics aside, there were bigger problems that took precedence." He gestured to the raptor that flexed its wings, bouncing on powerful hind legs.

"How could we in good conscience bring back Earth's extinct animals when the current ones were dying off left and right. We killed the last black rhino--the last pod of orcas washed up, emaciated and full of plastics; polar bears, tigers, grizzlies, pollinators—one by one, and then in matched bundles as the ecosystems collapsed."

His dark eyes sparked with outrage, lips pressed into a slash across his face. "We had no chance to bring back these creatures."

Theresa opened her mouth to reply, head tilting to the side and features twisting in confusion. "Wait…are we arguing?"

Donovan paused, expression shifting in response to the question. "Umm-uhhh, we are if you are—"

Theresa laughed, turning her grin towards the hologram raptor. "No, you misunderstood… or I said it wrong. I'm asking if you can make it work. Integrate them into a modern ecosystem here on Mars?" Her eyes widened as she grew more attached to the idea. "Have you worked out the problems such that these could survive and thrive without, well, being a threat to all the other organisms in the web?"

He nodded his head. "Yes. Because Mars needs predators. And as I've designed it, this will work as well as any; better, in fact. Anyone who wants to question what I'm doing as the planet's ecologist might want to ask themselves whether they want me to create a well-manicured garden, with a child-safe petting zoo, or an actual ecosystem. But I'm arguing again, aren't I…?"

He frowned, tucking a stray lock of hair behind one ear and then smirked. "I mean…I had all the arguments ready, so…I'm just gonna say this. Look at the stats for my raptors, and try not to get it mixed up with your library of classic sci-fi and monster movies from the 20th century."

Theresa bit her lip, holding back laughter. "Donovan…I'm not about to stand in the way of this or any other of your animals, so long as I don't suspect you are making them to keep the human population in check."

Donovan cracked a smile, relief showing in his eyes. "Got a little worked up, didn't I?"

Theresa held up two fingers as if pinching air. "Just a little."

"But that, that does, um…bring up another important topic."

"Yes?"

"Isn't it past time for you to put a cap on *human* reproduction unless you want ah--a repeat of Earth? You *are* head of reproductive matters on Mars…"

Theresa blinked several times. "Well…we are pretty far off from taxing the planet, especially when everything is being designed for minimum impact and maximum sustainability…"

Donovan nodded, pacing towards the door. "Even still, the numbers need to be in place; how else do we set a precedent for everyone to get used to, keep it from snowballing, if you will?"

"You do have a point. I'll take a look at all the data for it."

Donovan flashed a smile before leaving. "And take another look at the raptor's as well; they're flawless, but I respect your creative eye. I could have them cooking before winter if we move forward at the same pace."

Theresa stared after as he left, giving a start as the raptor hologram took flight, opening its narrow jaws and releasing a high-pitched shriek.

She laughed, shaking her head and flicking her wrist at the hologram to end the program for the time being, mumbling to the empty room. "Raptors now, and then what, huh, Donovan?"

Theresa dug one hand into her lab coat pocket, retrieving her handheld. "New messages please."

A tinny female voice answered back with what sounded like a smirk in her tone. "The only messages you have are from Mars. Would you like me to list them at this time, or put a call through to Earth?"

Theresa frowned, brows knotting together. *Two messages out to Richard and an attempted call…And how many days have passed?* She tapped each finger in the air, counting out: six days. *Uncharacteristic for Richard.*

"Put a call in to Richard Brant, please."

The VR-comm felt heavier than usual against her scalp along with the weight of worry that was settling itself into pockets of tension along her jaw, neck, and shoulders. Minutes passed, and she stared ahead into the spinning colors of the VR screen, waiting.

"There is no response. Would you like to try someone else?"

She wet her dry lips. "Um—ehhh, no, I guess not for now."

The worry coalesced into sharp, hot lances of anger, spurring her into motion. She paced, taking large steps across the smooth red Martian floors.

"Record message to send—Richard, you haven't answered in several days or sent a message of your own. I'm worried. I'm just checking in, but without a reply I'm picturing worst case scenarios. Send."

Theresa dropped the headset onto the desk and paced to the adjoined room that belonged to Abby, pausing as she remembered that the room would be empty. Abby was hiking with Deimos.

The sand spread out in front of them, like a vast ocean painted red and onyx by a vibrant sunset. The sand dunes and volcanic rock outcroppings standing in for towering waves served as the only landmarks through the eastern desert on the far border of the Martian colony. But it wasn't nightfall, and the red and black of the sand was not a trick of the light. Abby ducked down, burying her hands and feet in the sun-heated grains of sand and relished the weight of it.

Deimos did the same, mimicking her motions as he always had.

Abby rose and faced the desert, feeling the shove of hot wind against her back, letting it push her onto her toes until it seemed she might be lifted up and carried away. The next gust pushed harder, speeding her across the sand in a full sprint, her long legs thinner than the knees that hinged them since her most recent growth spurt.

She felt Deimos follow and smiled; he would always follow. She ran faster, pumping her legs harder and more quickly until her breath came in ragged, heaving pants and her muscles began to cave beneath her.

Abby fell down in the sand at the crest of a large dune, this one a mix of red and black sand in alternating patches like the stripes along an arcanue's back. Deimos fell down next to her and she rolled, letting gravity take her all the way to the foot of the dune, where she held her breath until the dust cleared…*Only difference between that and Mars is the color of the dust.* The errant thought was absurd and out of place, which meant it mattered to her. *Gavin didn't want to come. How many others didn't…?* She closed her eyes, listening to the sound of her own breath and the echo of Deimos's next to her. Reaching across the sand, she found his hand, but remained silent, eyes taking in the dilute indigo blue of the sky above. A twinge of shame needled at her. She was giving in to distraction—brain chatter, instead of thinking. Genesis would be disappointed if she were in her head today.

Abby pushed at the worries, sliding them across her mental landscape into one corner, hoping they would stay there. She resolved to think instead of play victim to brain babble.

A shower of sand fell off of her clothes as she sat up and pulled Deimos up with her. None of the words would cross her tongue and find voice when they met at the edge of the desert, but the run had knocked them free now and she needed to voice them. "Richard isn't answering mother's comms or mine; neither is Bram, Aurelia, Gavin, none I've tried. Not even Santana, and she always answers."

Deimos waited for anything further until he saw that Abby was looking over, waiting on him. "So you're worried about them." Abby tilted her head to listen for her own thoughts. "I think so. But it might just be her worry and I feel it. It's only been a few days. I tried to Dream Speak Gavin because we argued. If he's angry still, he might not answer, but then I called others when I saw her try and just…nothing."

Now that the words were spread out across the sand, she could look at him without seeing her own thoughts and was glad she did. His eyes were like Genesis's. Not the color, though that was the same as well—it was their demeanor, a measured stillness that made his face like a mirror when he was listening, reflecting back what she needed to see more clearly without judgement or reinterpretation. Like Genesis's but warmer, his humor less sharp and cutting. Clever and teasing at times, but never cruel.

Deimos smoothed the sand in front of him like a blank canvas. "What can I do?"

"Mmmmm…tell me why I can talk to you and to Genesis, my siblings, most of the time at least…but no one else."

He was drawing in the sand between them while he listened,

and Abby watched the twists and spirals form, tracing the same paths with her eyes.

He paused before answering her question. "What does that have to do with the unanswered calls?"

She scrunched her nose up in a freckled scowl. "Nothing, I guess. But I can't seem to master my head today, so that's what came out."

Deimos nodded, a knowing smirk on his lips before he fell back to tracing shapes in the sand. DNA spirals. It was idle, done to keep his hands busy while he listened. The next strand of genetic code trailed all the way to Abby's bare toes in the sand, so he took a handful and covered her foot to finish the last segment and then shrugged. "Because, you're Abby. I always assumed you talked to who you wanted to and ignored the rest, until you started feeling bothered by it."

"Ugh, because I'm Abby… That's too simple, Deimos. I need an answer that'll make it easier."

He brushed the sand off of her foot and erased the double helix, meeting her eyes with his own yellow-gold ones, entirely serious now. "You want to change it, then. For you, or for my mother?"

"Um…Both. I want to choose and not feel stuck, limited…to master myself."

Deimos nodded once. "Fair enough. Everyone has something that's hard for them." He recited it as if by rote. "Hasn't my mother said it a million times to you as well?"

She thought a moment, searching her memory for what Deimos could find hard. He didn't enjoy his mother's training like she did…but there was nothing Abby could see, nothing that he couldn't at least do. He didn't freeze like she did and lose his words. "What's hard for you, then?"

He turned away and then looked back; his eyes were shadowed when he met hers again, sharper like Genesis's, and the tone of his words matched. "Being kind."

Abby waited for more and then wet her lips, a frown was building at the bridge of her nose and she smoothed it away with one hand. "But you do it. You're kind almost always. More than I am…people don't like to be ignored, so I hear."

"Sure, okay. But do I really? Or does what's in my head count? And what about the times I slip?"

Abby was pouring sand over her own feet now, feeling the sand-fall with her toes. "Who do you think things about then? Me?"

Deimos laughed, pushing her over into the sand and getting up to brush off. "Maybe. Why?"

The three tallest outcroppings of rock were visible over the next rise and he turned to trot up the high dune in front of them, black sand slithering down behind him with a hiss.

Abby raised her voice to be heard as she ran to catch up with him. "Because maybe I want to hear what you think…"

He looked startled when she came up next to him at the top of the dune, and like he didn't believe her. "I don't think so, Abby."

"You asked what you could do to help…it won't work if I can't help too. Talk to me, tell me what you think even when you don't like it, and you help me find a way to get unstuck."

He opened his mouth to reply and then closed it, brushing a shower of sand from his short black hair with one hand. "I dunno, maybe…I'll try."

Abby turned to face the cliff of stone in front of them as if this was the challenge she couldn't seem to rise to and then reached for the first low crevices to get a grip and start the climb. Deimos found his own hand holds and climbed in tandem with her, silent now as they focused on the way up.

"Timeline is moving up and you need to be ready for it, is all I'm saying at this juncture." Genesis's contact stood before her in VR Comm without cloak, mask, or face scrambling. And what she saw on that face was hard to decipher. Was the narrowed corners of his eyes and the pinpoint pupils fear or excitement? And what of the subtle tick that he likely thought he had suppressed, a tilt of neck and cracking of the jaw that was fast enough to go unnoticed or read as insignificant by anyone else. Was he nervous?

She stepped closer, shifting from confident smile to brows upturned with concern.

"And that's all you plan to say? I need more than that."

She cocked her head to the side and placed a hand on his shoulder, meeting his eyes full-on and locking his to her own. "You've explained numerous times that the children are not ready to interact in a closed system when the stakes are so high. Rough edges still being worn smooth, you've said…" Her eyes widened in alarm. "Could the Reproductive Council have convinced the WGC to terminate, or is this something else? Some reason of your own?"

Richard unfolded his arms. His otherwise stillness made him resemble a statue of marble, staring with close to immutable features as if not registering her presence. "Genesis, just do it. Prepare for their arrival and be ready to run a lot of interference. If you can't lay down enough narrative in advance, they'll show themselves to be a problem well before they've earned trust and affection."

His veneer slid aside for no more than a moment as his thoughts seemed to scatter, or perhaps to be drawn elsewhere by some sound or distraction on Earth where he was projecting from. "I have—a lot to deal with here, and there are too many factors in the air for me to explain. If it falls through, you'll have started readying the colony on your end, and that can't be bad, can it?"

Genesis shrugged. "I suppose not. Just bear in mind that you keeping secrets impedes my function—go on, then; deal with whatever needs to be done on your end."

DRASTIC ACTION

Bram stared at Richard's back, arms crossed and brows knit over eyes dark with worry.

"Aurelia isn't back from her excursion, and it's been days." He popped his fingers one by one blinking with nervous tension as he awaited reply.

The screen that held Richard's attention appeared to feature lights winking on in rapid succession, forming a large and growing cluster of luminosity. Richard kept his attention on the screen, without pause, giving no indication that he was aware of Bram's presence.

"You knew she was going out to replenish her rat supply."

Bram flinched as if startled and tucked his hands into pants pockets.

"She was, uh—well she said, anyway, it was just a quick in-and-out dash. No more than an hour."

"And you didn't say anything to myself, or Gavin, even?"

"Gavin knew as well. And we've—well we've been keeping tabs on her—tracking, but she's gone off the network."

"Oh? And where was she last?" He glanced back, brows raised, at the boy who was now flicking his gaze around the room as if to avoid resting on his guardian more than a second.

"WGC East Wing—Gavin thinks decontamination, but that's not the only thing in East Wing—ah, could be the Census department, or Reproductive licensing and placements or—"

"She *is* in decontamination; rather, quarantine. And likely to remain there should she survive."

Bram's voice emerged after several moments, in subdued tones, his brows pulled together in a deep crease. "Should she survive." The echoed phrase was barely above a whisper and followed by another long pause. "Then she's gotten into something serious this time."

Richard turned around, sliding on VR gloves for precise manipulations with his hands. "She has. And it would seem it's going to be a tougher fix than I expected." He gestured towards the screen where a rod-shaped organism with numerous waving, hairlike projections was displayed before them.

"That's it then?"

Richard nodded as Bram stepped closer, staring up at the large diagram of a bacterial cell.

"What treatments have been tried? It resembles Yersinia Pestis, doesn't it?"

Richard gave a half smile. "Resembles but is not. This one here is also gram-negative and a member of Enterobacteriaceae. Now Yersinia Pestis, one of my favorites, prevents aggressive treatment once it's gone too far—otherwise we lose the host with it as it releases its toxins. Septic shock kills the patient. Luckily, this one seems to be slower to reproduce in the host than its forebear, but it is somehow evading full eradication with antibiotics, causing relapse."

Bram scowled deeper, staring at the data surrounding the unknown cell. "She's in quarantine—it's contained, then?"

Richard's laughter came out of a sudden, bursting forth like a geyser but without mirth.

"Contained? No, no. It is spreading quite rapidly. It would

seem to be very communicable between rat and human, as opposed to needing another organism as intermediary, and it is pneumonic in nature…spit droplets, breath, mucus. Survives an uncanny duration outside of a host." He began to pace, gesturing with rapid hand gestures as he enumerated the qualities of the pathogen.

Bram's lips were pressed into a thin line, his skin blanched of color.

"How far has it spread then?" "How far?! It's in this very building. It is contagious well before notable symptoms set in, and perhaps during the in-between phase after it seems to have been treated, before relapse."

Bram grew silent and still, contemplative. He rubbed the tips of his fingers across his lips, eyes sparking with some sudden realization. "If it's already here and spreading, then Aurelia couldn't have brought it…"

Richard nodded. "Correct. It was already here, under our radar, spreading silently. It was caught and treated as an isolated outbreak of run-of-the-mill pneumonic plague among the surrogates. Quarantine, treatment, relapse…none have since recovered. They are dying, and it's all over the city as well, not isolated to this continent, according to WGC Eurasia."

Bram's words came slow and cautious. "We are designed to withstand more, our resilience is high, our immune systems efficient."

Richard nodded again. "Indeed. Aurelia is holding out—ill, but it's progressing more slowly. She is feverish and perhaps delirious—and still alive."

"Then we use her as a template for the treatment!" Bram was animated with excitement.

Richard shrugged. "This isn't a fantasy scenario where we play God and save the world. There is no time to rebuild the population's immune systems from scratch. And while Aurelia may be holding out longer, she has not responded yet to standard treatments for Y. Pestis or others in the family. She has not recovered like the other cases who later relapsed. If we remain here trying to cure this ourselves with no exit plan—we will lose people."

Bram's eyes widened, bright and clear with shock. "Mars, then?"

Richard turned to face him, eyes shining with a fever borne not of illness but sleep deprivation and focus. "Mars, then. But well before we are ready, so don't look so pleased. We'll have quite a bit to set in motion to make this happen. And if I cannot solve this thing sufficiently before the ship comes for us—" He gestured towards the holographic virus rotating in front of them. "It'll fall upon Mars, Theresa—the others there, to either cure it or make the call to leave us."

Bram nodded, a quick, awkward duck of head that highlighted the fear freezing him, locking his joints and slowing his movements. "And Aurelia?"

The corners of Richard's lips creased as his face tightened against any further expression. "That depends on her status in 48 hours' time."

"Can we—uh—can I see her? In quarantine..." The boy's voice was strained with concern, stumbling, his sensitive eyes large in his pale face.

Richard flicked a glance his way. The expression in his eyes was nearly unreadable, cold, but Bram knew the look well. Richard's surface was still, but underneath the sharks were circling. Bram dug in, searching for the words he himself would want to hear. "She's—uh —gonna be fine, Richard. You'll help her."

Richard seemed to ignore Bram's attempt at comfort and instead opened up a new window labeled **Quarantine Security Live Feed.** He gestured with a flourish of one hand towards the screen. "There, see her. It won't be a comfort to see, but maybe it'll serve as a cautionary tale. She wouldn't be isolated from us if she'd followed my rules instead of sneaking out, exposing herself to unnecessary risk—to their protocols." The words were sharp and biting, hinting at the uncharacteristic well of anger boiling underneath.

Aurelia was there in a small room with a medicot, curled up against the wall. She twisted her hair around her fingers, pulling strands into her mouth to bite. Her other hand was drumming the exam table as she rocked herself.

Bram winced, withdrawing mentally as if what he saw on the screen had burned him. His jaw tensed, brows pulling up and together as he watched her shake with a fit of coughing that seemed to go on forever before it tapered off, leaving her exhausted and shivering.

He wet his lips and looked away, but found his eyes pulled back to the screen. He had to see her, even if she couldn't see him. That was Aurelia suffering there, scared, alone. Her skin was mottled and glistened with fever sweat, eyes closed now that the coughing had taken her energy.

Her voice cracked as she spoke, too quiet to hear at first but then louder as she tried again, the same words on repeat. "Richard… please…Richard…"

Bram turned an anxious look to Richard, whose eyes were on the same screen as his. He was so still, staring. He seemed to flinch when she whispered his name for the third time and then he turned back to the other screen.

"Is there any way we can…?"

"No." Richard's voice sounded tired now, strained. "They took her handheld. Quarantine is on complete lockdown."

Bram's eyes darkened with alarm, as he watched Aurelia double over again with coughing. His own throat itched in sympathy and he cleared it, noticing a soreness that wasn't there before their conversation began. "But how will we—"

"I'll have the access codes before we leave. Here—you need

this, and then sleep."

Bram cleared his throat again, frowning at the discomfort there.

Richard's eyes softened for a moment and he placed a large hand on the boy's shoulder. He reached out with his other hand and Bram saw the pressure injector as Richard pressed the small device against his exposed inner elbow and activated it. It dispensed its contents with a cold, stinging, hiss, and Bram rubbed the spot on his arm. He watched with growing alarm as Richard held another injector to his own arm. *Is he sick too...?*

"As for the rest of us, we were likely exposed quite some time ago, based on the cases I've uncovered in the WGC complex, so we have a countdown of our own." Richard's smile, likely meant to comfort him, was too full of the stark reality of his words to have any such effect.

She was being moved. These end effectors were more like robotic arms, with silicone padding meant to simulate a human touch. They lifted and repositioned her on her stomach, placing and adjusting straps across her back, around ankles and wrists, then cinching them tight.

Aurelia's vision blurred and the light that had remained constant before for so very many hours of countdowns shifted each time she opened them.

She startled, flinching as if falling in dream from the vertigo that came as the medibot moved down a corridor.

This new room was darker, soothing to her aching eyes.

Aurelia coughed. It was a deep rattling sound that grew wetter with each involuntary spasm. Her sallow brow furrowed in pain and she turned her face to the side to swallow, despite the swellings on each side of her neck that throbbed and choked her.

Her eyes drifted shut again as the movement of the portable medicot that she was strapped to slowed and then stopped. She pulled in another breath, struggling to accomplish the task without setting off another fit of coughing. Still, the cough took hold again for several moments, leaving her weak and heaving, something warm and wet coating the side of her face.

She reached up to wipe it and then examine the source of wetness but met resistance. Her arms would not lift, even if they had strength remaining, but instead remained strapped to the bed at her sides.

A deep growl grew in her throat and she grimaced, fighting again to regain control of her limbs, alternating between growls and shouts of rage as she succeeded in rocking the well-balanced bed back and forth with no further effect.

One of the robotic arms that extended from the exam bed reached out, pressing against her back as if to still the heaving with a touch. Its voice was firm and authoritative, but with a note of conciliation. "You'll exhaust yourself and hasten your decline. Please, do not struggle. The straps are to keep you safe."

"Safe!!" Aurelia's voice became a screech, her eyes wide with panic and fiery rage that set them to gleaming in the dim. "Safe from moving myself? From wiping my face?!"

Spittle flew from her mouth, tinged red. The side of the mattress in contact with her face, once white sheeted, looked as if it was speckled with vivid crimson paint, flicked from the end of brush bristles.

Aurelia saw it and registered the blood in some distant part of her mind, but the rest took no notice. Letting out a guttural roar, she rocked the bed harder than even before, her wrists and ankles beginning to redden from the struggle against tight bonds.

"If you cannot calm yourself, I will have to help you to do so. Treatment will be impossible if you continue to struggle."

Aurelia's eyes widened in panic. "Richard!…Riiiicharrrrd!!"

Her scream choked off into a sob.

Another arm emerged, this time with two different effectors. The first attached a tube, clamped on by strong suction to the vein in the crook of her right elbow, the second dispensed a pale-yellow liquid into the prominent vein of her other arm.

"The first will calm you and deliver medication, the second hydrate and sustain." Aurelia's struggling slowed gradually as the sedative took effect, until her head slumped down into the mattress, eyes still staring with frenzied intensity at the wall, and providing a clear view of the swollen and dark-bruised lymph nodes on either side of her jaw.

Her mouth still moved, but, aside from the rasp of labored breathing, no sound escaped, the syllables she mumbled lost between mental impulse and sedated tongue.

GROWING PAINS

Donovan pulled off the VR Comm and turned to the guests gathered in his lab. The room was dimly lit, walls covered in row upon row of ovoid objects hung from a network of simulated veins and arteries contained in tubing. David and Emily stood listening, in front of the AUC chambers that ranged in size from ones designed to house smaller mammals and birds to those built for large grazers like the arkanue and prairie predators. A few hung empty, but the rest of them held an embryo or fetus, some too young to distinguish species and showing only the amorphous shape and features of all embryos, including the universal tail that would recede to non-existence in a human.

Donovan paced under the amber glow of the AUCs, pulling a strand of his twisting black hair, allowing it to return to its spiraled shape as he let go.

"Now, here's the thing—ecosystem stability requires good timing and attention to the balance of species, from microbial life all the way up to the largest organisms—forests, large mammals and reptiles. Each one equally important." He paused, grabbing the same ringlet and twisting between thumb and forefinger. "We have —copious data detailing the population levels for everything I have seeded on Mars, as well as many of the organisms that were started and took hold before we arrived, primarily the lichens, lichen-grass, rat-tail seaweeds, and microorganisms. But—and here is the point you were waiting for me to get to."

David chuckled from where he leaned between two empty AUCs labeled *Raptor*.

Donovan inclined his head towards David and half-smiled. "Yeah, I know—We also have drones doing much of the seeding for our insect and plant life—But the last time we went on a seeding mission in-vivo was two years ago. The surface has changed big-time since then, and we need to see it, touch it, smell it—be in the ecosystem we're building. Get a real feel for it. I'm going out for an extended trip in a week, and you are all team-members I'd like to have along. David, Emily?"

David nodded and pushed a hand through dark brown hair that had grown long and shaggy since arriving on Mars. "We've talked about this a bit, and I agreed it's a good idea." A smirk grew on his face, sharpening his already angular features. "Nothing more satisfying than getting my hands in the soil and leaving behind just the right seedlings for the spot. I'm going, but how long are you talking when you say 'extended?'"

Donovan shrugged, and then placed a hand over his lips, mumbling as he did the mental math. "Three —three months, give or take. Travel is fast with the drones, but we need to spend enough time on the ground getting a feel for things, and I'd like to go past the Eastern desert and make a circle equidistant around the colony—and then we'll see, I might—I might just stay out longer myself, explore the area around the second original colony site— not the close dome complex we're adding now, but the one on the other side of the East desert, and start prepping it for when we need to expand out from this one."

Emily pressed her lips together, brow creasing in concern. "So by extended, you mean you don't know when you're coming back?"

Donovan tucked both hands into lab-coat pockets. "We—er,

if we all go. And then, yeah, I might be gone a long bit, but the drones can make it a back-and-forth thing as needed." He shrugged again. "Who's in?"

David raised a hand. "I'm in. But hey, what about Carla? She was in on the last one."

Donovan glanced over at Emily. "Well, if Emily comes Carla won't, right?"

Emily shook her head to back up his assertion. "Kendra is temporarily out of commission so, no. But I think you should invite Carla." She looked away, avoiding eye contact. "I'm going to stay. If you need someone for tech, I can send my apprentice, at least for the first half."

Donovan pinched his lips between two fingers, nodding his head as if to convince himself that this was expected, until he could stifle any look of disappointment.

"Alright —uh, alright then. Then we'll see if Carla is in, and that makes a team. Leaving in a week's time."

The dust collecting in the halls was thick and red as everywhere else on Mars, the same color as the massive red stones being 3D printed by construction drones. They were nearly silent, but still Melissa could pick up the faint hum and the vibrations they sent out through the new complex.

Pacing deeper into the sunlit corridor, the Head of the Martian Governing Council pulled out a handkerchief and covered her nose and mouth. The footsteps that approached from the Western hall that adjoined the old and new domed complexes were slow and deliberate, with a faint click of heel.

Melissa smiled underneath the handkerchief, picturing the oddity that was Genesis's signature footwear for meetings. They were not high like the stilettos of Earth, but still higher than the flat, more physiologically appropriate options that were favored by most on Mars and, for some reason, these had metal on the heels and toes, giving an exaggerated click-clack.

Melissa lowered the handkerchief as she turned to face Genesis.

"The construction is, well…" She gestured to the smooth walls and archways that enclosed them. "Coming along as expected, but I can't see why we'd want to meet here unless we had intentions to tend to this dust or—"

Genesis gave a quick, amiable laugh.

"Just to make my point clear. A field trip of sorts. Construction here is nearing completion…And it's time we began making definitive plans for how and by whom it will be inhabited…"

Melissa narrowed her eyes, head tilting as she struggled to discern the direction of Genesis's thoughts.

"I don't think I follow…This complex is for an increase in population—which we do not have at this time. The first is still accommodating the full population."

Genesis nodded, turning in place and making a click-clack with one shoe. "It is and it isn't. Families have grown. And when the children of these families pair up and want a bit more space— we won't have it."

Melissa frowned, still evidencing her confusion. "But that will be a while, and then this complex will be available to them."

Genesis opened both palms and gave an apologetic smile. "Let me be clearer. The longer a family remains in one location, the more difficult it is for them to move elsewhere. Delay spreading out and it will get more complicated. Consider also that tight quarters causes bickering, and there has been some increase in social friction."

Genesis paced the hall, gesticulating to punctuate her words. Melissa followed her movements with her eyes, allowing the words to soak in; somehow the strength of Genesis's vineberry smile punctuated and brought further credence to the idea she continued to elaborate.

For a moment Melissa lost track of the words as the spark in the speaker's golden eyes drew her gaze. Melissa shook her head as if to shake away the spell and focus on the words formed by the lips instead of the lips forming the words. She twisted a dark brown wisp of hair between two fingers as she listened.

"Picture this: we relocate half of the colony to this new location, still only a corridor away, with full access to resources and friendships, and everyone settles in with more space and any new additions can intersperse."

Genesis paused in her pacing in front of Melissa, leaning in with tilt of head to give a conspiratorial air to her words. "Set up the new central gardens and hint that it's closer to the beaches, and you'll have volunteers."

Melissa pulled in a breath, mirroring the grin Genesis offered, a warm flush on her cheeks. "So, extra space, ease of expansion, decreased friction—we move one half to the new complex, perhaps consider the more distant complexes already in place but uninhabited as well? Am I hitting all the bullet points?"

Genesis wet her lips, dry from the dust that covered floor and wall alike, and gave her companion a look of warm approval. "Flawlessly. You've taken what I brought to you and adapted it beautifully. And if we do things as you've laid out, it'll ensure that the youngest of the community are not expected to set out and run this and any further complexes on their own without oversight of the first generation."

Genesis took a step back, breaking the intimate mood that her proximity had created as she instead leaned against an arched doorframe with hands laced behind her head.

"Now, what of the Pinnacle's preparations for retaliation against Earth. Is it truly ready, and is it well equipped enough to succeed?"

Melissa's eyes widened and she sputtered, the words that escaped jumbled and half-incoherent. "Ahh—um, Neil, rather, Captain Neil shared that with you?—It isn't common knowledge yet—won't be likely. It's the Captain's project."

She pushed the front locks of her hair back in nervous frustration.

"Captain Neil says it's ready and well equipped. He wouldn't be taking a chance on—"

Genesis stepped closer again, click-clacking as she advanced, a focused frown pulling her features into something resembling disapproval. "I didn't ask what the Captain thinks about his ship…I asked what you think, because you have a discerning eye and a cool head."

Melissa's expression became one of deep concentration, taking on a near blank expression as the nervous smile dropped. "I think—I think that the ship is as ready as it can be, and his mission could go either way."

"Then why are you letting him do this?"

"Mmmm…Because he needs to regain his confidence and have a larger focus outside of Mars and family, and there is a good chance he won't take that last step and fly her to Earth once he has waited long enough for the 'right' time. He has an infant to tend to with Kendra…"

Genesis was close again, close enough for Melissa to smell the mix of spices and Martian plumeria she wore. Genesis's laugh was quiet but mirthful, filling the space between them.

"You're playing mother to the Captain—let's hope it doesn't back-fire and plays out how you anticipate. A tool is only useful if you can aim it, and I'm not sure you'll be able, if he surprises you."

Melissa's eyes hardened. "If he surprises me, then I won't envy the Council on Earth. If he surprises me, I'll hope for his safe return, but won't lose sleep over the consequences of his decisions should he fail."

Genesis brushed a lock of Melissa's hair back with one smooth hand motion and smiled.

"Well then, you seem to have this matter well in hand. I'll leave you to it. Care to discuss your approval ratings within the colony next?"

Melissa raised both brows at the change of topic. "Yeeeeesss, but outdoors, please. The dust is—distracting."

"The beach then?" Genesis followed Melissa out, click-clacking as she walked with one hand placed on Melissa's shoulder.

BABY STEPS

"Yes, I would say we want a large selection of saplings, seeds, sprouts, what have you. The full range of each plant's life cycle, including soil bacteria, fungus, and especially anything you want to take hold across this land mass."

Donovan wore his VR Comm visor for video chat so as to experience David's expressions and avoid miscommunications of tone.

"I'll be taking more detailed data snapshots of each area we stop in to add soil amendments and sew in more organisms as needed…it's an art, you know; you know that, or your drones and apprentices would be the ones getting their hands dirty. We'll have those as well, of course."

David nodded several times, following along. "Yep, I've already loaded up the drones and several crates of greenery." He grinned, rubbing both hands together. The smile lit his dark brown eyes with excitement. "You know, it's too long since we've been out there!" He rubbed one hand over his short-cropped beard. "Oh, and I have some news! Carla's coming along after all. Emily convinced her, wants to be treated like she can handle the births, and Kendra is up already."

Donovan flashed a smile, glancing away just as he did so. "I'm glad Carla'll be along for the trip. She's good company and helpful. Alright, back to preparations for me…I'll forget something if I save it to the last minute."

David gave a quick wave as his VR image froze and then faded into a blank screen. Donovan pulled off the headset, struggling to free a tangle of hair from the curving arm on the device.

"Emily requests entry, would you like…?"

"Oh, um—yes, just, let her in."

Donovan began to scroll through the data lines for his lab's AUC units. Many were recently birthed, the rest longer gestating such that he would not miss any extraction days.

Pulling up a virtual control mid-air, Donovan set to adjusting presets for external stimulation protocols, and hormone surges.

"Donovan?" Emily stopped just a few feet away, turning her attention to the AUC protocols in front of Donovan. "Couldn't Theresa monitor these while you're away?"

Donovan continued to enter commands, moving groups of AUCs to new categories for hormone levels on preset days.

"Sure, but better to preset them. She has her own things to attend to, and this is mine—the apprentices can monitor and adjust, but they don't know all of the nuances yet. I won't risk lives being lost."

Emily nodded. "Sure. Probably how Gran feels about going off on this trip and leaving me to tend to the midwifery needs."

Donovan looked away from the hologram panel and met Emily's gaze. "Um—you've been apprenticing much longer with Carla than my apprentices have—if they'd pick a thing and focus on that instead of hopping apprenticeships, they might be ready." He shrugged, closing out the holographic controls with a flick of wrist and turning to face her. His voice lowered to a subdued murmur, as he reached out to flip a lock of red hair that rested beside her face.

"But you aren't here to discuss the trip."

She shook her head.

"No. I hoped we could talk about a dream… If you have a minute."

"Okay." Donovan took both of her hands in his and pulled her to sit on the long, cushioned bench against the nearest wall. "The same dreams? About a child?"

Emily bit her lips, pressing them together between her teeth. "Yes. Sometimes a boy child, this time a girl, and they lead me into the dunes…this time there were bones, dead and dying things…some of the—" Her voice caught and her features pinched together as she looked up trying to fight off the tears that struggled to free themselves from her eyes.

"The bodies of my lost ones unburied…and then the child is gone—and I feel like, I just feel like it means if I try again it'll end the same. Or I'll have them a while and then lose them somehow…" Her voice hitched, and the tears that had threatened welled up again, falling like rainwater collected on the undersides of leaves.

Donovan's voice was impassive, but his eyes were warm and damp. "You believe your dreams are prophetic?" Emily scrubbed the back of a hand across her eyes, violently blue in contrast to the tear-reddened lids. She gave him a sidelong glance. "No —yes. I know that they aren't because I don't believe in prophecy, but that doesn't shake the feeling, the anxiety that makes my heart race, the sickness in the pit of my stomach every time the thought recurs."

"Which thought?"

"That I'm going to try again. I'm going to have a child, if I can."

A wide smile took over Donovan's whole face, and his eyes grew bright. He hesitated a moment, uncertain, and then reached out, pulling Emily into an embrace. "I'm so happy for you. When? When are you planning? You—you need to stop avoiding Carla and talk to her…let her help you with the fears—the dreams and all that."

Emily bit the side of her lip, frowning at his suggestion. Her response was slow, begrudging. "I will, now that I've decided."

Donovan's grin returned again, full force and he squeezed Emily's hand. "I know how important this is—"

Emily looked up at him from under her brows. "I know you do—but there's something else. Something from the dreams so I wanted to—wanted to just ask…"

"What is it?" Donovan's expression shifted to one of curiosity—puzzlement.

"Sometimes—sometimes in the dream, they are Jonathan's…but sometimes they are yours and I…"

Donovan's eyes widened. "Oh…"

Emily continued without further hesitation, filling the air where Donovan tried and failed. "I know that you've already had your one replacement child of sorts, Alicole…but she is a girl, so you haven't really replaced yourself…and Mars can handle—"

Donovan frowned, lips creasing together. "That's not how it works, and population control, even at this time, sets a precedent…I won't be party to what Earth was."

Emily looked down at her hands, voice low but insistent. "Then why do you want this for me? Why would you support me having my own progeny all this time—even push me to—if you are really so worried that we're over-breeding?"

She looked up to catch his brown eyes with her own and hold them.

Donovan sighed. "Because you haven't replaced yourself, and it's what you came here for…and you lost Jonathan, so you could replace you both—"

"Then what does the genetic make-up of the child matter? Except for principle's sake."

Donovan spread his hands pointing to each finger on his right hand as he laid out his arguments. "The example I set as planetologist matters…and if we don't start drawing a line somewhere, it'll go too far."

Emily copied Donovan's gesture, pointed to one of her own fingers and then the next. "No one is going to look at you as an example of wanton reproduction; two, set the rates too low and humans don't succeed in colonizing Mars. And three, you've only replaced yourself…a couple replaces both partners together…"

Donovan grew silent and then leaned in to place one hand on Emily's cheek, pulling her face close enough for their lips to meet, tentative at first and then clinging, the warmth of their breath intermingling between parted lips. He drew back to catch a breath. "I hadn't thought of it that way."

Emily gave a wry smile. "Neither had I until I said it to you. How long till you leave?" She scooted closer, leaning her forehead against his.

Donovan smiled and kissed her again. "I have a little while. A week."

Theresa's brows were tightly tucked together as if seeking support from each other's proximity, and her hands moved with restless energy, tugging at and straightening stray hairs and the edges of her clothing as she struggled not to blurt out further questions before Genesis could reply over the VR Comm. "Genesis, please…have you heard from Earth or not?"

Genesis's VR representation had gone still and nearly expressionless, implying a vast distance to travel from thought to reply.

"I have, but not much, and what I've received back as answer to my questions has been…vague." She looked away, and once again went silent, distracted. It was obvious that only a small portion of her attention was on the conversation.

Theresa sighed through grit teeth, the feral expression belying her otherwise kempt appearance. "I cannot reach the children, or their caretaker, Richard Brant. It has been over a week, and while that isn't long, it is beyond abnormal…I know you have contacts on Earth, and that you have means of accessing databases there that I do not. Is there something going on within the WGC or the Reproductive Council—"

Genesis raised a brow. "You are speaking from anxiety, Theresa; assuming danger when—"

"It's possible they've renewed attempts to harm the children. They could—"

Genesis shook her head. "Unlikely. I'd suggest a political upheaval or natural disaster first at this point. And the WGC is seeking to make amends with Mars, so it's unlikely they'd allow threats to what is ours…"

Theresa paused, taking in this new information and adjusting her flow of thought to include it. "After all this time? How would they benefit?"

"Remorse? Or calculated assessment of their chance of survival on Earth or Mars without cooperation, perhaps?"

Theresa frowned, shifting her shoulders and crinkling her nose as if shaking off the distraction. "And what of the dropped contact?"

Genesis fixed Theresa with her full gaze. "I'll see what I can find, yes? And in the meantime, I'm sending you a questionnaire of sorts…"

Theresa's nose crinkled and she licked her lips, a rough laugh escaping. "A—ah, questionnaire—for?"

Genesis laughed. "There are things going on outside of your stew of anxious, paranoid spiraling. I've been tasked with preparing the colony for an influx of settlers—your spawn —and while it's still a couple years off, gradual, regular preparation is key to a smooth transition. The questionnaire will clue me in to their unique needs and what sort of things the colony can expect and do to support them and you. Abby is the oldest of the children on Mars, and she is just one—and generally solitary. I'd say we are unprepared for one hundred youths, arriving all at once, without established relationships or exposure to Martian culture, climate, or terrain. I'll be sending preparatory curriculum to their caretaker as well, once you approve it."

"Oh…good. That sounds like a good thing to be doing."

Theresa's eyes were calmer now, less panicked and more fatigued in the aftermath of her initial fears. She sighed, removing one hairpin and replacing it carefully. "Please, let me know when you find anything out."

The questionnaire that appeared on Theresa's wall screen several moments later was comprehensive, allowing for input of information on each of the hundred children, their likes, dislikes, strengths, weaknesses, projected career paths and preparation to those ends. Psychological profile questionnaires were attached along with all medical and psychiatric testing results.

Theresa stared at the screen, uncertain if she had the energy to focus on such a large task or if this was a blessing of sorts, considering how much time and concentration it would require and how little room it would leave for dwelling on the communication silence that sent twisting brambles of fear up from the pit of her stomach and along her nerves each time the thought to call recurred in her mind.

She opened the first attached file and read the name, a small smile pulling at her lips as the mental image of a child she had only seen and touched through dream-speak with the VR Comm came to life in her thoughts: flashing grey-blue eyes with orange flecks and angular nose and jaw that gave an elfin quality, wisps of burnt-honey hair and a compact frame that was strong for her age. There was little to no resemblance to Abby or herself, or even Greg, but such was the way of genetic selection when placed in the hands of a geneticist such as herself and the others on the AUC project.

There was more in Aurelia of Theresa's intellect than appearance, gene packets enhancing and encouraging the traits that would make her most successful in life, specialized, resilient…It was a part of the AUC project mission—*To alter the original genetic makeup from donor parents to better allow for greater genetic diversity while maintaining racial ambiguity.*

Theresa's hand-held chimed a message from Genesis and then another almost simultaneously. *"It's a lot, I know. But it'll improve their chances of assimilating here."*

Theresa gave a verbal reply without looking away from Aurelia's growing file. "Message reply, Genesis: Yes, I see that; thank you for the work you're putting in."

Theresa could picture Genesis's amused smile on reply. *"Their success is our success."*

She was focused in now, pulling up visual representations of all pertinent information mid-air and inserting it in the file. A third message chime sounded and Theresa continued to physically manipulate the file holograms, opening some to review before adding them and dropping others into the file without second thought.

"Read message aloud and prepare for verbal reply to sender."

The AI secretary replied with a serious business-like tone. "As requested, Emily's message reads: Theresa, I'd like to come by this evening, please, to discuss my reproductive options…if you have a block of time. I'd like to move ahead quickly. Carla will attend as well if you have this evening free. Thank you."

Theresa paused, staring off as she processed the message and its tone without Emily's vocal patterns to give better insight. *Was she planning a child—now for some reason? Hmm…Hopefully not like last time—*

Theresa saw Emily as she was then, so many years ago, shaking and desperate, begging for an AUC progeny of her own to fill the void of the pregnancies she'd lost, one after another.

Unease and curiosity percolated across the intervening years and the snippets of memory; Theresa had tried to broach the subject with her, to offer help, and was met with either avoidance or denial of any need or desire for it.

She mumbled under her breath, turning attention back to the files. "No need for an AUC now, unless—she loses more." The idea made her flinch and she flicked her head to the side as if to shake out the onslaught of thoughts, disturbing possibilities of a recurrence after all of the work they'd put into making pregnancies viable on Mars, all the healthy pregnancies and births in the past nine years.

Still…Theresa's eyes strayed to the prototype that took up a large, recessed space in the curved wall beside her viewing screen. The modified AUC unit had gathered red dust, bringing a twinge of shame.

Why did I set it aside, huh, Theresa? Caution? Carla would say fear—Carla would be right, then.

She stepped forward, leaving the holographic files to wait, and ran a hand over the curving silicone body of the unit, the translucent tubing that formed the four-armed frame of the artificial uterine chamber. The original design was not hers, but this adaptation was, altered to accommodate Martian gravity levels only thirty-eight percent of Earth's, radiation, and the ability to shift hormone exposure levels moment to moment without her inputting the change in advance.

This one had a coating that allowed viewing inside by projecting imagery from the interior onto the outer surface without allowing light in to disrupt the fetus. Theresa's smile was wistful as her mind grasped eagerly for the creation that was, as yet, untested, and may never be—except for Donovan's animals, smaller and larger versions like the ones submerged in the caves by the seaside for the finwhale's first generation.

Restless ennui threatened to take hold as she pushed back the urge to move forward with the technology. *It had risks…moral implications—but who would be arbiter of those risks if not her?*

Theresa sighed, forcing focus; the files needed transferred and Emily deserved a reply, as well as her full attention when she arrived.

Theresa stepped away from the prototype and returned to her files and questionnaires.

CRUMBLING FOUNDATIONS

The VR version of the council room was a wildly embellished hodge-podge of mental constructs. Each attendant, unconsciously or consciously, added in elements to the room that overlaid the bare bones of the WGC council headquarters architecture.

What was in actuality an amalgam of recycled materials, 3D printed to resemble stone walls and wooden flooring in amphitheater style, in this corner became brick and crawling ivy and, in another, silken, antique pillows with Persian carpeting.

Richard paced beneath the carved pillars, one residential Corinthian and the next Doric. Council members were arriving at a trickle-in pace.

Morton Steiner appeared to his left, looking more like a waxen doll wearing layers of paint to cover blotchy skin and sweat drenched hair. Richard cleared his throat. "Your construct is ragged—clean it up."

Morton closed his eyes, opening them almost immediately as if whatever the darkness behind his eyes held might come out after him if he stayed long. He looked down instead, taking a shaky breath to focus on what he was projecting into the VR Comm.

"Better?"

Richard bit back his first reply. "It's fine. Let's get on with this before we all fall apart."

He put a hand on Morton's shoulder, more old habit than genuine sentiment, and searched the room, assessing numbers in attendance and identities. To his right a construct came into view, disheveled, shifting, hands shaping into long tubules that wrapped back around the owner. A name appeared and then disappeared from view next to the humanoid shape that struggled to consolidate itself within the VR Comm.

Richard adjusted his signal, attempting to create a more direct link to the struggling council member. "Focus on my voice. The council chamber is around you, silicone ceiling letting in light, columns shadowed by the circle of arches. Your shape materializes here, hands clasped to still the shaking, the coughing can't reach you here…See yourself as you were, poised, consistent, present…3, 2, 1…"

Richard focused his own will into the link, filtering out his own thoughts lest they intensify the self-doubt and struggle.

Flashes of dark and light, flooding with sunset red permeated their shared mind space. Skin touching, caressing, the scrape of nails, beads of blood upwelling from unexpected cuts. Gums pulled back to reveal teeth broken and misshapen, tongue wrapped around to twist through the empty eye sockets of a face he recognized. The face that matched the name. The sound started low, a guttural mumble, a chant—built up into a scream, there were words beneath it but he couldn't catch them.

Richard pulled back, stepping away physically as well to fight the pull of the mind he'd reached out to just moments before. *Surely, just moments…*

He stumbled, shoving back against the reaching, misshapen arms, the crimson-sunset fire. He opened his eyes again, raking a hand through disheveled hair with deliberate, calm movements.

The figure was gone, leaving an empty name slot in its place. There were several more around the room. Sixteen of thirty absent from their designated spots at the World Governing Council meeting.

Diadonna stood at a dais, central to the other landmarks in the room. Her violet-grey eyes, framed by blue lashes, and smooth twilight peach cheekbones with undertones of sienna brown, were preserved from what around the room appeared as a collective struggle to create cohesive and meeting-ready mental constructs, whether it be from illness or lack of ability to focus in crisis.

"Council Members… It would seem that we have reached another point in Earth history where we are faced with our own fragile mortality."

Richard's eyes narrowed as he listened to her begin, her voice smooth and without the expected hesitations of a mind under siege. The same that he could feel beginning in the subtle misfiring of synapses, the thoughts that resurfaced, refusing to connect to logical frameworks instead attempting to reshape perception, and set off pulses of fear…anger.

"A pathogen, previously unknown to us, has achieved a wide spread of infection and a level of lethality that is threatening our future on Earth."

She paused, eyes searching the collected officials for something that was not present. Creases appeared beside her lips as they tightened, and her nostrils flared in a subtle tell of rallying mental resources.

"Many of you have already been infected, and some on the council lost to us. The WGC council complex is under full quarantine, as is the reproductive council…but it has come to our attention that these measures were taken too late, or possibly—this contagion arose in several locations at once. All Earth cities are affected. All continents.

"As you may know, I've instituted worldwide stay-at-home orders with our governing council and research teams as the only exception. Access to personal medibot units is universal, with some delay in distribution of broad-spectrum antibiotic component refills and repair for older units. Measures to alleviate that inequity are already underway and our broadcasts are ongoing, with key steps to survive this. Stay at home. Self isolate. Begin antibiotic treatment by medibot at the start of first symptoms and complete the full course. No assignment is as essential as avoiding loss of life."

Morton's voice was low, but came as the only interruption, despite the disjointed murmurs that could be heard inside the comm, half-muted to prevent vocal chaos.

"I've already asked this in private, but it bears repeating…Was it one of ours?" He shook his head, carefully arranged features flickering to reveal a deeper panic than his construct showed. His eyes gleamed with restrained fear, teeth clenched to measure his speech and tone. "I'm not seeing the God-damned breadcrumbs…pardon my outburst…that make this ring true. All Earth cities?! Reads like a fucking VR Sim fantasy unless we planned it… seeded it, hid it…Or someone else?"

Another voice sounded clearly in the comm, mumbled curses clearing into a question before devolving again. "Did Mars cook it up and send it? You know we well pissed them off, and nothing from them since?!"

Diadonna cleared her throat again, louder this time, and placed a full-stop on interjections without her direct approval to speak. "We have a guest speaker…Dr. Brant, here to explain this event. He is an expert in a number of fields, including research-focused microbiology and genetics, and previous WGC position holder.

I'm giving him the floor." Diadonna's construct stepped down from the dais, taking a seat among the other council members to allow Richard to take up the speaker's space.

Richard's voice projected out from the back of the room at full volume, causing those assembled to turn, eyes wide.

"One sickened animal can infect a complex, a full colony of them, you might imagine, could infect cities. Earth's emptied ecosystems have been repopulated with a far more successful species than we ourselves. Rats, notorious for their ability to share their epidemics with us, and famous for surviving them better."

His pacing was slow and measured, keeping tempo with his speech as he wove his words into their receptive minds.

"Did we start this one? Perhaps, but I could not say when, unless it was through centuries of antibiotic resistance, viral research, and ecological insult…biological warfare? Yes… but recent or present, intentional or accidental, is a moot point."

The council member's comm contributions were still silenced, but their eyes and physicality showed enough. Eyes alternately wide or narrowed, brows furrowed, teeth bared or mouth slack.

Richard laughed at the silent reactions. "What we have now is an opportunity to prove our worth, or go dark and let the rats take it…they are already on the recovery, while we burn ourselves out. Submit yourselves for full quarantine and treatment under my remote care for access to new treatments, then we can manage the rest of the population; shut down all unnecessary government functions, and with as much as we can automate, that's all of it, and you might pull through, if we find a better treatment quickly."

Diadonna stood before speaking, features showing a calm that only twitched with irritation. "All those who are symptomatic have and will continue to report for antibiotic treatment. It is not as widespread within the WGC headquarters as the Reproductive Council.

Richard tilted his head to the side, raising a hand to his lips in exaggeration of thought.

"Forgive me for the contradiction, Diadonna, but that is both incorrect and lacking foresight. I guarantee they can already feel it, based on their shoddy constructs and inability to hold their tongues without a mute switch…I suspect you feel it, too—unless you isolated yourself well before any threat was known to the rest of us."

Richard directed mental command to his VR Comm to open

simultaneous, private discussion with the Head of the WGC. *If she isn't compromised, she'll be capable of two streams.*

"*Diadonna, you have to know this is far past any need to calm them…ding dong—grim reaper at the door…their only chance is to submit to being test subjects.*"

Diadonna's response felt like a shout muffled behind a thin pillow of moldering insulation foam. **"There is always cause to remain calm. I choose to maintain my poise as council lead. Despair won't help them recover."**

"*No one exposed and without my—upgrades, is coming out of this…But okay, let's humor them, sure. You're letting them think that a course of antibiotics has or will set them straight, when it's obvious that many of them are moving into stage two of this infection, a gradual onset of psychosis, relapse, death. We don't even know, yet, how long the antibiotics can prolong that eventuality. But real-talk now, Diadonna: I am getting me and mine off of Earth while I work on this thing. When are you jumping ship, so to speak, and are there any others unexposed to go with you?*"

Her mental voice came through with icy tone intact. **"Did I not make it clear? There is a quarantine in effect. No one leaves, no one enters until this is solved. Communications to Mars are restricted, and have been for quite some time for anyone outside the WGC complex with the highest clearances. You think we need Mars panicking and rushing out to collect their long lost grandparents and siblings and bringing this to Mars? All communication will shortly be disallowed to prevent just what you describe."**

"*Huh, and your ship leaves…?*"

"I'm staying."

"*Fine…but I prefer not to force my children to watch the Earth infrastructure fail and play pick-up the pieces on a mortally wounded planet. You know they were intended for Mars.*"

She spoke each word with equal emphasis as if explaining to a distracted child. **"I won't. Allow. This. To. Make it. To. Mars. And I am not a part of your pet project. You are not on the** *council any longer, and the council lead you had in your pocket is not here."*

Richard hesitated, voice cold with restrained fury. *"If Mars is your concern, then—we need to get there."*

"Mars is already colonized successfully. Your services are no longer needed there."

Richard sighed, pausing before responding, voice shaking with the restraint he held tightly in place. *"Fine…okay, a number of my children are on assignment outside the Council walls, I need to collect them for treatment…is that something you can support?"*

"Call them back."

"Some have already fallen ill and I've lost contact. I'll go get them."

"Send medical drone pick-up."

Richard allowed a rumbled growl to come through the comm. *"You may be well now, but what are the chances that will hold?…I will not continue to research a cure or transfer my data to any of your other teams, should they stay functional, if I don't get access codes. I'm uploading my list of necessary codes to you for departures and returns, medibot protocol overrides, security footage, mag-rail transit."*

The pause on Diadonna's end was long, allowing Richard to focus on the disjointed discussion still taking place in the Council meeting proper. They had been unmuted, in staggered groups allowing discussion, and most that he caught stank of fear, words and tone evincing a deep-seated panicked turmoil that meant they had little time left before they lost full control.

"You are not the only one researching this for us…" Her tone lacked the conviction of her words.

"But you know I'm the best here—and the only one able to carry on multi-stream VR Comm despite signs of advanced infection. Your epidemiology team and the one in WGC Eurasia is infected and plagued with infighting."

He felt the startle reaction, the growing shock and alarm in her mind, and he continued before she could respond. *"Yes, I am— and keeping the effects at bay quite well…**send me the codes** and tend to* *your governing council while it still stands. I've calmed them some while we argued—fed them the more comforting bits of information about this infection, and there aren't many—but now I'm signing off to continue my research. I recommend you have everyone sent to intensive treatment in the main quarantine center, where I can remotely alter their treatment as we discover more. It's the only chance for them."*

Diadonna grew silent and still, indicating a shift in focus from the comm to some external activity, and then the codes came through; not enough to break the communications blockade, but enough to get them to WASA.

Richard made a formal bow with crooked grin. "Thank you, Diadonna, I'll be checking in on you and the council before I depart."

CHANGE OF PLANS

"The WGC—what is left of them—and the Reproductive Council are in agreement now."

Genesis raised both brows, keeping her expression otherwise conversational. "What is left of them?"

Richard waved a hand as if shooing some insect for providing a nuisance. "Yes—keep up. They are fewer in number and will continue to—decrease. Still, they are in power and believe they are handling the situation. They intend to cut contact soon, no comms in or out of the headquarters, and none off planet, certainly—I just left the meeting, and they are decidedly more optimistic than they should be. I think they have some back-up plan unmentioned."

He allowed a look of disgust to gleam in dark hazel eyes, as he scratched a recently unkempt beard. "They may well hold on until they lose the ability."

Genesis folded her hands in her lap where she sat among brightly colored silken floor cushions. "Richard—"

Her contact turned a sharp glare on her before smoothing his features. "Don't—call me that. That's not the way I want Mars informed of our—interactions."

Genesis nodded in apology. "Fine. Dr. B, then. You—haven't explained this 'event' that you are now referencing as if I'm up to date—I am not."

He looked angry now, impatient as she had never seen him, the glint in his eyes sharp and sardonic.

"Extrapolate, then—I don't have time for you if you can't keep up."

Genesis glared back, matching his fury with her own and allowing the words to emerge with venom.

"Losing our cool now, are we? Doesn't reflect well if you cannot calm your fit long enough to use your resources. Call me back when you are done with your tantrum…"

The man snorted, allowing a pained smile to join the irritation in his expression without lessening it. He cleared his throat. "The contagion affects mood regulation—provokes outbursts. Many did not make it to the WGC meeting simply because of 'outburst of temper.' They are not even aware they are still infected, as yet."

Genesis grew still, eyes narrowing.

"And you are?"

"Yes. As are the children, the ones here, anyway. Many were away from the headquarters on trainings. It is…a slow burn, I think, colonizing hosts, and quite contagious well before illness could be suspected. Not a sudden onset like we initially thought. It builds to a peak in stages before breaking and either taking the host with it or…I'm not sure of the other outcomes yet."

"If there is going to be a gap in communication, you need to compile all of this and send it. We can't help if we don't have that, and certainly not if we can't coordinate."

"I'm handling it."

Genesis turned a sharp glare on him and leaned in. "For how much longer? Don't be arrogant. If your mental capacities are compromised, you had best use your resources. And contact Theresa yourself or I will tell her…everything."

Richard stared forward, some war raging and flaring behind eyes that flickered with competing emotions, alternating with shadows of fatigue. He licked his lips.

"You have access to my data banks; I'm sending the codes. You can access until they cut off all comms. I'll reach Theresa as soon as I can, but I need to focus on Aurelia. She's coming out of this with me one way or another. Just…give Theresa something to hold her until I can…focus."

"I've already done that—you're forcing my hand."

She rapid-blinked, taking in the extent of his compromised state.

"I have this under control—on Mars anyway…just—get yourself stabilized."

Genesis cut contact, dropping the VR Comm as if it was scalding hot. She frowned, searching her inner landscape for justification to the emotional reaction that gave an edge of urgency to her thought processes. The role he filled for her was still—new in her experience…first her contact, *something like a mentor. The attachment stems from our genetic similarity.* It was an understatement. *Shared genetics, really.*

The thought brought a comforting framework. Urgency was acceptable in this case, so long as it didn't impede her logic.

How long had she known now, without either of them addressing it? Their connection…it hovered in the back of her mind like snow falling on silent pines. Her oldest memories had surfaced in the VR therapy sessions with Theresa and Carla, most of them cloaked in mental metaphor, thankfully, or something to confuse with an allegory for current events. They didn't expect accurate memories—her caretaker towering so many feet above her with those squirming, vulnerable pseudo-humans in large glowing chambers, like a ceiling full of living lights. He smiled at her, lifted her—the memory resolved into snow.

Snow and pines.

There was a second wolf in the cave when they found her. Theresa stared at the heavy-bodied canine that seemed to be grinning, standing there behind the wolf she recognized from previous therapy sessions, David's gaunt, hungry-looking avatar in Genesis's mindscape.

They flanked Genesis but didn't show any further aggression, instead waiting for some signal from the sleek, black wolf between them, a she-wolf who stepped toward Theresa, a low growl in the back of her throat.

Theresa took a step back and flicked a glance at Carla and Genesis. I found them, now you do your thing, Carla. Carla nodded and turned back to the Genesis that stood next to her, composed, smirking, unchanged from when she had arrived on Mars. She cleared her throat. "Where is it, Genesis?"

Genesis stared at the midwife with no more than a faint echo of curiosity on her face. The black wolf growled louder.

"Where is what?"

Carla gestured towards Genesis's slim, muscled figure, flat abdomen with no sign of pregnancy. "Where is your Progeny?"

Genesis looked irritated. "This is a VR augmented mental construct, Carla; my Progeny is right where we left it. In my body."

"Really, because I don't see it…"

Genesis rolled her eyes. "We already discussed the split focus and representations of myself here."

"The wolf doesn't appear gravid."

Genesis's composure faltered and she looked angry. "How the fuck should I know, Carla? Maybe it's in the back of the cave in an AUC? Why don't you go look?" She gestured towards the wolves, two silent and one growling with increased aggression.

Theresa bit her lip and caught Carla's attention. "Is this how we build trust…?"

Carla doubled down, stepping closer to Genesis until she was a step away, directly facing her. "You're only lying to yourself. The thing is, I don't think you've ever had anyone call bullshit on you."

Genesis was scowling at the older woman in front of her. "If you're going to bring—"

"No, Genesis. You spin your stories, gather up all the most convincing bits of truth to piece together until it isn't even a lie anymore, but a woven tapestry of reality, rearranged how you want it. It's impressive, but it isn't helping you with this. So just listen."

The reply came as a half growl, Genesis's eyes a mix of anger, confusion. "If I wasn't listening, you wouldn't be in here, Carla."

"Good. This split isn't a choice. It's a reflection of what you're doing to yourself, in here." She tapped her own forehead instead of Genesis's.

Theresa was watching the wolves while she listened to the tense exchange. The tall black female with the yellow eyes was approaching Carla, with that low growl in the back of her throat.

"If that's true, then what difference does it make if you can't fix it?" Genesis's eyes looked raw, unguarded for a split second.

"Carla…" Theresa's voice was a whisper.

Carla sighed, and reached behind herself, offering her wrist for the black wolf to smell. The she-wolf sniffed at the midwife and then sat down, seemingly disinterested. "Take us into the cave and we'll see what's there."

Genesis stopped at the mouth of the cave. Theresa and Carla were a step behind. Would they push her if she stopped? Her feet felt heavy and cold, and a body wide ache was settling into her. Surges of irrational emotion welled up with each reluctant step and were answered by a rising tide of anger. There were memories fighting to fly free around the darkness of this endless trek downhill, but she wasn't alone; they were in her head, and there was nothing to keep them from seeing.

Something crunched under foot and Genesis reached down to see it closer. It was a small brittle sphere, damp and decaying, with pin-prick teeth along a jaw frozen crooked. She flung it aside. Bones in the dark. *Skeletons in the closet…*

She moved on. It was Tigger's skull, of course. They didn't need to see it.

"Are you okay?" Theresa was whispering in her ear. Did she stop again? Yes, she was thinking, drowning in this dark that was the dark of thoughts, instead of actual darkness that her eyes could pierce.

She cleared her throat. "Of course."

There was a growing light ahead, pink-tinged like the beginning of a soft dawn, but it didn't cut the darkness, just grew larger.

Genesis slowed, shying away from the light, while Theresa pushed ahead, crossing the distance with excited steps.

"Come see it, Genesis; it's beautiful."

She already saw it and it wasn't. It was barely formed, visible when it shouldn't be, something people turn away from, something they feared and disposed of.

Carla was there next to Theresa, next to the glowing AUC chamber. They were smiling, touching it, and their faces filled her with rage.

Out of the dark, the black wolf came forward, growling once again, advancing, snapping and forcing them away from it.

"Don't touch it! Just, leave it alone!"

Theresa was beside her, hands on her shoulders. She flinched and pushed them off, shoved at her. "Don't touch me!"

"Okay, okay…I'm sorry…just—look at it. It, he, is ready to come out."

Genesis glanced up and took a step back from what she saw.

"It isn't…"

But it was, she could tell. It looked like Phase One at the end. Genesis felt a rush of terror fill her veins with ice water and freeze her in place. She reached down and felt the actual swelling of her lower abdomen, felt the fluttering movements there, the deep gashes from her own nails. *I tried to dig it out…*A wave of nausea joined the other emotions spinning in her gut, mixing there into something she couldn't recognize. They were here to make it stop, make the pain stop, not the pregnancy.

She turned and found Theresa there, and Carla, the pink light of the glowing AUC illuminating their faces.

Genesis stood and grabbed hold of Theresa's wrist and Carla's, pulled them with her to approach the AUC.

It was warm, pliable, and when she pressed, he pressed back. But it wasn't beautiful.

Flashes came with that nudge. *She was watching Phase One sleep and the lab tech found her, his eyes, blue orbs in the pink glow of the AUC lab so full of disgust for her…and he called Dr. B to come get her…*

Genesis's eyes widened as she saw into the dark, no compartments here to shove the memories, to hide them. "Theresa, I don't want you to—"

"I'm not leaving, Genesis. I'm right here with you."

She was almost asleep from the rhythm of his step, carrying her back to her room. His voice was stern, but it soothed. Soft cotton of the white sheets he tucked around her face… A kiss on her forehead, his dark hair and the collar of his lab coat tickled her cheek…

Genesis was shaking, fighting the memory. Carla's hand on her back was firm as if to shore her up.

But Tigger was there, under the edge of the covers where she could pet him. He was beginning to smell, though, and Dr. B, he sniffed the air, pulled the sheets back. His eyes were heavy with something she couldn't give any name to, the quirk of smile he gave her just before laying her in the bed was gone. It was the last one. Tigger gone as well. Dr. B, gone. She felt revulsion building up in her gut and turned to run.

Theresa grabbed her hand and pressed it back to the AUC, the other she placed on Genesis's own abdomen.

"This is not me! I can't—be this!" She dropped to the ground and curled in on herself.

Theresa looked over Genesis's head to Carla.

The midwife's voice was low and soft in the small circle they made around her. "You are not the first, and you won't be the last to hate this, and feel inadequate."

A sob broke free from the roiling pool of mixed emotions in Genesis's gut as Carla continued.

"You won't be the first to come from nothing—or something painful—and pick your own legacy."

Genesis glared up at the AUC hanging over their heads. "I can't be one of those things." The tears were flowing freely now.

Theresa leaned in and caught Genesis's eyes with her own. "Okay…when this is done, we can terminate it. I won't let anyone force you to do this to yourself."

Genesis stared at her, all thoughts and emotions gone still, frozen. Theresa stood up and pulled her onto her feet. There was a control panel on the right side of the AUC chamber, and Theresa guided her hand to the right keys to expel the progeny within.

"We'll do it here first—so you'll come out of this feeling ready… knowing what you want."

Genesis's hand crept across her abdomen to the deep gashes there, her other hand toying with the controls. "Okay."

She pushed the sequence and watched as the arms on the sides of the unit tightened on the lower segment and then the upper making rhythmic motions until they grasped the opening on the underside of the AUC and stretched it open around the progeny's head. The process was slow, methodical, and the finality of the choice made her unable to look away. Carla guided Genesis's hand to the opening, the head hanging there as fluids drained from the small gasping mouth. She reached up and touched the damp wrinkled scalp, the strands of black hair, that hung down as streams of amniotic fluid poured out and the progeny slipped free into her hands.

She crouched down and set it on the floor, and its arms and legs flailed out, a cry erupting from purpling lips. The black wolf sniffed at the damp head, pink tongue flicking out to lick the crying child on the floor of the cave. Genesis stared for several long moments, then lifted it and the crying stopped. She pulled it closer, inspecting the dark hair and dusky skin and then pressed her lips to his scalp, inhaling his scent.

Theresa sat down next to her and reached for the progeny, but Genesis pulled him closer, out of Theresa's reach, and the black wolf growled. "He smells like—like he's mine."

Genesis shifted her eyes away before meeting Theresa's probing gaze full on with a conciliatory smile.

"You requested I try to reach Richard, or someone else in the WGC building. Someone who would know more about the radio silence, as it were."

"Yes—?" Theresa stared, mahogany eyes unblinking as she listened with an unwavering focus. The screen that held file after file on the AUC progeny in a glowing map with pictorial representations went to sleep, shifting to giant swells of green Martian waves. Abby sat at the desk with a stylus sketching through VR, her eyes flicking their way any time they seemed distracted enough not to notice.

Genesis turned towards Abby and then back to Theresa, satisfied that the information she had to impart would not faze the girl who was likely listening, even with a VR headset on.

"I was assigned a contact on Earth for Human Relations. That contact was changed not long after our arrival on Mars and, as it turns out, he is someone you are familiar with."

Theresa scowled in concentration, eyes still locked on Genesis's face so as not to miss the visual tells that could give more context for her words.

Genesis hesitated and then plunged forward, words crowding together as if to avoid the listener's likely reaction. "My contact is your Richard Brant—I only found out recently, as our interactions were without name or true face for quite some time."

Theresa's eyes remained blank and her stillness deepened until she broke eye contact, piecing her words together as if selecting them from a bag of Scrabble tiles. "You—have a contact—on Earth and it happens to be Dr. Brant—and you've reached him when I could not—continue."

Genesis nodded, complying without hesitation. "He has been unable to contact because it's become necessary to move up the timeline for transport to Mars. I haven't a date, but it's soon, if I understand correctly."

She paused, watching the mental tug of war in Theresa's eyes. "He plans to contact you shortly with further details—he asked me not to worry you. But I thought it best you knew immediately. You've *been* worried, and it isn't fair to you." Genesis placed a hand on Theresa's shoulder and the other woman flinched, eyes distant and full of thoughts like bodies surfacing from underwater.

"Worry me?" The intensity of her glare made Genesis step back. "That ship has sailed and it's captained by a damn fool—I fail to see how moving up the timeline is connected to the lack of communication—unless they are under duress?!"

Genesis watched as Theresa grew increasingly agitated, pulling at the edges of her lab coat and fidgeting with her hands with a deep telltale scowl between her brows.

"Why now?! And without my input—"

Genesis lowered her eyes and sidled closer, catching Theresa's gaze before continuing. "I don't doubt that you know Richard much more intimately than I do."

Theresa sighed, shaking her head not in denial but irritation. Genesis watched her reactions, gauging them as she formed her next phrasings.

"But he is stubborn, yes? And needs to keep his own council until he has formed his own framework and interpretation around an issue."

Theresa was nodding now, her eyes focused on the words that rang true.

"You know where his motivations arise from. His priorities. If he had to go silent, I think we can trust that it was out of necessity."

"You spoke with him. How much more are you holding off from sharing?"

Genesis laughed, the humor dry and subdued lest it come off as mockery. "Only things that he was holding back from me. We— are going to be needed in this shortly—I suspect quite urgently. It's best we don't waste energy on anger, or on parsing the details of what has already passed."

Theresa turned away to stare at the green waves on the screen, sucking in a shaky breath and exhaling slowly as the rhythm of the water seeped into her raw nerves. "The children's files—you knew we would need them compiled for their arrival."

"Yes."

"Fine. They'll be ready by tomorrow. All one hundred, and then they'll be off my mind so I can focus on the next steps."

Genesis smiled, the combination of approval and mirth lighting her eyes with warm humor. "Good, then we'll be ready when he contacts again."

Genesis turned to leave and then paused, turning back to face the other woman. "Theresa?"

"Hmmm?" She was already back to work on the task. Genesis's smile was warm and revealed an uncommon vulnerability. "Thank you for trusting me on this."

Theresa blinked, uncertain how to respond, grateful that Genesis had already turned to leave. "Um, sure."

LOOSE ENDS

Emily folded and unfolded her arms with nervous energy, pulling a lock of pale red hair between her lips, but her eyes held a resolve that often evaded her.

Theresa waited for her to begin, glancing over at Carla's patient figure where the older woman sat on the floor, stretching her quadriceps to fill the time without appearing to rush things.

She glanced at her handheld, silently chiding herself with the knowledge that a silent alert in the wrist band and lab coat collar micro-processors would signal any messages coming in from Earth. Even the main AI in her room had instructions to allow any incoming communications from Earth to bypass her private meeting settings. There was no need to check or think on it, but still she did. Emily was here and deserved her attention. She let out her withheld breath and turned her focus back outward.

Emily caught Theresa's eyes and smiled. "I expect to be in the early stages of conception—rather, I am, because I checked my implant. Ovulation occurred two days ago."

Theresa blinked, a slow smile forming. "Oh!…I expected you to need my help—" Emily blushed, glancing over at Carla who looked faintly puzzled, and then wet her lips. "I do. I have a very specific request…If I'm going to do this—to try for this, then I want to—to have the two at once. Jonathan's and my child and this one, born and raised together. A mix of past and future instead of either going backwards or—or forgetting…"

She paused, growing silent as she stared at her hands in her lap and the room went quiet with her. "Okay! Of course, I can help with this."

Theresa paused, tilting her head as if deep in thought before she stood and paced towards the AUC unit against the wall.

"There are some options to consider…You are already carrying one. Fine. Do you want to try to carry a second simultaneously?"

Emily frowned, blurting out her reply before Theresa could finish. "It has to be at the same time…that's—important." She looked away as if pausing, but instead of continuing with explanations or justification, she allowed the silence to hold and keep her motivations.

"Fine, yes. But does it have to be you?"

"Well—not a surrogate."

Theresa pressed her lips together, hands tugging at her lab coat as she took a breath to renew patience. Earth was forefront in her thoughts, warring with her excitement over this new prospect.

"Not a surrogate. Your own AUC chamber. It could be installed in your own living space and controlled and monitored by my computer system remotely."

Emily's eyes widened, alarm and confusion sharing space in her expression.

"Why? When I requested that before—you refused. Why would it be an option now?"

Theresa looked over to Carla, whose lips were pulled to the right and eyes narrowed in withheld judgement that was both skeptical and intrigued. "I'd certainly like to hear the whys and wherefores of this option myself, Theresa…" She pushed her silver braid over her shoulder and leaned forward in a stretch with her face resting in her hands.

"Of course. What we had before was the AUC technology from Earth, with all the flaws of that program inherent. And without any alterations to account for the requirements for successful gestation on Mars."

Emily nodded, still listening, now leaning in as if mesmerized by the possibility presented as Theresa continued to elaborate.

"This is my design, and proven to have equal success rates to natural gestation on Mars."

Carla's deadpan voice interrupted. "With animals—you haven't used it on humans, unless you have a little miniature Abby running around that I've somehow missed—" She opened her eyes wider and turned her head this way and that as if searching for a phantom child.

Theresa laughed, the undertone of tension clear. "No, no human children have been grown in it yet…but thousands of other organisms." She looked from one of them to the other. "It's just an option. I'm not trying to sell anything, but it could be insurance, should anything go wrong. And it would set a precedent that we have all of the options on Mars."

"Mmmmm…" Carla frowned, turning from inspection of Theresa's face to Emily's. "You're offering another basket for the eggs, but the one she has is just fine."

Theresa sighed, a quick exhalation of irritation.

"I know that. What happened before—the losses—were due to our collective unsuitability for Martian gravity, er—lack of it. But you know that twin pregnancies are harder on the one carrying…"

Emily stood, walking over to the four-armed AUC unit and raising a hand to press against the firm yet pliable outer surface. "But—will it feel the same? One inside me and the other in this…? What if they're lonely or can't feel…loved?"

"Fair questions. They'll have as much interaction as you choose to give, plus your voice, your heartbeat and breathing patterns, walking motions—all added in through the computer, and then interaction with you from the outside. Your pattern of hormone fluctuations can be programmed in as well through monitoring, with slight delay."

Theresa approached Emily, standing next to her in front of the AUC.

"If it helps…I only ever experienced Abby in one of these, and then in the RPU attached to my chest. I didn't have a physiological gestation with her, or any of the children, but at least she couldn't feel more like my child."

Emily's voice was a low whisper. "On Earth, I would have considered it a gift, better than no child or having one placed with me. Now, I see that it is, but it's—"

"It's a lot to think about on the spot—you don't have to answer now."

Emily turned back to Carla and smiled, tears forming at the corners of her eyes. "No, I think if you both feel it's safe enough, then we should do it. Set a precedent, as you say. There are plenty among us who can't experience pregnancy or wouldn't want to— but would want progeny."

Theresa's excitement showed in the shimmer of her eyes, but her tone was careful, measured. "Are you sure?" She glanced over at Carla who was standing now with hands resting on hips.

"It isn't my decision."

"Well, no, but do you trust my assessment of the safety?"

Carla gave a grudging nod. "As much as I can. You'll have to tolerate my questions if you're doing this. I know your technology is not like the sort that I had to fight against on Earth in my youth—ineffective, undermining and demeaning women…but my gut reaction is still skepticism."

Theresa nodded. "But it isn't an interference or replacement for human gestation…it's an option, a safeguard, should the future require it, and an equalizer."

Emily's voice took on an air of urgency and breathless excitement. "Can we start now? I don't want this one behind."

"I already have your genetic material. You can be here for as much of the process as you want…and if you want any changes made to their genetics, we can discuss."

Emily shrugged, watching as Theresa opened up virtual representations of the male and female gamete banks. "How much do you want left to chance?"

"Everything…just so long as they are strong enough to survive."

"Fine, fine. The Martian Adaptation is already a part of your genetics, and these are fresh enough."

Carla placed a hand on Emily's shoulder with a warm smile. "Em, I'm off to pack and plan for Donovan's trip, unless you want to have me stay back while you do this…for support? We leave tomorrow if I go…"

Emily shook her head. "No, I want you to go, and I want to do this as if it's simple, normal—even if it isn't. If you hover, I'll worry more."

Carla snorted. "Yeah, I know it. But I had to offer…I expect regular updates, and I hope you'll let Kendra be there for you. Does Donovan know? Is it planned?"

A smile pulled at the corners of Emily's lips. "He knows…just not that it's definite yet. And not about this other one." Emily peered into the empty AUC once more, the smile on her face softening and turning inward.

The sun was low, glowing deep purples and reds through the dusty atmosphere and setting the Eastern dunes alight with somber fire. The favored trail skirted the dunes, remaining on higher ground to give a solid running surface and some shade from tall outcropping that emerged to the West and eventually gave way to a steady rise that became the lower edge of the West mountains.

"Yeah, I checked my messages." Neil barked a quick laugh allowing his breath to fall back into the tempo of trail running before continuing. He turned his head, running backwards a moment for Melissa to catch up.

"All right, long-legs, that pace will bite you in the ass after a few miles and then we'll see who's still going."

Neil laughed, turning back around before a rock could trip him up.

"So…inbox full of, 'Thank you for your years of excellent service to Earth, Captain', and 'Please forgive our accidental betrayal, Captain…' and…can we give you our latest tech, Captain…?'"

Melissa pulled up closer, quickening pace. "And you've replied…?" "Not a damn thing. I'm not interested in their lies."

Melissa gave him a sidelong glance. "Not interested in making them believe you have an accord—and wouldn't consider retaliation at this point?" Her tone was light, but the sharp look in her eyes gave clear subtext.

Neil shook his head, laughter coming out with each huff of breath. "You've been taking notes from Genesis, haven't you? Watch out, or she'll have you in bed with her and David as well."

Melissa rolled her eyes, laughing and pulling ahead with her cheeks reddening further, from the exertion or from the suggestion.

"A little guile is useful, you know. And Genesis is not the only one versed in playing for advantage. I earned this position before I had her support."

Neil slowed the pace, falling into a loping jog as the trail turned back towards the colony. He stretched his arms across his chest and then overhead, adjusting the weighted vest and tightening the closures.

"You did—you did…I respect that. So tell them all's forgiven? Sure, why not."

Melissa nodded as they approached the outer wall that led into the complex of domes. "Yes, but gradually—make them convince you, so they can trust it when it comes."

Neil laughed again, leaning in for the security scan.

The gate security AI had a warm, sardonic smile to her voice. "Have a good run, Captain?"

Neil wiped a hand across dry lips to remove the frothed spit that had formed and dried there on the long-distance run. His breathing was still heavy. "Yeah, thanks. Request entry please."

"It's been a while since you had a good run, Captain. You slowing down on me?" The AI teased him before opening the gate.

Neil's smile was melancholy. "Wouldn't dream of it." The gate opened and they entered. Melissa watching Neil's back as she followed in, a pace behind. None of the other AI's bantered quite like this one.

"Neil?"

He cleared his throat and took a drink from the water reservoir in his weighted vest. "Yeah?"

"Why not reprogram this one, now? It's been a while. You don't need to do that to yourself."

He shrugged and headed into the garden and towards the door to the inner hallway. "Nah, it's fine. It's good to be reminded." He tapped the side of his head. "Not as if they aren't all in here reminding me anyway. You too, right?"

Melissa wet her lips, flicking her eyes away. "Yeah, they are."

The Martian landscape blurred beneath them, the transparent floor of the transport drone allowing full view of the passing terrain. Rust-reds, lichen-black, and mottled, subdued green and yellow hues of lichen grass, quaking-aspen, pines, ginkos, Martian plumeria, and cycad species formed a distorted checkerboard at this speed of travel.

"She's told you, then?"

Donovan glanced up at Carla from where he stared at the shifting landscape far below them. He nodded, an amused half smile appearing before he turned his gaze back to the floor. "I wasn't surprised about the speed once her mind was made up, only…the staying back, not coming along on this."

Carla shrugged, memories flickering across her grey irises like clouds. "Suppose she'll explain when you get back. I think she needs to get past that same point without me holding her hand and staring at the health of her skin to watch for signs of weakness—or so she imagines." Carla tapped the side of her head with one finger. "And then the dreams she's been having…"

Donovan nodded. "I know a bit about what's going on there… She told you about the dreams, then?"

Carla snorted a laugh. "No. No she didn't. But I can tell when she's not sleeping and when she's avoiding me. Only thing that keeps the dreams away for her is that VR sleep-aid program she uses."

David rubbed a hand across his jaw with a scraping sound. "Not my convo, but…is there reason to keep closer watch on her now?"

Carla licked her lips, shaking her head. "That's a resounding no. She's as capable as the others, but she's had a harder road— The infertility was Earth brainwashing. The losses were Martian gravity caused. Now there's just lots of programming to overcome…physically, she's as fit as the others."

David nodded and fell silent, turning to his own thoughts and quiet observation of the data collected and compiled as they flew over patches of greenery, each with its own unique ratios of assorted plant-life sprouted after initial Martian terraforming efforts centuries ago like the lichens, and lichen-grass, or seeded at their arrival like the aspens, ferns, and later cycads.

"First touch-down point approaching. We are 436 miles from the colony proper, approaching grassland with a moderate sized body of water. Young trees have been transforming the microclimate to suit more abundant growth of flora and fauna."

Donovan watched the rush of color with interest as if he could discern the health of the ecosystem from nuances in hue, despite their speed of travel.

David glanced over, a smirk lengthening the smile that rested between narrow jaw and sharp chin. "You see that blur that passed on the left, my plumeria, spreading fast and furious under your aspens. Not even the Martian winter stops this strain—Plumeria Martis Rubra."

"You're mocking me."

David held up finger and thumb, pinching air between them. "Just a little. There are things I can tell from the landscape, but probably not that kind of detail."

Carla chuckled, looking up from her messages and joining Donovan in his inspection of the blur of landscape. Her eyes were bright with excitement when the Drone's AI spoke again, and the craft slowed and then shifted direction.

"Beginning our descent. There is ample shade to set up camp on the edge of this grove, roughly 123 young trees and 605 saplings."

Donovan stood, retrieving a discolored green work belt with numerous pouches, then fastened the buckle. He held on to the handgrip above the right window and waited as the drone lowered itself into a smooth landing and stopped. He was the first out of the door when the seal released and it slid open with a hiss.

David followed just behind, breathing in the smell of algae and moist greenery, tasting the tang of iron-rich soil. Donovan was crouched in the grass, a hand up to stop further movement.

Several feet in front of them, in a small clearing, were several grazing animals. Their coats were pale sienna-brown, with a coppery sheen that blended well with the Martian dunes. Faint stripes of a darker shade adorned their backs, making them hard to notice among the shadows.

Carla stepped out and dropped into a low crouch next to him, freezing in place.

One of the creatures looked up, its long slender neck giving it an ethereal quality. The eyes were a darker shade of copper than the coat, framed in lashes the same color as the dark twisting horns that topped its small angular head. It twitched cone-shaped ears in their direction, moving further beneath the copse of aspens with a casual air, as if it knew of better grazing elsewhere but had no cause to hurry. Five others of similar size followed after the first, putting greater distance between themselves and the drone.

"These are my gerenuks, second generation by the size of the horns—and no young with them yet. And this far from the nearest drop off point!" Donovan's statement came out in an excited rush and he stood, pulling sample files and soil meters out of his many pockets. "I've counted six species of my animal life just on arrival—the numbers will show in the drones computer banks, but I can estimate just based on what's visible." He paused to catch his breath and bent down to fill a small capsule with topsoil to insert into the meter for analysis. He held it beneath his nose, waving it and sniffing at the vial, then pinched a small portion between two fingers to feel the texture. He nodded to himself, mumbling notes into his hand-held.

Carla was already farther off, hands cupped around the blooms of a red and yellow blossomed plumeria. She pressed her face into the fragrant cup her hands made and inhaled. David approached the same shrub, reaching for one of the thick, glossy leaves and assessing the color and texture of it. He raised his voice for Donovan to hear several feet away.

"Your grazers aren't eating them—too bitter from the alkaloids. It's a mild toxicity, but could build-up to an effect in large amounts…"

Donovan frowned. "Good; should stay that way so long as the aspens and other forage are abundant."

Carla rubbed her hands together, her smile infectious in its energy. "Alright, David, what are we putting in here?"

David, who was on hands and knees inspecting a large cluster of aspen seedlings, chuckled and brushed his hands off on his pants.

"These are suckers as opposed to true saplings—coming up from the roots of the larger trees. That's fine, but saplings put in a good taproot faster, so we could extend this stand of trees further out with my saplings…add in some gingko and some Albizia Julibrisson, and I'd like to see more ferns."

Carla pulled a yellowed leaf from a young sapling, the green veins showing up in sharp relief. A frown pulled at the corners of her lips and she held it up to the sun. "How's that soil sample, Donovan?"

He paced over, turning the screen of his handheld for her to see. "PH is too high, iron all bound up in the soil. That's why the chlorosis is happening here. Looks to be resolving on its own as the leaf litter decomposes and thickens in this area, but we can speed the process…microbes, more iron, turn in some more humus. The drones'll do most of that."

Carla nodded, allowing the yellowed leaf to slip through her fingers, and turned back to the transport drone to collect the saplings that were already being carried out by smaller drones built to assist with planting.

A chime sounded on her handheld and she ignored it, jumping up onto the ramp. Once inside the chime sounded again three times echoed by the drone's message system alert. The sound repeated in a cycle that would not end until the message was played. This particular pattern was reserved for urgent messages.

Alarm filled Carla's face with heat, her thoughts speeding and ricocheting around one theme. *I've been ignoring them… Emily is there and 6 weeks pregnant*...The thoughts recurred but didn't find purchase. This had to be bigger. David and Donovan stepped up into the craft, expressions mirroring her own.

DESPERATE TIMES

The halls echoed the sound of his feet against tile back to him as he ran. The empty corridor lit with a dim blue glow that gave an abandoned quality to the many off-branching hallways and undisturbed doors.

The visor of Bram's VR Comm was down and active, still allowing enough of the visual input of the corridor he ran down through the comm visuals for him to navigate. Another figure was there with him in the comm, bearing resemblance to himself but with larger build and darker, highly curling hair.

"He agreed for you to go and get them, yes?"

"No, he didn't. He's preoccupied and it needed done." Gavin's image swaggered a moment, brows raised in emphasis, before his face grew serious. "Who better to do it than me? They are already exposed, well before leaving, and some are sick. I heard him say it; I told you that. I'm bringing the stop-gap treatments we're using at the least—refills. And I feel fine, so I can help them get back."

Bram sighed, keeping up the loping pace as he turned

corners, pausing only to reorient towards the room he sought using the landmarks he knew only from the maps displayed in the VR headset.

"But you should have cleared it with him anyway…" A flash of irritation sparked in Bram's eyes flickering there as he continued. "Aurelia, you, Octavia, Feldon… perhaps if you stopped breaking rules for every fucking whim, he'd trust us and we'd have already left for Mars. Have you considered that?"

Gavin raised both brows and whistled. "Temper getting to you though, isn't it? That's another symptom, little brother…. Has it occurred to *you* that he is not the arbiter of all truth, or that maybe I'm in less of a hurry to get to Mars than you and he are?"

Bram growled in irritation. "Fine. You're just distracting me. Get them and get back here; I need to get Aurelia—*as directed.*" The last words held a note of accusation. Bram closed the VR Comm, cutting the link with Gavin, and stopped in front of a door. Richard's face appeared within the visor, and Bram leaned in for a scan.

"Scan complete, authorization code required."

Bram intoned the code Richard had provided, Richard's simulated voice layering over his own. "*3286990-Abandon ship before the rats come out.*"

Bram flinched at the mental image. Richard's codes and ever-changing passwords never made sense, but the tone was ominous and left a pit of unease in his mid-section.

"Access granted for entry. Further authentication required upon exit."

The door slid open with a faint sound, like the rustle of snakeskin against dry grass. The lights were dim and red here as well, to avoid disturbing the sleep of patients within.

The musty smell of sweat and fear enveloped him, along with the metallic, sea-salt scent of blood and urine. There was another smell, stronger—antiseptics, and something sweet. IV fluids and…something else he couldn't place.

Bram covered his nose and mouth with his sleeve, searching the large room quickly from right to left. It was divided into twenty small compartments, each just large enough to house a robotic exam and treatment beds—medicots and the requisite equipment for one patient. They were not labeled by name but by number, the unique number encoded into each citizen's DNA at conception.

He scanned his hand-held for more information, more codes, the cheat sheet to retrieve his sister.

"AUCPH4269BIO…"

He searched the top row of units for the correct designation. There were sounds emanating from some despite the insulated walls, low moans and guttural mumbles; the one next to Aurelia's echoed with the sort of sobbing that came from deep in the gut.

Bram paused, hand in front of the sobbing unit. His calm demeanor faltered for a moment and then it passed, creased brows smoothing out. *Beyond help…Aurelia was different.* She was fighting it, her immune system waging a violent war against what had taken hold; otherwise, the antibiotics would not be helping her when they had ceased to help the others after relapse.

Code entered, Bram stepped back as the seal broke and the multilayered doors opened.

She appeared to be sleeping, breathing heavy and

irregular, but without the rasping that previous videos of her showed. Bram brushed short twists of hair back from her face, revealing the mottled and swollen skin at her jawline. She stirred but did not wake, lips smeared with red that flaked and peeled as they moved now, forming words he couldn't place.

Bram cleared his throat, pressing his lips together to steady his expression before addressing the medibot security. He glanced at the hurried notes Richard had transferred to his handheld.

"AUCPH4269BIO is being transferred to my care. Please deactivate security and uh…release the treatment field for transport."

"Do you have an access code for patient records and discharge?"

"Yes…uploading now…"

Bram waited, brushing his knuckles against the edge of the bed with restless energy. He leaned in close to Aurelia's cheek.

"We're getting this figured out, you know…it's not your fault. It started before you went out. And some of us aren't even sick."

The light in the unit shifted colors and then faded down to a dim neutral yellow, signaling vacancy.

"The patient's records have been transferred to Richard Brant and you are now free to take custody of her. Thank you."

Bram provided a new destination and followed close behind as the automated treatment field navigated the halls until they reached Richard's laboratory, where he was waiting.

Richard placed a hand out to steady himself against the wall. *Stood up too fast.*

A surge of anger flooded his mind and he closed his eyes. The red of capillary blood behind eyelids somehow enhanced it and he opened them again, searching the room for some point to ground his thoughts and combat the rushing hormone-fueled tidal waves of mood fluctuation.

The objects in the room seemed to mock him, outdated, sparse, conjuring sharp, vivid memories that reared up in his mind as if occurring in the present moment. Morton was there, laughter raucous and full of life, and Theresa—his Theresa…

The physical impact of the mental images she conjured caught him by surprise. He could feel her skin beneath his hands, the very texture, a small, raised scar on the underside of her right forearm, the tickle of hair follicles. Her skin was cool from winter chill but radiating warmth as his touch fired her blood. Flashes of memory rushed forth, bringing with them the memory of tactile input, taste, the glimpse of smile she gave when she was correct and gently mocking him, pedantic words that he could count on should he fail to give a literal reply to questioning.

Richard's whole body heated, a crucible under influence of flame. He shook his head, gritting teeth and then released the tension in his jaw, beginning the count of breath that was a last resort before the medication. *One…inhale…two…exhale…* He continued to ten, allowing thoughts to pass through, forcing attention to his breath.

There was no rasp there yet, no heaviness. There was time before it overcame the antibiotics.

Richard lowered one hand to his throat, just below the jawline.

The pulse of blood felt faint, obscured beneath swollen glands, but it didn't sound weak in his ears, a throbbing rush instead of the stream like trickle beneath his first two fingers. It matched the pulse tracker on his climate-control undergarments. Pulse rapid, blood pressure low.

He sighed, calmer by a small margin, and then pressed the medication applicator to the bend of one elbow, forcing it through the skin there with air pressure. There were bruises still fading there, and some fresh. He placed the VR Comm that was waiting onto his head, lowering the visor over his eyes.

"Record visual and send."

Another sigh escaped, breath shaking as he inhaled to begin.

"Theresa, forgive the delay in contact…"

The silicone capsule was large for what it held, but time would change that. The minute organism within was enlarged, and clearly visible through the outer surface despite layers of membranes and fluids, and the lack of illumination.

Emily's eyes were damp as she ran a finger along the tiny cluster of cells, tracing the place where it was implanted in the biological substrate inside of the AUC forming its own capsule of amniotic tissues. It wasn't even humanoid looking yet, the tissues still splitting and differentiating into what would become fetus, placenta, amniotic sac. Emily covered it with the tip of one finger, smiling at the image of her progeny. Her other hand rested over her still flat abdomen as she let out a shaky sigh.

"It helps to see this one, doesn't it?" Theresa watched Emily's expression shift at the question, embarrassment, gratitude, and grief warring behind her shadowed eyes. There was something else there when she met Theresa's own—something that was small and embryonic, the size of the offspring she was cultivating, but growing just as steadily.

"Yes, it does. This one I can see, and this I can feel—the changes in me, anyway. It's like confirmation any time I get frightened again…"

"You know you can see them both…the implant has video capabilities, and you have access to that."

Theresa's voice grew animated as she explained the details of the new technology, eyes lighting up as if reflecting several of the nearest stars at once.

"This one isn't bothered by our observation either; no more lights, just the nano-camera, same as your implant. The real-time footage is projected onto the inner surface of the AUC to simulate seeing within. You don't have to wonder this time."

Emily raised both brows as she listened, smile growing in mirror of Theresa's excitement. She shook her head, looking back at the tiny creature that would soon resemble her or Jonathan…perhaps some mix of the two. "You…love this more than anything, don't you? It's not just an assignment, is it?"

Theresa's mouth opened and closed and she grasped for

words. "It's me…I do what I'm assigned—but this is me. These chambers, the act of creation, the joining of genetic fragments into someone new, and watching, monitoring, sustaining them in this wonder of human ingenuity…"

"Your ingenuity."

Theresa frowned at the compliment, tilting her head side to side with a shrug and pull of teeth across lips.

"At this point, much of it…but I was a child when the first were designed by Rick Branson and the first research team…but this one, this one I've changed so much that it's practically re-envisioned. The process is magic—like researching and crafting some potent wizardry and setting it into motion, guarding it until the most spectacular result is achieved."

Emily smiled. "Like Abby."

"Like Abby, and all her siblings…you know I never— never got to interact with the other phases once they were born. They weren't mine genetically, but I—I tended to them like this, the whole way through. Then they went to caretakers."

She shrugged as if to brush off the memory that still held sway behind her eyes. "I didn't see any need to see them after—if I could have. But it felt…hollow." Another shrug. "Do you have names chosen? Is Donovan involved, or just donating?" Theresa flinched at her own question. "Sorry, that's not something I needed to ask—I mean…"

"I might have names, but I'm waiting to see if they fit…when we meet. Donovan is—involved. We just aren't sure how yet." She bit her lip. "We're still figuring that out ourselves."

Theresa's AI chimed a message and interrupted. "As per

previous direction: apologies for the interruption, but you have an incoming video message from Dr. Richard Brant. Play message now?"

"Not a VR Comm? Just a recorded message…"

Sharp lances of alarm and anticipation pulsed from gut to every nerve ending in Theresa's body causing a sudden tremor as she scowled and held her handheld up to view. She glanced over at Emily, gesturing with the handheld towards Emily's viewing screen. "Do you mind?"

Emily shook her head, registering the urgency in Theresa's movements and expression.

"Link to this system and play message."

Richard appeared on the screen and Theresa's arms dropped to her sides, eyes widening.

His hair was unkempt, brow glistening with sweat, and there were purple bruises beneath both eyes and along his jawline. His eyes were his own, bright with the same intelligence and humor that shone there before, but somehow intensified with raw urgency—fear.

He cleared his throat, words coming in measured tones, staccato instead of with his usual ease, as if the effort required was slowing him.

"Theresa, forgive my absence. I've been preoccupied, as you'll soon see. A contagion—previously unknown, at least in this form, is spreading through the population. I am infected, the children are as well; the side-effects, or perhaps primary effects, negatively impact mental faculties and emotional regulation." Richard's eyes went blank, mouth hanging for a moment between words as if all of his focus was shifted inwards. Shadows of emotion crossed his eyes and he closed them, shuddering and squeezing them tight before he reopened them with renewed clarity.

Emily stepped closer to Theresa, placing a hand that went unnoticed against her shoulder as the recorded message continued.

"I have—been directing my energy towards finding a solution and will continue to that end as soon as I finish this recording. I cannot maintain the focus to VR Comm at this time or I would. For now, I've given Genesis access to data that could help on your end, but I have something to ask…"

He looked away, standing as if with nervous energy that could no longer be buried, like insects hatching and flying free before their wings are fully dried.

"We need transport to Mars. If you want us to make it there as we planned…it needs to be now, please."

DESPERATE MEASURES

The silence of the central dome amphitheater was pervasive, even small sounds somehow not registering in Theresa's awareness despite the large numbers present.

The red-orange tones of sunset were deepening now to deep violet and indigo, the progressive dimming of the room compensated for by automatic lighting sensors in the high domed ceiling, shifting quality of light to that of a cave lit by numerous torches.

Feet shuffled against the floors that held and radiated back the day's sun as the thick walls did. The room held the Martian colony in security, exuding memories made and relationships forged within its walls; still, there was a damp, creeping chill that came not from outdoors, but from within the colonists themselves.

Theresa squeezed her upper arms through the lab coat she wore and rubbed the fabric with her nails, shivering despite the warmth. There were small sounds that hadn't registered until now. *Thoughts are louder in this room…*

Fabric rustled, feet against floors, and there were the whispers, children and others around the room coming out of a careful silence cultivated by the suddenness of the meeting.

Richard's recorded voice started again after a long pause and finished with the words she had already memorized. His voice held a note of desperation and fatigue that sent off sharp thrills of worry every time they played, aloud or in memory.

"We need transport to Mars. If you want us to make it there as we planned…it needs to be now, please."

The playback ended and Theresa stared down at her hands where they rested in her lap, frozen, aside from the tremor she could feel extending out along her nerves all the way from her core, where a mass of fear was building and shifting like a hurricane still over sea. She sat in the circle of Martian Council members, already briefed before the other colonists arrived for emergency council.

Melissa's voice broke the relative silence, taking lead of the Council.

"As the Council sees it, there is only one course of action to take—and I don't doubt we can come together as a colony and rise to the occasion, move quickly, and prevent as much loss of life as we can here."

Melissa's face held a grim determination that was still bright with hope, the combination making her eyes shine with a sharp glint.

"What we need to get creative on and direct our energy towards is the how. It's easy to ask if we should, or why not to, even who should we—but how, that's where we need to focus. How will we get as many survivors off of Earth and to Mars as possible? How will we ensure that this contagion doesn't take hold on Mars? How will we maintain the ability to reach Earth in the future? We have assigned teams to tackle this as quickly and effectively as possible."

Melissa glanced over at the circle of council members, catching Genesis's eye and noting the slight nod.

"Genesis will address what may be most pressing on your minds at this time, and then we will assemble into our teams for immediate action."

Genesis stood to take up a position closer to the assembled

colonists, her face a study of calm concern.

"You are all likely wondering about your own on Earth. The ones we left behind and expected to carry on without us. Theresa may be the most directly impacted, as the number of surviving family she has is inarguably the highest and they are her progeny. But most of us have people left on Earth. And that matters. It's going to affect us if we lose them."

Genesis allowed a trembling frown to supplant the calm smooth expression. "I saw a number of you fire off communications on your hand-helds at the first mention of trouble on Earth. Understandable. But communications in and out have been blocked by the World Governing Council of Earth. I have been informed that their decision is to wait out the pandemic while attempting to solve it themselves, and contact or transport to Mars has been forbidden."

There were murmurs among those assembled, and Genesis hesitated long enough to catch them and adjust tack.

"Could go and collect them…no, I'll go myself if no one else is—they'll have a team for it though—"

"How will we get to them—?"

"How many can we carry?"

Theresa smiled at the questions she heard, so many of them 'how' questions and leading from the precedent that Melissa and Genesis discussed before the meeting began. Multiple choice—and leaving Earth to fend for itself wasn't one of them. Direct their energies towards problem solving. Now we see if Genesis can get them past the panic over their own people—despite the possible lost cause.

She watched Genesis's face as the woman made mental adjustments and directed conversation.

"This contagion is—fatal, by all estimates, at 93%. And that is a best-case scenario, with quick, comprehensive, and ongoing treatment. And because its treatment is confused by shifting symptoms, with surges and relapses, and they have yet to find an effective treatment method—we can't expect survivors."

She held up a hand for silence before any outbursts could take hold in the room. The Martian colonists were restless and agitated, growing more so as evidenced by the increase in sound in the chamber and the quality of the interactions.

Kendra's youngest was crying again, the sound similar to the bleating of a small lamb, laaaa—laaa—laaaaa. Theresa couldn't help but stare, the sound of infantile hunger breaking through her distress.

Kendra caught the child's cue despite the distant, pained expression that pinched at her features. She stood and moved to the side of the row she sat in for room to sway as she latched Askia onto one breast, dancing with him as she listened. Neil was in the circle of council members, but stepped down to sit next to their three older children, lifting Jasrie onto his lap. Genesis hesitated a moment more for them to settle, and then continued without sign of dropped focus or irritation.

"We can't expect survivors, but we will go to every length reasonable to retrieve any that we can find. That's one task we all have—create a list of your connections on Earth and give their previous locations, genetic ID codes, contact information. We can't transport as many as we would like, but we can get ours out."

Theresa glanced towards the nearest exit. They'd be at this for a while longer, until all of them, or as many as possible, felt a sense of direction and purpose to counter the fear—like the busy work Genesis had requested of her while Richard kept her in the dark. Anger ignited her thoughts like hydrogen gas next to flame. Fear for them, that was the flame. *He kept me from knowing, from helping them.*

The exit was right there, and she was through it without further thought or hesitation, the voices of the whole colony in serious discussion following her until the door slid shut behind her. Genesis was turning the crowd over to Neil, for talk of the

Pinnacle and its rescue capabilities, no doubt.

To anyone else with such acute hearing, the council meeting would likely feel like an overwhelming din—better than many before this one; they'd fine-tuned their ability to steer the tone of an emergency meeting, but Genesis separated the sounds and other auditory and visual cues one by one, sorting and collecting until she had a feel for the room. They were scared, badly, but they were focused, just like she and Melissa had discussed with the rest of the council beforehand.

She caressed the room with her eyes once more, resolute sympathy a placeholder on her face as she watched for anything that would need managed, responses that she could massage in one direction or another. The colonists were predictably ready to meet this challenge, mission accomplished—and then she saw Theresa stand, face ashen, and turn for the door. Genesis watched her leave the room and quirked a brow before smoothing her face.

Either their presentation was so effective she was off to tend to her part in all this or, more likely, the pallor meant she was struggling. Genesis noticed a surge of protectiveness at the thought and filed it away. It was an expected reaction now, even in the face of Theresa's continued rivalry with her over Abby, the mistrust and resentment that boiled under the surface. There was more to Theresa's reactions towards her than that...but it was inconsequential, for now.

A moment of indecision froze her and then passed. Side thoughts and doubts were just mind chatter and she silenced them. Her core perceptions told her this path was important. Theresa was important...in the impossibly dark cave of her mind, the VR therapy induced close-quarters they shared for nearly nine months,

Theresa had offered her an easy out as if she mattered more than being the first test-subject for pregnancy and birth on Mars, as if she mattered more than the experiment she'd made of herself.

When she was in labor, and she called out for Theresa and Abby to be there instead of Carla, or Emily, or Kendra, Theresa came with Abby in arms and stayed until the end.

The feel of Theresa's hand in one of hers, David's in the other, the smell of pine oil filling the cave—the room was dark as a cave, at least—was burned in her memory and it stuck there. It felt as if she would break apart and nothing of her would be left in the aftermath, the fear growing so large it filled the air with a reek that overwhelmed her senses.

This thing Theresa was facing now was the same. Genesis pulled away from the memories, feeling a sudden urgency to follow after.

She caught Neil's eyes down in the seats with his children and gestured him over. He was back on the stage as quick as could be expected after disentangling himself halfway; Jasrie he carried up to the dais in one arm, gesturing to her with finger over lip: *no talking*.

Genesis stood close and leaned in to speak between the two of them. "I have something to see to, if you're ready to take this on." She indicated the enclosed amphitheater full of colonists with a sweep of her eyes.

He was nodding, any trepidation he might have felt over what was happening buried deep under his usual captain's level-headedness and bravado. A look of concern crossed his face. "Sure thing...You looking in on Theresa? Or I could send someone..."

"I've got it." She touched his hand and smiled before taking up a brisk stride down the stairs. If Theresa was leaving in the middle of this, then her mental state wasn't good. Even Neil, buried in his own little problems, saw that.

Theresa heard the door open and close again and picked up her pace. If anyone started asking her a million misguided questions about an illness she knew nothing about, she'd be hard-pressed not to correct their assumptions that every field of science is the realm of any and every scientist they could corner and question on the subject.

The footsteps drew nearer.

"Wait…Theresa." Genesis caught up with her, falling into lockstep and placing a hand on her shoulder and then gesturing to the garden door.

Theresa's inflamed thought-scape vacillated between refusal and acquiescence, stuck and unable to think clearly. In the absence of a decision, she allowed herself to be led out into the heavy wind that would be bringing towering clouds of dust and then the seasonal rains before long. The Martian plumeria that Abby loved was still blooming, surrounding them in its strong, sweet scent with undertones of nutmeg and cinnamon. It should have been soothing, but instead heightened Theresa's agitation.

Genesis spoke first, using one hand to gather up whipping tendrils of her long hair out of the wind's grasp. "I already sent you the little data that Richard sent me. We'll get them here—every one of them."

Theresa's voice caught in her throat and then escaped, carrying more of the withheld anger and fear than she meant to express.

"You can't guarantee that. You can't. Neither can I—are you going to collect them personally?! Transport them yourself when any crew we can put together succumbs to it?!"

Genesis's eyes widened for a split second as she took in the force of Theresa's anger. "Yes. I am. I'm going myself, with whatever team we put together. I'll carry them into the elevator one by one if it's necessary." The vehemence in her tone and sincerity in her eyes matched Theresa's own.

Theresa's voice took on a dark note of cynicism. "Why? Why care about a hundred progeny you've never met? You don't need to curry my favor for any reason I can think of. For Abby? To collect a whole clan of impressionable followers?"

Genesis blinked, her eyes going cold, closed off. "Why do you hate me still?" She stepped closer, yellow-gold eyes locking onto Theresa's. "Jealousy over Abby—but we have her affection in common. Competitiveness? Why? When we could be stronger working together. Do I threaten you? Do you even know?" She shrugged, as if to push for a like response.

Theresa shook her head, eyes clouding with confusion in the face of such close scrutiny. Genesis's proximity was unsettling, the force of her personality distracting. "I—I don't know. But I don't trust your definition of truth. You bend it, twist it, mold it to your liking and your purpose."

Genesis nodded. "Hm. And my definition of trust? What of that one? Because yours needs an update, unless you enjoy pushing away potential friends and allies."

Theresa scrunched her nose, confusion warring with irritation, impatience at Genesis and the conversation. "I need to get started on my part in solving this illness." She turned away only to be stopped by Genesis's firm grip on her shoulder. The wall was at her back and Genesis blocked her path and then released her before she could protest.

"Please, you need to listen before you go off to single-handedly take this on—again."

Theresa's eyes flashed but she remained silent.

"Trust means knowing a person will act and react within their known capacity. Know the person and you can trust." Genesis tilted her head with a faint smile, her eyes inviting Theresa to take the cue and laugh with her. "You've been inside my mind. You and

Carla. Seen my demons and faced them with me. And I'm better for it. Stronger. What about you? Who gets to see your demons and stand there with you? Who gets to hold your hand through the hurricane?"

Theresa broke eye contact, wetting her lips, dry from the harsh wind, and swallowed as if to push back the wave of emotion that was rising. Genesis pushed further, leaning in and straightening Theresa's lab coat as she'd seen the other woman do hundreds of times before. "You know me. Any voice that says otherwise is paranoia—anxiety. Self-defense against rejection. I know a few things about that voice."

Genesis pulled out her handheld and opened a graphic. It glowed to life, projected above the small screen, a rotating DNA sequence. "Why do you and your progeny matter to me?! Here!" She thrust the handheld into Theresa's hands, her eyes wet with unshed tears that soon left brick-red Martian dust tracks down her cheeks. "Here is that kernel of truth that has you so afraid of me, so paranoid. My selfish ulterior motive: a commonality, when I have none with anyone else. We are the same, your children, you and I. Shared genetics, family in a way that I've never experienced." Genesis grabbed hold of Theresa's hand and, pulling it towards her face, pressed her index finger against one pointed eye-tooth hard enough to draw a drop of blood. Theresa pulled her hand away and pressed the wounded finger to her own lips in reflex.

"How many times did Abby draw blood nursing once these sharp canines came in? You put them there, and so many other things, when you designed her, a residual trait from the DNA packets you chose. We are the same, even if I was made first, and closer to sister than daughter."

Theresa's lips curled into a feral scowl even as tears reddened her own eyes. "They could be here already, but he refused. Disagreed. All these years, needing them to be bigger, stronger, for space travel. Abby traveled still a developing progeny and survived it, and now they won't all make it. No matter what I do, I could lose them. If Richard was your contact, and you cared about their survival, then why not convince him to travel sooner?"

Genesis's voice was low, subdued. "I don't think I could have." She shook her head stepping, closer once more, but this time she leaned into Theresa with an embrace.

Theresa shuddered, leaning her forehead against Genesis's hair. "We were planning the trip soon. I can't get this close to having them here and have it ripped away."

"Then don't. Find the answers we need. Do what you do and I'll do my part. I meant it, that I'll be on that ship. And I'm here for this if you'll accept it."

Theresa stepped back and looked into Genesis's eyes. There was no flinching away, no shadows of guile. She nodded, pressing the cuffs of her lab coat against her damp lashes and glancing towards the door. "I'm going to get started."

Genesis gave a tentative smile and gestured towards the door, as if to agree that they'd argued in the windstorm long enough. She wet her lips, ignoring the grainy feel of dust on their surface, and stepped toward the door ahead of Theresa. "Okay, good."

The meeting was still ongoing, and Abby stared with rapt attention at Theresa's laboratory viewing screen. Neil was standing at the dais now, with Jasrie in arms. His words were blurring together as her thoughts wandered, but the important ones stuck. *Three days...departure in three days...* They needed time to remove extra equipment from the ship, fit more passengers.

She glanced at the door, feeling the urge to check her handheld for Theresa's exact location. She had left the meeting—Abby saw her stand up and leave the circle of council members—there wasn't anywhere else she would go but back here to the lab or their other rooms.

Neil was still talking. It wasn't important now, just the fillers, tags, and placation tools that people were so fond of and that normally fascinated her. They stood out from the real-talk that people used so much less often, like neon signs in a dark sky, equally glaring and demanding notice but contributing little value.

She turned back to the door, wondering for a moment why it hadn't opened when sufficient time had passed for Theresa to cross the colony from the central amphitheater to their apartment.

When it still didn't open, she turned back to the screen and tried to listen. Melissa was answering questions now, and Neil and most of the council were gone. The room was hollowing out…and it seemed fitting, like performers leaving a stage, leaving behind an empty theater that would echo if she spoke. But the room wasn't hollow, she was.

By the time the door opened, she could feel that stuck feeling, like too many words had built up at the loading dock in her head and now there was no room to let them through.

Theresa stood there a moment, just inside, allowing the door to slide shut behind her, and then she turned and walked over to the wall unit. "Spice brew please. And another with sugar." She retrieved the steaming mugs and placed one next to Abby on the desk. Abby could smell it as she approached, bitterness, sweetness, and the warm undertones of cinnamon and nutmeg.

Sitting down next to Abby on the bench, Theresa leaned over, rested her forehead against Abby's. The smell of the gardens outside clung to Theresa's hair, wind whipped Martian plumeria, spicy lichen smells and rain in the distance, and Abby breathed it in, letting it fill some of the hollow space. "It's a lot, isn't it?"

Abby imagined her own expression matched Theresa's: lips frozen and expressionless, eyes overly wide and bright. It felt that way. She sighed, finally managing to nod once. The movement shifted things and she felt like she could answer, but the spice brew demanded her attention with that tantalizing smell that was so rich and soothing all by itself, and she lifted her sweetened mug for a careful sip. She held it there in front of her face feeling the heat radiating off of it and into her cheeks and fingers. "You're going?"

Theresa drank from her own mug, watching Abby over the rim of it through a curtain of steam. "Yes. In three days. It will be, at the least, three months."

Abby nodded. "Can I come with you?" The answer was clear in Theresa's eyes, unflinching and without compromise. "No."

Abby felt the hollow spot grow in size and depth, and she fidgeted with the rim of her cup, tracing the top edge with a finger and then gulping the hot liquid too fast. She covered her mouth with her hand and swallowed it anyway, wincing at the heat. "Okay…"

Theresa brushed Abby's hair out of her face where several strands stuck to the spice brew and set the cup down for her. "Do you want to…ask anything?"

Abby shrugged and reached for the cup again. Her hands felt empty and cold without it. "Won't know what to ask until you're gone."

"Slower this time, please—" Theresa gestured to the spice brew Abby was sipping at again. "But you'll be able to comm with me and with Genesis."

Abby lowered the cup from her face and licked her lips clean. She blinked several times and then set the cup down again. "Genesis is going?"

Theresa finished off her mug and stood up, pacing to the other side of her desk to begin pulling out items she would need, equipment that was already calibrated for her so she wouldn't lose time setting up what was in the ship's small laboratory space. "Abby, I know it's worse that we're both going...but Genesis is…well, she'll make sure we get everyone we can safely back here."

The hollowness was still there, but filling up with other things:

Theresa's fear, all the things she wasn't saying out loud but that Abby could fill in. Genesis was competent, resourceful. They needed her. They needed her and Theresa because this wasn't the cheerful passenger flight she expected to bring Richard and her siblings home. This was very different.

And precarious.

THE CLOCK IS TICKING

Beads of sweat along her hairline collected into larger drops and ran down the sides of Aurelia's cheek and jawline, where a multi-colored roadmap of bruising remained as evidence of passing infection.

She stirred, eyes opening without light of recognition kindling in their glassy surfaces. Her lips moved, but no sounds emerged from the raw tissues of her throat.

Bram glanced from her, to Richard, and then the mid-air representation of her latest blood samples.

Richard scowled. "They deployed specialized nanocytes during the first 48 hours of infection, and yet have not formed a clear picture of this infection—why the relapses, where it's hiding, how it is different from Y. Pestis we've previously encountered."

Bram stepped closer to the hologram, grasping one of the rod-shaped bacterium between two fingers to rotate it and examine closer. "But we have this: it's decreasing in number, infection clearing from the last round of antibiotics."

Richard shook his head; Bram was there beside him with blood pooling down his shirt, eyes absent from the dark sockets that should have held them, and then he wasn't. He was several steps away, brushing Aurelia's hair out of her eyes, his own still intact.

There was a sharp throbbing in the swelling bruise on the right side of Richard's jaw and he lifted a hand to gently press there, providing counter-pressure to the pain. He cleared his throat.

"But look at her. At her and her vitals. Fever, restricted movement in the neck, the wincing against the lights—photophobia, low blood pressure but rapid pulse. We're fighting *this* thing. But I don't think it's the full picture."

Bram scowled, rubbing the crease of his brows between thumb and forefinger, giving the illusion of many years more age than the eleven he'd lived. "It's clearing from her bloodstream, now, and her lungs…"

He trailed off, going still aside from lips moving in subvocalization, eyes lighting up as he glanced at the bacillus hologram. "We need to look for something other than this then. Maybe a secondary infection?"

Richard sighed, covering his eyes as if to lower his field of vision without closing it off in its entirety. "If there is something else there, her immune system clearly isn't recognizing it, and neither are the nanocytes. But I don't think you're wrong."

His voice was strained, either from fatigue or the effort to modulate his responses in the face of surges of what felt like violence distilled into liquid form and poured into his veins.

He pushed a hand through his hair and strode over to Aurelia's bed and the Medical drone that was attached. "I need another dose of LPC-073 as well as the full complement, adding in another antipsychotic symptom control—Bram, you as well."

Bram was staring at the floating magnification of Aurelia's blood sample still. He rubbed a hand across his eyes, then stepped towards the medical drone and sat down hard as if controlled by an impatient puppeteer.

Richard leaned closer from where he sat, grasping the side of the boy's face and manually opening one eye wider to assess pupil dilation. They were dark, pupil enlarged to obscure much of the iris.

"List your symptom picture, Bram."

Bram fidgeted in his seat, eyes flicking back and forth as he searched for focus.

"Hot flashes, lassitude, synesthesia—there um…there are images… colors, when you speak, and they distract me from—everything. Lightness, I feel light; I can think clearly, but it's like reacting in dream."

Bram looked away from Richard's probing gaze, cheeks flushing even more than that caused by his low-grade fever. "There are flashes of—of things that aren't there."

Richard nodded, eyes softening with sympathy before the sharp glint of barely contained anger returned. He spoke in controlled tones. "You'll need what I've been using to control the hallucinations—that is what they are." He paused to collect the thoughts that were again racing through his mind, surfacing and then fading too quickly for him to collect most of them. "I haven't found the source. There are a number of toxins released by the bacterium, but none should induce all of the effects we're seeing. Psilocybin, Cathinone, other unstudied psychoactives, a murine toxin, fraction 1. Perhaps the combination is what is triggering—violence, rage, sexual urges in those mature enough, as opposed to…well, simple euphoria and altered state of mind, which psilocybin is known for."

His voice took on the tone of teacher as he continued. Bram appeared to be listening, but may have been lost in thought, as he gave no sign of following or processing the words. He didn't move at all until he winced at the ministrations of the medical drone.

It pressed the end effector of mechanical arms into the depression between upper arm and forearm to administer the requested medications, moving from Bram to Richard.

"Dammit all. I don't want to travel with an invalid, with several, can't travel like this." He gestured to Bram, then to the monitors that cycled through separate rooms, each containing one of the fifty-nine children present and quarantined in the building. Some paced, others rested, but each of them were attended by a medical drone administering medications every two hours.

His hair fell loose and greasy into his face, the grey streaks darkened by perspiration. It caught when he shoved it back, cursing at the tangles that were so inconsequential and yet provided fuel for his impotent rage. *The antipsychotics haven't taken effect yet. Breathe, dammit.*

"If the ship is underway, then we have about two months. We don't have to make our exodus yet."

He pulled in a breath, holding it and then releasing slowly, allowing the speed of his pacing to taper off. "We still have time to use the lab here, to review blood samples from all of the patients in quarantine."

Bram's voice was distant, as if he had already made transport to Mars and was communicating across the void of space. "Secondary infection could have taken hold anywhere: lymph nodes, along with the enterobacteria—lungs, bladder, spleen, heart, brain even." He trailed off. His hands moved in the air out of sync with his voice, tracing structure and location of body systems listed.

Richard rubbed his eyes, scowling at the fog that descended as the anti-psychotics took effect. There were still break-through flashes, residual symptoms of the cocktail of psychoactive bioparticles released by the enterobacteria. *Several rounds of antimicrobials and still it surges up—there's a pattern, there's always a pattern.*

Aurelia's breathing was rapid, lips dry from the quick passage of air between them. He glared down at her, seeing the others superimposed over her face at the same time. Many of them were asleep with eyes open, breath coming like overheated animals reduced to panting as they tossed on their beds. They were stronger than this, weren't they? Not meant to be dropped by any pathogen, unless the adaptive immune system upgrades were not enough. They were alive, though, unlike the whole of the surrogate program now- likely more of the WGC. *Clock is ticking—we have time—but not much.*

Aurelia's eyes opened and followed his movements. She didn't see him.

"Medibot 241: record and apply to records for cross-reference. You're going to need to be my record keeper and my critical thinking…The unknown enterobacteria is advancing in a cyclical manner somehow. Surging and receding as symptoms shift, blood and lung sputum clearing only to reinfect short hours later, either between doses or after multiple days clear and after discontinuation of antimicrobials. The surges occur even with continued antibiotic administration, but muted. The same effect was seen with broad-spectrum antimicrobials among the surrogates—recession, surge, recession, surge. In their case, sudden resurgence was followed by emergence of more acute symptoms, sudden psychosis, and subsequent lack of response to further treatment or death."

The screams echoed in his mind, reverberating and gaining strength as they found weakness there in the grey-matter that was Richard Brant. Fear blossomed in multicolored flowers, twining their way down his arms and legs, stiffening his spine and making the muscles bunch as if the threat was one he could run from or fight through.

The screams played on repeat, shrill and panicked and laced with pain, others weaving into the song, something more base and guttural, the raw, blood-surging tones of anger boiled over into a stew of rage. The screams continued and Richard bowed his head, raising his hands to cover both ears, then lowered them and opened his eyes to ground himself in what was there. Still there: Aurelia, eyes flinching from the light despite their lack of focus, and Bram resting next to her in a light doze under effect of both the antipsychotics and a sedative.

The medical drone's voice held the same cool, metallic tone that felt reassuring before the jangling of his nerves rose to such a loud clamor. Now it was ominous and set off sparks of fear.

"The data you have entered matches the overall clinical picture over the course of diagnosis and treatment."

"Good. Fine. Send nanocytes to assess all organ systems and bodily fluids. Package data for quick analysis and transfer."

He watched the screen as clips of data appeared, grouped and sorted by organ system. It would be like combing through sand to find microscopic seashells. But if the nanocytes were missing something he would have to find it. *Theresa could…*He grimaced at the thought, the mental images and sense memories conjured, painfully distracting.

But she could. Need to break the communication blockade now— Santana would see to it if she was well enough. Richard directed the AI to display vital signs and security cameras for Santana's room.

The camera showed a child sleeping on the floor next to the antique wooden bed frame that stood against one wall, in sharp contrast to the streamlined, automated features of the room.

She was shivering, short cropped dark hair long enough to fall forward across flushed forehead and form unruly spikes everywhere else. Her breathing was rapid and skin flushed, eyelids twitching in dream.

Richard turned to assess the readout of vital signs: a high fever, swollen lymph nodes but no current signs of hallucinations. *The early stages —*

He cursed under his breath, turning back to the security camera display of 100 beds, 59 children, all in various stages of illness. The other 40 were absent on a research trip, their beds empty, except for Gavin.

The room that belonged to the largest and strongest of the children was empty as well, security lock deactivated. The scowl that began at Richard's eyes deepened, the side of his jaw twitching with restrained anger.

"Where is Gavin?"

His personal AI answered, accessing records from the building security AI.

"Gavin was granted permission to exit the complex on the fifteenth and has yet to return."

"Granted permission by whom?" "One Richard Brant, yourself, gave permission to exit using private access codes. Would you like me to connect comms with Gavin?" Richard exhaled slowly, and stared ahead of him, waiting for the intensity of anger to recede and his thought processes to find completion. The room shifted around him, arcs of light and wavering shadow augmenting the landmarks around him. Bram and Aurelia were still sleeping there on the medical cot, except when they weren't for just a split second and instead stared eyeless back at him or screamed as the surrogates had.

The world wavered, as did his perception of it, but his mind remained calm, save for the undercurrent of visceral anger that pulsed there, ready to break the chains of his self-control.

"No—don't contact Gavin yet. Connect with WGC lead, Diadonna. She might like an update."

FINAL PREPARATIONS

"I knew you were going, you know. Gonna go over there and stir something up again."

Neil flinched, and then lifted his eyes to meet Kendra's.

"We were going to talk about this. Before I made any move. I was waiting until things evened out here with Askia."

"That other thing, going after them for what they did, much as they deserve it. I might have tried to talk you out of it. But this? We don't have much choice."

Kendra's smile was sad when she unlatched the tiny bow lips, breaking the seal around her nipple with one finger. She handed the fussing infant to Neil, nuzzling the soft cheek as he settled in against his father's bare chest.

"You're going to miss so much of this though. *He's* gonna miss it." Her sigh was resigned as she leaned her cheek against his shoulder, joining in with the swaying bounce that was lulling Askia to sleep.

Neil pressed his face into Kendra's soft tawny curls, breathing in her scent, a hint of spice-brew and frangipani, with a subtle undertone of mother's milk.

"I think I wasn't going to go. I'd have put it off again and again, trying to find the right time to leave you all here. When is the right time to miss a full four months of a child's life? Probably never."

Kendra nodded. "We'll show him though. Video comms every day, and you'll do this thing right."

She looked up at him, eyes fierce with determination and advance threat should he fail. "You'll get those kids, and anyone else, and you'll get back here. Understand me? Because I'll be waiting and Askia, and Jasrie, and the boys—they'll be waiting."

Neil bent down to pull her lips against his, in a deep clinging caress. His eyes were wet when he pulled back, but so were hers.

"It's going to be fine. I'm writing up the mission plans. Nothing left to chance under my command."

He turned to face the large, curved screen mounted on their wall and addressed the AI while still holding Askia, now asleep against his chest. "Open up comms with the Pinnacle and pull up schematics."

The screen glowed to life and the feminine purr of the ship's AI answered the command as schematics appeared in 3D in front of them.

Kendra let out a long whistle, shaking her head as she came closer to the rotating representation of the Pinnacle. "Those are quite some serious upgrades you've put in on her."

Neil cleared his throat. "Deactivate and begin removal of SX69 Guns and the Big Screamers, also 56BG1s." He turned back to Kendra.

"Going to need that carrying capacity for as many passengers as possible." Kendra's lips pulled down and tightened, eyes taking on a hard glint. "What if someone on Earth doesn't want you picking up survivors? They said no contact with Mars, and no evacuation, didn't they?"

"I'm not taking all the guns off of her—just the big ones. I mean, it's unlikely they'll have the muster to be hostile, too busy trying to survive if Genesis's reports are accurate. But if I'm wrong about that, I'm not gonna be unprepared."

Kendra's scowl loosened and she reached out for the sleeping infant, to tuck him against her in the bed for the night. "Good." She pulled a light sheet up to her waist, using the Martian Mural blanket gifted to them to cover Askia's legs and bare chest.

"And Neil? Come to bed when you're done. I want as much of you as I can get before you do this."

"If they're going, then Neil is going to need me. He has no second in command without Trina. I can come back with Carla, and Donovan will carry on here."

Genesis shook her head. "Not necessary. You are on a mission of import yourself and I intend to go with him as Second. Everything else will be automated, and anything that breaks down he can fix. Theresa is likely to come as well. I'm not certain if she wants hands on to work on her research into the pathogen, but I don't think anyone could stop her from doing this herself."

David's figure paced in the VR Comm with a grimace, teeth showing like a coyote assessing the wire around a chicken coop. "Why you? I could go in your place or as well. Neil and I work fine together, and I have leadership experience as well. Deimos won't feel good about you gone so long, and the risk involved; he'll know what's at stake."

Genesis laughed, the sound replete with wry humor. "Deimos will be happy with the break from my guidance. Keep him busy assisting Theresa from here, or have him join you out in the wilds cultivating flora and fauna—I wonder, are you worried about me and the Captain working too well together?"

Now it was David's turn to laugh, the humor setting his dark eyes alight and alleviating some of the tension. "No, I'm not. If that ship was ever going to sail I'm sure you'd have already dropped anchor."

Genesis wrinkled her nose "Dropped anchor? Is that even a thing? I think you've been out with Carla too long. You're picking up her penchant for incongruent metaphors."

"Now, Melissa, I might worry if she were going. The way she blushes at your whispered advice is a bit…obvious. Though I suppose you and she can get up to anything you have in mind planet-side better than you can in zero-G."

Genesis ran the tip of her tongue along dry lips to wet them and widened her eyes in feigned innocence.

"Don't you trust me? Or are you jealous?"

"I'm not jealous, Genesis; that would be a waste of energy and an insult to us both. I know where we stand—I trust you to act within your capacity and satisfy your—predilections."

Genesis's eyes narrowed and her smile deepened. "That's probably best."

David shrugged. "If I'm not needed, then I'm not, but I won't say I'm not worried about you going and being exposed to whatever they bring on the ship. Or that I'm not itching to help with this."

Genesis cocked a brow. "I am the least of your worries. My immune system is adaptive in a way that yours is not. If anyone is going to be useful in keeping things together while we get the Pinnacle back to Mars, then it's me. The Captain, and anyone else with the common immune system, on the other hand, is going to be a concern."

David nodded. "Fine. Sometimes I wonder just how many secrets you have locked up in your genetic code." She shrugged. "Look it up. Pretend I'm one of your plants—Venus fly-trap?" She laughed, pleased with herself. "Theresa has it all on file, if you know what you're looking for."

They cut the comm and he pulled off the headset, tossing it into a patch of lichen-grass a few feet away so he could continue with the seedlings he had ready to put in the ground. The holes were dug, so he grabbed the first two and placed them, filing in and compacting the soil around them. Another handful of dark red soil rained down onto the seedling's and he looked up. Donovan and Carla weren't due back to this site yet. It was Joanna, of course, and she looked worried; still smiling, but he could see it in her eyes. "What are we upset about, Jo? The trip?"

"No, we're okay…" She dropped another handful and patted it down.

David gave her a look that said he wasn't buying it, both brows raised and a slight smile curling his lips as he shook his head. There were two more tiny trees in now.

"Okay—Yeah, worried about you being alone here without her, and about her going…"

"I don't get to be alone, Jo. You know that." "I'm not really here, though." She looked confused when she said it. It must be a strange thing to say about yourself, even if it was true.

"And yet…here you are, and here I am talking to myself." He chuckled, pressing down with some of his weight behind it to force any air bubbles around the roots out. "I do just fine, Jo."

When she didn't say anything else, he looked over at where Joanna sat. She wasn't there anymore, and, for a moment, he wondered how far she had gone so quickly. The thought was followed by a rolling wave of unease. *She didn't go anywhere…she wasn't there.* He brushed the sweat from his brow, trying to tuck his hair back with his elbow, then gave up and pushed it back with a muddy hand. *But she was there.*

He grabbed another two saplings and buried their roots with swift movements, and then another two, and another. "No point arguing with yourself… Just put the plants in, David."

✧✧✧

Theresa couldn't hear the others with her VR Comm on unless they spoke directly into her link. Each of them worked in the VR matrix, analyzing fluid samples the slow way—*the slow way, but not the old-fashioned way—has he tried tissue samples and cultures? It could work...*

"Fuck, fuck, fuckity." Theresa yanked the headset off and paced over to the wall unit for spiced brew. She cursed under her breath, glancing up at the others who seemed unfazed, having caught none of her outburst.

Laughter bubbled up like a bottle of uncorked champagne and she stifled it with her wrist. It was comical from this vantage point. Each of them interacting with the VR interface, reaching for and manipulating objects that were not there as if engaged in hallucination.

Theresa felt the edge of hysteria in her mind. *No ongoing data from the patients—no contact—no new samples.*

The musical trill in the tune of an old song emanated from the discarded VR Comm headset, the sign that her auto call was attempting to get through to Earth again...*Get your boards out, get your boards out. Blood tide's rollin' in. There're bodies in the surf, and smoke on the wind. Oo-Whoa-o-o —now!*

Theresa's nerves electrified with anticipation as the tune came to an end, and then fizzled into disappointment as the silence drew out with no answer to the auto-call set every half hour.

*Still blocked...*Theresa reopened the old footage sent from Aurelia's nanocytes. This was lymph fluid, full of white cells and the biological debris left in the aftermath of cellular warfare.

"Let's do this again, then—" She glanced over at the rest of the team. Some were cataloguing Aurelia's blood, others the lymph fluid or urine, saliva as well. Virtually grasping, copying, and identifying every particle foreign or native to Aurelia's body. B-1,3-

glucans, mannans, melanin, Pla, YopJ, all present in high concentrations along with Y. Pestis bacteria. Theresa frowned at the growing list of proteins, molecules, cell fragments and bacterial agents in her VR simulation. And then there were these trace psychoactives, cathinone, psilocybin, several others as yet unidentified. They were present with this new version of Y Pestis, but were they derived from it?

The message chime of incoming communication sounded but she didn't hear it. There was something here she should be seeing, something that was setting off memories of earlier research from during her apprenticeship that she couldn't place. It would come clear if she zeroed in long enough.

Grasping a new protein she hadn't noticed in previous samples, along with several labeled ones, she placed them in a virtual file, a collection of puzzle pieces to make sense of. The excitement was building like a frenzied focus that would not abate until the picture was complete.

The message symbol flashed in the corner of her screen on repeat.

Theresa felt a hand on her shoulder, it was insistent. Some portion of her mind registered, the rest assembled and reassembled protein fragments and categorized free-floating toxins and psychoactives.

The hand shook her and a voice spoke in her ear. "You have a message."

She bit down on her lips, pushing down the irritation the interruption elicited. With deliberate and methodical set responses, she nodded and gave silent thumbs up to Dr. Alexander, and then opened the message, feeling a thrill of excitement as she saw the name attached.

Richard Brant
6257RGAUG WGC Center

Theresa,

What follows is as much data as I could get at this time to supplement what I sent before. It's a complicated and shifting symptom picture, yet I feel we are on the verge of figuring it out. If I could just reach it faster.

I can't VR Comm. While my focus is laser sharp and lucid, my mindscape is unpredictable and unsettling. You don't need that, and I may be unable to maintain the connection.

This is reaching you courtesy of my skill with persuasion and Diadonna's temporary magnanimity. But she is infected as well now, and her good will may not hold. If you have a response, I recommend sending ASAP.

This message was relayed to your whole council on Mars, but I recommend you ensure it was received. We will leave for the pick-up point either as soon as I have stabilized the children enough to move or have despaired of doing so. I WILL bring them under any condition necessary.

Yours,
Richard

Theresa scrolled through Aurelia's updated symptom list, and found her eyes widening and then narrowing, brows shifting position as she took in the drastic shift in symptom picture.

Rapid pulse, pupil dilation, fever, outbursts of anger, apparent neck and head pain, stiffness, lack of lucid interaction, subvocalizing between outbursts, intermittent laughter, vomiting —

There was a heaviness in the pit of Theresa's stomach, but it didn't touch the rapid firing of synapses in her brain as she made connections from the previous data to this. And then she went cold, the realization like ice-water running in her veins. The Pinnacle would be leaving in three hours and she was going to have to be on it to do this, she...and Dr. Alexander, if he would go.

The sandy red soil was thicker around Carla's roughened heels, growing more loamy and full of organic matter as she neared the original dome complex and its new twin that extended along the curve of coast.

A wave of deja vu colored her approach with memory. The uninhabited dome complex far East across the desert was identical, and the current campsite for their planetary ecology expedition, Donovan's expedition. She was needed back here.

The garden gate opened at her request and scan, admitting her into its balmy interior. David should be proud of this: soil built up and enriched by the compost of the colony's wastes, painstakingly planted and tended until it resembled fairytale forests from old Earth illustrations. His plumeria grew tall here, carpeting the ground with fallen petals and filling the air with their rich sweet scent that had an undertone of something darker: nutmeg or allspice, maybe. Carla glanced up at the clouds overhead as she picked up a trot. Soon the transparent overhead hail shields would be opened up to protect the gardens from the hailstorm, and not long after there would be more children here. Theresa's brood...if they could see them safely here.

Carla nodded to herself, picturing what would be like a field of children. She grinned at the mental image. They'd be popping up like dandelions in a lawn, resilient and strong, one could hope. *One can hope—though somehow, I don't think hope is needed for these ones to thrive, assuming we get them here.*

Carla brushed a hand across the powdery bark of Emily's gravesite aspen, under which her great-grandchildren rested, and then paused in front of the door that led into the colony's inner complex. There'd be a lot of frightened and overworked people inside. That was her part. Bolster them up, decrease stress, keep them working without a terminal burn-out. Theresa wouldn't come see her before departure; she'd bottle it until work was done.

Carla sucked in a breath and, with a final glance to the West Mountains like a quick prayer before embarking on the gods' work, stepped inside.

UNDERWAY

Rain fell in fat warm drops that splashed and ran in rivulets down the sides of the large geodesic dome that served as arrival and departure terminal and entrance to the space elevator. The Pinnacle was docked high above, just out of Mars' atmosphere, waiting for its crew.

The elevator stood open as if waiting for those leaving to step across the threshold...and those remaining to let them go.

Askia's eyes were open, a crooked smile accompanying the squeals of delight. Neil held him up above his face as if to toss him but didn't let go. Jasrie, Nile, and Grant stood around him, watching Kendra's and Neil's faces.

"Now, you get them out and you get right back here, okay?" Kendra's smile held strong, but her eyes were wide and overly bright with moisture.

Neil kissed Askia's rounded cheeks, one after the other and then his forehead, before tucking the cooing infant back into Kendra's sunset-colored wrap carrier. She leaned in to receive kisses of her own, then crossed her arms over Askia to sway and bounce him back to sleep while Neil knelt down to give parting hugs to their other three children.

Jasrie jumped into his arms, knocking him back onto his heels with the force of her hug, small, soft arms wrapping around his neck. Neil laughed, stroking her tightly curled brown hair back from where it tickled his nose.

"You be good for your mother, Jas baby, and I'll be back. All three of you be helpful with the baby." Jasrie nodded, still tucked against his chest, and he extended the firm gaze to his two older sons.

"We will. And no fighting while you're gone. Promise." Nile held his hand up to swear, and Neil laughed, pressing his own palm, three times as large, against it.

"Good boy."

Neil moved to unwrap Jasrie's arms from his neck, but she clung tighter.

His voice was a whisper as he worked to keep his eyes from tearing up. "I gotta go now, baby. Go to mama."

She released her grip and he hugged her once more before standing and locking eyes with Kendra and mouthing silent words. *"We're coming back."*

Kendra nodded back, unable to trust her voice. She brushed the back of one hand across her eyes and smiled silently.

"I mean that, babe."

Neil scanned the room with his eyes, showing a reassuring smile to the colonists who stood back from the loading dock to witness the departure without crowding the families of the departing. Abby and Deimos were closer by and he walked over, reaching out for Deimos's shoulder but giving Abby space. "Wanted to see if you two could look out for my older ones…they look up to you—especially Jasrie, Abby."

When she didn't answer, Deimos stepped in. "We will, Captain. Both of us." His smile was earnest and apologetic at the same time.

Neil ruffled his hair and then smiled at Abby, not waiting for a smile back, but getting one, a half-smile that looked a bit forced, but it was there. "Thank you. I'm gonna get everyone back safe, okay?"

Abby nodded, eyes wide and dark. She looked as if she would freeze and Deimos tugged her arm, pulling to an empty space near the exits.

Melissa stepped out from the crowd of colonists here to see them off and leaned in to whisper to the Captain, "That's quite a crew you have there. I want to see every one of them back with you—you make the calls you have to, about Earth *and* the mission, so long as ours come back." She turned a sharp look to the elevator.

Neil looked over his shoulder at the gaping mouth that awaited him. It was full now with everyone who was going along, save for himself: Genesis, Theresa, Dr. Alexander, Dr. Spanner, five medical apprentices, and Emily's apprentice Sean for engineering tasks, should they become necessary.

Neil nodded to Melissa, mien serious. Closely guarded memories of the last time a crew boarded the Pinnacle, only to be met by flames and suffocation, crowded his thoughts. He shook her hand with a firm grip of reassurance before he reached back to squeeze Kendra's once more in parting, then he turned to the elevator, stepping across the threshold and strapping himself in before giving the command.

"Take us up, please." Anticipation lent a subtle energy to his movements as the mantle of command settled over him. A smile grew on his face, giving a spark of true excitement to his eyes. He blew a kiss and waved as the doors closed, then turned to the handful of colonists that would serve as crew and rescue team over the next few months.

"There are two treatment centers along the way, and the

departure station itself has a medical facility. It would be best for you to get everyone in a transport ASAP and meet us there. Gavin?"

Richard spoke though the voice comm without the VR function. He stared across the lab that had served as place of work and dwelling since the Phase Four progeny were brought forth from their AUC chambers and placed officially under his care. The walls resembled marble, as in all the official buildings. Marble that was made from a conglomeration of recycled materials, melted and fused into a smooth surface with ghostlike remnants of their past identities.

Most of what was here belonged to the WGC. They wouldn't have further need of anything he chose to take along, but he had no use for most mementos of Earth. Mars was a new chapter to begin fresh, without bringing phantoms of past decades.

A small backpack sat open on his desk, awaiting something to safeguard. Richard stared into it for long moments, a tired smile hanging on his haggard face.

The bag was still empty. He glanced at the time displayed. Several minutes had passed as he waited for reply. "Gavin, are you receiving?" The reply came after another moment's delay. He could hear other voices in the background mumbling, raised voices it seemed, but too jumbled and distant to make out the words. *Was that Feldon, and perhaps Caris?* Feldon's eyes sparked like lightning behind clouds when he was angry, which was often, and Caris seemed to revel in instigating an outburst. Anything to provoke the rages that she found so fascinating to witness—that would not do on Mars. Richard listened closer, trying to catch their words. Something about a sky-boat, jumbled words he couldn't place, and then the words came across clear as day but with no context for processing — *"found them bleeding each other out."*

Richard frowned at the strangeness of the phrase. Found who? Bleeding each other? It was like something out of an old newsreel.

"They are not fit to travel." A fit of coughing interrupted Gavin's reply. It was wet sounding and followed by wheezing. Richard winced, concern pulling his brows into a deep scowl. Gavin's voice sounded hoarse and weak coming through now. "I'm not so fit for it myself. But I brought the antibiotics and other meds for symptom management to get us back up and moving. Already distributing them, actually."

Richard spoke quickly as if some invisible clock had started ticking at the mention of illness away from his ability to help.

"It advances quickly. Better to treat while traveling. And stay on top of the antibiotics or it can overwhelm before you are aware that it has even repopulated itself. We can stop there to assist. We have other stops to make as well, collection points for others that have people on Mars."

"You think anyone will make it to a collection point?" His tenor voice, normally colored with a deep sense of amusement, was incredulous.

"No, no I don't. Not unless they haven't been exposed yet. And they won't last long once we expose them. It simmers in our bodies while they burn out. But I've been asked by the Martian Council Leader to collect them, and I'll try." He shrugged, the gesture more weariness than lack of caring.

Another fit of coughing came across the line. "Don't stop for us then. You have enough, and it's about time I put the things you've taught me into practice. We can meet you at the Stairway to Heaven—at WASA."

Richard stared at the small statue in his hands that hovered over the travel bag. It was ovoid and made of silicone and glass, a prototype of an AUC in miniature, complete with minute fetus suspended by a translucent umbilical cord inside of simulated amniotic sac and fluid.

Memories spread from the thing into his hands like hot water poured into a cold bath. A young Morton Steiner laughed and clapped him on the back in that obnoxious way that he had. He didn't see the significance of the project, but he did see the scope of at least what Richard shared with him. He saw the acclaim they'd both get, with Morton backing it on the political front to make sure support for the project stayed consistent long enough to work the bugs out.

The prototype and its apparent failure—*he hid her well enough, though*, and each phase that followed, with Phase Four as the crowning glory. Theresa's beginnings in the AUC lab, still half child herself, but with the raw genetic material to co-create the culmination of it all.

Morton, again that well-known face, swollen now with power and twisted toward different priorities, imagining that he could stop the project they'd started together. And where was he now? Unconscious in a quarantine now most like, or dead. Has it been a week? *How long has it been?*

"Richard?" The item was still in his hands and he tucked it into the bag with shaking fingers, clearing his throat to speak. It felt raw again, itching and coated with mucus, and that heaviness building deep in his lungs again—pneumonia.

"Yes."

Gavin's voice was impatient, sharp with irritation, somehow still holding the echo of itself that was long displaced by years and maturity. For a moment it was the high-pitched whine of a three-year-old child, precociously claiming a tone of authority well beyond its years, and then it was the voice of the man-child again, matured and cloaked in patience. "We will meet you at the Stairway to Heaven, yes?!"

He cleared his throat again, signaling the medibot for an earlier dose of antibiotics. "Yes, we'll meet there—just, call for help if you can't make it."

"Fine."

The call ended on Gavin's end, leaving the room around him silent aside from the buzz of anxiety the call left scrambling across spent nerves.

Theresa gripped the handrails in the back of the large conference hall that held their small crew, allowing her feet to float free with the lack of gravity. It set the pit of her stomach squirming with memory of the last time she was aboard the Pinnacle: Abby stowed away in the RPU hidden under her travel uniform, heartbeat to heartbeat, as she lost her grip and collided with one of the cafeteria walls.

Captain Neil was talking at the front of the room, and his voice carried fine, but did not penetrate the wall of interwoven thoughts that populated her grey matter. The words made it through but were filed away before she could process or attend to them. Instead, the microbial research that had become her sole focus continued to scroll through her head as she worked on building a ground-floor of knowledge to jump off from. Dr. Alexander was the only one on board with any background in epidemiology and infectious disease, but it was not his specialty, and research was hers. It was like learning a new language, and so she would study it whether consciously attending or dreaming.

Genesis's voice cut through the stream of her thoughts. "The only ones leaving Earth with us are those who show up at W.A.S.A headquarters. Dr. Brant has been tasked with collecting as many of ours on the way to the pick-up point as possible, but it won't be many."

"It needs to not be many." Captain Neil opened his mouth to explain and then closed it before starting again. "I don't like how that sounds either, but the ship does have a maximum capacity."

Theresa's heart kicked up its pace, the lub-lub of it sounding in her ears as she sucked in a breath, eyes wide with worry. "There are a hundred, including the children and Richard before we start bringing in other survivors. How many more can you fit?"

The Captain cleared his throat, the sound strained and uncomfortable as if he might choke on his own answer. "Numbers? That's going to put us above capacity. But these are children, so weight is gonna have a little more leeway. I have some more options to massage the weight in the right direction, so don't stress it."

Theresa pressed her lips together in a tight line, triple blinking at his response. *Don't stress it? Ha, ha, ha.* She stared at the face of the man that brought them from Earth to Mars, then saw them through colonization for two full leadership terms. Mistakes aside, he could make this work as sure as anyone, and what other option was there?

Shadows of fear appeased, Theresa's focus shifted back to the problem at hand. She slid the VR Comm visor down without leaving the meeting hall. The others were still in discussion, but it didn't matter. Let them plan, and prepare for arrival, and all of the logistics of descending to Earth, collecting survivors, and the return trip. She and the others on the team would have to cure this. She paused the analysis of foreign bodies in fluid samples to send a message, and then focused in.

Dr. Alexander appeared in the simulation a moment later, in miniature next to the hovering protein fragments, polysaccharides, and psychoactive molecules.

"You requested I join you…" He was already staring up at the sea of particles, reaching for the nearest to collect and categorize before he turned a sharp eye back to Theresa's avatar. "You aren't just sorting these anymore, are you? You're looking for something in particular. I can tell when you're on the trail of something, it's like a bloodhound on a scent, or so I hear. I've never met one." He smirked at his own joke and then grew serious. "Put me onto the same trail and we'll track it down."

It was a moment before she answered, so intent was she on

the patterns that were only visible within her own labyrinthine mind. And then she responded without a glance over or any hint of inflection to her voice. "The infection moved, or set up a secondary locus. Meningitis—"

"That's uncommon with Y. Pestis—because it kills quickly…"

"Mmmmm…it's a pattern. And this isn't Y. Pestis, exactly, is it? Something derivative of it, another strain, correct?" Theresa flicked a token glance his way for confirmation.

"Yes, yes, that's quite right. But the antibiotics that Dr. Brant was using to some effect should kick it whether it's in the lymph, the blood, the brain…especially at the doses being used."

Theresa went silent for another long moment, grasping a fragment of destroyed white cell and setting it aside. "I think there is a secondary infection with something else. Something opportunistic that's come in on Y. Pestis's coattails—"

Dr. Alexander cocked his head to the left and narrowed his eyes. "That would make sense, except that we aren't finding it."

"I think it's here and I'm going to keep looking. And you are too. I need lists of what all of these fragments are part of. I want every possibility, every candidate that fits what we have, even if it's in small amounts."

He looked skeptical, pushing a long-fingered hand through white streaked black hair above deeply tanned skin. "Okay. You run the research and I'll tell you what you're looking at—if you need it." Dr. Alexander winked even though she was still not looking his way, and, turning back towards the presorted piles of organic matter, began labeling any that were still unnamed, He made copies and regrouped them by possible use and origin.

TREADING WATER

It was cacophonous. A surging wave of sound, motion, and shifting expressions, conflicting body language, that reached a crescendo as the elevator car faded out of sight into the storm heavy cloud-cover.

The elevator station that allowed transport up to the Pinnacle was filled with colonists.

Abby backed away from the empty shaft that towered far above. Theresa was gone, and Genesis, with all the others, and there was nothing left for her in this building. Deimos stood next to Kendra, surrounded by Neil's children, making good on his promise. She could join him, but the idea of being hemmed in by their energy made her skin itch, and a sense of panic built in her head at the thought.

The others were cheering for some reason…For the return of her ninety-nine siblings perhaps bringing sickness and death with them, that and the unknown? Unlikely. Perhaps for their distant family members and friends on Earth—distant but not forgotten. That was likely a waste of sentiment, considering survival rates coupled with the rescue team's resources of time and human-power.

Abby stared a moment longer. Melissa waved at the void

above as if there was anyone to see and then fell to rubbing her own arms, goosebumps forming in the chill.

Kendra was busy with her children. Two of the boys were crying now, adding to the noise, literal and energetic, in the room. And the other two were dancing for Deimos, vying for his attention.

Carla stood next to Emily with a hand on her shoulder, her grey-blue eyes searching the crowd and then stopping on Abby.

Abby flinched; there was concern in the midwife's eyes; concern, and questions.

She would speak her comforts, ask her questions, toss out her incongruent idioms like so many choice crumbs to a flock of birds, and Abby's voice would freeze up, not rolled up in her tongue or buried in her throat, but locked in her mind where too many thoughts and many more collected observations gathered and argued for her attention. I can see her later.

Abby spun on her heel and fled, allowing the wind to envelop her as the landscape blurred into its constituent colors, rusty-brick red, mossy browns and greens, and dusty black.

Her eyes were half-closed, letting in just enough to guide her footing but still block out what was too much.

The colony would be empty, but the ocean was what she needed. There was no one here to caution her against diving from the whale song cliffs…

Abby turned off of the path, shifting direction with her shifting thoughts. The whalefins might be there and swim with her. She stripped as she ran, pulling off weighted tunic and folding it before tossing it into the red sand at the top of the cliff.

She paused at the precipice to pull the ends of her soft brown leggings over her feet, then stood at the edge to survey the deep green water below. It was frothy with sea foam and algae where the towering swells met smooth red rockface. No sign of pale iridescent bodies beneath those shadowy waves, no darting of Martian sardine, the primary food source of the larger sea-life.

Abby sucked in air, breath ragged from the sprint that had turned long-distance as well as uphill to reach this frequent haunt. She fought back the sinking disappointment that sapped energy from her limbs that was there just a moment before. The water would have to suffice by itself.

Another breath and she leapt, arms overhead like the beak of a small dolphin pointing towards the depths below.

The water was cold on her skin, removing all traces of heat from the day's sunshine and that built up by her run. She blew the air in her lungs out as bubbles, watching them dance back up to the light of the surface before she turned and dove deeper to inspect the caves under the cliffs.

The light couldn't find its way in this deep, not into the winding caverns. She pushed off of the sides, feeling her way along the familiar rough and smooth patterns of volcanic stone until her lungs burned and ached for a breath.

The sounds of underwater singing greeted her before she opened her eyes, and the waters became visible even in this inky blackness. The unintelligible crooning soothed the heavy ache in her heart, but not her burning lungs. She kicked off again, barely noting the misplaced ankle that scraped rough stone and would bleed into the cold water.

A small patch of light shimmered far above and she made for it, pushing through the water with all of her remaining strength.

They were all around her when she broke the surface, gasping at first and then forcing her sounds of struggle to calm lest she frighten them.

Abby's eyes widened, their tapetum lucidum shimmering in the darkness as she took in the many glistening white bodies. They were rolling on the surface and then ducking under in the gloom. Only a small crevice above allowed any illumination, but she could see them even in near-dark. She cupped a palmful of water and brought it closer to isolate the smell that was filling her senses. It was pink-tinged and smelled strong and salty, with a musk to it. The smells of birth, and also fresh colostrum. A grin pulled at her lips.

There were new whalefin progeny in the cave, some hidden behind their mothers; they were smaller and even more iridescent than the larger whales. *Their newborn skin, even from here, gave tell to a smooth, pliable texture that would be soft to the touch—like all newborn things…not roughened by wind, and sun, cold and sand—Donovan would want to know…*

Abby climbed out of the water onto a small ledge just overhanging the dark water. It was narrow and didn't allow her to stretch her legs all the way out, but it would keep her far enough away from the newborns to avoid angering their mothers. If it would…*normally that's nurture, not nature—human raised animals, more tame and less cautious around us, but not these ones, he said.*

A lock of salty, damp hair held captive between her restless fingers served as fidget. She brushed it across her lips, back and forth like the pointed end of a paintbrush. How long would the whalefins stay here? How long could she?

The thought renewed her smile despite its impractical nature. There was no food or fresh water. And it would grow colder at night. And the others would contact Mother and worry her. The smile dropped from her cheeks and she shoved at the drenched auburn locks that hung heavily towards her face. It was unruly when wet and tried to cover her eyes, or wind around her ears.

A newborn whale fin rolled onto its back a few feet from the cave and lifted its pointed beak towards the ceiling. Light from the opening in the ceiling, a hundred feet up, illuminated its belly, turning it into a glistening rainbow before it ducked back under the water.

Abby stared after it, eyes gleaming in the artificial gloaming, all time forgotten. The cave and dark water within and around it were like a time capsule, closing her off from everything and everyone above, almost like her mother and the others aboard the Pinnacle surrounded by the vacuum of space.

"Shhh…" David lifted the kicking creature by the nape of its neck, unwrapping the exposed roots that entangled it as he soothed. Its coarse, tawny fur, more red-brown than yellow, dropped showers of matching sand as it struggled and kicked long back legs like a kangaroo's. The ears were equally noticeable, long like a rabbit's and mapped with capillaries visible through the thin skin.

"Shhhh…That's it now. Your buddy Donovan isn't back at camp for the night yet. 'Course you probably haven't met. What are you? Third, maybe fourth generation ratbit?"

He glanced back at the dry sinkhole the animal was trapped in. Most likely opened up by a flash flood. But when did this little beast get ensnared?

It still had fight in it, the oil-drop eyes darting around as it continued to wriggle. He was looking for a good bit of cover to turn it loose when one back foot managed to make purchase in the palm of his left hand so that it could turn just enough for the long front teeth to bite into his thumb.

David's hand let go as the sharp pain registered and he pulled it into his chest. The juvenile Giant Red jerboa darted under a rock and into a hole. The darker red stripes on its back allowed it to blend with the shadows of coming evening and escape David's visual tracking completely.

He sat back against the tree and looked over his hand.

"Huh. No thanks, eh? A wave…a handshake…guess that was your handshake." David smirked at the blood welling up. Five cuts, one from the bite and the others from the back claws.

"You can't be so lonely yet. Genesis isn't that long gone."

There was a gentle warmth in the voice, a voice that was immediately familiar.

He glanced over his shoulder to where Joanna leaned against the same tree, crouching down to his level. He smiled with the same level of comfortable warmth and then tended to his hand. A bottle of spray antiseptic combined with liquid graft would set it straight quickly, regrowing a protective layer of skin over the next few minutes so the cuts could heal faster underneath without pulling open or becoming infected.

"We both know I don't need to be lonely to talk to the wildlife. I just tend to stick with the greener, leafier sort, you know?"

A soft chuckle escaped her lips before she kissed his cheek. He could feel her warm breath against his neck like a desert breeze, and he leaned towards it.

"Why not imagine Genesis here with you while she's gone? Why call me back?" David frowned, pulling one of her small soft hands over to press against his cheek so he could turn and look into her eyes. They were sapphire blue, uncommon, and clouded with concern.

"Maybe I should ask you that, Jo—why you and why now? Because I don't think it's voluntary. One minute I'm alone and the next, there you are."

She spread one hand, the other still trapped against his cheek. "Maybe I'm a ghost—or you're crazy." The last bit was said through a laugh.

He joined in, shaking his head and releasing her hand before standing and brushing the dirt and lichen grass debris from his clothes. "Yeah, maybe. It's in the records, after all. Why now, though? It's been—a long while."

Joanna tilted her head. "Do you believe her? What she said? That I'm dead." David started to speak and then stopped, confusion warring with certainty in his eyes."

"I—uh—I dunno."

Joanna stood and stepped closer, interlocking her arm with his while they walked back towards the campsite.

"Am I on the list of kin?" David nodded, still frowning at the ground and the pebbles he kicked with each step. "You are, but, it's your old name. They'd have changed it if you were saved and reassigned, hidden." He cleared his throat. "It doesn't matter for us, you know. It's been too long. I'm not the same."

Joanna nodded in agreement, her answering voice somber. "Why put me on the list, then?"

David shrugged. "You shouldn't be there if it's as bad as they say. You and anyone that's with you."

She nodded again. "Okay."

"You're past every one of the losses, you know. Does it feel— better?"

Carla placed the large end of the fetoscopic heart-tone amplifier just above the small swelling just above Emily's pubic bone, angling it downward, then right. The sound came through the speakers before she could make any further adjustment. Thump, thump, thump, thump, it was like a fast drumbeat beneath a pillow.

A grin spread across Carla's face, bringing up age lines that still didn't show her century and counting. Emily mirrored the grin, tears of relief illuminating her grey-blue eyes.

"It feels different, maybe because I feel different." Emily looked away and then down at her hands in her lap. "It always felt more like a fantasy before, imagined more than real—as if, as if I was willing something that wasn't ever going to be there." A sigh from deep in her chest sent the forelock of her hair fluttering back from her face.

"Like a phantom-pregnancy where there is no child but the one in your head. But with this, I can see it—"

She stood and paced over to the AUC that hung in the center of the room. "And this time I can feel all of the changes. I'm still scared, I think, but I know it's real."

Carla nodded as Emily spoke, following her granddaughter's narrative without interjecting, lest she plug the flow of sharing with her own story. *Better to listen until nothing else comes than to cut her short and leave an unlanced wound to fester.*

A small laugh escaped Emily's lips as she leaned in to catch a glimpse of the tiny form, floating in a sea of amniotic fluid, arms flailing as if to swim even at so early a point in its development.

"They're not even a half inch long, and already seem to have a personality. Heartbeat faster than this little one in me, and look at those butterfly flutters."

Carla chuckled, noticing the sparkling in Emily's eyes when she looked into the AUC unit. Theresa was right to suggest this for the second child. At least for Emily's sake. So long as all turned out fine, despite Theresa's sudden absence. A shadow crossed Carla's face. Three weeks since the Pinnacle left, and things were fine, but if they didn't stay that way, there was no real expert to set things back on track.

Theresa swore she could do it by remote monitoring or send instructions to them. Time would tell.

Emily wrapped Carla in a sudden hug, squeezing hard enough to surprise the older woman.

"Thank you."

"You're welcome. I said I'd be here for this, didn't I? Before we ever left Earth."

Emily nodded, trying to cover a frown that pulled at her lips unbidden. "Gran, what about mother? She thought I was silly to keep trying but—do you think they'll bring her from Earth? That she'll make it…I have, I have dreams with her, and the children."

Carla's jaw tightened, lips pressing into a tight line. "I don't know. If she makes it here it'll be like a second chance, but, well, some trees don't transplant well and others do. I think she'd have come with us before if she wanted to. Epidemic or no."

Emily sighed, resting one hand on the flesh of her lower abdomen and the other on the silicone side of the AUC, and glanced up at Carla with worry covering the joy that hovered in her eyes just moments before. "And the birth? How will they both come at once?"

Carla shrugged and then placed a hand on Emily's shoulder, feeling the faint tremble that was always there when her granddaughter was uneasy. "Twins don't come all at once. They have to wait their turn. If I remember correctly—and I do—there's a window of prime timing to birth an AUC baby, whereas this one you're carrying will choose the time, likely first considering the conception came sooner."

"Theresa isn't here, though…"

"She isn't now. But unless things go very wrong, she will be then." She said it with a voice firm with certainty, the sort she used on patients that needed that extra boost of confidence after being shaken bad by some trauma: a death, a bad birth, an injury. It was like using her own steel spine to shore up theirs, if only until they could regrow their own. Carla added a smile to soften the tone.

"And if she isn't here, I know how it's done. It's mostly automated, and the settings are already programmed."

"It could fail, go wrong, and then—"

The shadows in her eyes had darkened, her glances turned furtive and haunted.

"You dreamed it, didn't you?"

A nod, followed by faint whisper. "Yes."

"Theresa cut the thing open to take Abby out before her time and it can be done again. I can't promise the outcome for you— you know that—life and death is a tricky thing, both natural, both still outside our fists no matter how tight we try to grab hold.

Water and fate always find a way through the cracks."

Hot tears fell from Emily's eyes to splash on the side of the AUC like a thunderstorm torrent in a heat wave. She scrubbed at them, the motion futile with the speed they returned.

"Better cry now than to let it twist up your guts and addle your mind. This—" Carla placed a soft hand under Emily's chin. "… is the surrender we talk about at the approach of birthing time. Surrender of control, of fears—it's that knowing that you'll be passing through a place where death and rebirth are cozied up together and you won't get to choose which one holds your hand on the other side."

Emily tried a trembling smile, despite the rain of tears that had slowed, but not ceased altogether.

"And I have another seven months for these thoughts and feelings." The laugh that escaped was incredulous, but also pregnant with wonder, as if the momentous nature of this struggle was not lost on her even in the midst of her storm.

Carla joined the laugh. "You do. But you have both a head start because of the ones before...and also an uphill climb, for the same reason."

Emily rolled her eyes. "Yeah, guess so."

Giving Emily's shoulder a quick squeeze before removing her hand, Carla flicked a glance back at the pink and red mottled cheeks that were finally drying before she cleared her throat.

"The dreams, Em…I know the VR sleep modules help you dream less and fall to sleep. But it may be keeping them coming back. Just a thought—you might have to go through them, to be done with them."

Emily's brows pulled together in a scowl, built of concentration and worry in equal measure. "I could try, but—I don't sleep so much without it."

Carla shrugged again, feigning lack of commitment to lower the pressure inherent in her suggestion. "You've been using it since before we came to Mars. Maybe try working through some of this instead of pushing it away. Dreams help with that, and talking. I'm not too busy." A crooked smile came up on her face as she made the offer.

Emily echoed the smile, reluctant but resigned. "You know you're busy. You're always busy when things are up in the air around here. And they haven't been this far up in quite awhile, with the Pinnacle off and Earth how it is."

Carla nodded, as she headed towards the door that led to her own rooms and office, attached to Emily's on the western side. "Sure, but still never too busy, if you need me."

RENDEZVOUS POINTS

The complaints, worries, and fears spoken aloud by his siblings were accumulating and would be a problem soon if he couldn't quell them. He searched for the words that normally flowed to his tongue with such ease and latched on to another quote without taking the time to check if it applied; it would get the words moving, at least. "Let our advance worrying become advance thinking and planning—we have the same treatments they have, at least for now. And he'll send updates." Gavin raised one brow in challenge, lifting it so high that it ducked beneath the dark brown curls of hair that fell down around his face on the left and were shaved into a short carpet on the right. It did fit, and seemed to soothe her, so he continued.

"This…this decision has been a long time coming, and you were all made aware of the choice you have. Follow through, or not."

He tossed one long arm towards the transport station across from the medical center, that waited with magnetic railcars equipped to transport them to the WASA Center or elsewhere.

The bullet shaped conveyances gleamed white-hot in the heavy glare of sunlight, wavering with heat distortion across the short distance. Daylight hours meant the windows of the Medical

Center were tinted to cut the transfer of heat and harmful UV rays into the building; still, the intensity of sun outdoors was obvious.

Gelsemium stared out the window, pale brown eyes a luminous amber as the pupils dilated. Her skin was darker than Gavin's, tanning into a warm walnut shade with sun exposure, not a trait from her main genetic progenitors but instead a feature from one of the genetic packages added in to supplement what she would inherit from them. Sweat dripped down her forehead despite the draft of air-conditioning in the room.

"And then, Gavin? When this illness takes—further hold. What do we do when they're off to Mars, and he's angry with us?"

Scowling and tilting her head to the side, she cracked her neck to release the nervous tension pent up there. A snake of hair tickled her, clinging to her damp and overheated skin and she brushed it back. It framed her face, chestnut brown with shimmers of red in the sunlight, as were the freckles that overlaid brown skin.

She stood, half a head shorter than Gavin and lighter of frame, and gestured towards the perimeter of the large treatment room they occupied with cots and medical-bots lining the walls.

"Geli, you think he'll withhold anything he and Theresa figure out—knowing we need it to recover? Hold a killing grudge on us?" Gavin laughed, the sound soft and incredulous.

She shrugged, lowering her voice. "You so sure he won't?"

He raised both brows in emphasis, turning his forehead into the high peak of a mountain range too high for inexperienced adventurers to climb. "I am. Once we really talk it through, he'll see it. He'll see it like I do, even if it sends him into a frothing rage first. It's the control, you know; he won't give it up until I take it."

Geli's frown softened into a look of concentration, leaving amber eyes distant, unseeing save for the maze of thoughts in her overheated mind as opposed to the boy in front of her.

"Then why not take it on Mars? Go along and then take the place he's planned for you."

Gavin watched her expression shift from concern to feigned

nonchalance. His voice was thoughtful when it came. "Because I have a different future in mind, and I see it so clearly it may as well be here already. Right now. And—" He lowered his voice to near-whisper to counteract the strain of emotion that threatened to break it. "And if I can see it like that, I can make it real. Manifest it here. Let the others shape Mars; we'll bring back Earth."

Gelsimium's lips tipped up at the corners in a smile that danced to the tune his words played, the passion infused into them. She grasped his hand and squeezed, flicking her eyes over to encompass the group of AUC progeny that occupied the space with them. "If you're going to stay for this, even still, then I'm staying, and we'll keep them as well. It isn't just your dream."

Gavin squeezed back, the smile that was a mere ghost on his lips setting his eyes alight with excitement, a dance of green flame that sent sparks showering into the shadows there as if his fire dripped with pine sap.

A sigh of fevered contentment passed between them as they returned to the space the others occupied. Gavin's voice was full of warmth and humor when he spoke, raising it to project across the whole room. Thirty-six sets of eyes, most a shade of brown or hazel flecked with orange and gold, a few a frame of grey-blue around a yellow sun, turned in his direction. Some that appeared to sleep shifted, eyes opening and lighting up with attentiveness without turning their gaze in his direction.

Gavin swallowed the smile that came from deep inside each time that he spoke to a group, channeling it into the words that would guide his siblings into correct action: action aligned with his goals.

Some could walk, but for how much longer? And why should

they? Richard stared at the long line of medical transport drones that snaked along the covered path from the WGC center that had been their safe haven for the past eleven years. There were too many of them, would be nearly twice as many once the others joined up with them at WASA.

He shook his head in slow motion, allowing a short sigh to escape as he watched them load into the first three magnetic railcars. They were sleeping, every one of them; not the sort of sleep that evinces a sense of peace and safety in the viewer, but the fitful sort that speaks of nightmares and delirium. Bram and Aurelia were the last. Aurelia's eyes were open again, but she only stared, lips moving with a steady stream of nonsensical subvocalization.

Bram, at least, appeared to sleep, in between bouts of violent thrashing that was contained by straps on the side of the medicots.

Light a match and they might all ignite. And why hadn't they ignited, combusted, plummeted into fits of uncontrollable rage, aggression, sexual urges…They were being treated more effectively than the surrogates or any of the others had been. And their immune systems had not given out despite the length of the battle—still, how much longer did they have? He scowled at the errant thought, stepping close to the nearest medibot.

"All medical-cots are to employ full restraints for travel, shoulders, wrists, thighs, ankles—neck as well. Immobilize it lest they thrash and injure something. Relay to all the medical-bots."

The bot seemed to clear its throat, more of a digitized precursor to speech to mimic human patterns, but it served the purpose all the same, and then gave a quick nod. "Commands received, implementation beginning now."

Thick flexible straps emerged, along with mechanical cuffs, from several openings along the sides of the cots. They swept out past the nearest limb, picking up its proximity by way of sensors, and then curling around and under the acquired body part and securing to the other side, tightening down and snaking around a second time to ensure immobility.

Bram, already strapped down, startled and attempted to sit up. His eyes flew open, wide with alarm and frenzied with fever as he tugged against the new straps and neck restraint with arms and legs, arching his back and bucking against the surface until he caught sight of Richard watching.

"Bram—Bram! We're transporting to the WASA center, I've restrained all of you for safety—it's just for your safety." Richard stood next to the cot and placed a hand on the panting, but otherwise still, boy's forehead. "You're burning up again—did you understand me?"

Bram opened his mouth to speak, eyes clouded with confusion and tears. His voice was hoarse and cracked as he spoke in a near whisper. "Going to WASA." He laid his head back against the cot and closed his eyes, blinking to clear them. "The straps are for safety…Richard, I'm fine. Sick, but functional like you. I can't help if I'm strapped down." His voice broke on the last word and Richard smiled. Such maturity, but still a child.

"You are functional for now, but Aurelia and some of the others are delirious and could hurt themselves or each other."

"But I'm…"

"You're ill, and could go downhill quickly. We don't want to wait until someone becomes violent to start being careful. That would be foolhardy."

Bram's nod was slow with reluctance and hampered by the neck restraint. He grew still and let out a shaky sigh.

An antique mahogany brown bag, weathered with age, hung from Richard's shoulder. He held it up to show the boy, who was no longer fighting the decision but looked as if he might begin crying again at any moment.

"This is for small personal effects. I'm going back in to collect them. It may seem unimportant now but will matter once this planet is just dust and memories to us. Is there anything I should look out for for you?"

Bram sighed again, the exhalation shaky and overly warm from fever; his breath had the fetid, bacterial smell of the sick and dying. "My books, if you can, and Aurelia's rats—the models, not real ones."

They both cracked smiles at the last statement, as if live rats should come along under these circumstances. It was absurd enough for a pained sense of shared mirth to well up in the place of more melancholy thoughts of their emergency departure that would soon hold a cold finality, should they make it off-planet.

Richard nodded as the smile cooled on their cheeks. "I can get those, yes. And something for each of the others—I won't be long, but if I run into trouble inside, I'll send you a code to unlock your restraints. In that event, you're to get them all to WASA and await the Pinnacle. It's already underway. I've programmed in a departure time."

It was cold inside, or perhaps he was hot from the fever. Both had to be true; if not, then the chill wouldn't feel so heavy and aching, as if it had seeped into his muscles and joints like many hundreds of liquid nitrogen injections, spreading within. His ears felt like a furnace in contrast, and a throbbing pain was beginning at the base of his skull. It reverberated and seemed to spread out with each step he took against the hard tile floors of the WGC corridors. The complex had so many wings that it housed the whole of the WGC and its many functionaries, as well as a branch of the Reproductive Council, with a Surrogate breeding and research facility.

It required little focus to find his way back to their wing. Muscle memory filled in for the many currents of thought that swept him away from the task at hand. They were more flashes of imagery and a sea of voices calling out than they were coherent thoughts. Some were memory, vivid as the red and yellows of a polluted sunset, flashing to the forefront of his mind one after another and carrying with them the same emotions that they held on the day they were stored away.

The children's rooms were more like barracks, holding sets of triple level beds with desks built into the surrounding walls with several computer screens each.

Richard found Bram's desk and paused, a light smile playing upon his lips. It was immaculate and organized with precision and care. Small desk-top shelves flanking the central desk held numerous books, clearly antique, with their peeling fabric covers and smashed corners.

Bram wanted his books, but this would be too many. Grasping a large hard-back on microbes, Richard tucked it into the bag on his shoulder and followed it with six others. It was worth transporting the extra weight if it would lessen the impact of this sudden uprooting and make the transition to Mars smoother.

Next, he acquired the thirty-odd rat figurines that hid in plain sight across the top of Aurelia's desk, posed as if scurrying, or standing on hind feet to sniff some invisible morsel dangled from above, or sleeping, curled into a small donut shape. Their poses and coloration were as varied as their living counterparts. He remembered these well. Bram and Gavin had designed the tiny figures with Santana and printed them as a gift three birthdays past. They'd done things for other siblings. Bram he wasn't surprised by, and Santana, but Gavin was charmingly thoughtless up until that moment.

Richard tucked the figures into a large side-pocket of the bag, noting the many cages on Aurelia's desk. It was hard to remember a previous time when Aurelia did not have at least one captive rodent in her cages. They stood empty now, as if awaiting fresh inhabitants that would never come.

Santana's antique circuitry, Gavin's coins, Gelsimium's dried insects and the accompanying poetry. Traveling lightly or not, they would each have something from Earth.

The leather bag grew heavy and unwieldy, the straps digging into the muscle of his shoulder where it hung. One bag was not going to suffice. He stared around the room, noting the disarray left by ninety-nine sick children. Many of them had made some effort to pack a bag when he informed them of the plan to make an exodus to Mars.

Richard dropped the leather bag onto the tile floor and strode from the room, muttering curses as he went. He returned several moments later with a wheeled cart, similar to the medical-cots but without the medical care features. A green light winked on and off on what could be considered the brain of the unit and a bright beam of headlight illuminated the dim room around him.

Blankets and clothing carpeted the cold tile floors in a muted rainbow and broken dish fragments crunched underfoot. Much larger cleaning bots would be needed to clear this away if anyone remained to implement such a task—but there would be no one. *The dead don't clean.*

The screens on walls and desktop were dark and silent, like many eyes staring out at the same scene of disarray that he surveyed. It called to mind images from the history banks of abandoned buildings in coastal cities worldwide, when humanity began moving inland to avoid the rising sea level that was breaking levees and the mega-hurricanes that were becoming a normal occurrence. Or farther back, there were the black and white images of ghost towns in Western America, shattered marbles and broken porcelain dolls strewn inside of wooden shacks, some lying in the streets, chalkboards standing in empty rooms with the final lesson in mathematics and grammar scrawled on their dusty green surfaces.

Richard held in the breath that he took in, refusing to let it escape as a sigh while he collected and loaded up each of the bags the children had ready, adding them to what he collected himself.

This wasn't the original plan for leaving Earth, but it would do. The sense of finality the plague added was almost fortuitous. A crooked smile pulled at his lips as he manually directed the cart to transport the baggage to the railcars waiting just outside.

He stared after the laden thing as it wheeled itself away to its destination, for a moment imagining himself following after and neglecting the final task that awaited further inside. He had a list, a long list, filling the screen of his handheld…and several more, if he scrolled down to see it in its entirety.

A strident ringing sounded from the self-same device and a message appeared there, preprogrammed to appear should his movements still for too long.

Next step awaits your action, Richard. Move your ass!

Cursing under his breath, he strode towards the medical wing. The names had drawn him in, with their many patterns and similarities to people he knew or might have known, and he'd gotten lost there.

The sedatives were still in effect then, and perhaps the levels of psilocybin had risen relative to the other psychoactives—evidenced by the nostalgia and lack of time sense.

There were sounds coming from the wide hall ahead. Doors lined both sides of it, and they shook with repeated impacts. Richard frowned, registering the sounds and trying to reconcile them with what he knew without a shadow of a doubt.

The nearest door rattled again and again. The thumping from the other side had a wet quality to it, like that of a dense, fluid-and-flesh filled object, propelled with increasing force against a surface that wouldn't give.

At least not before the object in question.

Richard approached it, eyes wide, luminous pools of morbid fascination. He reached out, placing a hand against the door. A flurry of blows shook that door, transferring their energy into the long-fingered hand that rested there.

There was no pattern to the assault, not a continuous one as one could expect from a preprogrammed movement like a medical-bot stuck in a command loop behind a blocked door and thump, thump, thumping.

No, this had that unpredictable quality that indicated a firing of synapses along human nerves. The banging on this door ceased and he stared, waiting for something, coming closer to listen so that his face approached the smooth metallic surface.

Rapid footsteps sounded, followed by an even larger impact. He didn't startle, but instead placed an ear against the door, and cocked a brow to listen. There was a shuffling of feet just behind the door and then a rain of fists that continued long enough to elicit heavy breathing but did not.

Richard took a step back and spoke to his handheld.

"Look up Medical Wing patient files." He glanced back at the door for a number. "Patient 1325. Status and name."

There was a pause and a request for access codes before the answers came. "Harper, Jim, age 36, assigned to surrogate breeding program. Heart Rate 416 bpm, Temperature 41 Celsius."

Richard wet his lips, leaning his face closer to the door again. "I'm going to open the door…If you'll step back and—"

The answering scream was gutteral, part scream, part growl and coincided with a heavy, wet sounding collision with the door. Moaning that rose in volume and pitch growing again and taking the shape of words. "Open it! Open it, motherfucker, Opeeeeeennnnn it. Ahhhhhh!!! Open it!"

The next thud was louder, and somehow wetter, as if raw meat, fresh from culture, were being rammed into the door, and spattering blood and interstitial fluids onto the marble tile.

The mental image flashed in his mind and hung there, expanding into a scenario where the door opened. He opened it and a bleeding, ruined face collided with his own instead of the closed door.

Richard squeezed both eyes shut, pressing knuckles against them and shaking his head as if to dislodge the thought. His right hand hovered near the door scan sensors that would open it and let Jim out into the hall with him.

He clenched his right fist, lowering it through force of will. Jim wouldn't be much help in finding survivors or dropping the communications blockade that was back in effect with Diadonna no longer answering texts or comms of any sort. No, he couldn't help, not with a pulse and fever like that, and not while ramming his head like a fresh picked cantaloupe into a sealed door.

He couldn't go on like that for long. He would crash.

Richard's mind offered up images of the children behind such a door, Gavin's high cheekbones shattered and bleeding where it joined his eye socket as he rammed the door, incoherent with illness induced rage.

He pressed his lips into a tight line, turning his gaze to the hall full of doors. This was only the first and there were sounds from most of the others. They should all be dead by now.

The children were not going to get this far gone. They were under more effective treatment and fighting it better on their own than anyone else could. He reminded himself for the hundredth time that they were different, he'd made them different. They would make it.

Still, Gavin's broken face hovered there, blood spilling from behind cracked teeth. Richard's hand shook as he shoved it into one pocket, searching for a vial, a cocktail of medications, sedatives and strong anti-psychotics. He twisted it into the pressure injector from the same pocket, a device that always called to mind a palm-sized mosquito with a wide blunt nose like an elephant, and injected the liquid into his right thigh this time.

The next inbreath was shaky, a sharp susurration that could not be held back with force of will alone. The out breath shook as well. Gavin and thirty-eight of the progeny were not strapped down as far as he knew, protected from themselves, and they might therefore not be fully medicated either.

"Call Gavin. And give stats for the next room over, 1326." He spoke aloud to direct his handheld computer.

The screaming from Jim Harper's door renewed at the sound of Richard's voice. This time the screams were unintelligible, but still punctuated by a pattern of impacts and a sharp cracking sound accompanying each blow.

Richard winced at what was likely the sound of bone breaking. The door would hold, Jim would not.

"Room 1326, WGC Councilwoman Aesa Rothechild. Deceased."

Richard's brows formed a gorge of incredulity around sweat damp eyelids and hazel eyes that gleamed with fever. He placed both hands on Aesa's door and rested his forehead between them. Too many doors bore the sound and vibration of an assault from within, and the hall echoed with a cacophony of raised voices, and shrieks of rage. Aesa's should be silent. She was dead. But there was a scratching there. A scratching that might be coming from the next door over.

The scratching intensified as he drew nearer. It seemed to grate across the inner surface of his skull as he rested his forehead against the cool surface. His voice came out in a hoarse whisper. "Aesa…"

The scratching stopped.

"Aesa?"

He pictured rats on the other side of the door, taking small bites from her pallid extremities, scratching. The whisper from the other side of the door replaced the image with a more vivid one. Aesa's short-cropped black hair framing a heart-shaped face and shrewd, dark eyes that gleamed with sharp amusement at her fellow council members. A smile that flashed small white teeth in approval of his side comments at the expense of the less gifted speakers.

"Aesa?" The voice was her own. It cracked and wavered, with a tone that was both questioning and forlorn. But it was her. He leaned in to the eye scanner and allowed it to process his retinal signature.

She would be standing there, ill, very ill but somehow well enough to make it through and board the ship. It stood to reason that some would survive this. Nothing has a hundred percent kill rate.

Her head thumped against the door, nails scraping. The voice came through again, tone unchanged. "Aesa?"

It was an empty sound, like an echo.

"I'm getting you out." It was meant as a comfort, reassurance, but his tone dropped into uncertainty as the picture began to form in his mind's eye. *Why just the name? She's said nothing else.*

The door slid open and she was there as he pictured her, short-cropped black hair framing her face, slight frame wobbling from the illness, ankles turned in as she came forward.

Richard took a step back, clearing his throat. Beads of sweat broke out on his temple and the back of his neck. Her eyes searched the space between them, eyelids bruised and skin mottled. Blood, still wet from an absence of clotting factors, ran from the corners of those eyes and seemed to seep from her pores blackening the skin of her cheeks and nose. The fingers that reached out to him were swollen and gangrenous. "Aesa?" The echo emerged from between her bleeding lips, hollow like the dark eyes that held none of her signature spark.

She fell forward against him, claw-like hands scrambling for purchase on his clothes, bare thighs wrapping around his and pressing her naked hips against him.

The urge to recoil warred with curiosity and he stood still amidst the internal tug of war, reaching up to grab the discolored face that was once colleague, once lover.

He forced the face closer, squeezing, pressing fingers into the marred flesh as he drew her face mere inches from his own and shook it. "Aesa?! Are you there?"

He stared into the glassy eyes, searching. They moved, shifting side to side in a dance of misfiring nerve impulses, but without direction, a ghost train with no conductor, no spark of intellect remaining.

Her mouth opened and closed, pressing forward, reaching for his own, just as her hands quested over his chest and downward, searching for openings in the garments with clumsy, fumbling gestures. Her hips thrust against him in coarse undulation, her unclothed pubic hair making a rasping sound against his pants.

"Aesa?! … you there?" Her speech wasn't the same forlorn tone as before, but instead a high-pitched screech that was nearly a mirror of his last desperate question.

Richard let out a shuddering breath, flexing the muscles of his arms and simultaneously allowing her closer, closing the small gap between her upper body and his, lowering his hands from the sides of her face where his fingers had left indents in the engorged tissues, to the sides of her ribcage. Reaching down, he gathered up her squirming, seeking hands and pinned them to her chest, crossing them there. She didn't struggle now that she was pressed against him, still moving in awkward, desperate mimicry of rutting.

Richard cleared his throat and spoke in a whisper. "Emergency security override for room 1326, code yqweip267109rg. Open on 3-2-1…" With all of the force he could muster from curled and flexed forearms, like a snake coiling before a strike, he shoved her forward as the door opened. Her right shoulder caught but she fell through, tumbling on the tile and leaving smears of dark blood on the patchy grey marble.

"And close on 3-2-1." The second command was faster than required. Aesa was still down, coordinating her limbs to push up from the floor. The screech was just an echo. "Aesa?!…you there?" But she sounded angrier than was possible.

The door slid shut before she could rise, and he could hear

her fists beat against it, nails scraping despite the futility.

The blood on his hands wiped easily onto his lab coat, already smeared in the same red-brown fluids. Glancing down the hall, he unbuttoned the coat and shrugged his broad shoulders out of the inflexible, soiled garment.

With one more glance at Aesa's door, he turned and strode down the hall past the many rooms, most occupants contributors to the din.

There was a bounce to his walk as he passed the remaining rooms without hesitation as if a weight had been lifted from his back. It didn't make sense, but he didn't need it to. There were no survivors in here.

The main control room was just ahead. Theresa would need to know this, and he would follow through, send out an invitation to Mars for the colonist's families. If they were dead or nearly so, they wouldn't hear it. If they were alive, they were unlikely to make it on time. He would send it, but Earth would keep her dead.

A CRY FOR HELP

A low growl could be heard escaping from between Gelsemium's clenched teeth. Her head was tipped back, a fistful of hair caught in Gavin's fist. His other hand held both of her wrists behind her back. They were slick with sweat and baking hot with fever, slipping as she wrenched her shoulders, struggling against his restraining grip.

"Geli, stop! You'll hurt yourself!" His eyes gleamed with panic and fever-madness as they searched the room for help. Fighting had broken out in more places than one. He could tell by the sounds of struggle and words spit out from constricted throats sounding more like the noises of too many starved animals in too small a space. If he wasn't quick they would draw blood, and more; they would damage their chances of survival.

One hand slipped, and the struggling girl lashed out, sharp nails finding purchase in the side of his neck. Gavin yelled, five points of fire erupted where she gouged, drawing blood as he predicted.

His own growl was deeper, white teeth with sharp pointed canines threatening as he leaned in closer to her face. The heat in his mind shifted past red to the white hot of starlight and it burned, igniting the shreds of reason he held on to just moments before.

If he shoved her to the ground in this position her neck would break on impact, especially if he followed her down. He could hear the echo of it, feel the snapping, see the stillness cloud her eyes.

She was still struggling, screaming for him to let go, and something about Richard. The words were hard to catch, either from her hoarse screeching or his state of distraction. Another scenario unfolded, one where he didn't let go but instead pulled her into him with the same violence. The fever intensified, his blood coursed and pounded molten in his veins, fogging his mind and distracting from her screams.

Gelsemium was crying now, the growls giving way to frantic weeping that shook her and wet his wrists with this sudden rain of tears. She was still speaking, and it dug into his ears like her nails had into his skin.

"I said stop! Stop it." His voice was a roar, overtopping the chaotic din of the room.

"Call Richard! Call—call him—call Richard." He dropped her. Not with violence or added force, but instead releasing her neck, then hands, before letting her fall to the cold tile.

She shivered and scrambled into the nearest corner, still repeating the same words. The rage that drove Gavin, that worked him like a marionette play-acting Dante's Inferno, subsided, faded into something thinner and colder, something heavily laced with fear. *To build may have to be the slow and laborious task of years. To destroy can be the thoughtless act of a single day.* The quote felt like a sharp reminder spoken in his hero's voice, and it replaced fury with burning shame. He stared around the room to see how much blood was spilled, taking in the whole of it in one scan. His heart raced faster as he did so, thrumming in a painful way at the back of his neck and radiating throughout the whole of his skull.

Tania had ahold of someone gone limp, Justinian. It was Justinian, no longer fighting back, no longer conscious. His right eye was bleeding, hanging loose as if plucked free by some scavenging vulture come for them now that they were succumbing to the illness. Others were injured, bleeding, some unconscious; Casper ran into the glass wall separating them from the outside elements for what must have been the tenth time, if the sound of it was the same he had been hearing all along without registering the source. The glass cracked, but held.

Gavin jumped into action, motions frantic and aided by desperation. There were medicots available for their continued treatment, restraints, but how many could he wrestle them into them before his strength gave out—*or mental faculties?* Geli bleeding on the floor beneath him flashed into his mind and he flinched, pushing the imagery back with some success. Still, the thoughts squirmed free and recurred at the forefront of his mind again and again, like stubborn goats being herded by an unskilled hand.

Tania first, then Justinian and Casper, that eye would need work…If you're going through hell, keep going.

Gavin activated the nearest medicot and came from behind, bear hugging Tania onto the cot, she was snapping and biting at the air, clawing at Gavin's arms, thankfully weakened by illness and half the larger boy's size.

Gelsemium would usually be helping. Guilt flooded him at the thought. She was still in the corner, mumbling. *Call Richard…*

He *would* call Richard, after they were all restrained—including himself, but only for new treatment protocols, because this wasn't working.

A rush of wind receded and then gusted forth in time with a slow heartbeat rhythm. It was a fitful, shaky sound that seemed to have many echoes, creating the effect of a call and answer. Aurelia could feel it hot against her cheek, as if a window had been left open allowing the dry gusts in to bake her in her sleep.

What sort of wind had an echo? Several of them, for that matter…and was this—it was summer, wasn't it?

Her mind fought for greater awareness, surfacing from deep submersion in the sensory deprivation tank of fevered sleep. The hot wind against her cheek was stale and humid; it smelled of old wounds left untended and blood clotted and dried under soiled bandages. *What wind had an echo?* The question recurred in her mind on repeat. And there was the same wailing howl that she had heard so many times before: a barking cough, whispered laughter, weeping.

It was breath, not wind. Her eyes opened, painful and raw, lashes gummed together and sticking to red-rimmed lids as she blinked, trying to clear the blurry field of vision. Bram was there next to her, only a foot away, hot, fetid breath of the acutely ill aimed at her face…and to his left, Santana; beyond that, Caspian. The medicots lined the sides of the magnetic railcar, stacked in columns of four to conserve space. And there was the wind's echo, the many labored in and out breaths of sixty youths, her siblings, all ill, strapped down, and sleeping, sedated, or delirious. Several pairs of eyes stared across the aisles and out the windows, stared unseeing as their gusts of breath rattled on without their awareness.

Aurelia went to lift a hand, to scratch the itch that was growing above her right eye, and to push aside the sticky tendrils of dirty-blond hair that matted there. *Dirty in the literal sense…*Memory seemed hidden in a thick bank of fog. She couldn't recall a bath or shower beyond cool rags against fever-hot forehead—not since the decontamination showers that were some indeterminate time ago. The fog had that as well, the passage of time, and nearly everything that occurred within it.

Her hand hadn't moved and the itch was painful now, irritating as only an itch can be once noticed but left unscratched. She tried to sit up, to see the hands that were not answering her commands, but could not. Something held her down. She stared over at Bram, tied down by the medicots's many secure harnesses.

She must be strapped as well. She strained against them, feeling no give as reward to her weak attempts, and then fell back the fraction of an inch she had managed to lift her body and limbs. Scorching tears welled up in her eyes, stinging with too much salt, and she squeezed them tight, blinking several times and drawing in desperate breath.

The breath came with ease despite her throat clenched with distress and the storm of tears, and she pulled in another, trying to turn her head left, away from Bram's CO2-laden, stale exhalations to reach the cooler air above her. Her head lifted as little as the rest of her, held near-stationary by a neck brace and she fought to control the rising panic.

She was alone, trapped, conscious and breathing clear again, the pain, tightness, and congestion having faded with the fog—but she was alone.

"Bram?! Hey! Bram, wake up please!"

The panic was there in her voice as she called out. He should have heard, would have heard if he could. Bram's breath hitched, held, ceased, no longer fighting against the swollen blockages for what felt like too long.

"Bram!?" His face was distorted by swelling, the lymph nodes on either side of his jaw large and blackened by the infection that raged on inside them.

Aurelia's eyes squeezed shut and she pulled in a long breath, the panic raced through her. A flash of memory took up the forefront of her panicked thoughts. She and Bram on Mars filled her mind's eye with more clarity than the room she had been in before closing her eyes. They were arguing. He screamed something, inches from her face, and she could feel the spit from his words impact her cheeks; his eyes were too wide, bloodshot with rage, and they were there in front of her. She could see his hands curling into claws, ready to grasp and hurt. Her blood would be there in a moment if she didn't move. Aurelia lashed out, hands forming the same gnarled claws as Bram's had as they impacted his face, digging into wide open eyes that shifted from rage, to alarm, to pain as the blood flowed.

An alarm sounded from within Medibot 26, the one attached to Bram's cot, and the robotic physician came to life.

Aurelia opened her eyes, staring around her and finding Bram, skin dusky from lack of breath, but eyes closed and unharmed. She was strapped down. They both were, and this was still Earth, not Mars. Her own medical-bot had come to life as well, a steady beep-beep-beep coming from its speakers as it injected something into the large muscle of her left arm. The spot ached and would for some time, a bruise forming where enough pressure was applied to force some medicine into the tissue there some unknown number of times now.

Bram's medibot raised the head of his cot and sealed a mask around his lips, endotracheal tube extending down into the swollen airways and forcing oxygen into his lungs.

Aurelia watched out of the corners of wet, panic-widened eyes, breath withheld as his was.

The tube changed function from breath to suction, and a wet struggling sound came from the device as thick, clotted, red-tinged mucus slid through the tubing and was cleared to make way for oxygen.

Bram's eyes flew open and he gagged against the tubes, throat contracting and then stilling as his eyes closed again and breathing, heavy and labored, but independent, resumed. The tubing retracted back into the mask, but the hiss of oxygen continued.

Aurelia let out her withheld breath. Bram was fine. Very sick, but fine. She swiveled her eyes to the very edges of her field of vision in all directions, searching.

"Medibot, where is Richard?"

Her voice cracked, dry and weak from sickness and lack of use. She cleared her throat before trying again when no response came. "Medibot 26, what are your current medical commands and protocols?"

The bot turned at the neck joint, spinning its uppermost sensor face and secondary processing unit to face her.

"You do not have authorization for medibot commands until time runs out."

Aurelia's heartrate made an uptick, and a sick feeling accompanied the rush of adrenaline as her cheeks flushed with heat. "When does time run out?"

"Time runs out in 36 minutes, when the trains will depart, or else when Richard's heart monitor indicates a pulse of either zero beats per minute or above three-hundred."

Aurelia stared at the ceiling, allowing the sounds of echoing desert wind, the labored breathing of her siblings to wash over her and overwhelm her thoughts. Someone was crying again, deep, choking sobs that devolved into coughing. There was a time limit that could come before he returned, and some risk of death, if he set a secondary trigger for their departure to his vital signs. There was wind outside of the train as well. She couldn't hear it through the thick, insulated walls of the train car, but she could feel the force of it, the slight swaying as it pushed at them. Her eyes searched the darkness as she waited for him, blurring out and stinging as long moments passed without her noticing the need to blink.

The wall of screens dominated the central intelligence control room in the WGC complex. The largest glowed with diagrams, and supplementary 3D representations of the same data were projected directly in front of Richard, at arm's reach, for his perusal and manipulation. He sifted through the list with one hand, the other pinching the back of his neck where skull met cervical vertebrae, providing counter pressure to the throbbing pain that seemed to increase along with an irritating stiffness in the muscles of his neck and shoulders. He flexed his jaw against the same stiffness and pain that spread into his face. The lymph nodes were receding now, a good sign…unless it was changing again.

He navigated through the virtual halls, represented by a glowing green framework. There was 1636 where Aesa scratched at her door. Jim's heart rate next room over had finally fallen below functioning levels, but motion sensors indicated he still threw himself against the door, like the many others like him in the medical wing.

Each virtual room had an overlayed display of vital signs and other sensor readings. It would do to sift through this way and read each manually.

"Set thresholds for living vs moving. Pulse rates between 40 and 200…no…not to exceed…400. Body temperature thresholds…" Each parameter further decreased the number of rooms visible, as the ones with inhabitants deemed moving but not living, winked out from view. Morton Steiner's room dimmed and winked out as the virtual tour passed it. Sixteen rooms remained after all parameters were entered.

Sixteen of seven hundred. The chill of finality that ratio elicited settled in. Less than two percent survival rates and the last sixteen were sick too. If they brought it to Mars without a cure, even onto the ship, it could end them. Even with himself and the Progeny—if they recovered—population numbers could go too low, especially if their survival rates were not enough higher when all was said and done.

The sides of Richard's throat stuck together, forcing a dry cough out into the silent room. And how long would they be contagious?

He searched the walls of the room for a drink dispensing unit as the cough receded. His lips were dry and cracking, with the sharp iron imbued tang of blood when he licked them. They were peeling, unnoticed until just this moment. The cough returned as he strode to the machine and selected water, collecting the glass and chilled liquid before pacing back to the display.

Sixteen remaining. They were ill, clearly, adjustments in treatment to match and even improve upon what he and the children were receiving might improve their chances, but enough to bring them along to Mars…perhaps not. They were, none of them, on the list of kin requested by the Martian colonists.

"Record and implement new treatment protocols for patients remaining by medibot. New protocols to follow by file transfer. Sending."

"New protocols received, implementation in progress." Richard stared hard at the screen, and the list of names. Diadonna was not on the list and was therefore not living or not here. He frowned at the sixteen names, none of them individuals that he knew, and put in a request for Diadonna's location and status within the council walls.

"Not found."

His frown deepened. Perhaps she had quarantined herself elsewhere, or used one of Earth's smaller ships to jump planet after all.

"Call Diadonna."

If she was off-planet, the call would be blocked. The call failed or was dismissed.

Fine… Richard typed in a message. His voice was still hoarse from coughing and didn't need the work of giving dictation and verbal commands for this search. Better the call didn't go through.

"Diadonna, you may have realized by now that isolating ourselves and waiting this out is proving quite fatal to the human race. But before I go on—I said I would check back in. Are you worsening or on the mend? Did you somehow avoid this thing altogether?"

The reply was slow in coming, so much so that he sat down in the chair in front of the holograph table. **"I'm sick. Treatments** are not helping. Do you have a cure yet?”**

Richard sighed, the gust of breath overheated and stale with illness and reluctant acceptance. He scratched the back of his neck as he nodded at the incoming information. Of course she was sick. At least that cleared her of any possible involvement in the spread of the thing. *“No. I have improved treatment protocols and some theories. If you are in advanced stages of the illness this won't help enough. I'll send you what we're using all the same. It won't help for you. The children, on the other hand, have a chance.”*

He could feel the pause, the hesitation from her end. It was likely the time same dilation that he had been experiencing, every action and meandering of thought taking twice as long as he realized.

“You have your access codes. Collect and treat them.”

Richard's brows pulled together, closing the gap in between them in favor of a proximity fueled by anger and tension.

“Yes, I have access codes to navigate the facilities and to get out and get the children. That's not what I need. I need communication with Mars. And you've closed off communications again.”

The reply was near immediate and came like a slap. **“No.”**

“Damn you! They have researchers on this who are not compromised. It's foolhardy to not avail ourselves of this resource. Please, they need our most recent data. They need to know what's happening with the terminal patients. And I need to know if they have a better treatment protocol yet.”

Richard paced as he typed the message in, cursing when his fingers fumbled at the antiquated method of message transport.

“Begging doesn't become you, Richard. Too much risk. If Mars goes down too, that's it for us. You think I don't know you'll bring them here?”

The growl that emerged from his raw throat came out in a stream of guttural murmurings and curses that culminated in a roar. His hands shook above the screen. He made a grating sound of disgust.

“Message Diadonna: *You are delusional. I would never risk Mars as well. That would be poor judgment indeed. I promise you, there will be no contact with Earth until the cure is in effect. Do you understand that? I just need their research because I…I'm too compromised—Send."*

Richard closed his eyes, squeezing them shut against the painful throbbing at the back of his skull. The stiffness was increasing, and a disorienting euphoria competed with the building fire in his mind. It was hot and growing hotter and filled his vision with flashes of what his hands could do were Diadonna in arms reach. Where he would place them, fingers curling into claws that would bite into flesh and pull her close enough for teeth to do the harder work of rending flesh from bone, allowing fever-hot blood to escape through his handiwork.

Richard stumbled, shaking his head against the imagery that was so vivid, so imperative. He could almost feel the softness of her skin and how it would give way, the popping and cracking of bone if he pressed long enough and hard enough.

He opened his eyes, unfocused as he fought to register the room he was in instead of that which hovered in his mind, pushing out room for rational thought.

"I think you are desperate. I know it. I hear it in your voice. Desperate men do stupid, stupid things. But I'm going to let you get through to them. After I send my own message. Agreed?"

The sounds of her struggling, ragged breath, the blood-filled gurgling, the styrofoam feel of a crushed windpipe under his fingers persisted in his altered reality and he fought for words, for coherence.

"Okay, yes—thank —thank you." His voice wavered as he spoke, sounding mechanical and devoid of emotion.

He needed to be strapped down with the children, needed a few more minutes of clarity to put in a call in once the comms came back on. Blinking back another rush of red-hued mental imagery, Richard pressed his hands against both sides of his head and squeezed. His fingers pressed against his scalp and furrowed temples as if he could rub and squeeze away the chaos inside.

The idea that hovered somewhere between the coiling snake of building anger and the vat of seething lust remained cloaked in a fog, wrapped in insulation that kept him from getting close enough to examine it. It hovered closer to his vision, then faded back into shadow.

He squeezed tighter, his fingers digging in, nails leaving bloody half-moons in his skin. It was a simple thing, not something he should have to fight for. *Medicate, record the message and send, restrain self.* There it was. He fought to hold onto the four steps and keep them from slipping away and dissolving into the molten pool of raw emotion and swirling confusion that was his internal landscape.

Richard pulled out another pressure-syringe of medication and shoved it into against his left shoulder with greater force than required. His lips turned down in a grimace, not of pain but disgust. It was nothing more than a band aid for this thing that had a hold of his mind, and it would slow his thinking further, incapacitate him.

There was time. Crossing the room with long urgent strides, he leaned in for a scan and gave the proper security code for the storage unit.

The medibot and automated transport cot inside quickly synced to his medical records with just a scan. He climbed onto it and rolled onto his side, letting out a shaky breath.

"Deploy restraints and transport patient to—" His eyes closed, as he spoke. "—to train 35762 at the docking station. Once restraints are in place, connect with patient's diagnostic nanobots. Direct to assess cerebrospinal fluid for meningitis, screen for viral, bacterial, and fungal. Treat as needed." Aesa's empty, hollow eyes and reaching, pawing hands hovered in his mind's eye. There was an answer there. He could feel it every time he remembered the hallway and the still moving human shells there, like finding a long-searched-for piece of a puzzle that will fit somewhere—somewhere forgotten.

There were 16 still alive in those rooms, now receiving the same treatment as the children, but already falling into fits of rage and hallucination, attacking the doors or themselves unless they'd been strapped down before they lost control. This was an opportunity that should not be missed. There was something here other than what the antibiotics could treat. Richard stared at the sixteen names displayed and pressed his lips together into a tight line and then wet them to speak.

"Additional treatment protocols for remaining patients. Note and implement. Add maximum dose of broad range anti-fungal, antiviral, and next choice antibiotic. Stagger implementation by six hours to record changes."

"Implementing."

Richard dropped his head back onto the firm surface of the cot. His handheld rested next to him, glowing faintly in the dim of the room as dusk showed itself through the large skylight, the sun having dropped below the horizon long since, leaving only a purple stain in its wake.

"Record audio and video and set to send every fifteen minutes to Theresa Marin, Pinnacle Command, and Mars proper."

He cleared his throat, still aching and raw from the coughing that seemed to have tapered off and stayed gone despite the emergence of other symptoms. Either the message would get through now or it would not. He could resume research once the sedatives wore off and he was aboard the train bound for WASA.

A soft beeping came from the Medical-cot and it jostled him. The rocking smoothed out as it completed the turn and settled into a steady roll down the empty echo filled halls where he would hear them again, Aesa, Jim, Morton, Greg, so many others. Diadonna would be counted among them soon enough, wherever she was. The rocking soothed him, but he forced his eyes open again and held up his handheld to record the message before the sedative could come on full force.

ASPERSIONS CAST AND DOUBTS RAISED

She sent it again. The message was set for auto resend, but somehow the time in between attempts felt too long now.

It had to go through as soon as the lines of communication were open again. They needed to know, or they might treat without this bit of essential knowledge. It had to be done just right.

Theresa gripped the handholds with hands and feet, lest she float off out of control. Zero-G was much kinder to her than it was the last time she was aboard the Pinnacle, for good reason. An RPU pregnancy was hard enough in a gravity environment without the complications of zero-G. Theresa sighed, a short exhalation that released only a fraction of the tension she held. There were other messages to check, treatment simulations to run. The first few had all patients dying from side effects of treatment. Not a desirable outcome.

The messages were all from Mars, now a distant speck on the rear-viewing screens. She opened the most recent video message from Carla.

"Hello, hello…this will be short and sweet as a cherry season in a hot summer. You've more pressing places to put your attention. I've been checking in on Abby as per your request. Not a word from her, to myself or anyone else here. But you must have expected that. You and Genesis both gone, that's quite a strain. But she is eating and drinking still, and studying when she isn't in the water. I wouldn't worry; just get the others and get yourself back here. Cheers!"

Theresa released her withheld breath. It shook and stuttered past her lips that were turned down in a scowl. *Needn't worry...But I will, won't I? I don't have time for it, though.*

And she *was* worried for Abby, and for a much larger cause. Her gut twisted in unease and her frown deepened. They would all have so much to adjust to—if they made it back. Ninety-nine children, old enough to be held to some standard of behavior but atypical enough to raise brows, just as Abby did with her silent stares and uncommonly discerning nature.

Theresa pushed a hand over her tightly smoothed bun before she could remind herself that the loose hairs would not be tamed without the aid of gravity. Her laugh surprised her in the silent room and she glanced around, embarrassed. She was indeed alone for the time being.

The crease between her eyebrows deepened into a sharp crevice of dismay. She stared at the screen of her handheld, imagining Abby as she was the day they departed, silent, set off from the group, arms crossed and plucking at the fabric of a soft brown tunic. Her eyes were distant, almost blank, and were unreadable to most. To Theresa the pain and worry there was obvious, even if submerged under several layers of protection.

She could send a message to reassure her, see if she would break her silence, task her with something that would lessen her isolation, perhaps with David. She grasped a handhold to the left, pivoting to change direction and grab hold of the next until she found herself at the door of the lab room. Dr. Alexander was waiting, still studying what they'd found.

The hall was empty, unsurprising for such a large ship with so few on board—*for now*—making it easy to navigate the hand and footholds quickly. There wasn't time to waste playing in the halls;

each minute wasted could mean permanent damage to Bram, Gelsemium, Aurelia, Santana…any of them.

A sharp repeating ring sounded over the speaker system and Theresa covered her ears. It was followed by Captain Neil's deep voice, less cheerful than his usual but still effective.

"We have a message from Earth, and I'd like us to go ahead and watch it together. Command chamber ASAP please. We're getting closer and it could be important. It's from the head of the WGC."

Diadonna's voice poured through the speakers with a virtual construct to accompany it on the large screen of the command room. It was similar to those conjured through mental image in a VR Comm, except that this was created in advance and saved to give visual to voice message with near perfect lip-syncing.

It was the perfection that gave it away, the lack of subtle tics and nuanced expression, the near-absence of the lines and creases that would appear during speech on any human. Diadonna's pasted-on smile seemed natural enough, as did the slight crease above her brows giving an air of concern. Not a strand of her wavy onyx hair, the same color as her eyes, was out of place as she spoke with hands folded in her lap.

Theresa stared at the image, unblinking, as if the intensity of her focus could force the message to skip the niceties and move on to the meat of the communication. There was a pause before the voice started up again, signaling change of topic.

"The matter that I have broken the communications ban for is of utmost urgency, and I urge you to take my words as seriously as you would those of your Martian Council Leader."

The construct shifted positions, standing and giving a more

commanding air to the speaker.

Theresa fought the urge to groan at the continued waste of moments, seconds, needed fragments of time slipping out of her grasp as she listened to non-essential pleasantries and prefaces. She pulled out her handheld, opened the files on the fungus she had found imbedded in the spinal fluid from Aurelia's nanobot data, and read the further entries Dr. Alexander made before they were called in to this. It wasn't Massospora proper, but a derivative, a modern relative adapted to survive, hide, and thrive in mammalian species with the help of Yersinia Pestis, plague bacillus.

She tapped the screen, opening up the file holding biological remnants from blood samples, categorized by probable source. Here the psychoactives were listed: cathionone, amphetamines, psilocybin, all manufactured and released by this fungus.

Diadonna began again, the concerned tone of her voice shifting to something more strained, urgent.

"I am lifting the communications ban because I am aware of your approach, and feel it only fair, considering our recent past history, to warn you. Mars's and Earth's priorities have aligned in a way that none of us could foresee until it had already begun. Survival of the human race and, more specifically, survival of the Mars colony, is crucial if we are to avoid winking out like a distant star, long since self-destructed."

She cleared her throat, and muffled coughing, a struggle to stop and catch a breath could be heard in the background.

"Please, hear me out. While we had only just begun to reopen the lines of communication between Earth and Mars, I assure you that what I say to you now is with our common goals—the survival of the human race in mind.

"First, a bit of history, as I had promised. I'd have rather relayed this to you myself without the use of an avatar, but illness necessitates this route. The program is splicing together multiple attempts to get this message across.

"To begin, it was not a well-supported decision to attack

Mars, but the short-sighted, impulsive act of one man who'd taken on the role of leadership and held it long after he'd lost our favor. His attack on your colony was his last act on the Council.

"The falsified research was a bit harder for me to sort out and find the source. It seems that it was set in motion during earlier stages of the colonization project, when support and resources for the project were still in question. False data bridged the gap, and record of it was erased, aside from word of mouth and memories I was able to track down. Names and dates are in the data banks you now have access to as the largest surviving enclave of humanity. I don't have the clarity to recall them anymore."

There was a long pause, a stumbling start that trailed into silence, and then she began again, speech slow and methodical.

"Now to the heart of my message. After this goes through, you'll have contact with Dr. Richard Brant. I know him as a friend, advisor to the WGC, and previous Council Member, Head of Reproductive Research at the Reproductive Council. I say this not to discredit Richard, but to ensure that his greater good does not supplant your own. His primary concern is for the Progeny from Phase 4, whereas my concern is for humanity in all forms it takes."

Theresa's eyes widened as she followed the list of credentials. *Head of Reproductive Research in the RC, WGC Council Member, advisor?*

A well of sickness pooled in her belly like viscous tar, waiting to swallow up what she knew of the man firsthand. *What do I know firsthand? What he told me…two meetings in person on Earth, years of long-distance VR Comm, dream talk…*

Theresa's fists balled up around the bottom edge of her lab coat, nails digging into the stiff fabric. She glared around the room at the others there: the Captain, Genesis, Dr. Alexander, their assistants, and cleared her throat in an attempt to allow the words that seemed stuck there to pass through with confidence. It came out just above a whisper, and sour as the churning pit in her stomach.

"She is on her deathbed with delirium, bear in mind…" Genesis examined her nail beds, a faint smile on her full lips, eyes unreadable. Captain Neil hazarded a noncommittal glance in Theresa's direction, nodding if only to appease the sharp tone her words carried.

"Of course, yes, we'll—bear that in mind." His gaze turned back to the avatar, his focus on Diadonna's words. His own came out in slow staccato, tapering off as if they no longer needed his direction to hit their mark. Diadonna's voice took on a strained quality, as if choked with emotion…or oncoming death. They were strident and ringing with warning.

"If you allow them on board without ensuring they are cured, not contagious, and…and that you have a cure for this should it hit the weakest among you, then you will succumb, and they will recover… You will clear the path—and they—will have Mars."

The message cut off. She was mumbling something still, something incoherent. *Not that her* words *were particularly coherent.*

Theresa fought back the cognitive dissonance Diadonna's words brought, shoving single statements and phrases into separate compartments for later examination until what remained was the core problem left to solve. They were all ill, and the success or lack thereof of her treatment plans would need to be tried and proven successful before they could come on board. Were they even at WASA yet? Were there were treatment facilities that she could reach quickly by way of the elevator if it became necessary—regardless of contamination? That's what open communication lines would tell her now.

"Theresa?" Captain Neil rubbed the knuckles of his left hand across his lips, the other hand and both feet anchoring him to a handhold. His hair, longer than when they were last in zero-g, drifted around him as if under water. "How well do you know Richard Brant? I'd like a better handle on this before I bring him on this ship and back to Mars."

The caution in his eyes irritated her, sparks of pale brown

worry flickering in their depths, and she let out a huff of breath before letting out a measured reply.

"I've known him for nearing twelve years. I know him well enough to state that the children are his priority, but if he was so morally defunct as to disregard everyone else on Mars, why would he have cared to take on the protection and raising of my progeny in the first place? He had no reason, other than being assigned to terminate the project. No reason."

The words didn't ring true in her own head. Pieces of the puzzle shoved to the side whispered their contributions, forcing together connections that she wasn't ready to make...*Head of Reproductive Research, WGC Council member and advisor...*

She licked her lips, shoving harder at the thoughts that held no bearing on getting everyone back to Mars where things could be sorted out.

Neil was nodding, Genesis silent still, until he turned to her with a hand gesture for attention. "And you have information on him, yes? Experience with him?"

Genesis glanced his way, eyes wide as if surprised by the question before she turned to include Theresa in her answer. The pause then was tangible, a pause during which her eyes spoke in her stead. Theresa's insides flipped again, intensifying the unbalanced space-sick pit of tar that had already opened up there.

"I do, yes. And I think we need to focus on getting Theresa's children and their caretaker well and on board." She disengaged from Theresa's pointed stare and turned a more casual look to the Captain. "Richard Brant is an asset: brilliant, experienced, accomplished, and devoted. There are few things that would make me advise against bringing him aboard. Our future survival could very well depend on him. But back to point—now he and Theresa's progeny are depending on us."

Theresa smiled, her relief palpable in the expression despite the tremble to her lips. *What did she say that refuted Diadonna's words…? Doesn't matter. Neil looks mollified.*

The pre-scheduled messages began to come in. Some messages and updates from Mars, many more batches of test data and research conducted by Richard and the medibots on Earth. There were 756 updates in all from the full course of communications black-out.

Theresa shuddered in excitement, tugging at the edges of her lab coat and smoothing loose hair that would continue to drift in the zero-g environment, a crown of fine seaweed streamers around her tightly braided hair that was wrapped in a crown around her scalp.

She grasped one handhold after another, pulling herself into position in front of the main holographic display panel and screen. "Sort by time sent. Display most recent tests run, treatment protocols and live footage, side by side, simultaneous. Two point five times real time speed." Dr. Alexander came up next to her, grasping the nearest hand holds and watching the screen.

"Time to see if your theories play out…"

Theresa grinned in his direction, focused exuberance taking the place of any uncertainty that Diadonna's words had instilled.

THE OTHER SIDE OF HELL

Call Richard…Call Richard…

Gelsemium's chant replayed in Gavin's head like song lyrics on loop. But the calls did not go through; there was no answer from Richard or the others.

The room was silent now and mostly still, thanks to the strong sedatives he'd ordered for them all. But what good would it do without further treatment? Without a cure for these rages, the flashes of anger and violence, hallucinations…

Gavin cringed into himself, squeezed his eyes shut to force away the mental images that came when he followed that train of thought. Gelsemium was close, still in the corner, but wouldn't look at him; instead, she stared at the ceiling, lost in the spin of fan blades that sent a cooling breeze onto their fevered skin, leaving behind a chill. She trembled; whether it was an effect of their altercation and the adrenaline overdose it elicited or the fever would be hard to say.

Gavin pushed off from the floor, forcing himself to stand despite the throbbing inside his skull and the disorientation it brought with it.

"There are still more…come on."

He leaned closer to Tessera, Blain, and Roan when no answer

came. The same fan blades had their attention.

"Come with me to get them back or it's your turn now… they'll hurt themselves out there—but get Geli first."

Tessera turned her stare in his direction, a scowl pulling at her features. "She's just sitting there. She'll probably stay."

He cleared his throat. "I'd think you an idiot if I didn't know otherwise. She's fine this moment. Would you like to predict for how long?!" The seething irritation that welled up was clear in his tone, a barely restrained violence that motivated action.

Tessera was up first, and then Blain and Roan, walking effigies of victims of the black death —but still walking despite the swollen sores, some broken open and weeping fluids into their clothes like red and brown watercolors spilled by a careless hand.

"Gelsemium?" Tessera's voice was gentle, coming out a hoarse whisper. "Come get in bed." She didn't answer. Her eyes were wide and bloodshot, pale against her skin and frame of dark tangles, her breath coming in a shallow pant.

"I'm gonna help you then, okay?" She reached out, one hand extended towards Gelsemium's wrist. There was no resistance as she grasped it, wrapping fingers around and bringing her other arm to wrap behind Geli's back and fold around her ribcage in front.

The medicot was close, the target mere feet away, when the screaming started. There were no more words, or pleas to call for Richard, just a keening screech that sent each of them reaching for their heads to cover their faces and block it out. Tessera faltered, near dropping her sister as she clawed at her ears with one hand. "Geli, stop! Agh! Stop it, stop it!" Her hand came down on Gelsemium's face, slapping first with stinging force that left red handprints, and then shoving down against the dried chapped lips and nose from which the sound came forth, muffling it.

The restrained girl struggled and bucked against Tessera, knocking her to the floor beneath her flailing form.

The burst of angry frustration that came from the space next to the medicot came out in a roar.

Gavin moved at lightning speed, grasping Gelsemium from Tessera and removing her hands by force. The next motion had her on the cot, arms held down for the restraints to set and lock in place. Her legs still kicked, one breaking free and striking him in the forehead before the task was done and he had all restraints in place.

His consciousness wavered, vision fading into a grey cloud of gnats and forcing him to put out both hands and lean forward over Gelsimmium before he fell into a full faint. Sweat dripped into his eyes and pattered onto the sheet of the cot. The air he pulled in in great gulps felt hot, intensifying the nausea that was building in his gut.

She was still struggling against the restraints, a low growl coming from her throat as she fought, and there were others still loose. Gavin surveyed the room. There were six left, nine if you counted the ones helping him. *Too many for me like this…I should leave them.*

Clark was pacing and muttering to himself; Aidan was trying to break a window with a large cast iron plant stand, making some progress judging by the fine spray of cracks that blossomed in the glass surrounding the main point of impact.

The scene played out in his mind: Tessera, Bain, and Roan confronting the six left, the six most likely to be trouble based on their stage of illness, body size, and personality type, and therefore saved for last. The images were vivid, near life-like: the blood that flowed as the heavy metal plant stand impacted Tessera's lower jaw, explosive and hot where it splashed the walls, covering Aidan, some of it reaching Gavin where he stood by, watching and waiting for it to finish, for the ones he couldn't pin down to expend themselves or take each other out.

The stand flew from Aidan's hands, hitting the glass another time. The cracks extended further this time, the inner layer of glass crushing and falling to the floor below it like shaved ice from a frozen cliff-face.

Gavin jumped to his feet, vertigo blacking his vision and causing a stumble. He pushed through, grasping the rails on the nearest medicots and propelling himself towards Aidan, who was now unarmed and off balance but preparing to collect the heavy metal object again. *Did he throw it or was it in my head…like Tessera struck and bleeding out…? Or was that the real thing?*

Gavin squeezed his eyes shut and shook his head for a split second as if he could shake away the conflicting memories like so many squirming maggots in a decaying corpse, the skull a sanctuary for feasting until the eye sockets were hollowed out and opened up like holes in a salt shaker.

Tessera wasn't anywhere near Aidan, nor were the others, but Gavin was, and he took full advantage.

Both of Aidan's arms were locked behind his back before he could turn from where he crouched. With Aidan pinned against him, Gavin reached one of his arms around and put Aidan in a tight headlock. The boy struggled and choked, wincing and fighting against the tight grip that pressed into swollen, bruised glands on both sides of his throat. A fit of coughing forced Gavin to turn his head away from the heavy, reeking smell of Aidan's breath. It had the smell of death to it; if not Aidan's death, then the death and decay of many billions of cells within him that were losing a war of attrition.

The nearest medicot was too far, and Clark had picked up the plant stand now and begun where Aidan left off, slamming the thing against already splintering glass.

White-hot rage filled Gavin's whole body, spreading like a raging wildfire from the tight cavity of his skull into his muscles. He squeezed Aidan's throat tighter, ignoring the struggling, shifting his forearm to press against the arteries on the right side where it was less swollen. *Ten…nine…eight…*

The struggling lessened, tapering off and then ceasing entirely as Aiden went limp against him.

Gavin let out a shaky breath and released the pressure with some reluctance. He dragged his brother across the room to the nearest vacant medicot and draped him across it, pressing the override for sending the automatic straps out to pin him down, programming could wait until later.

A cheerful chime sounded from inside of his pocket. *Too little too late, Richard…*

The thought bounced around in his mind, a discarded marble on pavement, colliding with his internal landscape and finding no place to rest, no coherence.

I brought us here…not Richard, and he'll be little help if I can't get us all strapped in and treated…might still be little help if he hasn't solved this thing.

The sound of shattering glass pulled him back to the present moment. The window-glass fell down in sheets of melted ice, the sound of it an orchestra of discordant notes, and after it, a hot gust followed.

Clark stood in front of the shattered wall, now open to the elements, eyes wide and without spark as if he'd failed to make any connection between his actions and the predictable outcome. His chapped and peeling lips brushed against each other with a scraping sound, mumbling something without words before he jumped. The pavement caught him, hard, not far down but still leaving scrapes and bruises on his wiry frame. He was up almost as soon as he struck the ground, up and running, down the ramp leading to the magnetic rail station that had brought them all here.

Gavin opened his mouth to shout, to call him back with a sharp tone of authority, but he closed his lips, trapping the words behind a prison of firm resolve.

His throat was raw and throbbing from struggling, shouting, breathing. It would do no good to shout and call back someone who was in the throes of this madness and already had a running start. There were going to be more losses before this was over. *I expected that. Planned for it.*

The air from outside was sobering somehow, soothing. Gavin turned, straightening his shoulders despite the heavy mantle of fatigue and self-appointed responsibility draped there like the battle-heavy cloak of a conqueror. Tessera was staring off at the open window, inching forward. He sighed, striding towards her and lifting her without hesitation or pretense and depositing her, dazed, and exhausted onto a cot. He brushed a strand of auburn hair back from her eyes, whispering an apology before turning away.

Six remaining. The fatigue was distant, a faint buzzing in his nerves, and a deep ache in muscles overused and shaking from exertion. *Strap them down and then myself…how many will move themselves now that it's quieter…?*

They seemed to have shifted again, from frenetic action and delusion to the rapid decline of illness, fever, swelling, bruising, bleeding sores erupting again as the levels of Yersinia Pestis rose inside them like the swell of a wave reaching shore again and again. *Another round of antibiotics would fight it off again…but how many times, and to what end, if it kept recurring?*

Gavin steeled himself for the next one. Bain looked ready to drop; perhaps he would, if Gavin brought another medicot up next to him and coaxed him in that direction. It was worth a try. They'd all be strapped down and ready for treatment, but it wouldn't matter if he couldn't get the access codes through to Richard, and even that might not be enough.

"Engage manual controls to redirect medicot…Please engage manual controls to redirect…" It played on repeat, in the vaguely humanoid voice with the smooth metallic tone mimicking the calm authority expected of a physician.

"Engage manual controls to redirect…"

There were other sounds that he couldn't place, desperate screams and shouts, moaning, barking sobs that seemed to continue on and on just as the medibot's message did.

Richard's thoughts were slow, synapses misfiring, losing direction, like minute silver fish darting through water only to find themselves suffocating in dry air. Suffocating, that was the word for it. He couldn't breathe. The sounds filling the hallway, *it was the hallway still,* were suffocating him from without and the slow meandering of dull thought suffocating him within.

The questions kept recurring with no answer satisfying or coherent. Who is that weeping behind the doors...? And the shouting, why are they locked behind doors.

He opened his eyes. The wall was directly to his right, near his face, where the pivoting back wheel of the medicot was stuck against the corner that led from one segment of hall to the next.

"Engage manual controls..."

Some clarity returned, and he groaned against the throbbing in his head and neck that threatened to shatter his skull with the feeling of pressure and sharp pain. He turned his face further to the right, feeling the pain-induced nausea build with his efforts.

The manual control was there. He could dislodge the back wheel.

A panel on the wall caught his attention, the controls for the numerous rooms in this wing of Quarantine and Treatment. Even the dim, pulsing, blue glow of the lights on the panel hurt his eyes and he closed them, but the mental image remained. All of the controls were there if one knew how to control them and had the codes...they were still screaming behind those doors, still trapped and untended to.

Richard reached for the panel without thought, his throat was raw but, still, he could speak the codes.

The doors slid open all at once with a scuffing sound of friction as they moved despite the press of bodies, the drum of fists on the other side.

The hall filled with them, and the smell of them, pungent with decay, rank with the bacterial reek of proteins rotting and the iron-salt smell of blood seeping through damaged tissues.

Richard stared at the ruined bodies that filled the hallway in his path, and some errant thought connected with another and then another. They were dead but still moving, from the stowaway that was now running them like bleeding, disease-spreading puppets, and they were in the way now…the train would leave him if he couldn't get through.

Aesa tumbled from her room and fell atop him where he was strapped to the cot, knocking the air from his lungs. A spark of anger and disgust erupted in his otherwise fog shrouded brain. *I let them out…I let them out.* A bout of coughing erupted as he struggled to expand his lungs despite the writhing body atop his own weakened one.

Richard managed a breath, fighting the urge to gag. Aesa's face was pressed against his, her breath mingling with his own even as he fought to regain it. He closed his eyes again, straining his neck further right, his face away from hers. Her cheek was damp and sticky where it pressed into his jaw, and he pictured it, swollen, blackened with dead gangrenous tissue, sticky with drying blood and interstitial fluids. His gorge rose again, and he vomited bile; at least there was no food there to choke on, and then found his voice, barely audible and cracking but it was enough.

"Medibot, release patient——restraint's, code——."

The straps released, and he didn't wait a moment more. He shoved the body off of him, reveling in the wet thud of its impact with the ground next to the cot; she would be slower to get up then. He pushed himself upright, using adrenaline to propel him off of the cot and to the ground, ready for a running start. His legs, instead, buckled beneath him, a shaking pile of starved, weakened, muscle tissue still half-asleep, as his brain was from the sedative. Panic set in as he sat there, one moment passing and the next as he massaged his right leg and then the left, trying to force them to stand, wobbling like a newborn foal beginning to walk for the first time.

There wasn't time for this, not to build himself up to running when his starting point was so far from it.

He wavered there, one elbow and forearm resting on the cot for balance. He couldn't ride it, as it wasn't made for speed. If he did, they'd fall on him or block the way with their stumbling, broken bodies.

A gleam of inspiration grew in the hazel eyes that were still uncharacteristically dim and bruised from fatigue and sickness.

Aesa stood on the other side of the cot and began to climb over it, wide brown eyes staring vacant and foggy at his face. "Aesa...?" Richard shoved her again, hard, the impact she made with the wall enough to drop her to the floor for a second time.

The cot couldn't get him there itself, motorized or not, but it would help. Grasping the front rail and bracing his arm against the surface of the medicot, he engaged the motors and walked sideways, using it for balance as he steered, directing it between himself and the flailing quarantine patients with his back to the wall.

They tried to follow, the nearest body that of a man with long damp streams of silver hair, and one wide brown eye—the other was missing entirely —that was now a muddy blue black in the whites. Blood and other fluids had seeped into it, drying there and beginning to decay as constricted arteries cut off oxygen, long before the rest of the body died. The same fate looked to have found the rest of his extremities, blackened and swollen as they were.

Richard knew the man: Jason Goddard, a premier scientist specializing in genetically acquired immunity. *You'd have been good on our research team...*The man shuffled closer, leaning just his face over the cot, discolored chin and nose jutting forward as he tilted his head left and right, once, twice, three times. Richard narrowed his eyes in disgust, rapid-blinking as he recognized the characteristic tic of the scientist that was now played out in gross caricature. He shuddered and leaned away, pressing himself further to the front right of the cot and shrinking against the wall to his back. The scientist reached a shaking hand towards him. It was a palsied tremor that jerked and stop-started as if his puppeteer had come in for work drunken and poorly trained. The hand pressed against Richard's hair in clumsy caress, tangling, pulling, and trailing a sticky dampness across his scalp before Richard could grasp the gangrenous face in his palm and shove. The man's skull made a wet sound of impact against the tile floor when he dropped, but Richard could hear him rising up again, hands shuffling against cold tile and pushing up to situate his weight over stiff legs. The door into the next segment of hall was close. He would reach it.

His legs shook but they held him, even when he braced them to push the next reaching grasping body out of his path with as much force as he could. They held him through the next hall and then the foyer and down the ramp, until the Railcar was in sight and the doors of the Council building were all that stood between.

He stopped, the cot pausing with him like a patient guide dog, and stared out into the dim cityscape. Sunset had come and gone, leaving behind a brown glow on the horizon and the haze of streetlights.

His eyes burned, still he stared, searching, adrenaline-fueled hyper-vigilance setting his senses on a cliff's edge, ready to monitor any and every detail for a threat. The concrete and glass landscape were damp and gleaming with puddles but otherwise still, the only sign of life the skittering of red-backed roaches gathering at the edge of puddles, waving long antenna as they went.

There were no walking puppets here, no bodies still moving despite previous demise, no rage fueled, rapid-pulsed dying, tearing at themselves or each other. He'd left them behind.

Richard's eyelids tried to close, his thoughts wandering,

drifting, all sense of urgency forgotten as shadows and light played games at the edges of his vision but somehow held no significance as consciousness began to elude him.

The air against his face, though cold and damp and smelling of the waste areas still being dismantled and cleaned by drones on the outskirts of the city, was soothing and lent a false sense of accomplishment, or perhaps that was another wave of psychoactive drug-induced euphoria from the illness.

He was still standing there several minutes later when a distant voice brimming with urgency forced its way past the farther outposts of his drifting consciousness.

The screaming was making her light-headed. It didn't matter. Aurelia glanced back at the countdown. Four minutes and thirty-nine seconds remained, and he just stood there. Completely in view through the windows, unmoving, eyes closed as if he had the luxury to enjoy the heavy fog that was coming in.

"Richard!!!! Richard, damnit! Richard get in here!!!" She was getting hoarse as well, but he needed to hear her and give her the codes, and get on the damn train.

*Crap. Crap. Crap...*She glanced over at Bram, who was sweating profusely, skin waxy and darkened, blistering with sores again. We'll die in here like this—or some will...

"Richard!! Rich—ard! Richard!!!"

He opened his eyes and stared again as he had done before. They were blank, wandering without any spark of recognition as they panned across the train. Two minutes and sixteen seconds.

"Richard!!!...Hey!" The last word ended in a hoarse sob. It was getting harder to scream as her voice choked on melting icebergs of panicked desperation.

There. His eyes seemed to widen and then narrow, and he had stopped scanning the area and instead stared in her direction, upper body leaning the same way.

He heard… "Richard, now!" It was strangled but maybe he'd still hear, maybe he could see her or had remembered.

One step, another…there were stairs, and he came down them now. The medicot propping him veered off for the ramp nearby and he stumbled, falling hard several stairs down. The pain seemed to galvanize his movements and he came on quicker now, forcing himself into an unsteady jog, then a run. One minute three seconds.

He was at the door, putting in codes, standing there next to her, breath heavy and ragged as he cleared his throat.

"Delay departure five minutes." He glanced out the door to see that his own medicot was trailing behind, heading for the open door of the railcar.

Hot tears flooded Aurelia's eyes, stinging like the salt of the dead sea had been poured into them. She wasn't alone, wasn't in decontamination, wasn't dying, and Richard was here.

"Please, the straps… I wanna sit up, please." The words were choppy and clotted with emotion but coherent.

Richard smiled, looking away only to guide his medicot through the doors as it arrived and climb atop it himself, lowering himself onto his side and letting a heavy sigh escape between his lips. There was blood on him, smears of it on his cheeks and in his hair, but he looked uninjured—though still very ill, eyes too bright now that they were open, their hazel depths sparking with too much life.

"Can't, you'll still need treatment." He paused to allow his breathing to catch up again. "You could relapse again."

Aurelia's voice was small but certain, ringing with no small amount of authority. "No, I'm better. I was sick first. You aren't, and you need me to speak for us, to make sure we get there."

Richard closed his eyes, resting his head back again with a

small inhalation at the pain in his skull.

"The codes, Richard."

He licked parched lips, tasting blood there. "In my handheld, just—use this one to access them. RB379xzgen."

He slid the handheld over to her and rested it on the side of her cot where she would be able to see it.

"Medibot release patient—restraints. Access code RB379xzgen."

The railcar slid closed, sealing the passenger car holding seventy survivors bound for WASA. It picked up speed much more quickly than what could be felt inside.

Aurelia sat up, taking care not to bring on any dizziness or nausea. When was the last time she had been able to sit up, or to take any food or drink by mouth? She let out a shaky breath, turning her neck in a slow circle now that the immobilizing brace was gone as well, and winced at the stiffness and residual pain.

Turning her focus outward, she looked towards the back of the train. Everyone who'd been here when she left was still here, except for Gavin.

A frown creased the still-bruised forehead that held evidence of the sores that erupted there not long before but were healing now. Questions bubbled up, colliding and struggling to reach her tongue first as if they'd been waiting in her mind, collecting for weeks, how long had it been, why were they traveling to WASA, *Gavin…where is he*? These and a multitude more. But Richard's eyes were closed, and he looked to have fallen asleep. His medibot's monitors confirmed as much.

Aurelia's eyes widened, taking in the magnitude of the situation for the first time since she'd lost track in quarantine. They were all sick now, some exceedingly so—Richard as well—and now they were on a magnetic railcar to the WASA center. She stared out the window at the blur of indigo skyline, stars and skyscrapers smearing together into an abstract tapestry of colors. The viewing screens displayed the exterior correcting for their speed. Towering to their right was the largest of the vertical farming structures that fed the city—while it still needed fed.

The thought occurred to Aurelia of a sudden, echoing with finality.

She shifted her gaze to the left where a solar energy power plant, equal in size and height, stood out against the horizon. These were the last bastions of the city, and beyond that the abandoned outskirts and the reclamation sectors loomed in a dusty haze, the only movement the reclamation drones, scaling the buildings like an army of ants disturbed by flood and carrying their pupa to higher ground.

They would be heading into uninhabitable territory now, a dead swath of land that would take them nearly to the West coast where the line would then continue South by undersea tunnel until they reached New Columbia and WASA.

UNSEEN ENEMIES

The data was all there laid out alongside the footage, and still it gave a conflicting picture, like so many water-logged puzzle pieces that were too swollen and misshapen to fit, their images faded and dissolving into a mass of indiscernible color.

Theresa sped up the video playback, moving blocks of data around the three-dimensional viewing space to connect bodies to vital statistics and time of events, along with treatment protocols for each patient. She blinked twice, sucking in a breath as she processed what she saw there.

Richard was in the hall examining a door, leaning in to listen to something on the other side. On the other side was patient number 45768w: Aesa Grantner. Vital statistics showed a rapid decline and eventual demise. Aesa stood at the door. Richard opened it and she emerged.

Theresa's pulse quickened and a heavy churning nausea swelled inside. It was secondary to the confusion. Aesa was clinically dead. She was also clutching at and gyrating against Richard in the hall. He leaned in close, staring into her eyes.

The next moment he forced her back into the room, his movements controlled but with violent force.

Captain Neil cleared his throat and Theresa glanced up to read his expression; horror, disgust, rage played across his features, his nose scrunching as his brows pulled down around flashing eyes.

"What is he doing? Isn't he supposed to be treating these people?"

Theresa opened her mouth to speak, hesitating over the correct words for the situation, then she shrugged.

"They're dead. The ones in this hall at least. And he has work to accomplish—"

Neil shook his head, confusion and irritation making his words come out with a sharper tone than was usual. "What? That's—why are you making excuses for this—I guess I can imagine why, but I still wouldn't expect you to. He shoved her bodily and locked her in, a sick woman half his size."

Theresa exhaled, struggling for words, for patience. "I'm not making excuses. I'm trying to explain—"

Genesis's voice sounded amused as she stepped closer to the display, gesturing to the vital signs that accompanied the video. "No, they are quite dead. See this…?"

She gestured with one hand at an absent heart rate despite brainwave tracings and let out a small chuckle. "They are moving, still, but not alive, as we'd assume."

Neil, looked from Genesis's amused half-smile to the numbers and charts superimposed over the footage playing in a loop, and frowned. "So, can I assume you have some way to make sense of this? Because I'm more apt to assume the numbers are wrong here and our man on Earth is not to be trusted. Especially considering the glowing reviews from Diadonna not a minute before we get this…"

Theresa looked deep in concentration when she answered, no longer making eye contact but instead focusing inward as she spoke, her hands animated and moving invisible pieces to her puzzle to illustrate her words.

"I suspected an opportunistic infection was accompanying the one we found—but we weren't finding it, manually or otherwise, and neither were the nanocytes searching inside the patients and sending us data. No other foreign bodies. So we kept looking."

Theresa glanced up. Neil was listening, nodding along despite the muddled confusion and disbelief that held in his eyes. Genesis's half smile hung on her face, eyes shimmering with interest as Theresa spoke. Dr. Alexander followed Theresa's words, hand gesturing along as she hit each point.

"One of the patients, Aurelia, showed signs of meningitis before we were cut off from contact and more data, so we looked there. Nothing, nothing, nothing. Nothing except for an ebb and flow—surges, really, of Yersinia pestis numbers, despite the aggressive antibiotic treatment—how much of this do you want to hear?"

She paused and glanced up again and then pushed ahead before waiting for an answer, speech coming rapid-fire as the words tumbled one after the next. "And then I caught the pattern. Once I had that, I knew what to look for, and it wasn't so hard to find. The Yersinia pestis is a decoy, a tool—an endosymbiont—uh, partner, and a decoy—I already said decoy."

"Not to rush you—but I'm wondering how any of this makes a dead woman walk and uh—grab hold like that. Assuming she's dead." He pinched his bottom lip between thumb and forefinger, forehead a study of creases.

"That's, yes—that's coming—just, yeah. So, it's a fungus. Y. Pestis is not the primary infection, it's secondary. Massospora is the primary, and Massospora wants to —uh, to control the host—so!" She gestured with both hands towards the replay of Aesa writhing against Richard in the hall for the tenth time. "So, it takes control of the brain and keeps the host moving, er, mating, fighting, transmitting infection." Theresa exhaled forcefully, a satisfied grin spread between her cheeks. "She's dead, they all are. These ones…"

The next set of testing data and samples came up on the

screen and Theresa paused, mouth falling open in concentration as the smile vanished and she mumbled to herself.

"These too, though. Most recent…different protocols." She cocked her head to the side and narrowed her eyes. "He used an antifungal on these ones, just an hour ago…and they're dead, like in the simulations I ran."

Theresa included the others in the room in a look and then cleared her throat. "Antifungals should work, but only the correct ones used—carefully…" Fine threads of worry darkened her fatigue bruised eyes and she trailed off.

"I need to treat them now." She grabbed handholds nearest a seat and strapped herself in. Fewer distractions from the lack of gravity would be welcome. Her handheld was already out. Richard should have received her last messages on auto send, but there was no reply here, just all of the data he sent after the channels were opened again. *Probably on auto send like mine.* Theresa shivered, a tremble taking up residence in her hands and shoulders as her bloodstream flooded with adrenaline, thoughts twisting and spinning with worry. She sucked in a breath. *He was alive an hour ago, and if they weren't as well, it would have been in the message, auto send or not…*

Dr. Alexander followed her over to the workstation and strapped himself in, leaning closer to speak. "I know you're feeling the urgency of this now. We are a ways off. They aren't responding. And these deaths…but those people are dead, either because it was too late for treatment or because he just fired in with a random anti-fungal in a last-ditch effort—or because he treated them too fast."

Theresa's eyes narrowed. "How do you mean?" Dr. Alexander nodded, further explanation already rolling off of his tongue. "Too high a dose, too effective. We've gone over how Yersinia Pestis kills a host. So what happened if the anti-fungal he administered cleared the advanced fungal infection?"

She wet her lips, biting at the dryness she found there. "That released our secondary all at once without anything to hold it back—endotoxemia and septic shock."

Dr. Alexander smiled, the expression holding a measure of melancholy appropriate to the topic; so many were dead on Earth, and more likely would be before they could do anything about it. "I'd think yes. It makes sense."

"So, we look at our best anti-fungals and use a cocktail of them and alternate dosing with antibiotics." "That's a solid plan considering our restrictions—time and distance, no real-time samples of what we're dealing with. Make sure their medibots are collecting more data and sending it all here so we can adjust fire."

"Yes." The one-word answer was all she provided, her full focus already returning to the streaming data from old messages still coming in.

"And Theresa…" He waited for some indication that she was listening and had to satisfy himself with a nod and a mumble. "With how long they have been sick with this, we are going to have to expect the worst—lesions in the central nervous system and the lungs, necrotic tissue in any and all organ systems, gangrene, lots of secondary treatment most likely…a long recovery."

Her eyes flicked over to his and then back at the screen, scowl deepening. "I know. That's unacceptable."

Emily walked the smooth red-clay floor of her rooms in figure-eights, the restless energy that she exuded through each and every movement evincing the storming internal landscape that moved her.

There was always the red sand in her dreams and the mountains in the distance, and then he would be lost. The scenes replayed behind her eyelids each time she closed them tight to cease the burning of sleep deprivation.

Sitting down on the platform bed and shoving disheveled hair out of her eyes, Emily glared at the discarded VR sleep-aid in the recessed shelf where she'd stowed it several nights before. The urge to put it on pulled at her hands, moving her despite any willpower she was using to fight it. The lavender fields that she used to drift off into undisturbed slumber and carefully-guided dream called to her.

She sighed, the sound rough with disgust and irritation. How would allowing unfettered dreaming help if it was all nightmare? How would it help if she woke again and again?

She stood again, pacing to the faintly glowing AUC unit that dominated her room with its presence and its purpose. Still small and hard to find in the sea of liquid without the magnification screens, she looked like a tiny doll, crudely fashioned as a representation of humanity instead of a true-to-life replica. The tiny finger-nubbed hands were rough, like unfinished clay with an almost webbed appearance, the facial features present but lacking shape and definition. And still, she could see the face it would become staring back. Was it the face from her more recent dreams, the girl-child smiling as she demonstrated a dance and then vanished after her brother, lost over the next rise of sand?

Emily sighed once more, this one deeper and accompanied by slow rolling tears. She pressed a hand against the side of the AUC, feeling the warmth of it. She was safe in here, and dreams were just dreams. Somehow this was harder than even the losses, more painful and raw even in its hope that was somehow too sharp, too precious to bear some days.

Her shuddering breath was humid with tears. There was never a chance of this on Earth, and she'd fought her way here, to this place, this time, this very sequence of events until these two could come through. Perhaps not the children she'd expected, and certainly not the way she'd expected—*Jonathan should be here*—but even still, she'd seen her way to this point. She could hold tight a bit longer, couldn't she, nightmares or not?

Her mother wouldn't believe that this time had come, maybe wouldn't want to. Emily scowled, still tracing the tiny shape projected onto the side of the AUC unit with one finger. It didn't take much for her own mind to fill in the sort of things she'd say. *You're making careless decisions again—flying off on your first thought— There'll be consequences, no doubt.* Emily bit her lip and ground it between her teeth in unconscious nerves as she'd done as a child, hands twisting and feet kicking as she sat through the gently chiding diatribes.

And who'll clean up the mess when you're all covered in it and overwhelmed again—eh? What if this one comes out wrong?

Emily pushed the memory-voices away. Her mother wasn't here, but back on Earth. A twinge of guilt and fear pulled at her just as soon as she became aware of the relief the reminder brought with it. *Back on Earth where a plague is raging…and on the list or not, the chances of finding and saving her were slim, they'd said.*

Emily paced over to her shelf for a different headset and put it on, manually directing the call.

"You okay, Em?" Donovan's voice was warm, even with the note of distraction that signaled he was working, gathering samples likely, still out in the field. Her smile was genuine, even though it shook as she curled up on her left side on the bed and closed her eyes. "Yeah, can't sleep though…Gran wants me to sleep without the VR. Better for processing thoughts and fears and what-not she says…Can you just, can you talk to me maybe? Tell me about your creatures or the scenery or something."

"Oh—uh, um, yeah. I could—I could do that. Just externalize my internal monologue, that'll put you to sleep."

Emily laughed, smile lines creasing the corners of her closed eyes. "Whatever you want to talk about, and I'll listen."

"Sure—Came across a new herd of gerenuks today, a branch off of the first herd most likely and these are young, all male and very skittish when I found them, well—really they found me. Ran up on me avoiding a dust-devil and—"

Emily's smile softened as she listened, allowing the words to form into pictures of the events Donovan described, until they blurred into a thin tapestry of sleep imagery that flowed on its own trajectory up and away from the words that still came.

The gerenuks were loping across the dunes the way they did, young ones and their tiny newborn offspring, still wobbly on their feet. Emily followed them, topping the nearest rise and looking down on their play. Her children were there again as well, all of them beckoning her to follow as they ran for the next rise of sand. But she knew what would happen now, just as in every other iteration of this dream. She'd top the rise and they would be gone, only red sand spreading out before her.

Donovan's voice was still filling her ears when she sat up, skin covered in a film of cold sweat, shivering and disoriented.

"Emily? You weren't out long, huh? Guess this didn't help."

She shook her head, negating his words and wetting her sleep-parched lips before she could speak. "It helped at first. Thank you—but then the dreams again. I have your narrative to thank for the leaping gerenuks this time, though."

"Oh well, well, that's an improvement, isn't it?" Emily laughed, shaking her head again. "I mean, not really? But they are cute though, the baby ones anyway."

Donovan's voice took on a more serious tone. "You know, I could come back from this trip sooner. If it would be helpful, I'd like to be there for you."

Emily frowned, lips turning down as her forehead creased up. "No, you are here for me already. See? You just put me to sleep. Just—just finish what you need to and don't rush, or I'll feel babied, and angry at myself for it. I don't need guilt to complicate things right now."

"Okay, yeah. But maybe just talk to Carla some more, let her help…"

Emily looked up at the domed ceiling, letting out a long sigh. "I can do this, you know."

"I know. But using tools that are, like, right there for you isn't weak. It's like using the knife in your pocket instead of biting a thing open with your teeth."

"I know that." She heard his hesitation, a pause that seemed to hold more words that he held back. She waited but all she heard on the other end was his breath.

"Go work, and I'll try and sleep again."

She didn't even have to close her eyes to picture the dream again…sleep would have to wait until she was too tired to fend it off.

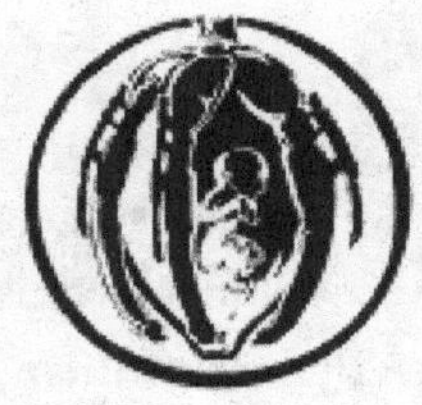

RECOVERY

Relief was the first feeling that washed over Theresa, after the nausea-inducing rollercoaster rush of adrenaline. *A response means someone is alive…*

She stared at the first non-automated message since the communications blockade was lifted and read it again.

"Mother, this isn't Richard, it's Aurelia. I'm in recovery, but I'm the only one. Richard is sedated or unconscious and sicker every hour. His breathing worries me, and his hands look terrible, bruised and swollen and covered in sores…I have all of his access codes and his handheld, but I don't know how to help—and some of us are missing. We are on the way to WASA, but Gavin, Gelsemium, Tania, thirty-nine of us are not here—unless there is another train. Are you coming to get us?"

She breathed out a rush of hot breath too long withheld. Alive and on track to be picked up, but where were Gavin and Geli and the others? They'd need the treatment as well unless they were recovering like Aurelia had.

"Okay. We aren't there yet, but we're getting closer. In the meantime, I can get you all on the path to recovery with the control codes to your medibots from the files Richard sent me—but do Gavin and the others have medibot codes, do they have access to treatment? Did Richard know where they are?"

Aurelia frowned at the message, orange-flecked blue eyes shining in the last rays of sunlight through the railcar's western windows. Gavin and nearly half of them were somewhere else. The blocks of memory from before quarantine started to emerge from the mists in her fatigued mind like icebergs in deep water. The others missing were the ones who were out on study trips, but not Gavin. He was at the headquarters still when she'd gone out for more rats. If he was there still after that, she didn't know. It was all a blur. *So, Gavin must have left after…*

She spoke into the handheld, giving clear instruction. "Locate messages to and from Gavin."

There were a few and she skimmed them, looking for the one that contained what she needed. He left without asking, met up with the others at a headquarters half-way to WASA. And there it was, the final message and an attachment.

"Strapped them all down, we are bad off—not in transit. Medical access codes to follow."

The smile of relief warred with waves of irritation, fear. They were sick and stranded, but at least the codes were here.

She forwarded the message to Theresa and stared at Richard on the nearest medical cot next to Bram. He was sleeping —or unconscious—and his breathing had a labored quality, his skin sallow and discolored where subcutaneous bleeding had begun and then faded with antibiotic treatment, treatment that had yet to cure any of them, except perhaps herself.

Richard's breath hitched and stuck in his chest. Aurelia's eyes widened, twin pools of alarm as she waited—ten seconds—thirty, for the next breath. Aurelia's heart raced with panic, alarms setting off along her nerves until her whole body bunched with tension, frozen in the face of an adrenaline rush that she couldn't respond to. *Help him…how?* She stood, slowed by the heavy feeling in her limbs and the reverberation in her chest, like a gong sounding in a damp cavern with nowhere to exit, building upon itself until its echoes filled the darkness.

Just as the medibot's alarms sounded, he took a shallow breath. It came as a constricted, wheezing fight, a tug of war on boggy ground until finally turgid tissues, inflamed and blocked by mucus and blood, gave way, allowing for passage of breath.

The medibot's control panel lit up with flashing yellow lights. "New treatment protocols downloading—pulsed release antifungal 362triaz alternating pattern broad spectrum antibiotic WTY41, 60 days intravenous."

Relief flooded her as she read the message. Maybe this could work now. They could recover, were already on the way to WASA, and would be met there for transport to Mars on the Pinnacle. *And Theresa is on the Pinnacle.*

A surge of excitement flickered through her, leaving a hollow feeling in her gut followed by a heavy sense of loss that brought the sting of tears to her eyes. She scrubbed at them, a surge of forge-hot anger burning away all other emotions.

Gavin and the others with him were not headed to WASA and had no sure way to get there on their own. *Dammit Gavin…Reckless and selfish, like my forays into the underground for rats.*

Aurelia stared out the window-glass, eyes unfocused as she pulled at her lips with restless fingers. She had the command override codes, and Gavin's location would come up if she looked for the last place he messaged from. It wouldn't make sense not to collect them now.

She cleared her throat, the healing tissues there still sore from prolonged illness. "Alter course for Gavin's last registered location. Override code to follow."

"Why are we stopping?" Richard's voice was hoarse when he spoke, unsteady and breaking the silence of near dark that had just begun to grey with the light of morning. "Is it WASA, then?"

Aurelia woke up from light sleep, eyes wide and startled in a face too gaunt for her bone structure. He could see the dark shadows around her eyes still, the pallor of her cheeks, and the weight she'd lost while kept alive by the medibot's nutrient solutions alone.

Her reply came in hushed tones. "No. No, this is where Gavin and the others are waiting for us. I rerouted for them."

Richard coughed into his sleeve, the sound less wet and strangled than before but still bringing up a stain of blood-tinged mucus onto his lab-coat. He smiled as he caught his breath, rolling onto his left side and rubbing at the muscles of his neck newly released from restraints. He winced at the pain there but still the smile grew, spreading and shifting to an incredulous laugh.

"What?" She looked worried, uncertain.

"My head feels clearer than for some time, quite different than my last recollection." He laughed again, wincing at a flash of recurring mental images that came with perfect detail from just before consciousness had left him. Theresa had joined them on the train car somehow and had climbed atop him. Her eyes were not her own, but instead were the lifeless, hemorrhaging ones of the woman from the quarantine sector. Richard pulled in a breath and waited for it to pass. When he opened them, Aurelia was at his side, the concern in her eyes magnified and exemplified by her chewed lips.

"It's not as bad as it looks. The flashes are still there, yes, so vivid still. But it feels more like a flashback—an insistent memory." He sighed then, closing his eyes once more. "What treatment is it?"

She shrugged, attention pulled towards the dark shape of the medical center just off of the magnetic rail and down the still active scrolling sidewalk that was resolving from darkness, shape becoming more solid and taking on an orange glow as the rising sun bathed it in light. "Antibiotics and anti-fungal, a very long course—Gavin and the others should be in there. She stared up at the many stories of windows, some broken but most intact, that seemed to stare back like dead eyes reflecting a mortician's examination light. "I can go in after them."

Richard gave a slight shake of his head, his eyes going distant again as a cascade of imagery from the treatment wing resurfaced in his mind's eye. He cleared his throat. "We can use the homing feature to direct their medibots here. Without going in."

Aurelia nodded, some reluctance warring with an uncharacteristic shadow of fear in her eyes. She held out Richard's handheld device, but he waved it off.

"You can do it. It's not complex. I'm not ready to have that back yet—in fact, can you message Theresa something simple from me?"

Aurelia nodded, staring down the sidewalk still. "Let's get them back now."

VITAL SIGNS

The message was so short that it was almost hard to process as she read it for deeper meaning and detail that just wasn't there.

"On the mend. Thank you. Meet you at the rendezvous point."

On the mend that quickly? Or just back from the brink? Four days means a quick effect. It means I didn't kill my patients…or allow any more to slip away…

She closed out messages to clear the space for the task at hand. There were new data sets for each patient coming in now, and she needed to follow their recoveries—or relapses. Theresa opened up Bram's newest data and stared at it with unblinking focus. He was still sleeping, it seemed but now his brainwaves showed normal sleep cycles and his fungal and bacterial loads were down. Four days was making a big difference for many of them.

She switched files and frowned at what she saw there. Santana was going to need more help; her lungs showed considerable damage, necrotic tissue, and poor oxygen transfer. Theresa pressed her lips together and rubbed her hands across her face. "What was it you were suggesting for Santana's lung damage, Dr. Alexander?"

The doctor glanced over, nodding as he finished a task at his own screen before moving over to Theresa's station, using the handholds to navigate the lack of gravity. He looked over her shoulder, reading Santana's latest data. "TNF-a. There's scarring beginning to form, so inflammation will promote healing. We increase TNF-a by maybe 30-50%, and it will help."

"Okay…thank you." Theresa felt his hand on her shoulder, a quick pat meant to comfort, and then he moved back to his own station. She hoped the gratitude was there in her eyes, even if buried under layers of sleep deprivation and stress, most likely. She could feel it boiling up, anger and overstimulation from hours learning new skills under pressure. *There isn't time to be out of my depth…*

"Connect with medibot 461 for altered treatment protocols. Increase TNF-a by 50% to heal pulmonary necrosis and decrease scarring."

Santana was the worst of those on the magnetic rail car. She should be fine with treatment and time, but she wasn't yet.

Theresa's eyes were tired, hollow. She placed Santana's file on the right side of the screen with several others who weren't responding to treatment as quickly or had complications that were going to need ongoing treatment. The left side held two files, those who were treated too late but were still moving, still showing brainwave tracings and erratic heart rates that would kill a living child and *had* killed *them*.

She tried not to let their faces form in her thoughts, a sequence of memory still-shots and live mental footage from their earliest moments of conception as she remembered them in their AUCs, magnified on the lab screens at first for her to view, and later, born children that she could only hold through VR Comm using dream-speak: Caspian with his honey-brown eyes and ready smile, Davina with her bird-like features and infectious baby-laughter that had evolved into quips of clever word-play as she matured. They were strapped down and heavily sedated now, undergoing treatment until the last bit of what was animating them died as well…or until the survivors became capable of dealing with them in some other way.

Next to the two files were twelve others that were completely dark, medibot codes attached to names but with no vital statistics sent or as far as she could tell, no treatment received. Had they died, or had their medibots shut down? Were they lost somewhere? These ones were in Gavin's group, so it was impossible to know until Richard or Aurelia responded to her again. Following that train of thought was like beating her head against a door while waiting for it to open. Wasteful, futile…She turned back to Santana's vital signs and then cleared her throat. "Dr. Alexander?"

"Mmm?" He sat nearby, tapping his fingers on the desk with eyes focused on the screen before a similar console with another set of files open, another group of the children needing further interventions to recover. "Yes?"

"I'm sending you, Genesis, and your interns the files for my worst ones for oversight…if you can handle more. I need that right now." Her eyes flicked away and she grimaced, voice lowering. "There is the other task to consider as well."

He frowned, turning to face her. "The losses so far have all been due to late treatment. They were beyond help, at least beyond our long-distance experimental help. Medibots are a fantastic tool, but not a full replacement for a team of experienced physicians."

Theresa plucked at the pockets of her lab coat, smoothing them against the white fabric as if they were not already unwrinkled and well in place. "Maybe, but if we don't work on the vaccine as well, there is a chance we'll lose some of our skeleton crew on the Pinnacle and be left orbiting Mars without approval to come down—and I wouldn't blame them."

Genesis nodded in agreement. "Send the files. I can cover more, and alert you and Dr. Alexander as needed."

"We'll both work on the vaccine and double up on overseeing our worst cases. If I miss something you'll catch it, and vice versa. Genesis gives us a third, and my team will pick up slack anywhere we need it."

"Okay, good. I'll focus on the Massospora and you begin with Y. Pestis. A month is a short time to create and test a vaccine. Though if treatment works, I suppose we buy more time in transit."

"Exactly, yes…" He drummed his fingers harder on the aluminum surface of the desk, making a hollow thrumming sound as he searched for words.

"And Theresa…" She looked over once more, finding his eyes restless…but also warm when they met hers. "Yes?"

"We aren't going to lose any more, but…it's okay to be afraid…and to mourn them."

Genesis was already monitoring Theresa's patients, catching up on their complications and current treatments, but she drifted closer to be heard. "You're doing everything possible here."

Theresa pressed her lips into a tight line and shook her head, denying any film of moisture that may have threatened to coat her eyes. "Not here and now, it isn't…later, when it's over, and I know how many I'm crying for."

He nodded, returning his eyes to the screen, and the others did the same. "Yeah, okay."

"I directed them correctly. You can double check me…but see? Several aren't moving. I have thirty-two en route to us and twelve others not moving. I'll just go see why the bots aren't responding."

The sun was above the horizon now, shining through the windows of the train car. Even with the tinted surfaces filtering the light, Richard had to lift a hand to turn away from the brightness that felt sharp and blinding. He shook his head. "None of the others are well enough to go along. Bram is unconscious, and I would be unwise to overestimate my recovery."

"We can't leave without them."

He turned to the western windows of the building that held the rest of the children. "Are their medibots sending and receiving data?"

Aurelia nodded. "Yeah, I haven't looked at them, but all of them show vital signs still and are sending data up to Theresa."

Richard hesitated a moment, opening his mouth to speak but instead blowing his hair out of his eyes. "That doesn't mean anything in this case."

It was clear by her expression and the tilt of her head that she was confused by his words.

Richard spoke quickly, refusing to delay further. "You've slept through much of this. Quarantine, unconsciousness, delirium…As the illness advances, it affects the brain and other physiology, eventually leading to death—but a death that leaves behind a functioning body. Brain waves…heart rate, movement. You won't know which ones are well just based on *presence* of vital signs."

Aurelia stared at him, looking as if his words were some disjointed gibberish or scrambled in her mind and needing translation. "But how would that work—?"

He shook his head. "Never mind. We have time for that when the train is moving again. We need to get them in here now."

The first of the medicots was on the path with a train of them following behind. It rolled on the scrolling sidewalk and then left the path to turn towards the magnetic rail boarding platform. It was Gelsemium.

Richard's words caught in his throat when he saw her, and Aurelia put a hand over her mouth to stifle a moan. Geli looked to be unconscious with her eyes half open, a thin track of blood-tinged saliva trailing from her mouth to the damp red puddle beneath her right cheek where it rested on the cot. Her chest rose and fell in exaggerated breathing motion.

Richard placed a hand on Aurelia's shoulder, restraining her.

"Shhh…look at her vital signs now, before we bring her in."

She looked ready to protest, but confusion won out in the internal war waged clearly in her eyes and she acquiesced, lifting Richard's handheld and connecting to Gelsemium's medibot.

"89…her pulse is 89, blood pressure 95/52. But you said vital signs aren't enough. It says she's sleeping." Richard released his breath, a light smile emerging from the smooth palette of unexpressed concern that he had held in place while waiting for the numbers.

"*Having* vital signs is not enough. Hers indicate that she is sleeping and in recovery despite her appearance. Let her in and check the next."

Aurelia opened the door, staring down the long line of medicots lined up between there and the building's exit doors. They appeared to be sleeping or unconscious like Gelsemium. A few had regained consciousness and appeared sedated but delirious.

She sucked in a breath, stepping aside for Gelsemium's medicot to pass through the doors to the train and with the same motion stepped out onto the path. Richard struggled to sit up, managing only to rise onto one elbow before the world spun and twisted inside of his head and he was forced to stop. He scowled over at her, twisting as much as possible to see her expression.

"You can't go in. Not alone."

Aurelia frowned and rubbed a hand along her jaw. "Pretty sure my ability to get in and out of a place I'm not supposed to be has been well established. Someone has to —their medibots aren't responding to remote commands."

His scowl deepened. "Don't release their restraints. What exactly do you plan to do if they have already done so themselves?"

Aurelia's eyes widened and she opened her mouth to answer, but then looked away, crossing her arms as her brows furrowed and she licked parched lips. "You aren't telling me enough if there is some way they are a danger."

He shook his head, clenching and unclenching his jaw. "You

aren't listening then. If they are alive and untethered, they could be delirious. If they've already passed, they'll again be dangerous because they move, and grasp—they'll be unpredictable."

Aurelia crinkled her nose and then reached into the side-compartment just inside the train's doors, pulling out a small crowbar meant for breaking glass. "I'll be careful."

The main lights in the building were off, leaving the many skylights and windows to provide any illumination that there was.

The building didn't sound empty, nor did it smell that way. A rhythmic clanging came from the corridor on the right along with other sounds. Voices, weeping.

Aurelia sucked in a breath and trotted down the dim hallway. If it was them making such noise it was either very good, or very bad, according to Richard.

Ducking her head and curling her arms closer to her chest, Aurelia took up a rat-like posture, keeping to the shadows as she started down the corridor. The sound of her heart thrum-thrumming in her chest competed with the incessant clanging and the clamor of distant voices, growing nearer as she ran, crowbar clutched to her chest. *Twelve of them....there were twelve missing. Which twelve? Did it matter? Who would she pick if she had to pick? If it wasn't already done and decided who was left there...*

Her breathing grew ragged and she felt a heaviness, a raw ache deep in her healing lungs. It transitioned to a cough that she covered with a hand. It came away wet, and a spray of blood colored her palm. The bright red set off an internal alarm that she quelled with platitudes. She wiped the blood off on the bottom of her shirt and, along with it, all but a whisper of fear in the back of her mind.

The sounds were louder now. She could pick out voices. Marilla's voice rang out above the others, plaintive, wailing. The words, if they were there, were garbled and unintelligible. Aurelia's throat clenched and the hairs stood up along her arms. It felt like a chill that came from within and brought with it that nerve-deep sting of fear, pulsing anew with each step she took closer to those sounds. That voice should have felt familiar, heralding her sister's continued existence and growing proximity, but it instead felt wrong.

Aurelia pushed past the fear and shoved it down. None of this meant Marilla was dead, that she wasn't okay. She was talking, even if it was hard to understand. The dead don't talk.

She could get to her and help. The thought got her moving. She picked up her pace and turned the corner into a large atrium style room that looked to be for processing new arrivals, but she stopped short of entering. The large space was in disarray, discarded clothing strewn here and there, toppled desks with shattered electronics scattered in their vicinity, clumps of water gel and root matter from a potted plant drying out on the dark marble floors.

A heavy draft that smelled of ozone met her as she stepped across the threshold. A window that had filled a quarter of the front wall was broken out, its shattered glass covering the floor with shards, shimmering in the emergency lights that were pulsing on and off in the dim of oncoming dusk.

Marilla was there next to the broken window, her auburn hair moving with the wind and taking on a bright red gleam each time the lights flashed on. There were five others. All twelve were here and accounted for, strapped to the medicots just like the ones outside boarding the train, only these ones did not appear to be sedated. There was Darius and Essex who were never apart, even now. To their left, was Nara, clutching some torn fabric in one restrained hand and worrying it with clumsy fingers. A little ways away, Wisteria arched her back, thrashing and opening her mouth with no sound; her violet-blue eyes seemed to stare without focus or direction.

They were all conscious, some of them crying, mumbling, Marilla wailing some word she couldn't quite catch. *Time….it sounds like time…*

"Time tooo goooo!" The stumbling, slurred speech was followed by a sob.

That moved Aurelia across the room, her feet pulling her across the intervening space with urgency despite the twinge of fear set off by the quality of that voice—grown large into an all-encompassing alarm bell in her mind.

She made a path to Marilla, feeling the glass crunch under foot as she drew nearer.

The girl was strapped down, her head fighting against a neck restraint meant to immobilize and prevent trauma to swollen lymph nodes. Her hands were held to her sides and clenched into twitching, flexing, claws.

Aurelia pressed both hands to the sides of her sister's face, stopping the thrashing.

Her skin was hot to the touch, feverish and flushed. It was mottled; patches of purple and blue bordered the hectic red of capillaries burst beneath the skin. She could feel the racing pulse that throbbed in her temples, faster than a hummingbird. "Marilla?"

The girl's motions stopped and her eyes found Aurelia's. They were unresponsive, pupils dilated to the extreme and searching as if Aurelia wasn't there. Marilla's mouth was moving now without sound escaping the chapped, blood-crusted lips. Aurelia thought of the blood that came up with her last cough and a twinge of fear twisted in her gut. Could she end up like this again?

Aurelia's eyes widened in confusion and alarm as she took in all of the conflicting pieces of information her senses delivered. *She's still alive. They all are. Is she delirious?*

Aurelia's gut wrenched as the fear intensified. She flinched away from that blank stare; the eyes were the same shade of brown that Aurelia had always admired, a lighter version of the red-brown of their mother's with a ring of even lighter brown in a starburst around the center. But the twin orbs in the familiar face were empty and without emotion, thought, or spark of recognition. They were bloodshot from hours of coughing, surrounded by dark bruising.

A sudden screech came from Marilla's parted lips as if her volume, turned down before, was pushed up with the jab of a finger. "Tiiiiime to goooo!! Time to go—time to…" She wailed the words in an endless loop in a voice that was like those eyes.

Aurelia's nose crinkled in disgust and she put a hand over her mouth. Tears welled up, stinging her eyes and her throat clenched. She felt as if she was going to retch, but her stomach was empty, hollow as that voice. It came from Marilla, and it was her voice, but still it wasn't. The inflections were wrong, somehow mechanical and plaintive at the same time, as if the meaning behind the words was lost on her even as they came from her mouth.

Swallowing the saliva that flooded her cotton-dry mouth and scrubbing the back of her wrist across burning eyes, Aurelia turned from Marilla to take in the rest of the room and the other medicots. Each of them was strapped down and moving against those restraints, their motions writhing and staccato as if their muscles would only obey them in fits and starts.

She froze there, staring. The medicots had no power lights, dark screens, an absence of vital signs being tracked. They weren't working at all, it seemed; perhaps they never were. She had hoped they just weren't sending data, not shut down, dark and letting them die. Her lie about their status wouldn't anger Richard as much as this truth would.

She licked dry lips, thoughts coming rapidly now. They'd had no treatment at all. No sedatives. Maybe they were just delirious, beyond treatment. Her eyes caught on Colin, who was weeping and clenching and unclenching his fists as he thrust his hips, arching his back off the surface of the medicot as much as the straps would allow. Her eyes were still burning and she rubbed at them again, angry, impatient, and then went into motion.

"Not leaving you here." Her voice sounded strange in the large room filled with incoherent sound and a wind that whipped through in gusts, pulling sound out with it as it passed through the halls.

The medicots attached to each other like train cars and could be set to manual control. One could pull the others. She tried Marilla's, setting it to manual and then trying all of the power switches. There was nothing. Two of the others powered on enough to show a flashing loading screen but when she set them to manual control they powered off. *No juice...*

She sighed, eyes flicking around the room for a charging station or any way to get these moving. Nothing. She could search the building...

Aurelia imagined pulling the medicots down halls with no direction until she found some place to charge. It could take hours. There could be sick—people—in other parts of the building, not strapped to medicots or otherwise restrained. She stared around the room, eyes darting and frantic now. Her throat felt dry, itching from what she hoped was healing, and she fought against the spasms of a cough coming on. She could push them one at a time, couldn't she? Try to push the whole train of them...? A wave of fatigue blurred her vision and she sat down hard, slumping against the nearest cot.

A sharp pain burned in her scalp as searching fingers twisted in her hair and clenched shut around fistfuls of the short blond locks that were matted and tangled from weeks of illness. Aurelia screamed and then clamped a hand over the clenched fingers that were wrapped in her hair. The fear that beat in her chest threatened to make her black out, sands of gray spattering her field of vision.

She closed her eyes and slowed her breathing, trying not to picture Colin's mottled, sore-covered hand twisted in her hair, where it indeed was.

The nausea returned with the mental images that forced their way in. She had to get up. His grip was so tight and twisted around her tangles. Several attempts to pry his fingers loose resulted in thick strands of her hair pulled out by the root and a rising panic that made it even harder to think.

She dug into his hands with her nails and felt hot blood on her fingertips. His grip didn't loosen. *No pain response.* Her mind, already that of a young scientist, fixated on that observation and became distracted by the connections she pieced together from it. *Something inhibiting the pain response: adrenaline…stimulants…something triggering endorphin and adrenergic neurochemical systems…*

His fingers tightened and she felt more hair pull from her scalp. Aurelia's eyes widened as she fought the urge to jerk her head away. Shoving her own smaller fingers between his once more, but with better purchase this time, she wedged them deeper until she could find some leverage. He only had one hand and she had both. The gap was large enough for her to extract most of the hair in his fist and her own fingers. She scrambled away, panting from the effort and stared at the hand hanging just over the side of the cot, clenching and unclenching in a rhythmic motion now that there was nothing to grab. She shivered and stood slowly, searching the room again for some tool she could use to end this. The crowbar she'd left next to Marilla, perhaps.

"Oh." Shame burned in her cheeks as she registered the shapes of three medicots against the far wall, in deep shadow. "Not very quick still, are we?" She shook her head and hurried across the room on trembling legs. These ones could work.

She held her breath as she accessed the controls and then waited. Two powered on. It would be enough.

The first she attached to the front of the train of medicots, the second she placed in the back, setting both to manual control.

They'd follow her lead and pull the others, avoiding obstacles with their sensors. She glanced back towards the dark hallway she came from and then at the large glass doors by the broken window. It was a closer route out to the scrolling sidewalk up to the magnetic railcar where Richard and the others waited. It would have made sense to take this route on the way in if she'd known about it, but the curve of the building had presented the front door as the closest entrance.

The air outside was cold now and damp; it smelled of ice and the reclaiming factories on the outskirts, the sharp tang of melting metal and the moldering dust of rubble unearthed after decades left sitting.

Relief flooded her as the rail car came into sight, even as she imagined Richard's sharp eyes assessing the blood on her cheeks and the tear tracks, then arguing whether to bring the obviously-delirious-and-perhaps-beyond-help husks of her siblings on board. It didn't matter; she wouldn't leave them. He wasn't the only one with steel in his spine. Who had put it there, after all? She could stand her ground.

DOUBLE AGENT

Theresa scowled at the data and gestured towards the screen with one hand as if it were the cutting edge of a blade.

"I don't like how slow it is. I don't like not knowing—STILL—if it's going to completely eradicate the fungus or leave hidden pockets in the brain, allowing infection to recur. It's not enough." Theresa pinched her jaw with the same hand, and exhaled through her nose, frustration flavoring her every movement. "And their healing time. Not good enough. Not for the ones with deep tissue damage in their lungs…fluid filled cysts in their brains."

Dr. Alexander nodded as she spoke. "You know…"

"What do I know?" Genesis looked up from the terminal next to hers, watching the exchange in silence, taking in Theresa's agitation and Dr. Alexander's attempts to soothe.

"Well, you've just hit upon the age-old quandary that every physician finds themselves in again and again, regardless of advancing technology."

Theresa's brows scrunched in concentration and impatience as she struggled to listen to his words, which came too slowly to keep pace with her agitation.

"No matter what skills, medicines, tools we have available, illness, and yes, sometimes death, outpaces us. We can't stop every death, cure every ill, prevent those nasty long-term complications, side-effects, morbidities…hell, sometimes we cause them—iatrogenic harm." His eyes were cautious, but also melancholy, and filled with a level of understanding that first-hand experience brings.

Theresa pictured Coli on the floor of the Mars Space elevator station, bleeding through their hands as they worked to save her and failed. By the look in the doctor's eyes, he was remembering it too, that and countless other patients lost on his table while his hands worked towards the opposite goal.

"I'm not a medical doctor. I'm a scientist. A geneticist. I don't fight death, combat microorganisms—I…"

Theresa froze, some new train of thought draining the agitation from her voice. Genesis watched some realization struggle to form on Theresa's face, and pushed. "Are you certain? Because right now, you're unfocused, lost—and floundering, as you said yourself, in a field you're trying to learn in a matter of weeks…"

The answering scowl was slow to form, warring as it did with this amorphous idea. Stepping closer, Genesis goaded her. "Go on, take the criticism and use it. I'm right. Now fix it before we lose more. You said yourself that this isn't working fast enough."

Theresa mumbled to herself, converting the scowl from one of irritation to raw determination. A sharp focus replaced the grief and fatigue in her eyes, and she subvocalized as if alone in the room, opening files and taking out representations of genetic material faster than Dr. Alexander could track.

"What are you thinking?" Theresa shifted focus from one sample to another similar one, speaking aloud now as she worked. "I'm not a physician, so why am I working from that angle…why?! Because we have sick people *now*, that need help *now*. The bacteria doesn't care about that, but I can *make* it care, because *that's* what I do."

The grin that spread on her lips was infectious, echoed by Genesis at her side, replete with amusement and triumph. "It sounds like you've regained focus."

Dr. Alexander looked to be a step behind, tracing a finger in the air and mumbling in an attempt to parse out what and how she would make the bacteria care for.

Theresa continued her monologue without prodding, fueled by the simultaneous work she was doing with her hands, manipulating virtual components to synthesize what they would need. "Why, Doctor, is the current treatment not fast enough or aggressive enough?!"

Dr. Alexander hesitated before realizing it wasn't a rhetorical question but one he was meant to answer. "We can't knock the fungal infection out any faster with safe doses of the medications we're using, and permeability of tissues varies for different cells making it possible for the Massospora to be unreached and persist for long periods of treatment…"

"Yes. Yes, exactly. So we need foolproof and easy access to the Massospora, and I know how to do it because it's what I do…no more playing doctor."

Dr. Alexander chuckled, listening now with enthusiasm. "Do tell."

"Massospora might hide from us, and from the antifungal treatments, but it can't and won't hide from its endosymbiont—Y. Pestis. Not even after I take a sample and give it new instructions."

"You're going to use the bacteria to kill all of the Massospora, a double agent…" Genesis's eyes were warm with respect and approval.

Theresa nodded and glanced over, blushing at Genesis's conspicuous attention. "Mm-hm. And first, it's going to shut off production of all but the psilocybin and psilocin they produce." She drummed her fingers on the desk thinking. "It'll be a docile little infection before it self-destructs."

Dr. Alexander was shaking his head and let out a low whistle. "Beautiful. But, how best to do it?"

Theresa frowned, the corners of her lips twitching as she bit at her inner cheeks. "I need the real thing…How many days until we dock above WASA?"

"Just three days." "That's soon. Maybe not soon enough, but it'll solve this thing. Once I have it, everyone we bring on board, and the crew, will be safe."

"We're bringing them in. All of them."

Aurelia's blue eyes shone with feverish certainty in the red-orange of the solar powered street lights. The flecks of amber in her irises sparked brighter in the extremes of light and shadow. Her jaw was set, brows high in defiance even as Richard's implacable face took on notes of derision. There were bodies moving on the loading dock, milling, some slamming into the sealed doors. Marilla and all of the others were loaded into the car and silent now, sedated but still struggling on their cots ensconced along the walls of the railcar.

"I don't think you know what you are saying, Aurelia. You're just—" He pressed a hand over his eyes as if the squeeze away his own fatigue.

Sweat beaded on her brow and her wide eyes were moist with threatening tears. He bit back sharp words, instead deliberately searching for a gentler way to say it. "You are not—yourself yet. Tired, overwrought from seeing them—like this." He gestured towards the window with the tilt of his jaw, towards the mumbling, wailing bodies just outside.

Aurelia blinked. "I could accuse you of overwrought too, Richard. You don't just call me emotional. You're not yourself either—we need to bring them. Some could be treatable." Shifting on the cot and staring into her eyes without giving any sign that he would acquiesce, Richard waited for her to look away, to fold, but instead her eyes took on a glassy, fervent gleam. She stared him down instead, fists clenched at her sides and, as he watched, the sharp glint in her eyes shifted into something both pained and furious. Through grit teeth she spit the next words. She widened her eyes and it seemed for a moment he could see into them before she flinched away, a visible shiver running through her before she opened them again.

He imagined what must be there in her head. She was no longer seeing him but instead some bleeding and deformed opponent in her own mind. *Flashbacks…she's still having them too.* If that was the case, her judgement *was* off.

The bodies of the dead were slamming into the glass with greater frequency now, like the ones in containment had slammed against their doors. Richard pressed his lips together and stared at Aurelia as if sizing up an opponent, still a child but never childlike, and even less-so now at eleven. He would have to discuss instead of command with her in this compromised state, and his head was throbbing again, phantom imagery, the ghost of his own hallucination memories threatening.

"I acquiesced to bringing your siblings on board despite their condition…they had no treatment while we were recovering, their medicots malfunctioning for whatever reason. If you unstrapped them instead of sedating them, they'd be just like those outside."

Aurelia doubled down. "We can't take all of their vital signs, can't separate them out if any are still living, at least not in the time we have left. But we can bring them and let the Pinnacle's crew figure it out. It's part of their mission, isn't it? You said it's part of their mission."

Richard sat up on the cot, swinging his legs over the side and then pausing to catch his breath. He looked out the window at the darkness that had descended, the heavy blanket of clouds obscured by the absence of light and blanking out the stars and moon like a layer of spilled ink. The Pinnacle should be close now, and he wanted to be there when it arrived. *We're wasting time…*Impatience colored his words when he turned back to Aurelia.

"To collect survivors. That's it. The mission is to get us off of this rotating graveyard and collect any survivors. These are not survivors and there won't likely be any, at least not any that are going to come out of hiding." He raised a hand before she could renew her arguments. "But fine, we'll drag dead weight to the WASA, and you can study them like your rats, yes?"

Richard quirked a brow and stood, crossing to the control panel. He selected the empty car behind theirs and accessed the doors. They slid open with an audible hiss as the seals parted, allowing the crowd of bodies to fill the car, and they did, flowing in like water through a broken dam. "Train car at capacity, doors closing." The Train's AI conductor spoke to them in pleasant tones, smooth, cheerful, and more appropriate for a picnic in the countryside than a forced exodus.

He sat back down, sinking against the cool glass and metal of the wall behind his cot. "Satisfied?"

Aurelia bit her lip and nodded, staring into the windows of the now full railcar behind them, flicking her eyes every few moments from the shadowy shapes that filled it to the twelve in her own car that mirrored their behavior. Richard watched her. He could see interest, fascination maybe, and a healthy dose of fear in those wide eyes, still ringed with bruised lids, chapped pink and bloodshot. They had a long way to recovery still, assuming this treatment protocol was ultimately successful and there was no relapse this time.

The train started to move again, slowly at first, and then picking up speed until the tall light posts on either side of the track blurred into thin streamers of orange light. WASA was ahead of them, and then the Pinnacle, once it arrived.

Richard brushed the tangles of dirty-blond hair back from Aurelia's forehead with an absent hand, still covered in sores that were dry and healing now. His voice was gentler than before.

"Aurelia, Sleep now."

He didn't wait for compliance, instead lying down himself and closing his eyes.

ON SOLID GROUND

The station was the same they departed from when they first left for Mars: expansive and built in a time when colonization and space exploration were at the forefront of human ambition. Now it was nearly empty, with only the necessary lights turned on, dark corridors and rooms the common theme.

The ground felt unstable, as if it wasn't really there beneath Theresa's feet one moment, and then the next was so certain and solid that she might end up crumpled on it like some boneless creature. The spinning sensation was the worst part. All she could do was pick a spot far ahead to stare at and hold onto something until it abated. The medications to increase tolerance for zero-g travel helped, they really did, but this was still an adjustment. *At least they aren't here yet. I can adjust and then get to work—if it's here somewhere.*

A thick-fingered hand rested on her shoulder and she opened her eyes. Brogan was visibly older despite longevity treatment, some white streaks in his hair and a posture that gave away his penchant for sitting and using VR in favor of more active pursuits. His barrel chest was thicker, his grin bright and full of fresh-kindled hope.

"Been hiding out in here, myself and three others running the station. Just a skeleton crew, really, since we locked up. But the WGC was broadcasting for a bit…and it's wild out there."

His voice continued to drone in and out of Theresa's awareness like the ground beneath her feet. She put out a hand to stabilize herself and then found she wasn't sure where it should go.

Brogan stepped into it, allowing her hand to come down on his shoulder. Theresa smiled with gratitude and then grew serious, holding the eye-contact. "I need to test you and the other three, see if you're carriers." Brogan quirked his lips and scrunched up a brow, scratching the side of his face and cocking his head. "You know we have that decontamination room…been in there several times since this all started, plus we locked it all down here. No one's been in or out for a couple months."

"Doesn't matter. I don't need it to make sure you're clean. I need a sample of the thing as soon as I can get it."

His eyes widened and then his attention moved to the footsteps echoing down the hall. Genesis stepped into the large reception and departure room from a side hallway that circled around the complex. She smiled at the three staff members that walked in a cluster around her, as if vying for closer proximity to her.

Theresa shook her head. It wasn't the form-fitting grey, ribbed spacesuit that captured or held their attention, but more likely the way her eyes fell on anything that walked as if she'd lovingly devour it in one way or another. *It must take a lot to have that turned on all the time—maybe it's her default.* Theresa felt a thrill of warmth run through her and wondered at it as if observing it in a specimen. *Arousal…anticipation, fear? Sometimes they're all the same…she's contagious.*

"Enjoy the tour?" Brogan was smiling in a way that mirrored Genesis's perpetual flirtation. Theresa wet her lips and cleared her throat before Genesis could answer. Her voice took on a sharp, all-business tone. "Let's take samples now. If none of these ones have it, I'm going out to find some myself, in a rat or a person, or the air. I'll catch it myself if need be. Richard's railcar is a day off from here still. I'm not wasting that."

Brogan grew serious, drawing himself up and redirecting his attention. "The lab's this way, down the hall on the other side."

He glanced towards the incoming elevator shaft that led up to the space station where the pinnacle was docked. "Any others coming down?"

Genesis shook her head. "Not yet. No need to risk infecting the Captain and crew before Theresa has this cure ready for us."

Brogan nodded, turning to lead them down the hall. "Be good to see Captain Neil. I took a liking to him. Used to see him off for all the missions before Mars. Bastard couldn't transition worth a damn though." Brogan chuckled. He continued to chatter as he led them down the hall to the laboratory, emergency lights coming on to give some illumination however dim. "Have to forgive the dark; we have the whole station set to conservation levels since this all started, which means any extra we get from the solar panels will be stored in case the whole system goes down."

Theresa's vertigo was fading, though her legs still felt weak, as if they would keep moving in the same direction and buckle with each step. The echo in the halls filled her head and gave rise to a melancholy that could not supplant the rising tension and excitement of the work ahead—and the children.

She'd see them soon.

They had stopped outside of a large, sealed door labeled in bold black lettering, **LABORATORY**. Brogan's cheerful voice was still talking. The lights were off inside the room, evidenced by the large windows that reflected back their own faces instead of revealing anything within.

"Now, in here should be everything you need. Not my area, but pretty well equipped, so said the last team we had here—was supposed to be another one sent—"

Theresa forced herself to focus in on the words that he was

saying, pulling her thoughts away from mental planning and halting the impulse to scan immediately and head into the lab.

"Wait—why isn't there still a team here? They could have been working on this."

Brogan's mouth was still open from being cut off, but he was happy to begin again. He shrugged, a wry smile creeping onto his face. "Weeeeell, WASA station was pretty low priority resource wise in recent years. They cut staff, disbanded our research team about six months ago. They'd been using us pretty infrequently with nobody going back and forth between Mars after things, uh…got tense?"

Theresa's polite smile dropped. "Got tense? Better you not say it that way to Neil. They attacked and killed our people after sending us to colonize under false pretenses."

Brogan's smile dropped as well, and he rubbed a hand on the back of his neck. "That's uh…that's rough. Was my understanding that it was mutual animosity—but I wasn't a part of all that. I just ran the elevator. The WGC makes all the decisions down here, ya know?"

Genesis quirked a brow at Theresa from where she stood behind Brogan and the three staff members, but she did not intervene with platitudes and easy words to smooth out the tension.

Theresa sighed, for once wishing Genesis would do that thing that, in all other instances, irritated her and then, losing interest in the disagreement, she put up a hand to cut the topic short. "It's long past...as is the WGC, I expect. Let me in this lab now, and I'll make sure we all get back to Mars."

Brogan's brow smoothed out. He looked relieved and put a hand on her shoulder. "You're good people."

Theresa gave an impatient smile and looked over his shoulder again at the staff members. "If you aren't research, then what do you do? Anything that gives you lab experience?"

The tall woman on the far left who identified herself as Jillian

Crantz gave a quick nod. "I'm engineering, he's station infrastructure, and she runs the agricultural department. WASA is entirely self-sustaining—er, was self-sustaining, before they destaffed us; some things might be a stretch for just us if we were stranded here long enough." She paused in her rapid-fire monologue to suck in a breath and give a nervous smile. "We were actually reassigned as well when this whole mess started, but it all fell apart before we could report, so we sat tight."

Theresa waited for her to finish, squinting as she struggled to maintain focus on the rapid stream of words. Her thoughts needed to be in the lab, and they were pulling her there with more urgency the longer she stood outside that door. "So that's a no. No lab experience. Just keep this place running, then—after I test you."

Genesis caught Theresa's eye as the others entered the lab ahead of them. "You know I can help in the lab as needed—after I set up a system to direct survivors here."

"I need you in the lab. I need more hands, more eyes, than I have, and we both know you have the head for it."

Genesis smiled at the grudging compliment. "As soon as you get samples of it, call me in. But I have to do this first."

Richard adjusted the ventilator mask to ensure a good fitting as soon as it emerged from the side of the medicot. Worry creased his brow, darkening the shadows that surrounded his eyes.

"Patient forty-seven, Santana, maintaining 88 percent oxygen saturation with supplemental oxygen." The medibot's voice was appropriately serious.

Aurelia stood nearby, only the wide stare giving evidence to her worry. "That's not high enough, is it? She's suffocating."

Richard glanced over at her and frowned. "You should be

resting. You weren't far off from this a few days ago." She wet her lips and continued to stare, giving no sign that she'd heard his words. "How much farther now?"

Richard looked back at Santana's face. Her skin looked dusky and bruised, lips faintly blue around the corners. Her breathing was loud, a crackling wheeze punctuating her inbreath and a whining sound like coyotes far off in the hills marked her out breath. He placed a hand over her ribcage, feeling the pulls of struggling lungs as her ribs retracted, sucking in in a desperate effort to pull in more oxygen.

"We are approximately thirteen hours out from W.A.S.A. If you sleep, the time will pass faster."

Aurelia looked left and right and made a face, scrunching her nose up and sighing as she climbed onto a cot.

Richard ignored it. No sense rubbing in the small victory, or it might be the last time she complied after this.

Santana was feverish again, unlikely from the Massospora X— that should be gone, or nearly so. But maybe from an opportunistic infection in her damaged lungs.

"Medibot 47, treat Santana with trimethoprim-sulfamethoxazole."

He stood and turned his attention to the other children, moving slowly and using the handrails on the sides of the railcar. Many of them were recovering. Several were sitting up, thin and frail looking, bruises under their jawlines and sores pocking their skin. But they were healing. Bram was one of these, small but strong. His brown curls were matted, and his face looked nearly skeletal with how dark the bruising around his eyes was, and how hollow his cheeks.

Others were doing less well, Gelsemium's vital signs had stabilized, but she hadn't woken since coming on the train, and was still strapped down so she wouldn't fall while tossing in her sleep as violently as she did. Gavin fared better than Gelsemium, waking twice. The first time he was delirious, raging and then weeping, but there was still light in his eyes—madness, yes, but not the empty stare of the screaming dead. He was lucid the next time for just a moment, a weak smile and an apology.

Richard placed a hand on the boy's forehead, no longer burning with fever. Their conversation would have to wait until he was well and they were settled into the W.A.S.A. Complex. There was more to him sneaking off to find the others himself and failing to return with them, and Richard had some idea what. Gavin was not reckless or impulsive like some of the children, regardless of what he might want to project so as to deflect questions or scolding. This was calculated. Gavin stirred and then resettled. Richard smiled. It didn't matter until they were well.

An insistent chime roused him from contemplation, startling him. They were messages from Theresa. There would be more now that the ship had landed, no delay beyond their own thinking processes. He tried his throat, clearing it and saying her name.

"Theresa—Hm." A residual cough made him wince. His voice was still a bit rough, speech painful—she would hear it. Written words would do better. He glanced over at the handheld. "Read Theresa's message aloud."

"Richard, we're still monitoring all the children's vital signs from here and many look good—better. But I'm not confident in the treatment, and Santana and some of the others need something else. Anyway, I have another plan, but I need samples of the infection and you aren't here yet."

Richard closed his eyes; a wave of vertigo hit him hard, a flash of eyeless faces wet with blood as their hands pawed at her, hips thrusting towards her naked body. He sucked in breath, holding and then exhaling slowly until the hallucination passed.

He whispered to the device, saving his voice. "You can wait. We'll be there in less than thirteen hours. Santana is on a respirator. The medibots are sustaining her and the others still struggling. Infection seems clear for now, but there is residual damage and I bet there is some other antibiotic resistant infection brewing—the cities aren't safe."

Her reply was near immediate, so much so that it startled him after years of having the distance between planets impeding their communication.

"I'm not going into the cities. That would take too long. This thing is widespread. I'll find it here. See you soon."

He groaned and flicked a glance at where Aurelia had fallen asleep, her lips slack with exhaustion, the repose of sleep taking off years and reminding him of younger versions of the girl.

"Your mother." He shook his head, a weary smile playing on the corners of his lips. "Theresa: Use the intermediate hosts, then. Bring a team if you leave W.A.S.A."

His head was throbbing again. He pressed the heels of both hands into his temples. When would the clarity return? The speed of thought? He struggled to push through the curtains of fog, fatigue and confusion, that made it feel as if whole portions of his brain were shut off, or the pathways connecting them blocked like freeways clogged with stopped traffic.

A lance of fear sickened him. It was like a gut punch, the sudden thought coming with the visceral force that every clear thought carried with it since contracting this thing. The weight of hallucination, and false certainty behind the most absurd ideas, bludgeoned them into the forefront of his mind like a carnival mallet. This thought seemed more significant than the ones before it, and the fear settled into his gut and intensified the throbbing headache. The damage could be permanent, his mind slowed, thinking altered beyond repair. It was a heavy thought, and he couldn't reason past, not with this headache. Twelve hours, seven minutes, and some burden might be lifted.

COLLECTION

Their nasal and throat swabs were clean, blood was clean, their lungs, spinal fluid, urine, the interior of the whole compound seemed to be. Fine. It was fine. Samples would be somewhere outside. If she had to climb into an old sewer, she would.

Theresa laughed at the absurdity of the statement. It was a wild, desperate sound, like the sort you'd expect from someone keeping silent watch for ghosts in an abandoned asylum. The sound of it made her wince, but it was absurd. There were no sewers here. The only ones left were in old cities and were gradually being torn out. This place was isolated and boasted only modern construction. For a sewer, she'd need old city territory, and that wasn't the best option just now. She needed to be quick, if she was to avoid herself and the others ending up with this thing before the end of it. Brogan and the other three were on preventive treatment, as was Genesis and herself, the same thing that she'd prescribed for Richard and the children. It wouldn't be good enough. Not by itself. In fact, this treatment might not even be effective for anyone other than her own offspring, or anyone without a next generation immune system like Genesis, but it would help. She hoped.

The doors leading to the courtyard outside of the central

dome of W.A.S.A station led first into a separate decontamination chamber. *That might have kept it out.* Theresa contemplated the likelihood that the decontamination would kill Massospora X spores as the outer seals released and the doors opened and closed behind her. *If it did, I bet the WGC wished it had installed a few more of these in their own headquarters.* But it probably wasn't just decontamination that made any difference. If they hadn't isolated, they'd have brought it in after getting infected.

The sky was milky in the darkness, stars and galaxies visible in the expanse of night sky above her in the absence of city lights, the air uncomfortably muggy and hot. It made her sweat through her lab coat and fog up the interior of her containment suit. The fine hairs around the crown of tightly-pinned braids stuck to her temples and the back of her neck. Her feet and calves felt hot from the warmth baking off of the scrolling sidewalk, even through the many layers of protective clothing.

The sidewalk carried her farther into the darkness towards the magnetic rail station just this side of the sparse, anemic tree line ahead. Theresa drummed the guardrail until the absurdity of her standing there and allowing the sidewalk to move her hit home. She almost regretted taking it. Just because it was there didn't mean she was at its mercy. Theresa took up a jog, taking advantage of the scrolling sidewalk's motion and amplifying it with her own. This was better, this was taking action. It felt like she was running in slow motion, as if her brain was sending the signals while her muscles responded with only a fraction of what they were asked for. *Probably about a third what I need.* Her joints ached as well, a deep throbbing everywhere bone met ligament met muscle. She'd slacked on the weighted garments the last few years on Mars, wearing them less and less, and there hadn't been time to build back up.

She was feeling it now, lightheaded, muscles burning and joint-ache deepening to stabbing pains and a weakness that made her right knee overextend and collapse under her. She caught herself with her hands, breath leaving her with the impact and sharp pains jarring up from her scraped hands to her shoulders. The gloves didn't tear, but still it hurt.

Theresa gasped, sucking in air and waiting for her heart to slow and the pains to abate. This was stupid—Theresa pictured the last text sent by Richard. *Just wait. We have plenty of samples on this train, probably in ourselves as well.*

And her answer: *No time, Richard. Santana is declining fast. Several of the others are declining. I can fix it.*

And the trees were close. There would be something there. If not there, then at the nearest city down the magnetic train route.

The sound grew louder as she approached the trees, walking now with a limp, a chorus of shrill voices filling the night with some unrecognizable, wordless song. It was too shrill and incessant to be crickets or frogs. Theresa paused, transfixed, and searched her memory banks for a name, a source. It was buried deep and came from sound clips played in a song like most of her memories were—linked to lyrics or melodies. The words spoke of another time: Earth, but not modern Earth. Far past. The voice was deep and warm, pushing out lyrics at rapid heartbeat speed.

> *One more chorus*
> *A song from the wild*
>
> *Risin up from our trash*
> *How to break the mold.*
>
> *Build something better…*

Theresa felt the beat of it deep within, the feel of the lyrics filling her chest with an ache akin to homesickness. It was tied to that sound, the smell of damp earth—not red Martian soil, but instead the thick, loamy, black jungle soil that had sustained humanity for so long. She choked back the emotion as her steps carried her to the edge of the trees. Everything felt somehow familiar, and yet foreign. Earth wasn't home anymore. The gravity was oppressive, crushing her. The night sky, too bright with moonlight. It wasn't home.

That sound, though. Playing on loop, inside and outside her mind. The sparse leftovers of what was once a forest was filled with that sound that made-up the backtrack of the song she remembered.

Cicadas. That's what it was. Not crickets, but the sharp trill of billions of cicadas out of their thirteen-year hibernation singing together and filling the night with it. Were they here when she left Earth? Were they so loud? She couldn't remember, but why would she, with Abby hidden in the RPU taking all of her focus. Maybe they weren't here, or were more numerous now. It was inevitable; there were years of work put into ecosystem rehabilitation by people like Donovan and David after the WGC took over, and cicadas might fill several niches until other species could recover.

Pavement gave way to the same dark, sodden earth that she could imagine the smell of, wet, musky, and thick with decay. She stumbled, already-aching gloved hands and wrists landing in boggy soil. The underbrush was speckled with some sort of blight, leaves mottled with patches of disease. Theresa crawled through it, slowly, eyes trained on the moonlit ground. Cicadas in many shades, taking flight from the underbrush with a buzz of rapid wings to escape her searching hands as she moved. One landed on her translucent faceplate before taking off with a sharp trilling whir and a tiny gust of air as wings brushed her mask and it escaped into the struggling greenery. There were so many. Theresa's eyes widened as a cloud of the insects scattered out from the next bush she disturbed; she whispered to her handheld that was mounted on her upper arm with a strap. "Record audio and visual and send to Donovan: Hear that? Cicadas. There are so many of them. Is that normal?…Thoughts? Comments? End recording and send." He needed to see it, and she wanted to hear his rambling on the subject.

Later.

She felt a surge of guilt for the distraction. Focus and speed was crucial. *But desperation and sloppy mistakes will kill them just as sure as my shiny-object syndrome.*

She moved on, a scowl building between feathered brows as the ground grew wetter, dirty water pooling around her knees and hands as they pressed into the ground. She lifted and shook off a muddy glove.

"Fuck."

Theresa stared at the retreating semi-translucent amphibian bodies with their loping progression into the darkness and the whir of more cicadas taking flight. She watched the dark water fill the hole left by her hand. Rodent droppings wouldn't be easy to find in this, and if there were live ones here they'd be hard to catch. Frog-shit wasn't going to cut it, or cicada crap for that matter.

She sat back on her haunches in a low squat, just high enough to keep the seat of her suit out of the water. The city was farther than she liked, and brought more risk. The footage from the inside of the WGC quarantine facilities replayed in her memory: the infected, delirious, and violent, moving well after their vital signs showed they couldn't be living. The woman with staring eyes grabbing Richard until he shoved her back into that room and sealed it.

She felt sick to her stomach, and her face itched from sweat and the brush of stray hairs she couldn't push away. Lifting one soiled hand, she scrubbed the back of it against her mask and pressed hard to appease the itch. She tried to avoid rubbing mud all over the clear surface. She was feeling light-headed and tired. Adjustment to gravity was a bitch. *That and long-term adrenaline exposure.* She couldn't smell the air around her, but she knew it would be unpleasant to breathe without the mask, the soil likely full of molds and all sorts of bacteria, fungal spores…she turned her hand over, inspecting her glove with a new excitement. A wild smile grew on her lips and she stared at the viscous brown mud. *That's what the smell would be: mold...spores. Why am I looking for rats when Massospora is a fungus?*

Because Y. Pestis uses rats as a host...

"Fuck." This time she said it with wonder, like I'll-be-damned rolled into one much simpler and infinitely more convenient expletive. *Fuck. I'll be un-damned.*

Theresa pulled an electronic test kit out and pressed the sensors to the soil sample on her hand. The results were almost instantaneous. Massospora X was here. Right here in this mess, but not inside the W.A.S.A station? Brogan said they'd been isolated. *That* isolated? *Whatever. I need to move on. But yes, that isolated. Self-contained and self-sustaining, clean to prevent sending undesirable microscopic hitchhikers up the space elevator.*

But the soil wouldn't do it. Most Entomophthorales couldn't be cultured that way.

"I need an infected specimen. And it doesn't have to be a rodent..." It was just a whisper in the darkness, barely audible over the chorus of insect voices singing for their prospective mates. Theresa reached into a pocket of her lab coat and she removed a large oblong specimen case, unsealing it before tucking it back into her pocket.

She smiled and lunged at the next patch of leafy undergrowth and it came to life with the exodus of small-winged bodies with large front arms curled as if ready to box. There were so many, it was as if the leaves themselves were flying away.

Moving quickly now, she grasped at the air that was alive with fluttering and closed her hands around the small retreating shapes in handfuls. She wiggled the specimen container out with full hands and released the small captives into it, sealing the tube and repeating the procedure with several more. She brushed her hands off on the sides of a tree, scraping off as much of the mud as she could. Decontamination would take care of the rest.

She felt tempted to try to run again but settled on a hobbling walk along the scrolling sidewalk. She thanked it silently now as it brought her up to the W.A.S.A complex faster than her weakened and aching legs could otherwise manage.

The message she sent to Richard was brief but triumphant. "I have it! Easy grab. No need to have worried."

Genesis sat at the large screen, every possible section of it isolated for a different task, with several more projected out from the desk in front of her for physical manipulation. The heading read:

CALL FOR COLLECTION

with each divided screen labeled for another mega-city or research and rehabilitation outpost. The message being sent out through all communication channels scrolled across the top of the screen.

Collection of all survivors for treatment and speedy recovery underway. Report by railcar or other most efficient means to W.A.S.A Station. Report to W.A.S.A station for immediate treatment and rescue. Evacuation to begin in one week's time.

Genesis sent the message out. Richard's login information, obtained from Diadonna herself, meant she could login as a member of the WGC and it would broadcast in each and every city on repeat until the Pinnacle departed, playing on every communal or personal screen by emergency broadcast.

But how many could they expect to come? The only known survivors so far were the AUC children, Richard. These four at

WASA were unexposed.

Genesis pulled up the data from the WGC North America headquarters, from the Reproductive Council Headquarters, and the WGC Eurasia Headquarters, in what was once Southern Soviet Union territory.

Their quarantine and recovery centers were full and alive, with bodies moving on camera. Some were strapped into medicots and others locked into rooms or wandering the halls. None displayed normal vital signs, according to the monitoring systems. None were alive by conventional standards.

Standing and pacing in front of the screen, Genesis stared with rapt fascination at those moving bodies, jerking and stumbling as if they'd stayed out too late drinking or else woken with a bitch of a hangover, clumsy, frantic, and unable to control their bodies.

She smiled and shook her head. It was an amusing thought, despite the gruesome reality that these stumbling fatalities put on display. How long would they move? How long would they writhe against any moving body that came close, as if even in death their lust couldn't be satisfied? Until they rotted, perhaps?

"Open file name: Mars' List of kin. Search by name, Genetic ID, and last known whereabouts for location and current status."

"Searching." The AI didn't sound excited to help. Some had much more human intonation. This one sounded either bored or indifferent to her search, and she wasn't sure if it was a relief or an irritation. The WGC Eurasia live camera feed was still displayed and held Genesis's attention as she awaited search results.

A woman with extensive mottled bruising under a curtain of auburn hair that obscured her face passed in front of the camera, head cocked at a sharp angle to the left. A patch of dried blood marred her right temple. Her eyes could have been blue, maybe green, but they were milky now, with half-mast lids obscuring them further. Her lips moved and a susurration of sound seemed to escape her dried, cracking lips, but it was too quiet for Genesis to make out any words.

Genesis scowled at the familiar features. It was not Joanna, but the resemblance reminded Genesis of her promise. The security camera face recognition software labeled this one as Ivanna Petrov, an apprentice in epidemiology.

Not that she had forgotten the promise. The thought kept recurring with irritating urgency, in fact.

She sighed, shaking off the urge to hurry, to rush off somewhere instead of conducting adequate searches first. She tucked her hair behind her ears and interlaced her fingers to stretch them before getting started. The records were accessible to her, at least with a little massaging. *Start at the beginning, or end, really. The end of David and Joanna.* Genesis's nimble hands moved on the touchscreen, finding, unlocking, and searching files. A small smile lit her face—the excitement of the chase. *That night at the hospital, the bleeding. David was sedated and Joanna died in surgery.*

She wet her lips and closed the case file. Their case was a well-documented anomaly, an example within the Reproductive Council; it was the only known contraceptive implant failure to result in a live child. But that was another search. A completely different rabbit hole to go down; they'd never have kept the child with its mother, if they had kept it alive at all. And would they keep a living reminder of such a stark embarrassment to the Contraceptive Implant program?

She shrugged for no audience but herself and clicked pointed nails on the front of the desk as she scanned over the rows upon rows of files. She clicked her tongue and shook her head before filtering them by date and location. *If Joanna did die…check all the deaths from that location and follow the trail…look for transfers, reassignments, name changes…or her genetic ID, uniquely hers but attached to another name.*

Her smile broadened and she let out a soft laugh of satisfaction. That was the best route, yes. Something about swimming through the Reproductive Council's records was uniquely satisfying, like solving a maze with a minotaur to seduce in the center of it all…

The search would take some time, but if it was here it would come up. Genesis moved the search screen to her upper right, watching mesmerized as Genetic IDs scrolled passed faster than the human eye could read them. She opened another screen, tapping into the Reproductive Council's foster placements for that year. Any that fit the time could be checked for their genetic contributors.

Genesis's handheld lit up and the AI intoned in a smooth, genderless voice that Theresa had messaged, and asked if she would like it read aloud.

"Yes, read it."

"Very well: Theresa states that she has found the required specimen and will be in need of your lab assistance shortly."

Genesis glanced up at the search screens, watching the information fly by for several seconds before standing and arching her back upward until she caught herself in a backbend. She held the stretch, walking her hands and feet closer together and breathing deeply another moment before pulling herself back up into a stand and rotating her neck in a circle to stretch the tight muscles there.

"Fine. Sync my handheld to W.A.S.A computer system and continue running the searches, lock station to control only by my handheld. I'll just do both for now."

A sharp ping sound came from the computer as she stood to leave, and she turned back.

"Match found for both ID searches."

Genesis's eyes widened and she stepped closer to the screen.

"Okay. Access video surveillance for first search subject. Work assignment and home." She waited. The Genetic ID displayed on the screen matched Joanna's. Her name was Joan Styles now. Not so different, or cleverly hidden, but who would have or could have looked for her?

Several streaming video files opened on the screen. Genesis paused all but one and manually manipulated the one she left running to zoom in on the subject.

It was a woman in her late fifties with longevity treatment, judging by the faint smile lines and a streak of grey in twisting dark brown hair that framed an otherwise youthful face. She was turned away from the camera, showing less than a profile as she paced the floor of a laboratory filled with plant and animal specimens.

Genesis tried to access other cameras, impatient. She could go there herself to get her if it wasn't far. She flicked a glance at the woman's personal data listed under the search. *Joan Styles, Nuevo Zacatecas, Old Mexico Environmental Rehabilitation Center.* Genesis did the math quickly. Roughly 2047 miles from here by magnetic rail would take at least 10 hours. She looked back at the video where Joan Styles was no longer in view.

"Access Joan Styles current vital statistics and display." A miniature version of the space elevator appeared on the screen with the shuttle traveling from ground to station and back in a constant loop. Genesis scowled at the imagery meant to occupy her while she waited. She growled under her breath.

Another sharp ping indicated the search had ended and the AI intoned an answer that intensified her irritation. "Vital statistics not currently available."

"Fine. Access Infrared."

This time the response came quickly. "I'm sorry, but the Environmental Rehabilitation Research Center of Nuevo Zacatecas does not have that capability at this time. Is there something else I can help you with?"

Genesis shoved loose strands of black hair back from her face. *You'd think there was no one left to maintain or troubleshoot this equipment on site.* A laugh escaped before she could catch it. She bit her lip, staring daggers at the screen as she wracked her brain for another solution.

"Access camera controls."

"Camera not responding."

It didn't make sense to be angered by the nonplussed, monotone of the AI, but she was. *Why?* The mental question caught her off guard. She felt a rush of uneasiness and confusion before shoving the question aside. This was what she was tasked with here. First priority was to collect Richard and the children, second was to gather as many survivors as possible, with a focus on the list of relatives.

Yes. Stating it that way was grounding and helped her regain focus. A small, confident smile pulled at her lips as she made her way to the laboratory.

STATUS UNKNOWN

The stars reflected on the midnight waves far below, sending shimmering galaxies to froth and foam against the base of the cliff. Deep shadow obscured the path back to the colony and the west mountains were lost in darkness, as were the domes, except for a faint glow against the central garden walls from the mushroom-shaped solar lights that lit the paths.

Deimos brushed a beetle from his wrist and then scooted closer to Abby to avoid the spines of a cycad and the insects its fruit were attracting.

"See them?" Abby was leaning over the edge, reaching out and pointing at pale shapes moving in the dark water.

"Yes."

She backed away from the edge and pulled her shirt over her head, tossing it aside. "I'm going in." The drop off was a few feet away and she stood just back from the edge.

Deimos hadn't moved to follow, and she stopped, looked over her shoulder. "Why aren't you coming? You need to say something, don't you? Something difficult." Deimos sighed, rising to stand next to her. He gestured towards the water below and then hesitated.

Abby prodded him, pushing his shoulder with one hand. "I

said I wanted to hear it. It's fine."

He let the words out in measured tones, trying to blunt the effect with his delivery. "You're using the whalefins…to not try."

She didn't answer at first but folded her bare arms across her chest; the cool night air was giving her goosebumps and his words stung. "I have tried, though."

"Nope, not true. You're doing what's easy. Avoiding the whole colony. Hiding in the caves or your room—even from me."

"Then swim with me." She pulled at his shirt and gestured to the cliff.

"No. Not gonna hide with you. And I won't help you if you ask me to like you did, and then hide from me."

They could hear faint whale-song down below in the gaps between their words and even as he spoke Abby stared down at the dancing shapes. "We could talk about it after we swim." She edged closer to the drop.

"Ugh. Stop it, Abby." His tone was sharp, eyes flashing, and for just a moment it was like Genesis was back. It filled her with excitement and something akin to homesickness, pulled her attention away from the water and the creatures in it. "You're acting younger than I am. Just say you miss them, or you're scared or whatever and move on."

Abby pressed her lips together and thought she would answer if she could. She tested the words to see if they would come and was relieved when they did. "I think…I don't like not knowing what to expect. I don't like hearing things when it doesn't mean anything—that sounds confusing. I mean hearing my mother say it's going well, or Genesis, or the colonists speculating and dwelling and none of it has anything to do with how it will turn out. So why think it? Why say it? So, I'm not hiding…I'm just waiting."

He shook his head. "You're hiding from it instead of filtering it out." Abby closed her eyes and took a slow breath. Her head was spinning, and she wanted the icy water around her to cool it away, to wrap her up until it was silent inside and out. But the last thing

Deimos said stuck. *Hiding instead of filtering…How can I filter my own brain chatter if I can't filter theirs…*

"Okay, I'm just tired—from waiting…I'll try not to hide. So could you just swim with me? Please?"

"Yeah, sure." He pulled off his clothes and tossed them in the sand with hers and glanced over the edge. The anger had gone out of his face and was replaced with a small smile. "They're still down there, swimming and singing. You first…"

Theresa wasn't waiting for her. In fact, she didn't notice at all when Genesis came. She was covered in a protective suit with an attached mask like the one placed outside the door for Genesis to don before entering.

"The searches are going well so far, though most of those on the lists are…"

Genesis stopped mid thought and stood next to Theresa in front of a station full of laboratory equipment. Theresa wasn't listening. She moved from centrifuge to electrophoresis apparatus to mass spectrometer and back, adjusting settings and checking progress without pause in her movements or time for thought, like a rapid-fire autopilot. Lidded culture dishes held dissected insects, their green and khaki colored bodies separated into their many parts, legs on one side, abdomen split in two with the lower thirds missing.

Genesis stared down at the dishes and then back at Theresa. "Cicadas are an intermediary host, then?"

"Yes. And rats. I thought of the rats first, most obvious. But here we have more of these to get ahold of." She glanced over at Genesis for the first time. "The search for survivors? Most of them are…" She drew the last word out expecting Genesis to fill in the blank and was not disappointed.

"Dead. Yes. Dead, or unknown status, like so many moving needles in a haystack painted silver. We won't find them, but we'll try."

Theresa was nodding, full focus returned to her equipment as she pulled the overgrown plug from the lower abdomen of another cicada for processing.

She grew animated then, gesturing with her free hand for Genesis to read the message on her handheld nearby "I sent footage of these to Donovan. You can read it, but basically what we have are two intermediary hosts, both of which can infect humans through bodily fluids, droppings, aerosolized particles, all containing spores because it's a fungus. Cicadas come out in thirteen-year cycles. These ones anyway. So their emergence with the hot weather would have triggered it. High temps were delayed here at W.A.S.A because of storms. It gave time for them to self-quarantine. That's what Donovan thinks. And with the rats feasting on these in high number, that gives another host."

Genesis read Donovan's more detailed theory of the life cycle and intermediary host relationship of this novel Massospora variety while Theresa continued. The two streams of information came together to form quite a picture.

She dropped Theresa's handheld on the desk. "What can I do to speed the process here? You seem to be doing all of it simultaneously."

Theresa snorted. "I'm used to that. But it takes longer."

Genesis smirked and licked her lips. "Going solo only takes longer if you don't know what you're doing."

Theresa frowned. "You realize I know far more than—" She cut herself off, her face reddening with embarrassment as she grasped the innuendo. "Just process these. All of them. These powdery white plugs and the tissue that comes with it. Don't bother looking for any ovipositor; it's obliterated by the infection. The ones without the plug, just take the lower third of their abdomen."

Theresa was still blushing despite her apparent focus. Genesis set to work, but not without chuckling at Theresa's red cheeks.

Theresa glared over. "The faster you process those, the faster I have this finished."

Genesis shrugged, hands already fast at work. "I can work and flirt simultaneously."

Theresa's blush intensified. "Well, I can't. I can't talk to you and focus. It isn't even Massospora we need most—well, I need both, but it's the endosymbiont bacteria I want, so I can put it to work for us."

Genesis nodded, demeanor serious aside from a warm glint in her eyes that Theresa did not look over to see. "Clever, clever. My hands are at your complete disposal until the rest of my search results are in or the children arrive."

Theresa's reply was delayed. She was looking into the mass spectrometer, eventually mumbling 'good' for whoever was still listening.

So close… They were only six hours off, and Aurelia could feel the anticipation building. Many of the others were awake now but still strapped down, Bram was sitting on the side of her medicot, pale and painfully thin, sipping a nutrient replacement pack.

They both cast furtive glances at the back of the train where Richard sat with Gelsemium, Santana, and the others on ventilators.

Bram spoke in a hoarse whisper. "You got Gavin and Geli and all of them back…"

Aurelia nodded, leaning against his shoulder and sighing. "I worried about you."

He smiled and took another gulp of the nutrient pack. "Guess this isn't the sort of thing to play copycat on. You started the trend, but in quarantine. Couldn't even see if you were okay."

"I thought I caused it…"

His brows pulled together. "With your rats?"

Another nod. "Yeah."

He shrugged and put an arm around her with a playful squeeze. "Richard says not. Just coincidence."

Gavin was awake and listening, head propped on one elbow on his cot a few feet away. His expression was troubled, hazel green eyes, dark and storming in the dim light of the train car. There was no sign of the perpetual spark of humor he was known for. His words were slow and cautious and he had to fight a cough to get them out. "We're headed to the space station, yes?"

Aurelia turned to stare at him and climbed down from the cot to put a hand on his shoulder as he coughed. He gave her a look of confusion as the cough subsided. Her eyes were damp with tears.

Gavin raised a brow and scrunched his nose at such open display of emotion. "Did this bug scramble your brains, or swap them with Bram's? You aren't the one I expect tears from."

Aurelia scowled at him, raising her voice. "You almost died. Gelsemium is still fighting, and there are twelve from your group who won't recover. That's enough reason to act out of character."

Gavin put up a hand, his eyes both startled and apologetic. "I get it. Sorry. It's just weird to see."

Her eyes flashed with barely restrained fury. "No. Strange is you running off when something like this is happening. Strange is not rendezvousing with us so you can be treated and get on the ship. Strange is—"

She jumped at him, striking out with one hand and leaving four bleeding scrapes in his right cheek. Gavin put up a hand to block any further attack, green eyes wide with shock. Aurelia's eyes were blue flame, her cheeks covered in hectic red heat blotches. She looked as if she would strike again, but Bram scrambled over and wrapped his arms around her back, pinning her arms at her sides.

Aurelia was stronger and she fought him. It felt like her mind was on fire, the surge of anger rising higher and higher, a runaway inferno with too much fuel to burn sending sparks and flames up into dry treetops and igniting them. "Let go. Let go! He got them killed. You know he did! Ugh—uhh!"

Aurelia broke free of Bram's arms and he fell back from the force of it and the train's motions. She was on Gavin again, her thoughts a cacophony of screams, and she tasted blood. Was it her blood? No, her teeth were locked on his collar bone and someone was pulling her off.

She opened her eyes wide and turned to fight whoever had her. Richard was there and he had her in a tight grip, both arms pulled behind her back. He had her on Bram's medicot before she could struggle free and the straps were on her, trapping her there.

Richard's eyes were more worried than she could remember seeing them. He stared down at her, mouth moving without sound. But there was sound, wasn't there? She just couldn't hear his words through her own screaming.

"Aurelia… Aurelia?! I don't know how I let this happen, but you weren't treated. I'm fixing that now."

She felt the pressure of an air injection on her right arm, the diffuse pinch and tingle that came with it, and then a slowing as if someone had switched her blood for cold winter sap and filled her head with it.

"I've sedated you as well. We'll be at W.A.S.A. when you wake." He was wiping at her lips with a wet cloth. It came away red with Gavin's blood.

CURE

The light in the windowless lab was the same, heedless of the passage of hours as they worked. The dismembered bodies of nearly a hundred cicadas in culture dishes took up one work station, like a buffet table for hungry insectivores.

Theresa's eyes were locked on the screen, as they had been for the past hour. The genome of Yersinia Pestis X was there now in its entirety, aside from the segments Theresa had set aside to work on.

Another screen held Massospora X and its biological make-up, including its full genome, and three dimensional images of it in all phases of its life cycle enlarged for clear examination.

"Theresa, I have to go now." Genesis was looking at her handheld, at the long list of names there. "I have all the search results, our Martian wish list. It doesn't look good, but I'm going to find as many as I can."

Theresa frowned, pausing to look at Genesis; any mistake now could cost her hours. "You're competent in the lab. Can someone else go look for them?"

Genesis shook her head and smiled. "No. I am the least vulnerable to this contagion. You don't know if the treatment you are using is good enough to protect older generation immune systems, and this other thing you are making isn't finished. I'm stronger, faster. I can get in and out of security systems. This is my job."

"Then wait for this. Stay while we finish it. We don't know for sure if the anti-fungal—antibiotic combo is enough for you either."

"Not true. It's kept the children and Richard alive and seemingly in recovery. But really, I'm not bringing anyone else with me, so just call some of Brogan's people in to follow directions. They'll do fine, if you even need them." She smiled, even as she delivered the obvious flattery.

Theresa shrugged and turned back to her work. "Okay."

Genesis turned to leave and then paused by the door. "So…I found Joanna."

Theresa froze. "David's Joanna?" "Yes. She might be alive." Theresa's attention was momentarily shifted away from the cure.

But Genesis was through the door before she could respond or question the sudden revelation. Joanna was alive and Genesis was willing to risk her own safety to collect the woman David had loved before her.

Huh.

The train of thought ended there in a mix of disbelief, confusion, and curiosity. She set it aside.

On the screen the simulation for her newly created Yersinia Pestis Novo ran again. If it worked like the simulation, this altered bacteria would be taken in by Massospora X, where it could then tag the fungal infection with a protein marker and inhibit the fungus's ability to change its outer wall against recognition by the body's immune system. Then it would turn traitor and attack Massospora itself. *No more hiding and coming back out in surges.*

Theresa rubbed her glove against her faceplate, scratching an itch as best she could, then stood back to watch the simulation again. "Shuffle songs from My Apocalyptic playlist."

"Absolutely, playing now." The AI sounded formal and expressionless when it answered. In a moment, music that only

Theresa could hear played on repeat in her ears.

> *Barreling down for the cliff ahea—ed*
> *I'll hang my mind —over bloody edge*
> *That's right*
> *Scraping off thoughts like useless scraps now*
> *Shaking 'em off like my hangers on now*
> *My words are road rash—mmm—mm*
> *Just an end of the line crash—yeah*
> *Toss me whole—toss me whole in the tra—ash…*

The music was somehow melodic and discordant at the same time, shifting abruptly and then picking up a new beat, this one frantic and dark like a labored heartbeat. It was her work under pressure playlist, the one that mirrored every struggle, high stakes, rushed deadline, and the most deep seated doubts and fears that might take hold.

Each hit was written in a time of upheaval or catastrophe and steeped with that desperate, bleeding, darkly triumphant sound that only such music could showcase. Theresa mouthed the lyrics under her breath without thinking.

Every run of the ten completed so far was a success; it would work. An automated lab space like this one could mass produce the cure without her hands in it.

Theresa nodded at the simulation as it ran again to the same end. There was no sigh or release of tension; Theresa's eyes were hyper-alert, showing no signs of wavering energy or pause. To the contrary, they were alight with a focus and determination that was sharp enough to cut through any fog of fatigue that might threaten after hours in the lab.

"Pull up vaccine notes and progress please on the left half screen—Alright, now. We just need our bodies to immediately recognize it from its mannan covering as well as the protein marker

I'm adding on."

Theresa read the data that appeared on the screen and then paused, brows knitting together. "I've figured out how you play peekaboo, but why the surge and recede, the alternation with the Y. Pestis? —Voice call Richard, please."

"Connecting…"

"Hey, Richard…"

Background sounds came through before any answer, heavy breathing, coughing, what sounded like an angry growl, terse words too quiet for her to decipher.

"Richard…?"

"Theresa." He cleared his throat before continuing, voice rougher than she was used to hearing it. "Yes. We're getting close."

Theresa smiled, a surge of excitement building with those words. "Okay, great, so am I. I have something I think will work better, dismantle the thing entirely and prevent possibility of reinfection by way of—"

He cleared his throat again to no effect. "Theresa, pause—I'm sorry, I just need to mention this before my attention gets pulled away."

"Oh, okay. What is it?" A lance of fear cut through any nascent elevation to her mood and she frowned, biting at the skin of her lips. The protective suit felt suddenly restrictive and claustrophobia inducing, and she flinched away from its sides.

"Aurelia. There was an oversight while I was incapacitated and I didn't have my attention drawn to it until now."

Theresa was gesturing for him to speak faster as if she could advance his words faster with the flick of her wrist. "She was recovering—is she alright?"

Richard cleared his throat again and she grit her teeth at the sound. "She wasn't ever treated with the new protocols, antifungals and antibiotics. Because she seemed to recover."

"Richard?" Her voice held a growing alarm that was insistent and required an answer.

"She's alive. But she had a relapse. It was sudden or… it seemed sudden, but perhaps it was simmering. She attacked Gavin. He's fine as well, lost some blood. The damn thing hides though, makes you think it's gone when it's not. I'm not sure if we've cleared it, or it's doing the same with the rest of us, despite the antifungals."

Theresa's stomach hollowed out and she sat down hard. "Okay. Huh. I'm looking at the way it surges and recedes now. I wanted to exchange notes—verbally with you. You have firsthand experience, but…rather, that's why I called. Is she being treated now?"

"Yes, and she is sedated—I'm worried about how long she's had a heavy infection and number of relapses. We need to talk about long term effects."

Theresa stood back up to pace. "No. I'm not ready to make mental space for that. It can simmer on a back burner, but I need us to get them all out of danger first. Remove this thing's fangs, and then we talk about long term recovery."

"Hm. Fine. The surging, then; what are you thinking?"

"Okay, think about the symptom picture, complex, shifting. That's part of what made me suspect a secondary infection, remember? But it isn't as complicated if we track when each set of symptoms occur. You following?"

Richard's reply sounded hoarser now, like it pained him to speak. "Yes."

"They aren't a complicated group of symptoms. It's two different sets for two separate microorganisms that are alternating. That's what I see. But I'm working on the why and some bits of the how. I have questions."

"Okay…"

"What were the first symptoms?" There was a long pause before any response came, so long that Theresa began to doubt that the connection was still good, the only evidence to the contrary the sound of ventilators and labored breathing punctuated by bouts of coughing.

"Are you okay?"

He cleared his throat again and then spoke in a whisper. "Yeah, sure. But my voice is tired. I'll write it up for you and send it. Everything I remember that is pertinent to your, line of inquiry, good?"

"Sure, just—get some sleep, and maybe up your dosage of the antifungals."

"I will. See you soon."

The call ended, the hollow sound of a comm line not in use replacing the sounds of struggle from the railcar that filled the background air space in their call.

Theresa's eyes clouded with worry, and she stopped pacing to look at the data on the split screen. The bottom right was processing all of the information Richard had gathered and sent before communications from Earth to Mars were blocked, as well as updates from the medibots treating the children now.

Theresa narrowed her eyes. "Search infection levels in all patients and report."

"Searching now—"

Theresa paced as she waited.

"Yes, infection levels have receded to below clinical significance levels in all patients."

"Even Aurelia? Bullshit. Not with the symptoms she is showing according to Richard—Massospora is what we need to track, not Y. Pestis."

"Tracking, but levels are indeed below clinical significance thresholds."

She shook her head, discounting what the AI was telling her.

Theresa had Doctor Alexander on the line before the simulation on a repeat loop could run again. "Hey, I need you down as soon as you are willing. I need more hands, maybe another brain. You could do a transplant or something. Or rather add yours on like an extra hard drive." She was the only one that laughed.

"What's wrong?"

Theresa exhaled a long sigh of frustration that came out almost a growl. "I'm worried about them. Not being paranoid. Aurelia just attacked someone, I can tell Richard is off as well. Some are on ventilators and not recovering, but the big thing is, they seem off, and I don't think systemic antifungals are going to knock this out, considering—"

"What?"

"It's in their heads, Alex. Fungal infections in the brain, we discussed how persistent they can be, and this one has obviously set up camp. I just feel like it's still hiding there, out of reach and ready to come back out at any time." Her words were coming like machine gun fire, spraying out bullets at a distant field of targets.

"Okay, slow down. But you were planning for this, your back-up is almost finished, right?"

Theresa shook her head, not to disagree but to channel the frustration. "Yes, back-up treatment. But I don't need a back-up, it looks like. I need a primary treatment."

"I've looked everything you sent over several times, and so has Erik and his apprentice back on Mars. We may not have an epidemiologist, but your theory behind this is sound, your sims confirm it'll work—What has changed is they need it a bit more than expected."

"What's changed is this treatment reversal. What I'm doing is complicated, too much margin for error. Fuck. You know. It's fine." She moved to brush hair out of her face and instead found her gloved hand stopped by the barrier of the masked suit and grit her teeth as she dropped her hand back to her side in irritation.

"It's just that the success of this is now crucial. I should have a team for something this multi-layered, but I don't. I have you. So get down here, help me train up Brogan's team members, and we'll do this. Get any vomiting or um…stumbling out of the way quickly, please."

Alexander laughed. "Got it—oh, have you uh, discussed with Captain Neil? Gotten his approval?"

Theresa shrugged. "He needs to come down too. Everyone we have needs to be down here now. Unless I've infected the complex with spores, they'll be fine. Brogan and the three down here with him have no symptoms with the anti-fungal plus antibiotics. Assuming this new treatment succeeds, we'll all be fine."

"Sure, but you tell him—and with more confidence than you just presented it to me."

"I've pitched new tech for approval or time extensions more times than I can count."

Alexander was nodding, a smirk on his face. "It was a joke, Theresa."

"Oh, ha ha."

Neil's hand hovered over the first sequence of a missile launch, the WGC and Reproductive Council North American headquarters already keyed in as targets. It would feel like retribution—fair recompense for their lies, and the attack on Mars that cost so many lives. He could wipe all trace of them from the surface of Earth from up here in orbit if he wanted to—and he did want to. There were two other headquarters: Russia, and the Antarctic. Three empty explosions for the lives they took, Jonathan, Eli, Trina… The urge to launch strengthened and he found himself justifying the idea, when moments before it was just an impulse. They were all dead down there, according to Dr. Brant, but maybe some weren't—maybe some of the ones responsible weren't. *Even one of the bastards would be enough to do it.*

His growing resolve wavered. It was possible there were still some innocents alive down there. Some on their lists, or not, that maybe they couldn't find or snatch up, but that deserved a chance.

He growled in impotent rage, squeezing the hovering hand into a fist and pushing off into a zero G spin towards the other side of the command room. *Maybe that shot is playing with my brain after all.* He licked dry lips and sucked in a breath, too fast to be calming but better than holding it like he had been.

It was time to go down to the surface to reset himself, and it wouldn't feel good. *I won't be running any marathons, anyway.*

REUNITED

The sun was rising red over a watery horizon, the gleaming surface of an inland sea broken by a sparse tree line on fire with reflections of crimson, amber, and coral pink. The elevated tracks of the magnetic rail system shimmered with the same light, far past the edge of the land and traversing the body of water thousands of miles across what was once the top of the South American continent and then Mexico.

The cicadas were singing still, their high-pitched trill filling the air around them with raw tension like a multitude of powerlines on the verge of overload.

Theresa squinted sandpaper eyelids, holding a suited arm up to block the sun from her face as she watched that shining track at the point where it faded from view.

There was nothing there that she could make out. Her eyes watered and blurred, and she closed them before flicking a glance at her handheld and the message there.

Ten minutes out.

Excitement, mingled with gut-gripping anxiety, traced a rapid path through her nerves and spun around in her belly, tossing and churning there.

"It'll be in view any minute now." Captain Neil smiled over at her and she gave him a terse twitch of lips in return.

"Shouldn't we see it now?"

Brogan leaned over and pointed at what looked like a pinpoint of light just where the tracks became visible in the distance. "See there? The speed is so fast that even far off is a few minutes travel. Watch how fast it gets bigger. I've watched these trains come in more times than I can count." His eyes shadowed with a confused mix of sadness and regret. "Never in a time like this though. Might be the last one I watch come in then, I think."

Neil adjusted the seam of his containment suit at the neck with shaking hands; his skin had an unhealthy pallor to it and there were dark circles around his eyes characteristic of space-sickness. He gave Theresa a quizzical glance. "Did you expect this when you left Earth with your stowaway?"

Theresa turned a startled look towards the captain and then back at the oncoming railcar, now the size of a large bird hovering over carrion on the ground below. "Which part? Which part could I have expected?"

He shrugged. "Coming back for the rest of them. Seeing them again. Not the rest of all this; that would be fortune-telling."

"Oh, no. No, I didn't ever expect to see any of them again. There was a good chance the Council was going to terminate them, and besides that, I never expected seeing or interacting with them even before the Martian transfer. That wasn't part of my assignment."

The train was even closer now, Theresa's pulse quickened and she clenched and unclenched her hands, fluttering her fingers in a rhythmic cascade in between to expend the tension and nervous energy that made her want to pace.

Neil was silent for a moment, the sort of silence that hung in the air full of unspoken questions, and Theresa frowned at him.

"What?"

He returned her look. "I'm just wondering how you could make them and not get attached, pass them over to someone else."

Theresa blinked, giving him a hard stare. "That was my assignment. To make them, not to mother them. But I didn't do that part very well, all things considered. I stole the one I could and conspired to get them all to Mars."

Neil flashed a grin. "That you did quite well."

Theresa's eyes thawed and she rapid-blinked to stop them overflowing. She unclenched her fists and moved to scratch her face, stopping herself again before the mask could block her. A bitter laugh escaped as she turned back to the silver, bullet-shaped conveyance that appeared to have doubled in size. "We'll see how well I've done that after we get back to Mars with the um—with the survivors." Her voice grew strained and trailed off, her eyes avoiding his.

The railcar approached rapidly now, its passage between the struggling trees along the track stirring up a wind filled with many thousands of winged insects. Brogan and his technicians stood at the loading dock with Doctor Alexander next to them. Theresa and Captain Neil hung back, waiting for the train to slow.

Theresa's mind ran through the many imaginings over the past eleven years, replaying joyful, awkward, and long-awaited first meetings with the progeny, *her* progeny. They would be shy, some of them gone mute with fear, or excitement, some of them jumping on her for the first hug, so many of them that it would take hours to make eye contact and exchange greetings. But was that an accurate term to use—her progeny? So few conversations with each of them, and only in dream-speak. She wasn't *raising* them, and now eleven years had passed with them out of reach, raised by someone else just as the other phases of the AUC project were. The early nightmares crowded into her memory: she was buried under a growing pile of crying infants, all attached to her by tangled fleshy umbilical cords, and she couldn't find Abby trapped somewhere on the bottom.

Theresa flinched at the vivid recall and watched as the train slowed now. It was a nightmare that was never even possible with the distance in between them. Abby was the only one who wasn't lost to her all that time. And what about Richard? Her pulse quickened again, taking up a rapid gallop as if to run and meet the train while the rest of her stood frozen, waiting. Richard was on the train. The last moment between them on Earth before she took the Martian assignment hovered in her mind's eye.

Her thoughts were such a racing quagmire of long-past, disjointed dreams, and long-distance communication that there was little time for her to prepare for the reality of the situation as the train came to a final stop. And the door to the first two cars opened.

Richard was the only one standing there at the opening, gripping the handrail with white knuckles. Theresa found herself frozen there as she took in his condition. His clothes and lab coat hung on him as if he had lost twenty pounds since the last video recording of him at the WGC headquarters; his skin looked dusky and mottled, his neck a sunset of fading bruises, including dark purple just under the jawline like he'd been beaten bad and lost the fight.

His eyes were bright, but weary and wavering in their gaze. He lifted his arm to cover a light cough that still sounded tight and painful in his throat, and when he spoke it was in a whisper.

Theresa forced her feet to move, overcoming the enormous block of ice she imagined holding them in place.

Neil was shaking Richard's hand and Richard was nodding with a warm smile that struck her as oddly familiar for a moment and she froze in place again. She looked around, expecting to find where she'd seen that same smile, and then dismissed the out-of-place thoughts. *It's Richard; you know his smile.*

Brogan was there at the railcar's exit, guiding out the first of the medicots and directing them onto the scrolling sidewalk.

He was speaking to the children with the same cheerful-tour-guide demeanor that she remembered from their first time at

W.A.S.A. *Probably giving the same speech too.*

It struck her as incongruous and she fought the laugh that threatened. A tour fleeing a pandemic. *There in the trees, you'll see the insect host for the devastating fungal infections in your heads, and up ahead is the proposed method for our hasty evacuation…*

The internal monologue drowned out Brogan's own words and brought the laugh closer until she forced her eyes down to the first medicots out. Gelsemium's mass of dark hair was matted with sweat and tangled in the straps of a ventilator mask, dark bruising and unhealed scratch marks across her face. Aurelia had the stillness of a coma that did not evoke peace the way sleep did, but instead made her seem gone. *Not gone though, Theresa, just sick and we'll fix it. We're fixing it. Is this how you meet your progeny?*

Nothing was funny about seeing them like this. She was still standing there, staring now as the cots drove themselves along the directed path. She was cold all over and fever-hot at the same time, her stomach doing somersaults. This wasn't how their first meeting was supposed to go. This wasn't the feeling. This was more like the nightmares. She had to move.

Richard was looking at her now, Dr. Alexander next to him with a gloved hand on his shoulder. She frowned in confusion. Where were Neil and Brogan? How long was she frozen?

Sucking in a breath of stagnant protective-suit air, she turned to find them, to orient herself. Neil, Brogan, and the three WASA staff members were at various points along the scrolling sidewalk, talking to any of the children who were conscious and making sure their medicots stayed true to the path, like she should have been.

She pulled out her handheld from the outer pocket of the protective suit and looked at the synced data feed from the children's medibots. She sighed, breathing out some small measure of tension and feeling her mental clarity sharpen as she processed each child's status. Heart rate, blood pressure, infection levels…the numbers reassured and gave context to what she saw as their cots passed.

The last cot was offloaded and she strode over to where Richard stood still. Dr. Alexander was following the last cot and gave her a nod as he passed. She ignored the questioning brow and look of concern he seemed to be aiming at her, and instead focused on Richard.

"The ones on a respirator, I have something I want to try: Dr Alexander and I were discussing increasing TNF-a again to use, along with—"

Theresa caught a glimpse of his face when she looked up. He was smiling again, but this smile was different, wider with white teeth showing, and it was directed at her.

She trailed off, staring back as he stood there, eyes full of humor. "You forgot the script…Hi, how was your trip? It's good to see you."

Theresa paused and scrunched up her nose. "But it isn't good to see you yet. Like this." She shook her head and gestured towards his painfully thin frame and the blood-streaked lab coat he still wore, and then at herself, sealed off in a full body suit to prevent contagion as long as possible.

Her voice broke and she paused until the tightness in her throat subsided. "I don't think this even counts. I think it doesn't count until you're well. Where is your medicot, so you don't have to walk?"

She leaned over, looking around his shoulder into the railcar. Richard's smile dropped and he put up a hand to block her. "Are there more still in there to move? I didn't count them all, who—"

Richard wet his lips. "Theresa, those are the twelve cots that were unresponsive, plus Davina and Caspian, who you knew about. They were with Gavin and weren't functioning when we found them. They didn't get any treatment. And one more—Clark ran into the city, and Gavin couldn't find him."

"You never answered when I asked about those unresponsive ones…"

Theresa moved to go in and he moved to stop her, losing his balance long enough for Theresa to grab hold of one arm and steady him. "Please don't. They didn't make it. Do you want to see that right now? They don't, um, they don't stop moving, even sedated. If we treat them like the others now, I expect it'll shut them down, but——"

Theresa grew still and then moved his arm out of the pathway. "I need to see or it isn't real. I won't have them just gone and not have seen them since their AUC gestation."

He frowned. "It could wait until after you don't need your focus so badly." Theresa stared at him, a tilt of head and a sneer pulling her face into lines of distaste. "I'm not going to do that, Richard. I'm not going to wait——" She pushed past him into the railcar and then paused, raising a hand up to her mask and then reaching over to grab hold of Richard's shoulder.

His voice was low, a pained near-whisper. He kept his back to the inside of the train car. "I wasn't implying weakness, Theresa. Just—The sedatives are wearing off and it's just—it's not something we should see."

Her face had blanched of all color and her feet seemed to be frozen to the ground once more, her voice a hoarse whisper. "The way they move is —" "Unnatural. Painful."

Theresa sucked in a slow, shaking breath. "The ones inside need us, so um—is there more sedative here? Are their medibots functional at all manually?"

Richard shook his head. "No. That's why they didn't make it." His voice was strained, a mix of anger and pain.

"Okay. Fine. Come with me then. We'll bring them in together, and I can obtain more samples from them before we put them to rest."

Richard cleared his throat and gestured with a lift of his chin towards the next railcar behind the one they were in. "You don't have to do that. There is a whole car full of nameless infected. It might be easier."

Theresa turned and looked through the window to where at least a hundred struggling bodies milled around in aimless marionette fashion. Her lips curled in disgust and she closed her eyes, lowering her head and placing her forearms against her knees for a moment to fight a sudden wave of nausea. She stood again and looked back at the children. "But they are tied down and those others are not. We need to bring them in, one way or another, because I won't leave them like this."

She stepped over to the lead medicot where Marilla fought her straps. She looked similar to the other children who had survived, except for the depth of the bruising and the lesions covering her skin that showed no signs of healing. Theresa placed a hand on the side of Marilla's forehead and turned her face to look down into her eyes. They were wild and unfocused, darting here and there, then rolling back as if the one controlling them was falling asleep at the controls in between fits of manic activity. It wasn't Marilla. The face didn't matter. It may as well have been a wax house replica. Her eyes were not the confident, intelligent ones Theresa knew and the way her mouth opened and closed as if about to speak or gag on her own tongue in a silent endless cycle, gag, repeat, gag, repeat, was something Marilla never did.

Theresa cleared her throat and turned away. "You ready?" Richard was staring at Marilla's face as well. He flinched at the sound of Theresa's voice and then squeezed his eyes shut, passing a hand over them before he looked at her again. Theresa's brows pulled together in concern as she helped him onto his own medicot, but he waved it away, gesturing to his head with a frustrated flourish of one hand. "It's flashbacks, I think—residual hallucinations. I've seen some of the children having them as well. Something we'll have to deal with."

Theresa felt a sudden impulse to reach for him, to bridge the physical and intangible distance...and then it passed. Layers and layers of protective gear was not conducive to comfort or any sort of intimacy. Instead she tried to construct a reassuring smile that she didn't feel and felt herself floundering, fighting to compose her features into something less transparent.

The medicots were already chained together, making it easier for Theresa to guide them to the scrolling sidewalk. She walked next to Richard's medicot with him on it, her eyes trained on the stream of vital statistics for the children that were now inside the compound waiting for them.

BREAKTHROUGHS

The sky opened up, sending fat drops of warm rain into Abby's outstretched hands. It was a different rain than usual, the storm system blowing in across the Eastern desert instead of the Western mountain range. Rather than the strong woods and spice smells of cycad, aspen, and Martian creosote mixed with lichen grass, this rain had the strong tang of iron and was warmer, heated by wind over sun-baked sand. It felt momentous, exhilarating; her heart beat faster, and each splash of rain on her cheeks forced a breathless laugh from her. The excitement of it seemed appropriate for what she was doing. Trying to do.

Trotting over to the small stand of aspens further back from the cliffs, she picked careful footing in the shifting sand and mud that ran red over her bare feet. Her bag and clothing were there, hanging from a low branch, and she pulled out the small wrist computer she'd taken off with everything else in her frenzy of excitement when the rain started. How would she know if he was coming if she went tech free into the water?

She strapped it on and opened the message tab, setting it to projection. It was harder to read that way in the rain, but she didn't care. *"Donovan, I've been watching the whalefins for you while you're away. Deimos said you arrived back with David this morning. Meet me at the cliffs before you even unpack, by 3:00 and I'll show you something."*

His reply was flashing below her message, unread. *"Okay. I'm excited to see…a good thing, I hope."*

Abby's heart rate galloped as she stared at the message. He was coming and she might freeze up again. Deimos's accusation admonished her as she recoiled from the follow-through of this plan: *You're not trying…*

The wind was whipping in sharp gusts, pulling and grabbing at her as it changed direction, unable to make up its mind about a final destination. Abby tightened her jaw and whispered into the rain.

"I won't be the wind today." She glanced back at the aspens, considering the way that they waved and bowed under the onslaught. It seemed the way to act in a storm if you can't be the rock-face.

Her heart was still racing when she looked down the path towards the colony. Donovan was far below, picking his way up the muddy path, as rocks slid out from under his weight. It would be easy to turn and jump from the cliff edge, but not yet.

Abby opened up her messages again, lifting her wrist closer to her face to combat the rush of wind and rain. *"Donovan, I'm at the top……"* The messenger AI sent her pause as well and then waited for her to continue. *"Just stop at the first stand of aspens by the biggest cycad and you'll see me."*

She watched him advance slowly and then lean in to his handheld to read and reply. *"Sure."*

The stand of aspens wasn't far off, and the urge to lunge for the cliff was still there. He was still climbing, at the steepest part now, forced to grab hold of a low branch on one of the first trees that was rooted in the rocky soil. And then he was standing at the large cycad, just past it, rainwater forming waterspouts off the tips of the sodden black curls hanging around his narrow face. He was fifteen feet away from where Abby stood, but she could see his expression through the rainfall: cautious, quizzical.

She felt the curtain of mental fog coming down, the urge to walk away, to crouch down and curl around herself in the splashing brick-red mud puddles, or instead jump over the cliff's jagged edge…but Donovan was there, waiting, and she had called him here. She was supposed to walk over, but her feet wouldn't move, she couldn't make them.

Donovan peeled some of the clinging strands of dark hair from his cheeks, still waiting, and then moved to step closer, pausing and calling out instead. "You okay? I can walk you back…"

She couldn't name his expressions anymore, but she could feel them, and it made her heart pound faster; the sensation of deja vu that returned each time she froze was overwhelming. She opened her mouth but it was a pointless gesture, the words weren't coming. Movement helped, movement always helped jar the words when she froze. It didn't matter why if it was true.

With one hand she waved at him and he waved back, a small, confused smile growing on his face.

That was worse. Abby squeezed her toes in the mud feeling it ooze between them and then lifted a foot, lowering it with a sudden splash; it was warm and wet, and made her want to fall down and roll in it. *That would be awkward*…An involuntary smile flashed out and shifted the gap between her words and her tongue. "I just…splashed myself." *Genesis fills gaps with smiles…*

Donovan looked less bothered now and more amused when she glanced up, and it made her think of the last time she saw him on the beach, when Genesis spoke for her, smiling, complimenting, making jests until he was fully distracted from her silence and his hurt feelings.

Abby smiled again, trying to recreate what she felt from the sudden splash instead of molding her face itself. It seemed to work and Donovan smiled back. She lifted her wrist computer to her face, still smiling, and spoke into it. "I jumped off the cliff after the

Pinnacle left, swam into the caves. They were all inside, birthing calves…"

She glanced up to see if he'd heard, if he was angry that she was swimming with them, and felt another surge of fear before she could decipher his face. Donovan's eyes were wide, startled, and then he broke out in a grin larger than her own. He forgot the gap she'd asked for between them and surged forward, not towards her but towards the cliff, crouching on hands and knees and then laying flat to stare over the edge and search the waters below. "I can't see them now…did they stay? Have they migrated yet?" His words were tumbling, rushed with excitement; the whales' tracking would have alerted him if they had moved on again.

"No, they're still there. I see them every day."

He didn't respond and he didn't need to. Abby watched his eyes searching the water, the smile beginning to fade at the corners as the moments stretched out. A sense of what she could do was building in Abby's mind and she grabbed hold of it. He was excited, glad she told him, and didn't seem to notice or care how many words she did or didn't force out, but he wanted to see them.

Backing up several paces, she judged the distance, the rockier spots between puddles and broke into a run with long strides. When she reached the cliff edge, she jumped. Unlike the mud puddles high above, the frothy green seawater was cold when she hit it, a sudden but welcome shock. The bubbles from her impact tickled her face as she kicked to the surface and searched the cliff edge high above. Donovan was still there, watching, and had risen up onto hands and knees to wave at her. She waved back and then spoke a message for him. "They'll come out…they're playful."

She dove under the waves and opened her eyes, searching the cloud-darkened water for any sign of their approach and then trilled into the water, a mimicry of the whale songs.

Her lungs were burning now, but she waited as blurry shapes, pale green under the water, rose up from the direction of the submerged caves. Blowing out the remaining air from her lungs, she dove deeper, swimming a circle with the first of the calves to reach her and then turned back to the surface for them to follow. She hoped they would surface where Donovan could see what she brought him for——see it better than she could say it. It wasn't a full conversation, but she thought it didn't matter so much this time.

The last rays of sun slanted through the small cathedral window on the western wall of Carla's office, leaving a purple sheen on David's near-black, shaggy hair and the short-cropped beard on his narrow jawline. He looked up at Carla from underneath troubled brows through that curtain of hair. *Longer than when we arrived, or even when he ran for council. Like a garden untended and left to run wild, wild roses gone to vine and grass growing taller than the vegetables sewn and forgotten.*

He was still pacing without words. That was fine. Sometimes they just needed to move and think in a space that was made for it, as if a therapist's office gave some sort of permission that didn't exist elsewhere.

He paused again and stared at her from under those heavy brows, a sharp glint in dark eyes that, instead of hiding shadow in their depths, allowed it to surface and dominate those eyes. She pictured the wolf from Genesis's thought-scape and smiled.

He cleared his throat. "I know your schedule is full."

She nodded. "Lots of people scared right now. But my schedule is clear for the evening. Maybe that's why you came so late? Unless you want a late-night gardening session."

He echoed the nod, chewing at his bottom lip. "Donovan is back too. He's worried about Emily, or maybe just about himself and Emily, not sure."

Carla quirked a smile. "You want to talk about Donovan and

Emily…?"

He took up pacing again and flashed a furtive glance in her direction. "No. No, I wondered how much of my personal information, my old files from Earth are accessible in your um, your psychiatric files."

"Oh, just about all of it I suppose. You can't diagnose a tree without knowing what's happening with the roots."

"Then you know about my previous diagnoses?"

"But I don't read them until I'm asked to."

He looked startled, confused maybe, and Carla laughed. "David, I know you. I've seen some things that we could talk about." Her lips curled as if she tasted something bad on her tongue. "I really don't like using files from back on Earth. Didn't like how they did things. And knowing what happened to you and Joanna, back there…I'd rather hear from you on the matter. So wear through my floor if it helps you talk, or pull up a cushion."

She gestured to the many casually ordered stacks of floor cushions that bordered the space where she listened and also held community health meetings.

David chose a large, overstuffed pillow embroidered with Martian plumeria and large black bumblebees. He smiled, seemingly lost in thought as he traced the greenery with the pad of his thumb, the roughness of soil and sand-built calluses slowing the caress.

He chose another, plainer, one and sat down on it, holding the embroidered pillow in his lap. "I see her sometimes. Joanna. And I hear her…we talk." He didn't look up from his contemplation of the largest bee on the pillow, but continued tracing it, following the gently curved antennae down the head to the thorax, and the wide abdomen, embellished with stripes of black and crimson.

Carla listened. She sat at the same level on a matching bee pillow, legs relaxed in a butterfly pose, face propped on hands and elbows. Should he have looked up he would have seen her nodding as she followed his words, face impassive and clear of judgment.

But he didn't look up.

"Sometimes I think about her, and I know I'm playing it out like I used to—it was how I lived with it for a long time on Earth. I'd replay our times together, every single word, laugh, expression. I'd live it like it was the first time, all while I walked or set up seedlings, adjusted the hydroponics, installed new light panels. I went through the motions, but I was living with her in my head." He looked up, and Carla met his eyes, hoping he'd see what was there and not read into her expression any of his own self-judgement. She leaned forward and placed a hand on one of his, giving it a squeeze and then leaning back again.

David gave a half-hearted, self-deprecating smile and shrugged. "At some point I started trying to come out. To live outside of my head, without her. I'd go for awhile, but everything seemed so sharp-edged and raw and I'd itch to get back to her."

He laughed, and it was laced with bitterness, like the green cambion layers of bark stripped from a fresh branch with one's teeth.

"It got to where it hurt not to sink into my own head and go see her. I needed it." He gave a pained smile and looked Carla right in the eyes then. "I kept trying though, going longer without it until I could stand the outside again, even if the air felt cold, thin. That's when I started seeing her, when it wasn't just memories anymore. It was things she had never said, but I knew she *would* have said. It was so good for a while that I didn't even care if it was real. Didn't matter—Carla, could you maybe tell me how this sounds so I can stop hearing myself talk for a minute?"

Carla cocked a brow and nodded. "Sure. Sounds like you were grieving and you found a way to cope. To let go slowly."

David blinked, shock registering in his eyes. "Is that how people generally grieve? I haven't heard anyone else wandering the halls talking to a ghost."

"Well, everyone finds their own way. The Captain flagellates himself in his own head and in all his actions and decisions. He programmed AI with the voice of his dead second in command…"

David laughed. "Yeah. Yeah he did. But he knows she's dead, doesn't he?" Carla's eyes registered surprise for a split second before she could bury it. "Do you doubt Joanna is gone?"

He opened his mouth to speak and then paused mid-grimace, his teeth reminding Carla all the more of a wolf. "You know, that's a good question." He scratched his head and shook his hair back from his face. "Kinda what I wanted to ask you."

Carla frowned. "I can't answer if you can't."

He grew still and his eyes turned inward, searching and uncertain. "When I see her, hear her, feel her there…It's like I can't agree with myself. One train of thought reminds me that it isn't real, that it's some kind of hallucination or memory replay. The other train whispers, like an undercurrent, that I can't prove that. That it's as real as anything else." He shook his head and caught his bottom lip between his teeth.

"That same part wants it not to end. 'But you're surprised when she is there, so how can it not be real?' SO god-damn irritating…and just unsettling." He pointed a finger midair, twisting it as if prodding some imaginary version of himself as the whispering thoughts did to him.

A deep sigh escaped between clenched teeth. "That I feel her touch, so how can it not be real? That her words come in her voice and not mine—" His voice lowered, each syllable stressed with an emphasis born of restrained emotion that was clear in his eyes. "She shows up even when that first voice is loudest, proclaiming all the reasons it isn't real and all the reasons we wish it would stop, and the whisper says, 'Hey, see that? Here she is. Obviously not because you wanted it. So how is it not real?!'"

He sighed and rubbed an itch above his left eye. "And honestly, Carla, I'm tired of fighting myself. Just so tired."

Carla was nodding, sympathy clear in her eyes and her voice low and gentle. "Is it worse since Genesis left?"

"Oh sure. Yeah." He threw his hands up in frustration before returning them to follow the path of thick-petaled Martian plumeria blossoms on the pillow's surface. "I'm seeing her more. Thinking about it. That doubt though, the voice that argues with me about it, is the worst part. I can handle seeing her, I'm used to that by now."

Carla wet her lips. "Does she always come around during times of stress, and the mental conflict? Side question: are you ever of one mind?"

David nodded, tipping his head to one side and then the other as if weighing the accuracy of each possible answer. "Stress, I guess so. Anytime there's a big shift—thinking about taking the Martian assignment and a lot after that, few times while I was trying to figure things out with Genesis, her pregnancy—lately."

"Did you put her on the list, David?" He looked Carla straight in the eye despite the flinching that she could see. "Yeah. Yeah, I put her on there. That other part of me was loud enough, insistent enough, until I was afraid not to, you know? What if she was down there, still, with this going on?"

David's eyes turned liquid, picking up the soft red lights of Carla's lamps as they teared up and ran down his cheeks. He didn't bother to wipe them away; it was just water, and Carla was safe.

"Now, today, I got this." David passed his handheld over to Carla for her to read.

The message was short and to the point, but Carla stared at it for several moments, allowing all of the implications to come together in her mind.

David,
I found her. Survival is unlikely but I'm going to look for her and confirm. One way or another, you'll know. Be good.
Genesis

Carla handed the device back to David and waited for him to break the silence.

His eyes were dry now but had a rawness to them. "Genesis is chasing a ghost for me because she thinks I need her to. Putting herself in danger because I have this—issue." He fell silent and, when he didn't speak again, Carla took the lead.

"Do you? Need her to find Joanna?" His answer was slow in coming, the sort that wasn't rushed or contrived but instead formed slowly in one's mind like the moon being revealed by the wind blowing away a bank of clouds.

"No. If she is alive then sure, get her out of there. If she isn't—more likely option—then that changes nothing." His lips pulled back in that same wolf-like grimace. "It won't get her out of my head, will it? Or at least just, make the memories just... memory."

"Probably not, so you want my help with a cause and a cure, yes? Do you want the quick-fix route, or the slow build?"

David laughed then, and it brought a bit of the usual spark back to his eyes, pushing back the shadows for a breath before they settled back in. "I'd say quick fix, but I know you'd talk me out of it." "Well, it's your call, but I think you know how ineffective it is to just apply antifungals and fertilizers to a vulnerable plant specimen without getting to the literal and figurative 'root' of the problem."

He smiled and shook his head at her humor laden smirk. "See? There you go with your convincing metaphors…"

"But really, David, let's go for both. Treat it like a chemical imbalance to get you some relief while we tease this thing apart and work from all angles. Medications are still the quick fix, sometimes—other times, they are the best option, but for full relief you're gonna have to work with me. See me every day for a while, and we'll work up to VR therapy like we did with Genesis. When the full medical team is back, we'll look for physical and hormonal causes. Does that sound like something you can go along with?"

David drummed his fingers on the bee pillow and pulled at a piece of dry skin on his lips with his teeth. "Do we have to sit like this, or can we get our hands in some dirt while we talk?"

Carla smiled, stretching her back and reaching her arms up above her head with a groan of released tension.

"I think we could arrange that, so long as you and the plants can stay on topic."

"Sure, sure…so, um, have you heard anything from the captain or Theresa?"

Carla stood and offered him a hand up. "No. Last was what everyone was told. Their safe arrival at the elevator. Treatment options being worked on. Search for survivors in progress. All vague."

"I'm not sure why I didn't just go along. They should have more people." Carla was putting on her hiking belt and weights. "I don't know your reasoning, but I know why they didn't want anyone else—we're the safe eggs back here, no need to overfill a basket with a rotting handle if you want to have an omelet, eh?"

David snorted. "Sure, one or two more eggs would've been fine. Isn't too late for a hike?"

It was Carla's turn to snort. "No, it's not. Starlight clears my head. I'll sleep in the caves tonight, but you need me you don't hesitate to message, call, or hike up there."

David nodded as they left. "Sure. See you."

HELLO AND GOODBYE

Emily pressed a hand to the side of the AUC, feeling the warm, supple material that felt like skin but stronger, like silicone made more pliable and without the sticky consistency of some polymers. She placed the palm of her other hand over her belly and felt for the fluttering that had started yesterday. They had moved in unison the time before—coincidence, of course—but it *felt* like more, as if her hands were a conduit between them and, so long as she kept her hands pressed above them both, they would be connected to each other, and to her. Silly or not, she closed her eyes and waited. It wasn't long before the soft fluttering, like tiny wings inside her lower abdomen, came again.

Emily opened her eyes to see her and Jonathan's child moving inside of the AUC, still small enough to be cradled in the palm of her hand, but with tiny arms and legs kicking. It didn't move far yet, its soft cartilage-filled limbs flailing with the apparent strength of an amoeba's cilia under a microscope. Soon those bones would begin to ossify, and the fluttering movements would turn into tiny bumps and nudges. Excitement rose up with an intensity that overwhelmed her previous caution, overspilling the compartments where she held back both hope, fear, and attachment in separate, safe spaces like some carefully partitioned and sealed Pandora's box. She allowed the tears to fall and trail over trembling lips, catching in their upturned corners and then falling in a spray as she released a sigh.

The AI security announced Donovan's arrival, and Emily approved his admittance without breaking the connection between her hands and the spaces where her progeny grew and developed with each passing moment.

He stepped up behind her and leaned in close to see the swimming figure inside of the ovoid chamber that was installed into the center of the room, with transparent pipes and support structures extending up to the ceiling and then following the walls to a power source and filtration unit.

"Hello, little bit of Emily and Jon. I see you've lost your tail now. No more confusing you with one of the fellows in my lab, eh?" He reached down and placed a hand over Emily's own, where it rested on her belly, and she pulled in a breath.

"And how, um…how is this one, Emily? And you?"

He placed a kiss on her cheek, slowly, as if to set it there for her to assess her level of hunger for it like an hors d'oeuvres on offer. Her voice was low, for his ears, despite their isolation.

"We're fine—better than I've been, I think." She turned to show him a sunny smile that only gave a hint of the sadness he could usually discern in that shadowed landscape. "We've made it farther than with any of the others, by weeks now—oh, and I can feel him flutter. You wouldn't yet, but I can."

Donovan grinned and kissed her again. "That's similar to, but better than, what I wanted to show you today." Emily's eyes widened and she dropped her hands from their vigil of contact with the AUC and her rounded belly, straightening the sky-blue tunic she wore that had bunched up around her seeking hand. "What sort of thing?"

Donovan lifted a hand in apology to halt any idea that the anxiety forming in her eyes was well-founded. "Nothing with Earth, and nothing bad. Good things, come…"

He grasped her hand and tugged gently, breaking into a loping run once they exited the garden gate, where AI Trina's dry, humor-filled voice bid them a good hike.

Emily had to slow him by tugging back, halfway up the steep rise. The wind was pushing against their faces and chests as if to bar their way and she was out of breath.

Donovan's smile at the top was sheepish and concerned. "Sorry. You okay?"

"Oh, yeah, yeah. Just a little light-headed and easily winded when I run. Low-blood pressure; it'll pass." Emily knelt at the top of the cliff and looked over the edge, searching the waters below. "Is it the whalefins?"

"Yes." He crouched down next to her and pointed at an area of the deep green water that looked paler, the wave patterns choppy and disrupted. "See there? I invited Abby to join me out in the field when I go back—Theresa asked me to, worried about her all alone, I guess. Abby messaged back that she wasn't leaving the calves, that I should come see them. I think she's been swimming in the caves."

Emily watched as the iridescent white bodies surfaced, turning and slapping the frothy green water with their long pectoral fins and tail flukes. The ones still under water were singing again; those that broke the surface were chattering with high pitched squeaks, clicks, and moans. There were nearly twice as many of the large creatures as before, the new additions much smaller and swimming close to their mothers.

"And here I thought you'd ignored me telling you not to come back to see me, and you came for your other babies."

Donovan's face grew serious without extinguishing the spark of excitement the whalefins kindled in his eyes. "Actually, I called it early and came back for something else."

"Oh." Emily dropped all humor and listened. This was about what hovered at the edge of their thoughts, regardless of how much they worked to distract. His tone said that more clearly than the next words he said would.

"Well, Theresa has been sending me data direct message."

"Why to you?"

"Maybe not just me, but I'm a planetary ecologist. Ecosystems are my thing. And the base of that pillar is built on microorganisms—virus, bacteria, fungus, etc, that then interact with their whole ecosystem." His words came rapid-fire, blurring together at beginning end like train cars as they did when he grew excited. "You want to understand an infectious disease, its success—its ability to…to kill off the human population—to make a pandemic, you find clues in the ecosystem that it develops and thrives in."

"Should you have gone with them?" "Ahhhh…shoulda, woulda, coulda? Maybe? But I'm not the one to do the rescue and medical work there. What Theresa and I have been talking about is how this affects Mars, now and far future."

The whalefins were still dancing and cavorting in the water below. Something had their attention; the adults were circling around the young creating a wall of swimming bodies.

The movement drew Donovan and Emily's attention again.

Far below at the entrance to their birthing cave, a small figure emerged from the shadow and stood for a moment, sunlight glinting off of dark mahogany hair that waved and twisted in the heavy wind.

The girl dove into the water and swam in a circle around the large pod of whalefins, diving under and then emerging with slapping arms in a close approximation of the animal's swimming behavior.

Emily's eyes widened and she leaned closer, shielding her eyes from the slanting rays of evening sunlight. "Is that Abby? Should she be doing that, so close to them?"

Donovan's lips were pressed into a thin slash, his brows tight with worry. Emily got the distinct impression that if he released the tension in his jaw, he would smile, and if he hadn't so many rules he might jump into the water and do the same as the girl.

He shook his head, the underlying smile fighting to emerge and making it half out of hiding. "No. No she shouldn't. They seem to be allowing it, though; see there. The circle is looser, gaps, some weaving around her now." His eyes were incredulous. "Well then, so long as she doesn't touch the calves, maybe. Theresa would not like this."

Emily bit her lips, nodding. "Definitely don't tell her."

If she didn't look at their faces, it might be easier. Theresa watched the readings on their medibots change. Brogan's team was quite capable. The engineer—Jillian—got the defunct medibots the children were strapped into working quickly and without complaint. Theresa was grateful for that. She didn't need anyone pointing out the state of the ones on the cots.

Their breathing sounded better than the other children's, with no cough or wheeze, and the mild sedation stopped their incoherent vocal outbursts. None of that could hide that they were not alive in the same sense that the other children were. They moved like wind-up dolls, and they reeked of fever sweat, infection, and decay.

Theresa flinched against the memory of first seeing them, stomach flip-flopping and eyes squeezing shut. Some of them had called out for her, or for Richard, and Davina kept laughing as if there was some joke the rest of them didn't understand replaying in her head. It wasn't funny.

The door behind her slid open and she turned, no small amount of alarm sending her pulse racing. It was Richard standing there, looking like a specter in the half-light, a patient's gown giving the look of a child in an oversized nightshirt up for the fourth time that night for water.

She cleared her throat, rubbing the cold sweat on the back of her neck with one hand. "You should be asleep."

He shrugged and walked over to stand next to her. "When this is finished."

"I could have—"

"I know."

He took one of her hands and gave a gentle squeeze that was more for him than her. "I have their things in my bag…Davina's sculptures, the smaller ones anyway. There's this one…an android of sorts, all tubing and wires, but the eyes—such human eyes she gave it." He cleared his throat, passing a hand over his own eyes. "Some other ones, and her carving tools. Marilla's writing." He pulled in a breath, and reached out to brush the clinging hair from Caspian's forehead. The boy's unfocused honey-brown eyes turned on him and Theresa watched the boy's parched and cracking lips curl into a grin without meaning or purpose. It was only there a second, the movement resembling a reflex, like the sort that makes a newborn child flash twitching, fleeting grins in their sleep before they are able to do it waking.

Theresa handed Richard a damp cloth and his eyes filled with gratitude. He wiped Caspian's flushed, sweating brow with it and smiled, hands lingering every so often as if expecting Caspian to brush his hands away, or to flinch from the touch.

Theresa watched his expression as he worked and felt a renewed wave of affection. His hands were gentle, eyes tender.

He looked up to find her staring.

"Did you start yet?"

She looked away, but not at the children. "No, I…well, I was about to, when you came in. I will now."

She fumbled for her handheld, entering instructions to trickle down to their individual medibots. They flashed to life, pressure application syringes emerging from the compartments in the sides of the medicot and hissing into the restrained arms of the progeny. Some of them bucked against the cots, arms fighting against the straps, teeth clicking together with nothing to bite. It wasn't really painful, so there must have been other cause for the behavior: an unexpected stimulus, an overreaction, something.

It might have been easier if she didn't look at them, but she did. She watched as their unfocused, rolling eyes slowed and darkened, all remaining spark fading until it was extinguished, their breathing slowing and stopping at the peak of a final breath. Their muscles' twitching and struggling grew more infrequent until each of them stilled.

Marilla's eyes were still open, dull marbles in the face that had retained the soft curve of jaw and cheek that exaggerated youth. Davina's jaw, now slack, and revealing pointed eye teeth, was more angular already, taking on the look of a wiry preteen, just entering the limbo between adult and child.

Richard was still mopping Caspian's brow even as the boy grew still and cold. He flashed a shaky smile at Theresa when he felt her stare. "He was anxious to meet you, you know." His voice was quiet and hoarse with emotion. "Most of them were—are, have been, I mean."

Theresa couldn't trust her voice, so instead nodded. The room was too quiet, no breathing but their own now that the sounds of squirming, rustling, thumping, the occasional shout, had ceased altogether.

THE LOST

It was wrong for the streetlights to be on. It wasn't a rational thing to think when it had only been mere days since the last communications with Earth. The ever-efficient solar power networks would last until all of the hardware broke, the panels shattered or covered over in decades of filth, and so it took some time for Genesis to place why the street lights needed to be out to still the uneasiness in her gut. The feeling was visceral and recurred each time she passed another light post or another broadcast screen scrolling with the final public message from the WGC and alternating with the message Genesis programmed in before leaving WASA.

Please stay indoors to slow the spread. Your medibot will receive the latest treatment guideline updates!

Update: Collection of all survivors for treatment and speedy recovery underway. Contact 845663 and report by railcar or other most efficient means to WASA Station…

The magnetic rail station was empty, just as the streets were so far; the slap of her shoes set off a chain of echoes as she ran down wet and puddled corridors that reflected the hulking silver shapes of buildings towering far above her and the orange glow of the streetlights.

Genesis stared up at the multi-story buildings; the windows were reflective to preserve a level of privacy that was no longer needed and was, in fact, going to prove counter to her mission. No, there was no way to know if there were survivors behind those windows, especially if they were lying somewhere, hooked up to a medibot and unaware of the updated message.

Her breath came in hot gusts and cool rushes, in and out with an efficiency made possible by rapid readaptation to the Earth environment that was coded into her genetics, just like the efficient immune system that would have a chance at keeping her alive during an infection, even without Theresa's treatments.

The environmental rehabilitation center was ahead. In contrast to towering structures like the multi-story apartment buildings and the vertical food production complex for the city, the environmental rehab center was spread out across several blocks, the roof of it planted and covered with greenhouse glass. The rain-wet surface of it shimmered in the city glow like a bright halo.

Genesis smiled at the illuminated garden. She could picture David there, trimming overgrowth with nimble hands and mumbling to the pollinators as he worked, or to Joanna's ghost.

Not a ghost if she wasn't dead.

She turned a corner and found herself directly in line with the building. The distant sounds of thunder boomed just above it, sounding like a track of stampeding feet over stone layered over itself a hundred times. She slowed from a run to a walk, cautious and a bit alarmed that she could not place the sound. It really wasn't thunder, that was clear now, and the reverberating, hollow quality of it didn't match feet on pavement. She focused in, isolating individual parts of the sound…banging.

She could see them now, through the transparent front plates of the building. At least fifty of them hammering at the glass, some throwing their whole bodies against it and leaving behind smears of blood along with a fog of hot breath.

Her eyes widened a fraction before she stilled her expression, tilting her head like a bird assessing some shimmering scrap of metal in the street. She approached the glass, hand outstretched and watched with rapt fascination as the moving bodies inside crowded towards her, flinging themselves with greater frenzy. She pressed her hand to the window, feeling for the start of hairline fractures. It could hold all night...or maybe not.

A muted voice spoke from behind the glass, and Genesis removed her hand and strode to the glass doors. The AI security was suggesting that they lean in for a scan if they would like to exit the building.

They wouldn't be able to do that; they were stuck there, blocking her path to Joanna until the window broke.

She stared at the many bodies that swarmed the glass, leaning close to see their eyes, to search for recognition, a spark. There was none. Many of their voices were still in use, and it seemed like a cruel joke to Genesis. Humans, in this case brilliant scientists, reduced to no more than a flock of parrots, repeating single phrases with incorrect inflection. *Clever bird. Clever bird. Let me out…*

She curled her nose in distaste and leaned closer to listen.

A woman's face, rounded from swelling and off-color with deep blue and purple in eye sockets and misshapen jawline, hit the glass right in front of her, busting the swollen caterpillar lip against the glass and rubbing there like a cat, smearing its own blood. "Oh I was there once! Oh was I…I there…"

The pock-marked face next to hers banged its head in profile, so that the large parietal bone on the right side served as a battering ram. In between impacts he wailed and mumbled, the words jumbling and unintelligible, but the man behind him, the man who wedged himself closer with each surge of bodies, only to be shoved back again, his speech was clear even if it lacked apparent meaning.

"This is the last thing then…Ha! Haaaaaaa—ha-ha…the last thing. I'm—bringing it up now! Ha ha ha…" The laughter was incongruous with the whole situation, the tone of it matching some other time, some other conversation where another person might have understood what was now just a residual echo devoid of meaning.

"Fake it to make it, I say…Fake it to—"

Genesis turned away, bored with the display and anxious to move on, to get inside.

They couldn't run the identity scan to get out, but she could. Crossing to the scanner at the side of the wide doors she paused, searching for an escape route. There were twin staircases leading up to the second story and continuing to the greenhouse rooftop. She looked back at the door, crowded with bodies--better they come out if she had to go in.

She leaned in for the scan and waited.

"Genesis, welcome to the Environmental Rehabilitation Center of New Zacatecas." The light above the door turned blue and she ran. The hiss of seal breaking and bodies forcing, stumbling, falling their way through, reached her as she topped the first flight of stairs. She could hear some following, but didn't look back. The second story was just one more flight of stairs. Her feet flew, muscles in her thighs forcing her faster, two, three steps at once. They weren't catching up, and Genesis grinned at the rush of adrenaline fueling her. When was the last time she'd been chased in earnest? In wolf dreams, the ones that came so often since Deimos was born.

The second story patio had the same glass front wall with sealed double doors. Genesis slowed—of course, she had considered this, but seeing that entrance clogged with a mass of bodies fighting to escape just like the ones that followed her now made her heart race faster. She turned then to assess. They were coming, but there was still a flight of stairs between them. What chance was there that the entrance to the greenhouse would be unblocked? It didn't matter.

She took the next three flights of stairs even faster, pushing herself towards a limit she'd never come up against. The footage of

Richard letting one of these touch him so that he could get close and examine it replayed in her mind's eye and it pushed her harder, the large muscles in her legs burning with fatigue now. To be caught by them, would it be fatal? Her stomach turned over at the thought, groped and assaulted, bitten, buried under the whole pile of them. Even with the gap between she could smell them, sour and sharp, like fever sweat and sickness in a closed room.

The doors to the greenhouse were there, four more steps, a sprint across the patio, the scanner. She topped the stairs and looked through the shadows even as she ran. There were columns around the door obscuring some of her view, but it was clear there was no teeming mass of wasted humanity there, and she huffed a sigh and stopped at the scanner.

The interior was shadowed by large shapes, tall trees with sweeping drapes of foliage and bushy shrubs, and there was movement between them. The tapetum lucidum in her eyes gleamed white in the faint glow from the street lights below; even in the shadows, she could see them clearly. It wasn't empty. There were at least three.

She grit her teeth, eyes flicking to the other set of stairs across the patio that would lead back down to however many were not following her. No, inside was the way. She scanned and took the three steps to the door in rapid strides. They'd have no advantage, no chance to surround her. The clumsy footsteps that served as impetus for her mad dash up the stairs were there now, just behind. The door opened at the same time that the AI greeted her by name. She wasn't listening. She grabbed the first set of hands to reach through the gap of the opening doors and pulled hard, bracing herself in a runner's stance and turning the force as soon as he was out.

Laughter came from behind. "This is the last thing then—" He was cut off by the sudden collision with the body Genesis propelled through the door and directed at her shambling entourage with their bird chatter. The second she did the same, ducking and catching the smaller framed woman in the gut to topple over Genesis's back and into the crowd. The woman let out a belch of stale air, rich with the same smell they all carried, the stink of bodies being burnt out by fever and swimming in their own ripeness. Better they smell of death and decay than this. Last one.

She side-stepped a clumsy lunge and thick grabbing hands and backed herself towards the door. The third was larger and male, twice her size. He was naked and pale, his bruised and pock-marked skin glistening a sheen of yellow-orange sweat in the lamplights. The swellings at throat and groin were blackened and gave him a misshapen look, as if his body were made of clay in the hands of an amateur sculptor uncertain of human anatomy. To Genesis's horror and amusement, the sculptor seemed to have been preoccupied with clay-man's genitals, not just swollen but engorged and painfully erect, veins standing out against the bruised, discolored skin as if they'd soon burst. He was like a gruesome fertility totem at the entrance of a newlywed's bed chamber. Genesis took a large step back and the door closed between them. He hit the glass, thrusting his exaggerated erection against the cold surface that in no way cooled his apparent ardor. Thrust, thrust…thump, against the glass. There was no pleasure in it, at least none in his eyes. As Genesis stared, she caught her breath, enjoying the cool gulps of air no longer polluted by that sour stink. Fake-it-to-make-it joined the clay totem against the glass, followed by This-is-the-last-thing and several others that mouthed words without sound and rushed the glass to form a new crowd of writhing, thrusting bodies, the only difference being they were out now—some still shrieking *"let me out"*—and she was inside.

The ceiling of the WASA station served as a skylight at night, arcing above them to form a seal around the base of the space elevator.

Neil was staring up at the triple-starred belt of Orion and then following the invisible paths to knee and shoulder, watching the subtle telltale flickers of the two brightest stars in the constellation, Betelgeuse and Rigel. He pointed up at the cluster of stars and then traced an arc across the ecliptic and down to a place that would be just above the horizon but was obscured by the walls of the station. He pressed two fingers to his lips and then pointed them towards Mars.

Theresa looked up at him, startled, and stood up from where she sat on the floor with her handheld in her lap.

"What?" He glanced over at her, and then continued tracing constellations with one finger. "I just asked why you don't go look at them...but I don't think you heard me clearly...eh?"

Theresa, frowned, confusion and irritation welling up and forcing harsh words onto her tongue. She didn't allow them to form, instead searching for reserves of patience and using whatever she could find. "I'm making sure they are all going to make it through, recover fully, double-checking the vaccine simulation progress, harvesting more Massospora X to process for treatments."

Neil crouched down next to her and gestured for her to join him. She mirrored him, still frowning. "You know I respect you, right, Theresa? The things you are capable of, your brilliance, integrity—" He shook his head. "Serious respect. But I think you need a nudge just now—Kendra would call it that."

Theresa laughed, but the sound was rough, fatigue making the edges of it jagged, her eyes were back on the screen of her handheld. "What would Kendra nudge me into?"

Neil tapped the side of the device.

"To put this thing down and go see them."

Her voice was distant, drawn out around the object of her attention, Santana's vital signs and toxicology data. "I have—seen them. But they're um…sleeping. All in the Medical wing."

"I'm gonna spell it out so we don't have to play tag with this and get confused. I see you so buried in the numbers that you don't see them when you're there, but I see their eyes open looking for you, watching. You can't just bottle all that stuff up and hope it mellows enough for you to look at eventually."

Theresa tucked her handheld into her pocket and stared at Neil's earnest expression. "I mean, I actually can… and I have to."

"The new treatment is working though, isn't it?"

His eyes looked skeptical, and Theresa grew angry. "Yes. And yet they are weeks to months from a full recovery—lung damage, brain inflammation, and suffering violent flashbacks. They are exhausted and depleted. There is time to bond when I'm not having to monitor their painfully slow inch-worming towards recovery—and when I can afford to lose focus."

"Okay, you know you better than I can. I just know if it were me and mine, I'd feel sick about it if I lost the chance to be with them. Maybe some of them would recover faster with your reassurance." He shrugged and stood up again, pointing out a constellation that looked to Theresa like a brachiosaurus with its long neck outstretched from a small rectangular body. Where were its legs then? She stared hard, searching for stars that could form shorter hind legs and longer front ones, reaching up so the weight of the dinosaur would rest on its hind legs and it could reach higher branches. She shook her head, realizing that she was almost nodding off.

"I'm gonna go compare notes with Dr. Alexander again. He's with them."

"Sure." Neil stood with his hands in the side pockets of his silver Captain's suit. When he turned and smiled, it was warm and friendly, with most signs of worry hidden now. "You know I was speaking as a friend, right? Not captain, or anything like that."

Theresa forced a smile and nodded; her eyes were burning now, and she felt a wave of nausea that was the special sort that came any time she forced herself awake on late nights. "Yeah, Neil, Sure." She wiped at the water that collected in a thin film on her eyes. It was the strain and fatigue. *Like onion tears. Nothing to cry about, no more deaths.*

She turned and walked away, leaving the Captain to his stars. The lights were dim, barely more than that distant starlight, energy conservation for the night hours. The medical wing was just as dim, even the bank of active computer screens giving off only enough light to be used. Dr. Alexander was there, asleep on a cot next to the station along with two of the station staff including Jillian Crantz. Engineering, and yet she was acting as whatever they needed her to without complaint. At least some good people would get out of here and come back with them.

Somehow that thought made her eyes tear up with a wave of disconnected emotion that burned just as much as the last one. She let out a shuddering sigh as the tears fell and pulled down. Tugging at the fabric of her lab coat, she crossed to the first row of cots.

One hand reached out for the first of her progeny in reach, stroking the girl's smooth, cool forehead and tracing down her cheek and jawline. She rested her hand there and listened. Santana's breathing was strong now. There was still a faint rattling sound to it, a cough that came every few breaths, but it was better, so much better than the tight labored wheezing that sounded as if it would stop after this breath or the next and she'd never pull in another.

She moved to the next cot and the next, rows and rows of them…like AUCs in the old lab, where they first grew under her care. Many of them were painfully thin still, to such a degree that protocols for the AUC program would have had her cull them. But this wasn't then, and the AUC program and its progenitors were dead; her progeny were half grown now, children nearing adolescence. The mental corrections didn't remove the eerie feeling of having stepped back in time as she paced the rows of sleeping children, her eyes and ears trained on the sounds of their breathing, the quality of their coughs, pulse rate, temperature, color, weight. The litany felt the same, and even while her mind was consumed by this compulsive tracking, she felt her heart soften and swell with emotion. Their still rounded youthful cheeks, the fall of messy tangles across sleeping faces, bowed or pointed lips parted in sleep—they were beautiful to the extreme, and it hurt. If looking at the face of one such child in repose and seeing the culmination of their years of grinning toothless awkwardness, successes, failures, tears down rounded cheeks, tracing the minute details and recognizing them from your own mirror-glass, if that could fill you up with love to the breaking point, then what would one hundred do to you? The question didn't need an answer with words. She felt it there behind the sharp sting in her eyes. *But there aren't a hundred here. There're eighty-four, Theresa.*

A heavy sob broke free and she tried to stifle it with a hand over her mouth. But she couldn't, not without stopping the breath that carried it, nor could she stop the next one. She squeezed her eyes against the tears that came like daggers extracted from a wound, constricting her throat and squeezing her wracking sobs to a high-pitched keening. She dropped to her knees crumpling with her forehead against the cot on the end of the last row.

A hand pressed against the nape of her neck, gently squeezing and stroking her skin. "Hey…What is it? Hey…" Richard's voice was a hoarse whisper.

He climbed down from the side of the cot with a grunt of effort, joining her on the floor. There were no alerts going off, no discordant heart-rate alarms or emergency interventions. Theresa struggled to suck in a breath to feed lungs that fought her sobs. She didn't answer as he wrapped his arms around her and cupped her cheek, the same way she had the children's.

"Shhhhh… They're doing better. They're going to be fine. Is that it?" Theresa caught a breath, forcing shaky words out with her tears. "It's there are…It's just…there're so many. But it isn't all of them…and. I… I wasn't here."

Richard pulled her in closer and she felt the heat of his body through their clothes, not fever but warm. His breaths were slow and rhythmic and hers followed. "I wasn't—here."

"Yeah, I know. You're here now."

"Yeah."

Theresa felt a smaller hand slip into hers and she turned her face from where it was buried in Richard's chest. It was Bram, crouched down next to them in a nightshirt, large brown eyes wide with worry. His whisper was rushed, shaky. "What's wrong, mom?"

"Hi, Bram." She fought the shaking of her voice and another wave of tears as she looked into those eyes and leaned her forehead against his. "Just um… just really tired and sad tonight."

"About Marilla, and Caspian, and Davina, and Irina, and Ishtar, Clark and…" He continued the list, each name giving Theresa a flash of the face of one she wouldn't hold or take out in the Martian waves, or up in the mountains on one of the Captain's hikes.

Richard's voice was still a whisper even as he tried to catch Bram's attention. "Bram. Bram, please don't keep—"

"No, it's okay." Theresa continued the list with him until all fifteen were named and then they grew silent.

"Yeah, Bram." She squeezed the small hand in hers and breathed the warm, familiar scent of his hair. It was like Abby's but different, somehow reminiscent to the amniotic fluid they grew in. It must be her scent. They all had it. Her thoughts spread out, farther apart until they only touched and connected to each other with tenuous strands like pulled taffy, spun spider-web thin, until sleep buried them, melding all thought into dream, disjointed and stress-filled, the sort that left a tinge of unease in waking hours with no cause to grasp upon.

JOANNA

What appeared to be a greenhouse from outside was on closer inspection much more than that. This was an ecosystem being built. *Now, it will languish, no doubt. If it isn't finished.* The trees formed a double canopy with tall, thin-trunked specimens reaching the top of the glass dome and blocking out much of the moonlight, a second layer below dominated by short, thicker trees with twisting, split trunks, their bark and branches draped with shaggy green and brown moss. Below that, a thick underbrush and leafmold covered the ground.

Genesis bent down and pushed aside the top layers of decaying leaves and found dark soil, damp and spongy with organic matter. She dug farther, eyes widening when she found more layers of the same instead of rooftop. She sat back and stared into the underbrush. Something moved, shaking a large fern several feet ahead and to her right. She moved into a crouch, ready to fight or flee as needed. It moved again, curled fronds bobbing as a dark shape emerged.

Genesis released her withheld breath and relaxed her stance. Two small eyes glowed white in the dim moonlight, staring out from a pointed face with long jaws full of pointed teeth and white fur. The creature hissed and backed away into the underbrush, trailing a thick, pink tail behind it.

She shook her head and stood, brushed the soiled gloves off on the side of her suit and moved on. More than a possum could have been a problem. It was all well and good to shove them out the door, but wasn't exactly something she could use if there were more trapped inside with her.

Genesis reached down to the ankle of her hazmat suit and unsheathed the knife strapped there. Its blade was long and serrated. It would do for one or two at a time.

The schematics for the building were in her head, a clear mental map, memorized on the train ride along with the city layout. The entrance to the lower levels with laboratories, cold storage for genetic materials and preserved organisms, and growing rooms was to the left. She took up a cautious jog, head on a swivel, eyes scanning to take in as much as possible.

This door was not blocked by bodies and there were none in sight down the hall. It was a good start.

The air inside was cooler, well-circulated by the automatic settings that were standard for every large building. How long would Earth's modern infrastructure continue running without a human hand in it? Scrolling sidewalks transporting rats and ravens at the step of a small foot; buildings cooled, heated, and supplied with filtered, running water with none there to notice. *If everyone dies off and there is no one left to hear the last body fall, does it make a sound?* She pushed the thought aside and continued counting hallways. The next was the turn to Joanna's team laboratory. Such thoughts were a distraction, inane brain chatter, the difference between herself and most. While they spent their time bouncing from one piece of flashy brain chatter to the next, she could sift, sort, categorize, and choose which to discard and which to use. That made it child's play to anticipate the thoughts and actions of most of them, once she had a small sampling of their thought processes.

The turn came up and she took it, but the hall wasn't empty. She paused without startling; she had already pictured the hallway under several scenarios: empty, without moving bodies, like this.

The stench was the hardest part: the sweet, overripe, complex aroma of bodies just beginning to rot like meat tucked into a cabinet instead of an icebox by mistake, unbeknownst to the distracted until that cloying smell could lead them on a desperate scavenger hunt for the source of maggots on the tiles.

And there were plenty of those here now. Genesis crinkled her nose as her shoe came down on one fat, white body, wriggling until it burst underfoot. She stared down at the clump of hair and tissue it crawled out of. It was long and black like her own, but matted with blood and not far off from the head it came from. A man with deep claw marks down the side of his face was lying there. The claw marks were so deep and ragged that it looked as if someone had tried to trace the same bleeding trails several times more and made a mess of it. He was undressed, except for a white undershirt, stained through with someone's blood in patches and sprays, a gory work of modern art. His eyes were not closed, but neither were they where they belonged. Only blood-obscured sockets, damaged lids, and portions of the optic nerve remained.

Genesis crouched beside the body, curiosity taking hold. Where were the eyes, then? She looked at the hands of the female corpse next to him, prying open the clenched fists. There was blood there, perhaps from his face, but no eyes. She scowled, irritated by the mystery. Their legs were entangled, both unclothed, but her posture looked defensive. If it began consensual, it didn't finish that way. They were both sick. That was clear. Their skin was marred with sores and bruised swellings under their jawlines, armpits, and groins. The maggots were enjoying the cause of the woman's death, or rather, the cause of her body lying prone in the hallway. Death was caused by Massospora infection, but what stopped her moving was likely the chunk of tissue missing from her throat.

Genesis's handheld shivered against the side of her upper arm where it was mounted, and she tensed against the insistent demand for her attention. She glanced down at the screen. Theresa was calling.

"Drop call and block incoming for the next hour." Her eyes were sharp with irritation when she turned back to the dead.

She wet her lips and stood, leaving the bodies on the floor. The man's mouth was bloody with what she had assumed came from the gashes in his cheek. That seemed unlikely now.

There were three more bodies, each with their own injuries and complex death narratives. Genesis registered the wounds, body contortions, positions they fell in, and constructed hypotheses before she could stop herself, but it was just brain chatter, pushed aside and tucked in another compartment. It didn't matter now. According to recent records and camera footage, Joanna was in the room ahead, as well as a computer bank she could access to help search the building for survivors. Mission accomplished, or nearly so.

She leaned in for a scan, expecting a greeting and whoosh of door opening. Instead, the light above the door turned warning yellow, and it didn't open. *"I'm sorry. This point of entry is code-locked. Use the keypad or speak the code for access."*

Access codes were just a game, something to exercise her logic and knowledge of human psychology, but this time she was impatient. There would be little thrill to it if there was no prize inside... and that remained to be seen.

She hovered her fingers above the touchpad at the door. Whose office? Joanna's, and according to her title as project lead, she was running it. It was her on the camera. Genesis glanced over at the bodies down the hall. This was likely her team. The lock code would be Joanna's, and it would be something personal. That's how people worked; most people, the sentimental ones at least, and, according to David, she fit the pattern.

The dates were all there; she didn't even have to search her memory. This was essential information for essential people, so their dates were all recorded in her mind. Birthdate…no, the day they met…no, the marriage…no. Those were obvious but not the right ones. *We need over-sentimentality coupled with cleverness, a touch of maudlin clinging…Numbers for their names, the date of the tragic end…yes. Now we play with the order and which numbers.*

It took three tries before the light turned blue and the door slid open. She didn't celebrate. It was expected.

The room was large, with many sprawling workstations between large vivarium habitats recessed into the walls or taking up desk-sized spaces throughout the room. One was crawling with large, segmented cockroaches, striped and curling antennae waving at her as she passed; the next held Armadillidium and other species of isopods, their many hair-width legs running along the sides of low branches and carrying them back into the shadows under piles of leaf litter.

Genesis was struck by the magnitude of the work being done here, the number of species of flora and fauna kept in these miniaturized ecosystems-the amount of research and progress that would be lost now. It made her dizzy for a moment and she put out a hand. It wasn't grief that hit her, but some sudden insight into the sweeping change that had come so fast here. From bustling work environment, with sharp minds progressing towards long-term goals, to a sudden standstill that would eventually crumble and leave behind nothing.

Genesis crossed the lab, following the curve of the room that spread out along a path the shape of a boomerang. Joanna was at the last and biggest workstation, bookended by two large vivarium spaces with miniature magnolia trees in bloom and dropping a rain of white velvet petals onto the leaves below.

She was swaying there next to the magnolias, her back to the door, an unsteadiness to her movements, almost as if she'd been standing so long, she was beginning to fall asleep. Genesis approached slowly. Joanna should have heard the door but showed no signs of noticing that or the approach of footsteps.

There was a hollow place in Genesis's gut, an uneasiness as she watched that languid swaying. A large, iridescent Pharaoh beetle buzzed inside the glass, colliding with the side of it several times before landing on the nearest small branch. Joanna's hand lifted. It had a tremor. She grasped at the side of the vivarium, fingers fumbling, slapping, making purchase. Her grip held and she turned, pulling herself forward with sudden force until her forehead impacted with the surface. It left a smear of blood there, tinting the droplets of condensation within a bright red. Joanna swayed away from the glass and then pulled herself towards it again.

The second impact did not come; Genesis was there before it could, and she restrained her. The limp arms she locked behind her back, legs she swept out from under her, breaking Joanna's fall and catching her against her hazmat suit.

The cut on Joanna's forehead was shallow but it bled, bright red droplets spattering on them both. She was saying something: more parrot talk, of course.

Joanna struggled to move but her attempts were weak, ineffectual. Instead of breaking free, she writhed against Genesis. She leaned up and pressed her bleeding face against the faceplate of the suit.

The heat from her fevered body baked through the protective layers, making Genesis sweat. She felt sick now, nausea filling that hollow place in her mid-section. She stared down at the face that was Joanna, beyond a shadow of a doubt. Oval, with pointed chin, fine lines around the eyes and a maturity of face-shape the only tells left after longevity therapy. The eyes were still a startling blue, but they were empty, unfocused, even as her lips mouthed words. "I told him…yes. I… then what was after. Even still—Well the newest was. Why not David? Why not? Yes, I said."

Genesis's face showed no signs of the shock that came from the utterance of his name. It was just chatter. Nonsense. A stream of surface thoughts, echoes really. And why wouldn't he be there in her head still?

Genesis scanned the room, there would be a storage closet, emergency supplies, the standard issue for all public buildings. There, on the other end of the room, a door without a security scan. Medicots were standard issue.

She looked back down at the writhing figure in her lap, staring hard into those vacuous eyes. *Why am I wasting time on the dead?* Genesis felt a wave of impatience and disgust with herself; hot anger rose up to meet it and she stood, dragging Joanna with her to the storage closet.

There were three, charged and functioning, with strong restraints. Joanna could lie there and squirm while she had a chat with the AI. Vital signs in the building would be available: body counts, assignment names, and genetic ID's.

She pictured the ones she'd let out of the building. Unfortunate, but if any were on the list of kin, they were probably still banging on the door to get in. She could use more hands for this task.

The computer system gave little resistance once she logged in as Joanna. A staff of two-hundred scientists ran the building; only thirty-one were present, with none alive, if she followed the patterns for advanced infection vital signs. They were all as dead as Joanna and, according to the AI, seven of them were counted dead with no movement or vital signs. *Like the ones in the hallway.*

There was no delay in reaching Theresa; the voice that came across the line sounded weary.

"One: I'd like as many as we can spare to assist with collecting next of kin and two: have you tried treating them after they seem gone?"

Theresa's replies were clipped and irritated. "If you could not go silent for unpredictable amounts of time, we'd appreciate that."

"Missing me already, then?" Genesis's retort lacked the usual flirtation. It was just words. *Parrot chatter…brain babble.*

"No."

"Fine, I can't answer calls while sifting through dead bodies any more than you can while hyperfocused on a DNA strand. Have you checked?"

"Yes. None have come back from it. We treat them and every system shuts down."

Genesis felt hollow again and angry. She looked down at the woman strapped on the cot. Joanna's full pink lips were dusky, the skin around them blue from cyanosis. She traced their contours with gloved fingers. David's stories stuck in her head on replay as she stared at a face that had become vividly real for her over the passage of years. She knew when David was hearing her; now she knew what he saw in sleep and waking dreams. A bitter smile pulled at the corners of her mouth and she shook her head.

"Fine. How much does it take to shut them down? Is the anti-fungal enough?"

"No. It takes a lot. We used the new treatment as well. They might reanimate with just the anti-fungal, because it doesn't knock it out completely."

There was a long pause before she continued. Genesis just waited, lost in thought. "Don't waste what you have on that. You might need it for someone who has a chance still."

"I know." Genesis ended the call. Enough wasting time on sentimentality. She stood and set the medicot to shadow her movements and then she searched Joanna's desk for something she knew would be there. Old, tattered manuscripts, delicate shears, and shaping tools filled the drawer. Genesis pushed them aside, lifting and digging until she saw it, a flash of gold. She lifted out the chain and locket, engraved with tree and thorny vine entwining and merging into one, a rose blooming where they joined. She pocketed it and left the room. The medicot followed her down the empty hall in a zigzag, sensors directing it to turn and avoid the bodies on the floor.

REQUEST DENIED

Three council seats were empty. The others were pulled close for quiet discussion with no larger audience there to listen. Only starlight came through the large skylight of the amphitheater, leaving it to the many recessed ceiling and floor lights to bring some illumination to the room.

Donovan spoke with confidence. It didn't matter that they were all listening to him, leaning in. He paused to look around the circle before diving into the meat of the subject, what he came back from the wilds to make clear. Yes, they were listening, and the tension that ran through them was palpable, moving from one to the next of them and building. "I know we skipped over this in the other meeting. I know why. But everyone here needs this, so here we go. What happened on Earth—it will happen here. Not yet and not with this thing...I think. But at some point."

Melissa lifted a hand for him to pause. "Didn't we come here clean, decontaminated at W.A.S.A? We all went through several rounds of that."

Donovan shook his head. "No. That's not how this works. No such thing, sorry." He lifted a hand, marking off fingers as we spoke. "We came with escheria coli, streptococcus, candida albicans, lactobacillus, coronavirus, influenza, et cetera, et cetera, and Mars was seeded with microorganisms well before we arrived as a part of the terraforming. There is no *clean* when it comes to living organisms, ecosystems."

Some of them looked startled, Melissa, even Emily. Carla was nodding. David looked tired, a tightness around the eyes as if he wasn't sleeping well, but he nodded as well. He'd already heard Donovan warming up for this in the field.

"And last, most unpleasant source of possible pandemics…Earth now. We can't expect them not to bring it back. They'll shed it; it'll be on everything in that ship. Maybe they'll contain it or kill it, maybe they'll bring it down and spread it. And hopefully Theresa will have taken the teeth out of it and it'll be harmless by the time they get here."

Melissa laughed and the sound of it was rough, nervous. "Did you call us up for this to induce nightmares, or is there a silver-lining?" Donovan cocked his head and opened his mouth to answer, an incredulous smile building. "Uhhh…No, no silver-lining. I mean, microorganisms don't really give me nightmares, personally, but you're all welcome to imagine them as oversized monsters if it gives you a good focal point for action, as it were…. Some are helpful, some are neutral. The problem comes when, in generations, as different strains pop up like this one—ones really, Massospora X with Y. Pestis as endosymbiont. New strains of previously irritating microorganisms are the issue, and we have everything here on Mars to set us up for our own epidemics."

He exhaled as if to punctuate his speech. The circle of council members didn't respond right away, when they did Melissa spoke first.

"If this is a threat you are aware of, and want us aware of, can't you eliminate the problem bugs? On Earth, historically, things were eradicated, Smallpox, Measles, Sars-Cov-2, others—right?"

"Sure, but it's more complicated than that. The ones we eradicated weren't until after causing mass casualties. You can't know what's going to jump species or go airborne. Some mutate too quickly; some we've just never been able to wipe out." He spread his hands out in front of him.

"We don't want a repeat of Earth to point out what we need to focus on. So, we prepare for this now, or after we burn the dead."

Melissa choked on the spice brew she had lifted up to sip. It sloshed as she set it down, leaning forward to cough and catch her breath. Dr. Eric put a hand on her shoulder, listening for the wheezing sound of her coughing to clear. Donovan fidgeted, running through everything he'd said so far in his head and biting a nail. He glanced over at Emily and shrugged. She didn't see; her eyelids were drooping from fatigue and, while she wasn't falling asleep, she looked like she should be.

Donovan cleared his throat once the coughing tapered off. "I'm not trying to be alarmist, but we don't want to be Earth Two. We need to be smarter than that." His tone shifted in intensity, rising in sharpness and volume as he dove into another monologue. " I um…I avoid politics, argument, usually. But I don't think any of us can now. Earth is dead. We have a small population that won't withstand an epidemic, and we also have unchecked breeding. Maybe that's good now, but what about later? We need guidelines, quotas, and we need infectious disease experts, a separate panel to prevent epidemics, plans to spread our population to avoid a rapid spread and wipe-out."

David cleared his throat and lifted a hand. "He's not wrong. Earth had an infectious disease team on the WGC and centuries of history to learn from, and it wasn't good enough. But you know, what Donovan and I were discussing out in the field was what Earth didn't have—what we're working on."

Donovan was even more animated now and he said the word at the same time David did, the two exchanging a wry smile.

"Biodiversity—enough species to compete for the same niches that none can overpopulate, enough predation going on to control populations from up top as well. Earth ecosystems were falling apart for awhile. Planetary ecologists like Donovan were working on it, but Earth ecosystems were a dumpster-fire waiting to happen—"

Donovan continued when David nodded in his direction as if passing a baton. "Cicada infestation worldwide, allowing for overlap with the uncontrolled rat populations in the cities, allowing years of interaction between Y. Pestis originating in fleas and prevalent in rodent populations and Massospora, originally a fungal infection only affecting cicadas."

Melissa had both hands on either side of her face, making her eyes look wider than they were. "So you're suggesting an epidemic prevention and response team, specialists—sounds like our botanist wants to be on the team with you, who else? But you lost me a bit on population control. Very mixed signals. Are you talking about curtailing reproductive freedom, or outbreeding an epidemic?"

"Both."

"Oh, okay, sure, that's easy." She shook her head in frustration. "We can't head down the same path as Earth. I won't start handing out licenses to procreate like on Earth, and if I tried, I think our citizens would try to reinstate corporal punishment because prisons or banishment wouldn't do it for them."

Donovan grit his teeth. "It isn't asking too much for humans to be smarter about reproduction. Animals can do it; there are species that won't breed in times of stress, species that reabsorb their young, bear the number of offspring the habitat can support. We aren't rats and we don't need to breed like them, but as I pointed out, we have to set quotas for a population high enough to withstand losses, I don't think I'm being unreasonable, am I?" He looked around the small semi-circle of council members. Emily met his eyes and spoke first.

"It's just, you have to remember where we're coming from. People are going to be jumpy when you mention population control."

"I don't have patience for jumpy. It's been eleven years that we've been exercising our rights to reproductive freedom. We can't go on being reactionary—I can so I will, again, and again, and again, and again."

Carla spoke just above a whisper, meeting Donovan's fiery eyes with her calm grey ones. "I don't hear Donovan saying we need to change anything by force, or even set a low limit where he'd like it to be around one or none." She looked back at him for confirmation, and he nodded, grateful. "If Genesis were here, she'd bring up things like the power of culture to set norms for behavior, community responsibility, consensus." She watched their faces as she spoke. There was more nodding, and Melissa's eyes were no longer wide with alarm. David looked momentarily distant, his eyes shadowed and dark with pain.

Melissa was nodding now, and she stood up. "Okay, we have a lot to think about, plan, discuss, and Carla makes a good point. We need our whole team here for this."

David spoke from where he sat, rubbing his hands together. "When are they expected back?" Melissa looked irritated when she answered. "I don't know that. They have the Progeny but no other survivors—sorry, four survivors: the WASA staff. Genesis, Neil and a couple from WASA are trying to collect any they can find in the cities."

They had all seen the footage Richard sent from Earth; delirious, violent, technically deceased but still moving victims in the WGC headquarters. It was a long, tension-filled minute before any of them spoke.

David got up to pace the floor. "Why not just call them back? How long are we going to have them risking themselves to collect people when they aren't finding any?"

Donovan cleared his throat. "I have to disagree, David. The longer they are gone, treating this infection, clearing it, Theresa making sure her treatments knock it out entirely, the more sure we can all be they don't bring it back with them."

Emily looked alert now, and frightened, but her words were calm and measured. "Anyone who has survived this needs to be picked up. We can't leave people."

Eric was frowning, looking at his interlaced fingers in his lap. "I don't think they'll find any. The death rate is too high, infection rate too high. The only survivors they have were Theresa's progeny under early treatment and the WASA people who were isolated. Not even the WGC or Reproductive Council headquarters were that well isolated, sanitized; no survivors there, according to Dr. Brant and their own leader Diadonna, before she dropped contact." His expression grew pained. "I'm a doctor. I don't support abandoning survivors. I just don't believe there are any."

Melissa raised a hand for silence. "We put this to a vote then. All in favor of calling them back within one week's time, make your vote on your handheld."

The votes came in quickly, Melissa watched as they did, a look of controlled focus on her face until each of the seven were counted. "Four to three in favor of calling our people back." Donovan bit back an angry response; he forced his breathing into something that didn't allow for huffs or sighs, but the crease between his brows was deep and he was pulling at another nail with his teeth before they all parted ways. At least they listened to some of it. It was too bad that some of the repercussions of bringing that thing here might not show up for years. The return trip was a long one, at least.

Maybe it would be enough.

Neil fastened the last straps on his hazmat suit, his movements forceful with barely restrained anger. His brown eyes flashed with it when he looked up at the others. "I know how to take orders, but I'm drawing the line on this. They're all the way back on Mars sitting on their hands, not knowing what to do with all that nervous energy, and they want to jump and call us home!? Before we've had a fair chance to accomplish what they sent us for? No." He shook his head in disgust. The others listened in silence. Richard was still reclined on his medicot, hooked up to a direct line of medications; Theresa stood next to it, chewing her bottom lip and fidgeting. Dr. Alexander was nodding, as he often did while taking in information, regardless of his agreement or lack thereof. If Brogan had any objections, he hadn't voiced them yet, and neither had his staff. They all looked tired, weary from stress and caring for sick children. Neil frowned and continued, what he saw in their faces only reinforcing his feelings.

"Genesis is in just one city, by herself, trying to do what we agreed to, and I'm not calling her back yet without a reason. I'm going to go help, with any of you that we can spare. She just found a survivor. If there was one, there could be more. As captain of this mission, I'm saying we give this some time…at least enough for our call for survivors to report to WASA to be heard and answered."

Dr. Alexander was still nodding, but it was unclear whether it was acknowledgement of agreement. "I won't argue with your decision." He looked around at the others. "I think we'd be unwise to. Two points. One, we still have people convalescing. And two, after seeing what this thing does to a person, I don't feel right leaving anyone who has somehow survived it up to this point."

Neil broke into a fierce grin and reached out one gloved hand to pat Dr. Alexander on the back. "Good. We'll find them, bring them back to you for treatment." He turned to Theresa. "How many do you need here for the progeny? Minimum? I want to take anyone else with me to the cities, rendezvous with Genesis, wait for contact."

Theresa was frowning, her brows pulled together into the telltale crease of concern that Neil knew well at this point. "So, I'm not disagreeing with you. But I think we need to agree on a cut-off…dealing with this thing—knowing that my progeny survived until we started some half-effective treatment mostly because they have a next-generation immune system—does not give me confidence that there will be any survivors out there, or any we can find."

Neil looked irritated. He pushed a hand through his hair and stared at Theresa as she finished and spoke right on the tails of her words. "Don't forget we have survivors already. We have the WASA staff here, Brogan, and the one Genesis found in New Zacatecas."

Theresa's voice was low and patient. "I'm not arguing with you, Neil. How long? That's what I'm asking." He twisted his lips between his fingers. He looked mollified by her words, the irritation fading as he focused. "That's partway on you and Dr. Alexander. How long until your kids and Richard here are going to be ready to withstand the stress of zero-G for a month and a half? We can't consider going until then, and that's what I'm gonna fire back to Melissa and the council on Mars."

Theresa glanced down at Richard on the medicot. His eyes were sharp, but still shadowed with weariness and moments of confusion. He was too thin for his frame, bones of his jawline and cheekbones too prominent and giving his skin a stretched appearance. He wasn't ready for space travel, the children less so.

"I think we need a month. And you can use that. We don't want to be stupid and rush them. Alexander?"

He was nodding again. "Give them two weeks and we reassess, probably will need two more after that. Let's take it a day at a time. I'm not going to fight to get them on their feet and then watch them collapse on the ship."

Neil's smile was resolute. He looked pleased with the outcome. "Okay. That's agreed then. Anyone coming with me to meet up with Genesis should suit up."

Brogan raised a hand, silently volunteering himself, but then pointed over at Theresa. "I'm gonna go, but my staff are staying here to help you with the kids still."

Theresa nodded, the look of overwhelm in her weary eyes saying more than her words could. "Okay, yeah—just, be careful, Neil, Brogan. We'll wait for any stragglers here."

She stared after them as they left. There weren't enough to care for this many sick as it was. Some of them were well enough to be restless or angry, but not well enough to take care of themselves just yet. *Should have brought half of Mars to wrap things up here. Not a handful of us.*

LEADERSHIP

Gavin held tight to the handholds even as the muscles in his arms shook. He rubbed his forehead on his sleeve to mop up the sweat of exertion. There were several paths up and over the climb wall, some easier to navigate than others. He narrowed his eyes, tracing the paths and picking out the most challenging, reaching for the next handhold that would get him there.

His fingers slipped as he shifted his weight, seeing his full mass into a swing. Grit teeth and determination brought him back to the hand and footholds closest, and he paused, panting and wiping at the sweat that stung his eyes again.

"Hey, Gavin! That's enough. Come down now." Captain Neil's voice sounded distant, far below on the floor of the WASA training gym.

The next handhold was close and he reached for it, using main strength to pull himself high enough to reach the footholds that were higher up than he could reach with his legs alone.

He heard the movements below him, Captain Neil climbing up to where he was, his ascent faster than Gavin expected. The older man was winded when he got there and locked out both of their climbing harnesses.

"You didn't hear me?"

Gavin pressed his lips together and glanced over at the path he'd chosen to reach the top. "I mean, I heard you, but I was climbing…why stop before the top?"

The Captain nodded, crooked smile coupling with an amused glint in his eyes. "Because you're tired, and you're still healing."

"I'm not tired enough to quit before I finish the course." He reached for the next handhold and then froze when Neil placed his own larger hand over his.

"You could climb this wall until you fall off of it and dangle from your harness with that determination, but you're shaking and slipping and it's not helping you at this point. Nothing chasing you—nothing to prove…"

Gavin's head felt hot, foggy and claustrophobic inside his skull, and his heart beat in his own ears. He reached up and released the harness with one hand, using the other to control his descent to the padded ground below. His hands still shook as he untied the harnesses strapped around his hips, and he grinned, stretching and clenching his hands to savor the warm heaviness of increased blood flow in his muscles.

Neil landed next to him on the mat and mirrored his motions, untying and removing the equipment. He gave Gavin's shoulder a pat when he'd finished. "You've outdone what anyone could expect at this point—still got bruises fading and lung damage healing, and you're in here every day."

Gavin shrugged. "I need to recover faster." He paused for a breath. "For things I need to do."

The Captain was nodding. "Sure, sure. We have a rough trip ahead. Space travel isn't easy, but you're gonna be alright—" Neil looked over at Gavin and wet his lips. "But you know—I'm not your Dad, but you might need to hear this, I think. That pride is gonna get you in trouble at some point. Thinkin' you don't need help, don't have anyone to answer to, know better than anyone—"

Gavin looked away. His hands were on his hips, his jawline, only recently beginning to take on some definition as the softness left his face, was tense and frozen as he listened.

Neil continued, voice softer as he pressed. "I'm saying that way of being gets you in over your head—"

A sharp glint lit Gavin's eyes when he turned back to face Neil. "Were you in over your head when you tried to attack Earth?"

The Captain's eyes widened and his mouth went dry. He rubbed a hand across lips and jaw as he held Gavin's stare. "Yeah, uh—yes I was, Gavin."

"When you got so many of your people killed…how many?"

"Nine people."

Gavin nodded, a tug of war playing out in his eyes before he spoke again. "I lost fifteen…Is that why you stopped leading?"

The question burned in his eyes as he waited for Neil to answer. The Captain cleared his throat and looked away. "You took a big responsibility on yourself for a kid, it was—"

"A miscalculation. But you didn't answer—Why did you stop leading? Because you got people killed?"

Neil grew very still and met the boy's eyes with his own steady gaze. "Yes, son. I stopped leading because I got people killed."

Gavin turned away to pace, anger giving a sharpness to his movements as he spoke. "But that's the wrong answer! Good leaders make mistakes, oversights…You can't just quit over every loss—'success is not final, failure is not fatal: it is the courage to continue that counts.' Winston Churchill!"

Neil spread his hands and tilted his head to meet Gavin's fevered eyes. "The price of greatness is responsibility…I had to take responsibility. Take a step back and evaluate my fitness to lead."

Gavin froze, a small smile spreading on his lips despite the pain in his eyes. "Success is the ability to go from one failure to another with no loss of enthusiasm…"

"Who are you trying to convince, son: me…or yourself?

Looks like we know enough Churchill to go on like this all night."

Gavin opened his mouth to speak again, to throw out another quote about success, about leadership in the face of struggle, but the words froze, locked up behind another quote that tumbled out instead. "Healthy citizens are the greatest asset any country can have…" His lips trembled before he pressed them together and then he shrugged as if to throw it aside. "Fifteen. I lost fifteen. You only lost nine…do you still think about it? See them in your head…hear them?" In his mind's eye, Clark jumped through the shattered glass again, Marilla, eyes glassy, skin covered in bleeding sores, bucked against the restraints of a medicot. Gavin closed his eyes for a beat before turning back to the Captain.

Neil was very still; his eyes were wet and too bright with intensity. Gavin scowled and looked down; he couldn't hold the eye contact any longer, not while Neil was looking back like that.

"Yes, Gavin, every day. Think about them, see them, miss them… and feel responsible for their deaths."

"Well, you were."

The older man put a hand on Gavin's shoulder and directed him towards the exit, walking next to him. "Yeah, I was. And so were you. But I shouldn't have stepped down. It was the wrong call, quitting like that."

"It was. I wouldn't have." Gavin's head felt clearer, no longer crowded with conflicting thoughts. He knew what to do now.

The infirmary was just ahead and Gavin walked backwards towards it, still facing the Captain to wave before going in.

Neil chuckled, but it didn't bother Gavin like Richard's did. He wasn't sure why. This laugh didn't threaten him; it was warmer, somehow, and less exasperated.

"Send another one out to rehab for me, will you, Gavin?" With a nod, Gavin turned and pushed the door open.

The infirmary lighting was dim but enough to walk by, and enough to see that the male doctor with shaggy brown hair—Dr. Alexander, was asleep on a cot now, as was Richard. Theresa wasn't there, probably in the lab tonight. Gavin paused and watched the door as if expecting her to come through it and then crossed the gap to Gelsemium's medicot. She was coughing in her sleep as many of them still were, that dry, irritated cough that lingers for months after pneumonia.

"Geli." He reached out and hand to shake her but didn't. If she startled, she'd wake others.

She opened her eyes wide and stared up at him, mouth working as if she would scream or shout, but she rolled to her side and coughed into her arm instead.

"Go to bed, Gavin."

"No." He crouched down next to her cot. "We need to talk and it needs to be now."

She didn't answer and closed her eyes as if she had never woken.

"You're avoiding me…ignoring me. That's not us, Geli; we talk about things. Even hard things."

She sighed but didn't open her eyes. "I can't—look at you, Gavin, without seeing that again. Remembering the way you—"

"How I grabbed you, slapped you, tore your clothes? Do you think that was me? Have I ever been that way before?"

She opened her eyes but didn't look at him, a shudder passing through her as she answered. "No. Pushy, cocky…irritating, but not—not hurting anyone."

"It was the sickness and I lost it, trying to get everyone on a medicot, get you safe…"

She wet her lips and looked at him until she trembled, face

curling in on itself as her eyes grew wet with tears and her breath was hitching. "Doesn't matter though, Gavin, because what I know isn't what I feel anymore. I see you and my heart races and I'm nauseous and I see things again—you grabbing at me, digging at my skin with your nails, choking me with your hands, and while I'm there it feels real."

Gavin was frowning, his whole forehead a study of creases and his eyes sad, voice a hoarse whisper. "I'm seeing things—things like that but different. But Theresa has something to make it stop, probably. I heard her tell Richard. They're going to try it."

Gelsemium stared at the wall over his shoulder. "Then talk to me after we try it, if you want anything different than this from me."

He cleared his throat and stopped himself from taking her hand; she would not want to be touched right now. "Please, it's quick but can't wait longer. Are you staying with me? If the others will? Nothing has changed here, since we agreed that we'd stay."

Her eyes narrowed and she met his gaze for the first time. "If I stay, it won't be because of that, or anything else you say. It'll be because I want to be on Earth."

His eyes flashed with hurt and he seemed to wince and swallow back his first thoughts, then he smiled and nodded at her, ducking his head. "Okay. That's good enough for now."

Gelsemium sighed and closed her eyes, fighting an involuntary shudder, and Gavin felt a new wave of guilt as he watched her fight what was in her head.

He stood and eyed the door again before taking any steps towards it and then crouched closer to her again, brows knitting and frown filling his eyes with an urgent, grasping sort of regret. "Hey Geli, I—I'm sorry, you know." She should have heard him. He was close enough even if it was a whisper, but she didn't open her eyes or acknowledge him.

He stood again and turned to walk away. "Okay, Gavin. Tell the others." Her faint reply followed him. It wasn't forgiveness, but it was something; it was what he needed now, and it wiped the tension from his face, replacing it with a faint smile in the dark as he picked his way back to his own cot.

BREADCRUMBS

Her shoes hit the pavement, matching the rhythm of her breathing, in—in—out, in rapid succession. Sweat gave a sheen to her tawny skin and her hair was braided now, twisted into a crown lest it provide a handhold for grabbing hands again.

The city was an eerie mix of sounds that somehow felt deserted and full at the same time, that slap of bare feet that chased after, crashes of breaking glass and toppling desks inside buildings, sudden random shouts of incoherent bird-babble talk, actual birds—ravens calling out with their clicks and caws. But the bulk of sound was missing: without the hum of a city full of life, the magnetic-rail cars traveling the whole city with their incessant hum, announcements, music, conversations—all gone silent except for the repeat of Genesis's call for survivors to head to WASA. She was growing used to it now, every sound registering now as predictable, expected, and eliciting no startle response.

She caught a breath and spoke into her handheld. "Neil? I'm two streets over from you and being followed by a small crowd. They give chase in quick bursts and then get bored, or tired. Just a sec—" She ducked into an alley and climbed onto the second-floor patio to perch on the railing out of reach.

"Alright, I'm on the patio, Sky Oasis Apartments. You'll see me. My entourage will dissipate in a while if they don't see you. Oh, but I was saying, they get tired. I've seen some just drop and stop altogether."

Her heart was settling in now and her breathing normalized, but the high of being pursued persisted, and her speech was animated and faster than most could follow.

Neil's voice came through when she paused to grab a breath and continue. "I see you up there." He chuckled, the warm, infectious laughter making her join in. "You look like one of the ravens perched up there like that. Hold on."

Genesis watched him change direction and circle around the other side of the building. It made more sense than waiting them out or knocking them down. She'd cut a few throats since arriving in New Zacatecas—the proof of it still colored her hazmat suit— but it wasn't necessary with most of them, and somehow she felt Neil wouldn't derive any pleasure from cutting them down. They were innocent, just people, and not in control of themselves.

Neil came around the other side at a full sprint, reached the ladder with a jump and pulled himself up it without using his legs at all as if climbing a rope. He was out of breath when he sat on the ledge next to her but grinning. "I think—I'm the only one wearing my weights at home the recommended amount. And this makes it all worth it. Still, gravity is a bitch."

Genesis grinned back. "You are enjoying this far too much. I daresay you haven't had this much fun in years."

He snorted a laugh and shrugged. "And you're not?" Genesis licked her lips.

"Honestly this is—disturbing, but it feels important. Exhilarating, sure, the chase, the challenge, we can expect to enjoy that. People like us thrive on it." She met his eyes and held them with her own. "Don't feel guilty for loving it. Doesn't mean you wished for it or wouldn't change it."

Neil's eyes were shadowed now, teared up. "I think you got it just right. It's a rush, but the kind where the pit of your stomach turns over and it just keeps hitting you." He looked down at the cluster of ten infected bodies that moved below them, looking up with blank eyes and incoherent shouts.

"All these people. How many even—will we ever have a count, or just a guess?" He went still and then turned a dark look on Genesis. "Makes me wish we'd come sooner. Figured out something was off when Diadonna was sending mixed messages, and it felt off, but I didn't know why. And I was too busy seeing the past to do anything but think it was more political bullshit."

"I didn't catch on either, Neil, and when I did get news that something was up I had no idea of the scale." She shrugged. "There was nothing you could do. Now, where's Brogan?"

"I left him two streets over before coming to you because I run faster. He's in a coffee shop waiting."

"Well, I'm about done with this city. Three buildings left. We get in, access security cameras and search for survivors that way—"

"What, no busting down doors and clearing rooms?"

Genesis rolled her eyes at him. "It's more efficient. It's what I do." She pulled the large serrated pocketknife from her ankle sheath and opened it up, tapping his knee with the flat of the blade. "This is just back-up. So unless you want to stay up here with me and get out of these suits for a bit, I'm ready to move on."

He raised a brow, and she mimicked the expression with her own. "Really?"

She shrugged. "Suit yourself…"

Genesis grabbed hold of the edge of the balcony, lowered herself, and dropped. There were only three bodies still standing nearby and they gave chase. Neil dropped down and overtook them, passing by and matching Genesis's stride with some effort.

"Three more and then where, Captain Genesis?" His tone was playful, but not without respect, and it made her smile. Teasing and verbal flirtation were almost as titillating as the physical sort.

"As many cities as we can hit."

Neil nodded, his pace slowing some as they turned a corner. "Fine. Where's your survivor? The train?"

Genesis turned around to face him, still running but slower for his benefit. "Yes. On a medicot, being treated just in case. He wasn't symptomatic, but it seemed the thing to do."

"You…know…Trina was always faster—than me. Especially after a space mission."

Genesis smiled in sympathy. "She was. So catch up, Captain, before the dead do."

There were footsteps from around the corner…or was it just a convergence of echoes? It almost sounded like a mirror of the steps behind them from the ones who followed or perhaps an echo of their own. Genesis felt a vague sense of disorientation as she listened for the source of each sound and tried to place them at the right location and rate of approach. The sound seemed to disappear underneath the louder ones that came from behind. A sudden crashing sound of breaking glass from the right and then as the alley way opened up into a side street, Genesis turned just in time to catch the source of footsteps in a full-on collision.

They tumbled over each other, Genesis and a woman of similar size but with a compact, more muscular frame. The woman thrashed and shoved at Genesis, screeching and incoherent, tearing at the mask of Genesis's hazmat suit, and Neil grabbed hold of her, hauling her off by the back of her shirt at the collar and ready to throw her.

"Wait!" Genesis was reaching for the woman, eyes wide as she grasped the trembling blood-spattered face between her hands. There were fresh marks dug into her skin by blunt fingernails, and they were still bleeding. The eyes a warm brown, darting left and right, alert but in a state of panic. Her vision appeared to blur, her eyes losing focus and closing as she drooped forward, hanging from Neil's grip.

"Neil. From both sides." Genesis drew her knife. There was no alarm in her voice as she gestured towards the direction that the woman had come and then their own path where a crowd of the infected were approaching. "Just handle her while I take care of these."

Neil had her up and in arms as soon as she suggested it and was drawing his own knife. "Fine, I'll get her to the coffee shop. Don't play games out here or I'll come back for you."

"No. I'll just slow them so they—don't—" The last word she punctuated with a forward thrust of one leg as the first of them reached her. It connected with the man's chest, shoving him backwards into the two behind him, and turned them into a writhing, grasping pile. There were more but they weren't close yet, so she followed, knife still out and ready when she turned to run backwards a few steps to watch them.

Kendra sat on the edge of Emily's bed, her adept hands pressing into her lower abdomen just above the upper border of her pubic bone. She inched her fingers gently upward and outward, following the curve of Emily's uterus, now two inches out of her pelvic brim, firm and rounded.

She looked over to find Emily watching with a small smile that glowed with confidence despite the shadows of sleep deprivation that ringed her eyes.

"Look at you beaming and glowing. You know it's just right. Why am I checking you? How many times have you done this already today?"

Emily's freckled cheeks blushed as her smile widened and filled her eyes. "Only several." She reached down and felt the grapefruit-sized mound of her growing womb, tracing the contours as Kendra had. Shadows crossed her expression but didn't linger. "I never got this big before, even with the longest one." She sat up slowly and leaned her forehead against Kendra's. "Thanks."

Kendra grinned at her friend and put a hand on the side of her face. "What are you thanking me for? You're the one doing this." Emily shrugged. "For being you and being with me, I guess. You can remind me we're fine when I wake up in a panic."

Kendra held her reassuring smile and nodded, patting Emily's cheek before getting up to pick Askia up off of the floor blanket where Jasrie was watching him. He started to fuss and root for the breast as soon as he was in arms, nuzzling against her clothes with open mouth before Kendra could move them aside. He latched on the moment she freed her breast and pulled him close in the crook of one arm. "There you go now. You hungry? Just starving' over there all forgotten—eh?" She sighed, settling in against the wall alcove that surrounded Emily's bed. Emily handed her a large pillow and helped her tuck it under the side she was nursing on for support and she gave a look of tired gratitude. "You ready for this?"

Jasrie had clambered up onto the bed and tucked herself against Kendra's other breast, with one hand there as if to stake a claim on it, not nursing as she was 'all too big,' in her own words. She was staring at Emily with huge eyes as if there was a question she was burning to ask.

"Yes. For all of it…the hard stuff and the pain, and the doubts, and the sweetness. I've been ready so long…I see you there, Jasrie; did you not get to check on my baby yet this time?"

Jasrie shook her head, crown of dark soft curls moving with her. "No I didn't, Emily. I was watchin' while mama did, but don't you know I had to watch Askia cuz I'm a big sister. But how am I gonna learn all this stuff if I don't feel the baby?"

Jasrie's small face was scrunched up and her eyes were serious. Kendra was chuckling and ruffling her daughter's hair. Emily reached into Kendra's bag for her and pulled out a fetoscope before lying back on the bed again. "Here, Jas; we didn't even listen to the baby's heart tones yet and Carla's still coming, I think. You listen first and tell her when she gets here. Have you used this one yet?"

Jasrie nodded, taking the two-part device in her small, dimpled hands, and holding a thumb over the touch pad as if she'd done it a hundred times before. The amplifier unit lit up with a faint hum and Jasrie grinned, flashing all of her teeth in triumph. "See that? I do know!"

"I see that."

The voice of the room's AI interrupted with its smooth female-simulated intonation. "You have a visitor. Your Grandmother is here thirty-two minutes late."

"Let her in, please." Emily faced the door and waved silently to Carla before gesturing with a finger across her lips and indicating Jasrie curled up next to her, the fetoscope at her ears and the other end against Emily's belly. A whooshing sound and a distant thrum of blood through arteries in time with an adult heart rate, thrum-pause-thrum-pause at about seventy beats per minute, came from the amplifier, allowing those in the room to hear what Jasrie was hearing through the earpieces. She moved the cup-shaped end to the left and right across the mound of uterus that rose from Emily's belly, brows pulled together in concentration.

Carla smiled and gave a silent wave in return before creeping over and sitting just behind Jasrie on the bed. She patted Kendra's calf and smiled at her younger partner, scrunching her nose in proud disbelief as she gestured to their smallest apprentice at work.

Jasrie moved the cup end again, this time a bit lower, and huffed out a heavy sigh of frustration that was bigger than she was. She moved it again and then paused. It was still Emily's heart rate, and she knew it.

"I can't find it." Her small husky voice was plaintive.

Carla reached a hand over Jasrie's shoulder and placed it over the hand that held the cup of the fetoscope, moving it lower and just to the left and then a bit further, and pressing in gently. Then she let go and whispered next to the girl's ear. "It's harder to hear this early even with the amplifier. Sometimes I can't even find it with this. Emily feels the baby and has no worries, so it's just practice. Patience is your friend when it comes to finding heart tones; just ask your momma." Jasrie glanced up at Kendra, who gave her a wink.

She moved the cup just to the right and then a bit more. The sounds changed again. First a loud whoosh, a crackling, and then the rapid thrum-thrum-thrum-thrum of a very fast, tiny heartbeat, like drums in the distance. Jasrie's eyes lit up but she didn't move, lest she lose it. She held her hand there over the fetoscope, transfixed as they all were.

Kendra placed her hand over Jasrie's and gave it a squeeze. She nodded in approval when those wide eyes found hers. "Look what you did yourself. You're gonna be a better midwife than me 'fore long."

Carla tipped her eyes and looked over Jasrie's head at Emily who was doing the same and then over at Kendra. "I'm sorry I missed some. A session ran late. Lots of sessions."

Kendra gave a half smile, her blue eyes shadowing as she looked away. "Lot's a scared people. Neil isn't even in charge but he's still their captain, I'd say. Doesn't feel right without him here. And not just for me."

Carla nodded. "I won't argue that. You can't uproot one of the bigger trees in a forest without upsetting the whole thing. Trees are toppling left and right with our people gone."

Emily chewed her bottom lip and reached out for Kendra's hand. "How are you and the kids?"

Kendra pulled in a breath to stall an answer but then shrugged. "Not great. He's not even back on the ship. Still collecting people. You know, they called them back, right? You're on the council—you know. But he says they won't be coming till they get as many as they can out of there." She shook her head, eyes saying what she wouldn't give words to, the raw fear and worry that was a constant companion now.

"Have you talked, dream-speak, or voice message?" "Naw. He's busy, I'm busy." She gestured at the two of four children that were in the room. "Don't have time for dream-speak. But I don't want it anyway. Don't want to hear his voice unless he's planet-side, you know? How else am I gonna fool myself into thinking he's on a long run, or a trip into the wilds with Donovan and David, or some other thing that isn't on Earth?" Her voice rose on the last word, her tone describing conditions on Earth better than any words could. She sighed again. "No end in sight, so I have to keep taking steps. Checking babies, attending births, feeding this one. Singing… better than talking about it or thinking about it."

She closed her eyes, running a hand across the sparse curls of fine baby fuzz on Askia's sleeping head.

Carla took her other hand. "Sorry for watering your worries."

Kendra chuckled and opened her eyes. "It's alright. Make me and Emily some of that rye bread of yours with caraway and we're even."

"Yes, please." Emily echoed the sentiment from where she lay, still letting Jasrie listen in.

It was Carla's turn to laugh. "That's a fair trade, I think. Though you'd be surprised how many similar requests I've had lately." Kendra pursed her lips and shook her head. She was already tasting those pungent seeds and sour bread crumb, and it made her salivate in anticipation.

"I'm not surprised at all. Don't you have some sort of saying about a full belly being the best distraction? Maybe that was just my best distraction?"

Carla laughed. "How about, 'a full belly numbs the brain, slows the thoughts, and dulls the pain?' I just made that one up…"

Kendra laughed deep and hard, the kind of tension release that brings tears to the eyes and just keeps coming until it finally tapers off on its own.

"You know…I do have a thing I think about that fits this thing on Earth—If we've all got one loaf of bread to eat then it's inevitable that we'll come up on the butt-end once or twice, and possibly choke on some crust."

Kendra's laughter had fallen off now and she was listening with damp eyes, closing them and smiling as Carla spoke. Emily was as well, and Jasrie had dropped the fetoscope and returned to her mother's arms, looking sleepy.

"Some folks get all worked up over the butt-ends…" Carla chuckled and punctuated her words with a wagging finger. "But uh, personally, I like to dip mine in some vinegar." She gently pulled down the hem of Emily's shirt to cover her exposed belly and placed one creased hand there with a warm smile. "Some vinegar… and rosemary, and then savor the hard work, even when I come out of it with bits of tender skin scraped off the roof of my mouth." She looked them each in the eyes, her own shining with unshed tears.

"That's when real growth happens, and after a butt end the soft middle is even more tender to enjoy…and I like to think that last butt end at the far end of life will be just as worth the trouble. This whole thing we're going through is kind of a butt end. Not the first or the last, so someone must've cut the loaf in the middle several places and left the damn thing out to get stale. Those middle bits had better be good and soft, though, when we cut through all this crust…" Her voice tapered off and she looked at her listeners. Kendra's eyelids had drooped and closed, and Jasrie was sleeping in her arms holding Askia's small foot. Emily was dozing off as well.

Carla wet her lips and smiled, patting the great-grandchild that lay under her hand, still growing and developing in its watery cocoon. "As it should be…what good am I if I can't talk my people to sleep and bake good bread? *That* would be the butt-end, wouldn't it? Running out of words, flour, and yeast before I'm done…" She was speaking to herself now, the words under her breath, as she unfolded two stored blankets and tucked them around her sleeping companions.

"Off to bake like the little red hen, only I know the power of serving. Feeding heart and head and belly with just these hands." She rubbed her sinewy hands together, making a dry whisper sound as if preparing them with flour to knead a fresh batch of dough. She was still mumbling as the door sealed shut behind her.

DEPARTURE

"How many have they found in this city?" Theresa paced the tile floor of the infirmary in the small section of floor that was not occupied by medicots. Richard leaned against the far wall, watching her pace and blowing on a mug of coffee that sent streamers of steam up to warm his face.

"Just the one more, I believe. Thirteen total from seven stops now. Why this has you restless like a tiger in captivity, though, I do not understand. The children are here with you and recovering; we are on the same surface for the first time in eleven years, and once this has finished, we'll leave together." His voice sounded exasperated and a little amused, making her hackles rise, and she bit back a sharp response. Arguing felt wrong, and she wasn't about to allow the harsh words on her tongue to spill out.

Instead, she paused in front of him and tilted her head. She licked her lips, hesitant to answer, and then placed one hand on his chest, feeling the warmth of his skin through the thin fabric now that neither were wearing a hazmat suit. He was still thin but had begun to regain the strength and vitality that the virus had sapped from him.

"Mmmm…" She was distracted now by his proximity and the twitch of lip-corners that he had when he was amused; it was charming, even when that amusement was at her expense. "I'm anxious to be back on Mars. Ugh…I don't, I don't know what this is—feels like being in some sort of limbo." She stopped to think as if the answer was something lost and she had to dig for it underneath heavy objects. Her next words came in a rush. "You know, we aren't guaranteed to make it there together until we do. I don't care if it makes no logical sense. Eleven years apart. I want Earth behind us now. And Mars ahead. No more waiting. No more in between places."

He nodded, eyes giving away that it did make some sense, more than he'd implied before. His voice was subdued and laced with what she thought sounded like guilt. "We were waiting for good reason, before and now. For the children to travel safely—then Neil's ship was broken—and now because, thirteen people, or more if we find them, are worth saving. Mars might have a population, but at this point I'd wager it isn't enough to ensure the human race continues. Every single person we collect and bring with us pushes those odds in our favor." He placed a hand on the side of her face, stroking her jawline with his thumb and making her shiver. "I also just can't feel good about leaving anyone here with this thing in their heads. Having felt it. Still feeling it, with the flashbacks."

Theresa's forehead creased together, and she bit her lips. She tugged at the hem of her lab coat, shimmying her shoulders to straighten it. "You know I have something for that if you're ready to try it. Feels grossly counterintuitive under the circumstances, but the precedent for it is there—"

Richard leaned down and pressed his lips to hers—only a moment's lingering, his warm breath mingling with her own, and then he straightened, smile flashing and then receding behind a more serious expression.

Theresa's lips were still parted, her eyes wide with shock. "I wasn't—we haven't…" She cleared her throat before trying any more words and Richard chuckled.

"It was the lab coat thing, and your speech—the way it gets when you're explaining something, so serious, monotone but somehow excited. Sorry, please continue."

Theresa opened her mouth to speak, still frozen for a moment, and then looked around the room at the medicots occupied by her progeny, grown stronger and more restless as their recovery advanced. None appeared to have noticed the kiss, or at least they showed no reaction. Some were close enough to listen but were making a show of occupying themselves. Theresa gave a wave and a smile to Santana, no longer on a respirator and sitting up again.

Theresa's cheeks were flushed with heat and her thoughts muddled, but she picked up the thread, words starting slow as she fought distraction, looking away from Richard's lips. "Right…psilocybin is used in mood disorders…depression, therapy assist. And for flashbacks like you and some of the children are having."

"So, basically, you want to use the good part of Massospora to repair the damage it did?"

Theresa nodded. "Pretty much. But not until we're back on Mars, preferably. Carla is better qualified to administer it, mental health specialist and all that."

Richard snorted and his smile dropped. "I might take my chances with you administering mine and playing therapist here and now."

Theresa winced and scrunched her nose, eyes softening with sympathy. "That bad?"

"Yeah."

"Seven days, if they don't get any more calls or decide to extend the search again—I know you think the search and rescue is important, and I'm not saying it isn't, but it's time to go."

Bare feet slapped against the tile floor with a muffled thump-slap in their direction. Theresa and Richard turned toward the sound. Gavin was there, a few steps away now, moving slowly as if his strength was still flagging. His auburn curls were tangled and unbrushed, his cheeks gaunt, but his eyes were bright and his smile the same she remembered from the first ones Richard shared with her in videos. His brows were pulled together and his jaw working as if chewing something bitter.

"Hey, Gavin…What's up?"

He shrugged and then squared his shoulders. "I was listening. But why is it time to go ever? Why Mars at all?"

Theresa's face registered surprise and then smoothed out like a clean palette to listen, but her pulse raced and alarms sounded in her mind. "Mars is home now. Earth is an empty husk…we've always been planning this."

Gavin answered with more force than she expected, as if the words had been simmering in his own head for weeks and were now boiling over. "Earth is home. Mars is a half-terraformed substitute for refugees. Bring them all back here and we have a new start, right? You left for reproductive freedom. Well, nothing is stopping that on Earth now."

Theresa answered slowly, picking and choosing her words, lest she forget that this tall, confident boy was still a child.

Her child.

"The ecosystems are unstable, failing. Most animals and plants won't thrive in the wild here anymore. And don't forget that the cities are filled with the dead that haven't even realized it's time to stop moving." Her expression was incredulous as she continued, but he seemed unaffected. "Mars is steadily improving, clean, growing, ecosystems being built up with care, and no one to damage it with our rules and values." She paused, searching his face and then changing tactics. "Are you afraid to go? The change is intimidating, I know; it was for all of us."

His eyes flashed with anger. "Intimidating, afraid? You left easily enough. We were still here."

"Gavin." The name was said with sharp warning and Gavin

flicked cautious eyes at Richard, wetting his lips.

He shook his head, eyes shadowed with words unspoken. "I'm not afraid."

Theresa's pulse had slowed from rabbit's pace to the deep and unsettling thrum of a gong. *He's holding it against me.* "What then, Gavin?" Gavin shrugged and flashed a grin as if all was well between them and his words a clever jest. "Just seems silly to toss out a whole planet." He paced back to his medicot, positioning himself to fall asleep with his elbow under his cheek. "The WGC is dead, and someone could fill its shoes. That's all." He closed his eyes and rolled over onto his back,

Theresa was frowning, thoughts coming one after another. Richard gave her hand a squeeze. "I'm sorry." He gestured with a chin tilt over to where Gavin was waiting for sleep to come. "That boy is—never easy."

Theresa pulled in a shaky breath and met Richard's eyes. "You know why I left." He nodded, lifting a hand to rub his forehead. "I do. Gavin does as well, they all do." He turned a sharp look in Gavin's direction. "He just needs to be reminded."

Theresa shook her head. She was calm again, but the sinking feeling had settled into the pit of her stomach and coiled there. "It's fine, Richard. There'll be time for us to work on it on Mars."

Theresa watched the children cluster in loose groupings, some flowing from one conversation to the next like migrating birds grouping on electrical wires, settling, flittering to an empty space on the next wire and then resettling.

They were all on their own feet now, most signs of recent illness faded over the weeks healing and resting. Scattered coughs passed through the crowd of them, some followed by nervous smiles.

A small cluster of them had formed around Santana and they watched her movements with caution. Aurelia was there, and Bram, Gavin close by as well, whispering to Gelsemium. They seemed to be close, a small pack within the larger one, though Gelsemium seemed to edge away from Gavin even as she tried to listen. Santana coughed, bending her face into the crook of her arm so that spikes of short, dark hair fell over and shook with her. The others around her tensed. She stopped and looked up with a grin, pushing Aurelia's shoulder.

Theresa shook her head at the exchange. It wasn't funny yet, wouldn't be for quite awhile. They tensed and watched her. Santana had come closest to death and hovered there the longest.

Theresa tried to skip away from the dark path those thoughts always led her on, but it was no good. Her mind took mental note of which were missing, their numbers, their faces. Marilla scrunched her nose in Theresa's mental landscape and she shuddered. Davina and Caspian were laughing…Clark. Genesis had found his body curled up on a fire escape.

The survivors were out of danger and gathering for departure now, all of them gone through decontamination again. The medicots had been sent up to the Pinnacle first thing this morning and loaded into the ship's infirmary storage.

Brogan, Neil, and Genesis were gathered in a small briefing for boarding ship. Genesis appeared distracted, her gaze moving between the children, Richard, and then flicking over to Theresa. Theresa shot her a quizzical return glance and she looked away. *Huh. Maybe it's the progeny.* So many of them and all having an uncanny resemblance to Abby and herself, despite some very obvious differences in skin-tone, hair color and texture. If Genesis felt a kinship to Abby, maybe it was the same with them.

Theresa's attention wandered to Dr Alexander and the collected survivors from the cities. They looked shell-shocked, staring with rapt attention at the doctor as if they were children starting their apprenticeship and struggling to take in the fire-hose delivery of information. What Dr. Alexander was explaining to them now was basic, she could hear most of it from here—why they were no longer at risk of infection, the treatment they were all on as a precautionary measure, how their antibodies would be used to refine the vaccine and treatment options should precautions fail and anyone on Mars catch this. His explanations were cursory and meant to answer questions, calm fears, but they'd been through a lot, arriving at WASA only the day before, with Genesis and Neil and the bodies they transported. The ones from the list.

Genesis's recounting of their time in the city played in her head, the ones that were there now, grabbing and chasing anything that moved and wasn't already infected. She pictured them like Marilla, but up and moving instead of restrained, and it wasn't fear she felt but a heavy sick feeling, something like sadness and disgust mingling in her gut. Maybe it was pity. She tasted the word and the feeling, trying to match them. Pity was too small a word for this.

"Do you not even see the resemblance when you look at them?"

Theresa startled from her reverie to notice Genesis at her side now. Genesis's eyes were unreadable and full of shadows. The yellow-gold of them locked on to her own, making it hard to look away.

"Um…the children. They do all resemble Abby in a way." "The children and Richard. It's too much for you to be oblivious. So, is it your refusal to see a lie that's making you dumb, or what?"

Theresa opened her mouth and closed it, floundering until Genesis continued.

"Look at Gavin. Those brooding brows and the eye shape, the smile he flashes sidelong when he teases. He isn't the only one…Santana, Aurelia. It's there in all of them. Maybe ask why. Maybe don't ask, and instead look into it."

Theresa's eyes narrowed and she found her voice. "He's been

raising them… their father, really, regardless of genetics, and that is a factor in the shaping of expressions, speech patterns…"

Genesis rolled her eyes. "Okay."

Theresa looked closer at her expression. She was angry, frustrated, something else she couldn't name. "Did he do something? Piss you off? He's your contact on Earth, you said, so—"

"I don't make emotional decisions, Theresa, but you've proven you do. Maybe now that you aren't ass-deep in lab equipment, take a minute to hear what I'm saying. Thirty minutes to departure, a month and a half in space, and then the two of you will be free to move ahead with your—whatever is between you."

Theresa was listening now, a tremble in her hands as she gripped the hem of her lab coat. "What do you want from this, Genesis?"

She slow-blinked, scowled and then replaced it with a soft smile. "What I want is for you to be on equal footing with him when you make your decisions." She reached out and smoothed a loose strand of Theresa's hair back into the braided crown at her temple, eliciting a shiver.

"Stop it." Theresa snapped the words louder than intended and Dr. Alexander glanced over, raising a brow in concern. She waved him away.

"Look, Theresa: love him, fuck him, collaborate. I don't care. Just start paying attention and hold him accountable for his secrets the same way you've done for me. I've made a decision, and I hope you understand it eventually." She looked sad, the chill of some heavy burden peeking through and then gone.

Theresa shook her head, eyes creasing in confusion. "Genesis, what is it that—" But a commotion was building where the children were grouped up to board. Richard's voice was low but sharp with restrained anger. Aurelia's voice was strident and she stood next to him, looking at Gavin who was flushed with that same energy of confrontation that had hold of Richard, but where

Richard's anger was cold, Gavin's was hot.

Theresa flashed a look of concern and apology to Genesis, then strode over to stand next to Aurelia, who had lowered her voice but was still louder than needed for the small gap between them.

"Just stop now, Gavin. You almost died over this and I got you back. You need to take it as evidence that you are being reckless."

"You're one to call out recklessness, Aurelia. Under the city collecting diseased rats and nearly dying in quarantine a few weeks ago, weren't you?"

"Sure, yeah. And I am capable of admitting when I was stupid, so yeah." She was shaking with rage and looked as if she would bite him again if no one would stop her. Theresa winced at the thought and watched Aurelia do the same, closing her eyes and waiting for the thoughts and images to pass, as Theresa had seen Richard and the rest of the children do often since they'd recovered. Maybe treatment for the flashbacks should start on the ship after all.

Bram's voice was restrained, almost gentle, but he shook his head in warning. "Gavin, stop."

Theresa was there now, standing next to Aurelia. "Hey, what's happening over here? We're supposed to be boarding. What's wrong?" She directed the last words at Gavin. Watching his expression shift, calm, as he redirected his energy from Richard to her. It felt like being in a dream speak with him, having those glinting, humor-bright hazel green eyes on her, the others gone silent. She pictured him younger, smaller, cheeks rounded and baby soft as he asked questions she couldn't answer well. Why she was on Mars, when she'd come back to Earth… she flinched at the memories and forced her focus back to the present.

"I told Richard I'm not going." Theresa turned eyes wide with alarm to Richard and then back to Gavin. "What? Why—where else would you be?"

He stood up taller, stretching his height, close to her own. "This isn't new. Richard knows. He knew I didn't plan to go. Earth is home and I'm not leaving. Neither are the others that were with me. We didn't plan to meet up—I was going to say this sooner—before we were sick. I'm sorry for that, but I'm staying." He did look sorry, a little, and it made Theresa's heart ache.

Richard's voice was still sharp with anger but sounded weary as he rubbed the groove above his eyes. "I didn't think you were still entertaining this idea of yours. The population is dead, the cities full of dead, and the ecosystem's unstable—giving rise to these kinds of pandemics. It'll happen again. Don't think it won't. We've been preparing for Mars—" The anger dropped out of his voice as he stared at Gavin's resolute set of jaw, the determination in his eyes. "And we're ready now. Shit, I should have seen this coming. Why is here better for what you see for yourself than Mars is?" Richard looked over at Theresa's face, the hurt in her eyes, and then threw up his hands as if he expected no good answer.

Theresa spoke again before Gavin could reply. "Gavin, please don't fight us."

His laugh was incredulous. "I'm not fighting anything. I'm telling you both—I'm not going. Think about it. Earth is not a dead planet, and we can make it stronger again, greener, diverse. The same way you are doing it on Mars. I'm staying to make sure that happens and when Mars doesn't work or something, Earth will be waiting."

Richard was silent. Theresa searched for something to say that would wipe this away, something to nullify the sense he was making that was still not enough to justify leaving children here. "Does it have to be you? We could send a team from Mars, people who want to be back on Earth…"

Gavin locked eyes with Richard. "Ask *him* why it has to be me. It's what I'm made for, isn't it, Richard?"

Richard's voice was low, a warning in his tone. "Not for

Earth, Gavin. Are you afraid you aren't ready, that you'll disappoint us in the colony?" He was reaching, trying to grab hold of anything. Theresa could tell by his tone that he was running out of arguments.

"No. I'm not anymore. Maybe last year I was, and all the years before. But I don't have to worry about that if I'm staying on Earth."

"It wouldn't be a worry on Mars now, Gavin. You're ready, we all are."

"Oh, *now* we are. I never heard you say that before, just how not ready we were and how much longer it would be if we didn't try harder."

Richard cleared his throat. "I was trying to teach you, prepare you for life outside our own bubble."

Gavin sidestepped Richard's explanation, his eyes hard and unaffected. He looked like Richard had a few moments before, until the anger fell out of him. "Will you force me? Drag me onto the ship?"

Theresa stepped forward just as Neil joined them. He didn't intervene but he listened, hands on his hips and eyes downcast as he took in the situation. "No. We won't do that." She looked over at Richard for agreement and found it. He looked tired again and a bit angry, the crease between his eyebrows was deep and shadowed but he held her gaze longer, giving a slow shake of his head before speaking. "Okay, Gavin, How many?"

Gavin's eyes lit up, shining with the sudden victory. He looked back at Gelsemium on his right and she nodded.

"Twenty-five, twenty-six including myself. Everyone that was with me at the station where you picked us up. They've already agreed."

One of the children in the group next to Gelsemium, a stocky boy with dark eyes and giant features, cleared his throat for attention. "Actually, I thought about it, and I'm going to Mars. So's

Elle, Mica, and Jasper. We lost too many under your direction. We're not up for more of that."

Gavin frowned and looked over at the others mentioned with a question in his eyes. "Is that true?"

There was a moment of hesitation as he waited for them to meet his eyes or respond in some way, but when they did their answers were clear, and they stepped away from the dispute.

He started to speak, to protest, but then closed his mouth and began again. "Okay. Twenty-two then." Theresa looked at the cluster of children around Gelsemium and her heart sank. Twenty-two of the children that she wouldn't get to know. Dream speak wasn't enough. She walked over to them, fighting for composure, but her eyes were wet already and stinging. "Are you sure. All of you?"

Gelsemium answered first. "Just come visit." Some of the others nodded. Bain gave her a half smile and shrugged, and Feldon wrapped his arms around her waist in a tight hug.

She caught her lips between her teeth and rested her cheek against his head. "Okay."

When Feldon let go, she went to Gavin. He and Richard were still talking. Richard was nodding and had a hand up, ticking off Gavin's answers as he quizzed him.

Neil was close by and he gave Theresa's shoulder a squeeze, and leaned in to whisper, "You okay with this?"

"No. But I don't think I can fix it myself. I don't think Richard is either."

"Want me to tie them up and toss 'em on the ship?"

Theresa gave a pained half smile. "Maybe. He likes you, talk to him."

Richard's voice carried even when he wasn't shouting. "That's fine. But it's a hole in your plan if you want to stay without mentors, guardians…you may be early apprentice age, but you are not ready to be alone. Not yet."

"That's my cue." Neil gave Theresa's shoulder another

squeeze and strode forward, coming to a stop next to Gavin and Richard, meeting the other man's eyes before kneeling down next to Gavin to decrease the height gap.

"You know, it's a good plan you have. Stay behind and rebuild here, keep Earth open as an option for us." Neil paused, giving Gavin a moment to digest his words. "I have some people on Mars that would be excited to talk to you about it, help you prepare. Planetary ecologist, and environmental specialists, botanists…"

Gavin's smile began to falter, suspicion building in his eyes. "You're trying to convince me not to stay."

"Do you think you would benefit from going to Mars? I mean, do you have what you need here? By yourself?"

Brogan was hovering nearby and cleared his throat awkwardly, drawing everyone's attention and then finding it more eyes than he cared for. "Er…I, uh. I didn't know about this little debacle, I promise, but if some are staying, I may as well do the same. My team and I…we'd settle on Mars, but it wasn't a thing I planned for, you know? Leaving Earth."

Neil glanced over at Brogan, irritation clear in his eyes. "Brogan would be a good guardian, but is he who you'd want to apprentice under? Or do you want someone who can teach more about leadership first-hand, maybe someone who can prepare you for actually rehabbing the ecosystems here?"

Gavin crossed his arms, confusion building in his eyes. "Are you offering to stay and apprentice me? Help rebuild?"

Neil gave that warm laugh he had and shook his head. "I'd be happy to apprentice you, but not on Earth. On Mars. I have family on Mars, so when I send a team back here to recolonize Earth, I won't be on it."

Richard knelt down next to them, his voice low, cautious. "But you could be. After apprenticeship and with all the resources Mars can offer at your disposal. A large team, full support for you and everyone who wants to do this."

Neil was nodding along as Richard spoke. Gavin looked frozen, his bravado beginning to falter. "But neither of you are in charge on Mars. You can't promise that."

Theresa came closer and stood next to Gavin. "Two of us are on the governing council, three if you count Genesis. We aren't lying to you, humoring you."

She could see his resolve waver as he listened, at least for a moment, but then his expression hardened and he stepped back from the three adults that stood of knelt around him like points on a star. "Do not let spacious plans for a new world divert your energies from saving what is left of the old…"

Theresa tilted her head, and Neil caught her eye. "Winston Churchill, smart man…but Gavin, I could reverse that right back at you. Earth is the new world now, Mars is home base. And have you considered what your long-dead mentor said about making attempts—there is always much to be said for not attempting more than you can do and for making a certainty of what you try."

Gelsemium had taken up a position closer to Gavin now, not quite at his side but where he could see her, glance over, and she finished the quote that Neil started. "…But this principle, like others in life and war, has it exceptions—but we could do this all night, trade quotes in favor of one side or the other. What are you thinking, Gavin?"

He looked startled at the sound of her voice, eyes wide and haunted before he closed them and pressed clenched hands over his eyes, a visible shiver running through his body. Gelsemium put several feet between them; she was shaking as well.

Theresa took Gavin's hand and whispered as he stood there, eyes covered and still trembling for a moment before he shook off the images. "It's just another flashback. Come to Mars and we'll fix this. I can—I can fix the flashbacks, for you and Gelsemium both, and the rest of you having them still. But we need time for that, okay?"

His eyes were clear when he looked at her again, but they were tired, "Okay."

"Are you sure?" She whispered so her voice would make it off her tongue without breaking into a thousand pieces she wouldn't be able to find and show him before it was time to board.

Neil was gathering them up in groups now, the ones outside of the circle of upheaval and debate.

"Yeah. I was never going there—until now. I thought you'd come here, though."

"I did, it just—took too long."

"Yeah."

She thought his lip trembled and curled on that one word. His eyes were bright but no tears fell. And then a brilliant smile lit those same eyes, a larger, more mature version of the same one that filled her memory. "I'm glad we'll have time first."

Theresa leaned her forehead against his and whispered. "I almost brought you too, you know, you and Bram. But I didn't think I could hide three." Her voice was breaking and it didn't matter; a sharp thin sob filled the gap, tears drenching them both along with her words. She closed her eyes and sucked in a breath. "I'm glad you changed your mind."

Richard reached out and pulled Gavin into a tight hug. There were tears running down his cheeks when he pulled away and walked over to Gelsemium and the rest of Gavin's group. Neil shook Gavin's hand and gave it a warm squeeze. "You're gonna apprentice with me then, eh?"

Gavin stood tall, his expression more triumph than grief as he accepted the handshake. "Sure, Captain Neil." Theresa waited for a space to clear and then took Gavin's hand. Not the soft, short-fingered one she'd have expected if this had happened years ago, but this wasn't the curly-headed cherub in front of her; it was Gavin on the cusp of adolescence, and she had almost lost him.

"Let's go." His cheeks were wet with Theresa's tears and she wiped at them with the cuff of her lab coat.

He cleared his throat and gestured towards the open elevator waiting for them, glancing around for Gelsemium and finding her too far away, with another group for boarding. "We better move."

She looked down at his hand in hers, without answering, and nodded. His fingers were still short like hers, but they were wider now, the palm longer. They walked through the open door. Richard and Aurelia were inside, and Bram, Santana, some of the survivors Genesis collected. It didn't matter if she cried in front of any of them now. But she wouldn't. A curtain of numbness and relief was already shrouding her from the worst of it, like a soft cocoon of spider silk locking her away from too many thoughts or memories. There was work waiting on the Pinnacle. She and Alexander would refine the vaccine they'd been working on, and the children would still take much of her time. She looked over at Bram, who was leaning against Richard's shoulder, eyes red-rimmed and damp. They'd almost lost twenty-two more just now; they'd need support.

Richard was leaning back in his seat, eyes closed, and she felt a wave of emotion surge to the forefront of her attention. She did love him. Genesis's vague warnings and Gavin's words resurfaced alongside that sentiment, and she shook her head as if discouraging the whine of a mosquito in one ear. *Not now.*

She leaned back and closed her eyes, savoring the beginnings of weightlessness as the elevator lifted them through Earth's atmosphere to the Pinnacle.

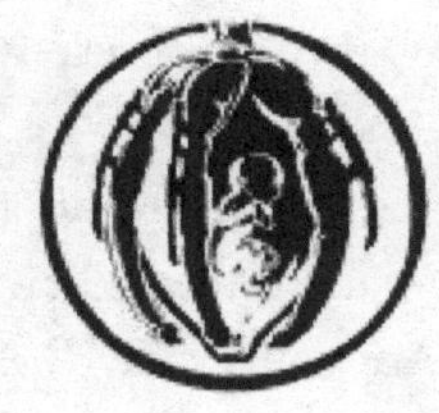

HOMECOMING

"We could swim in the caves." Deimos waved a hand between Abby and the replay of Theresa's message.

Abby's mother looked tired and pale, puffy-cheeked from built up fluid and pressure with purple bruising under her eyes. She was hovering in zero G in the message, with Captain Neil, maybe Genesis, and many dozen others blurred out behind her. *'We're three weeks off, Abby, and I don't know if you're accessing the updates we've sent to the council. I wasn't sure whether to share this out loud before I could be there, but I'm telling you now so you don't hear it first when we see each other. We're all well as can be expected and past any threat, but we lost fifteen. The list is attached. I love you and I'll see you soon."*

It started again as soon as it ended, but Abby didn't open up the list of names this time as Deimos had watched her do so many times before over the past weeks.

She didn't look over when she answered him. "Not until they get back. Then we'll take them—Donovan says the whalefins will migrate soon, so we'll wait to bring anyone in until then."

"We could swim somewhere else…"

"No." She stood up and paced the floor. The restless motion was a new thing since the message froze her up. It was still replaying. There was a soft chime from Abby's handheld, echoed by the smaller version she'd taken to keeping on her wrist, but she didn't seem to notice.

Deimos cleared his throat for attention. "You um…you have a new message."

A slight frown creased her brow and then was gone again. "It's just Carla. I said I wanted to see her. She's scheduling me."

"To talk to her? Are you…okay?" Abby paused in her pacing and smirked at her friend, but it had a bitter quality to it. "It's just to talk, Deimos, for practice with her. How else can I know what to trust from her?"

Deimos raised both brows, not trying to hide his shock. "Oh. You *are* trying. Not just with Donovan."

Abby shrugged and turned her eyes back to Theresa on the screen…*and past any threat but we lost fifteen. The list is attached…* "Fifteen is a lot when you count each one by their face in your head…multiplied by every word they said, and the ones I said back, and the ways their smiles curved, or brows creased, inflections, gestures…" Her voice trailed off and then she turned back to him.

"It is a lot."

"I was always trying, you know. I just…figured something out about how to look at it."

"From when you talked to Donovan? What was it?" She rolled her eyes at the memory. "I talked to my wristlet in front of him. It was…a thing. But not that. I can't explain it out loud, but I'll show you if you come with me to see Carla."

"We're three weeks off, Abby, and I don't know if you're accessing the updates we've sent to the council. I wasn't sure whether to share this out loud before I could be there, but I'm telling you now so you don't hear it first when we see each other. We're all well as can be expected and…" Deimos wished it would stop replaying, but he wouldn't turn it off if she wouldn't, so he spoke over it instead. "It's only three days till they get here. Two and a half if you count today half over."

It made Abby smile, with less shadow in her eyes so he counted it a victory. Nine years of his life she'd talked about them coming, three days—two and a half—wasn't very long, but it would feel like it.

"You look thin. Did you go off your feed for me and Joanna?"

David startled, almost toppling from his crouch into the row of tall, purple-leafed tomatoes behind him, and then he stood, taking long loping strides to where Genesis stood in the entryway of the greenhouse dome.

He pulled her hard against his chest and gripped the back of her neck and one hip in firm pulling caresses of need. His lips pressed into hers with urgency, suckling, biting, and drinking in the faint cinnamon of her breath in greedy gulps until they were both short of breath and flushed, hands roaming, mapping and retaking, reclaiming the contours they'd memorized but spent months without physical reminders.

Clothes fell away with urgent, impatient tugs until flesh joined flesh. Genesis backed David into a wall and he pulled her up to his hips and then turned, pressing her against the wall and thrusting their hips together. He pushed his face into her neck, nipping the sensitive skin and she moaned and arched her neck until he bit harder.

"Yes! Please, ye—es." She bit the lean muscle of his shoulder and bucked her hips into his in a frenzy of unmet need.

He glanced at the door and then back to Genesis, panting his words into her ear. "Where is Deimos? —sent him to meet you."

"With—Abby and the others. Shut up…"

David growled back and nipped at her lip and they laughed as they came. The floor was hard but cool against their skin when they sank down, still breathing heavy.

Genesis rolled over onto her back and rifled through the pockets of discarded clothing, producing something in her hand. She grabbed his fist, uncurling it, and dropped the locket and chain into his palm.

David rolled over onto his side and looked at the gift, smile dropping from his face, spent desire replaced with dawning horror. His brown eyes flew up to find Genesis watching him with calm interest. "You really found her?"

"Did you think I made it up? I found her and—and it was too late."

Tears rolled down her cheeks without warning, a sudden deluge from a clear sky, and David shook off the shock to pull her into his lap, arms tight so she wouldn't get that skin crawling sensation and push him away. "It's okay. It's okay. I didn't think you'd find anything at all."

Genesis snorted but the tears continued to flow. "You aren't supposed to be comforting me. It's supposed to be the other way…I held her like this, and I tried. I brought her to WASA, I tried everything Theresa had on her."

"Shhhh…" He squeezed the back of her neck, massaging against tensing muscles.

"I was supposed to bring her for you—all I have is ashes. In—in my jacket pocket. You can plant them, or something." Her eyes had run dry, but her voice was hollow and tight with pain. "I decided, if she was there, I'd get her for you—"

"You did. You did get her and now we know. No more wondering. We can bury the dead. That's all I expected."

Genesis grew silent and her breathing slowed until she pulled out of his grip and stood to dress herself. "You do look too thin. Still fuckable, but are you okay?" She grabbed his narrow waist where there had been something softer to grip before.

"Yeah, I am. Been talking to Carla a lot, instead of myself, and it's helping." He looked down at himself, noticing the way his muscles and ribs showed beneath his skin in a way that he hadn't noticed and gave her a sheepish smile. "Just missing you, I guess. Worried."

"Okay, well, we need to report to the doctors for preventative treatments for you. It's for everyone, just in case."

She walked towards the door, expecting him to follow, and then paused to watch as he finished dressing himself. "When we're done, we need to talk. Not us stuff—things about the children and Richard and myself. I'm gonna need you to have an open mind."

David pulled on his weighted vest and followed her out. "Yeah, okay—open as a book."

The sun was up only a few minutes before Theresa; a Martian lark that was nest building with soft scritch-scratch noises against the outer ledge of her window had announced the dawn, and grabbing hold of the fabric of her interrupted dream proved as difficult as holding onto the wisps of fading darkness.

It was a city, winding streets: some stone, others paved for a short distance and then giving way to red sand—a mix of Earth and Martian construction with Mars-red skyscrapers and ratbits lounging on sprawling carpets of lichen-grass between the magnetic-rail stations and scrolling sidewalks. But the city was empty aside from wildlife and decaying corpses grown over by vegetation.

Theresa closed her eyes, searching for more. The rest was foggy, lost on waking, except for the feeling that she was running from something and searching urgently for something else. The remembered sensation made her stomach turn a quick somersault before settling.

She turned over and moved her face onto a different part of her pillow, relishing the feel of the cold fabric against her skin as she watched Richard's bare chest rise and fall in the predictable rhythms of sleep. His lips were parted, slack, and the relaxed features of his normally stern face, devoid of expression or tension as he slept, looked years younger. Theresa frowned, brows pulling together in characteristic bird-wings of concentration as the resemblance became more and more clear to her. She knew the subtle details of his face, not from VR Comm, or memories of their first meeting, but from Abby, from eleven years of watching her progeny's face grow, change and mature.

She reached out her hand across the empty sheets to where he lay, trailed a finger just above the bridge of his nose, across the profile of his lips, feeling his breath across her hand, and down to the curve of his jaw where the skin was no longer smooth but roughened from a night's hair growth.

Richard stirred at her touch, dark hazel eyes opening and fixing on her as he rolled onto his side facing her. He smiled, reaching over to touch her face as she had his. "I like this better."

The center of his eyes around the pupil was the same mahogany red color as Abby's, but the outer ring was a deep pine green with patches of lighter olive—central heterochromia, like many of the children had. The crevice between her brows deepened, so lost in thought that she didn't grasp his meaning. "What do you like better?"

He reached farther, sliding his hand to the base of her skull and pulling her closer as he leaned up one elbow, speaking his answer against her lips between light feathery kisses that made her breath catch. "Mmmm…proximity, touch… It's much better than VR sims."

He paused, quirked a brow, then released her, leaning away as he scanned her face. "But you have something on your mind. It's palpable when you're upset or preoccupied, so thick in the air I could pluck your thoughts from the ether." He chuckled, reaching up and grasping some invisible object and trapping it in his fist.

Theresa shook her head at his attempt at humor, trying not to echo his smile. "It's just, some of the things that Gavin said, and Diadonna before that, and Genesis, made me start to wonder—to think, and I couldn't fall back to sleep."

"Then let's hear it, if I'm robbing you of sleep already." Theresa looked away, pressing her lips together as she gathered the words. It would be easier if he was still asleep, or at least not looking at her. But one option was absurd and he couldn't answer, and the other she wasn't willing to ask for. Instead, she let the moments of dead air space spread out between them until she could speak.

The dappled light of morning filtered through aspen boughs made puddles of liquid sunlight on the bed between them. Richard leaned up on one elbow, an indulgent smile on his lips, as Theresa's words tumbled out, sped along by anxiety. "I'm not sure if any of this is going to make sense when I say it out loud—well, except the one thing, but—"

He started to rise and then paused to gesture at the window. "Keep going." He sat up onto his knees, allowing the sheets to slide off and uncover bare skin as he reached for the window latch and pushed it open. He inhaled the air that came through the window, fresh with salt-seaweed, and wet sand smells as it blew in across the bay, and then turned back to face her with a brighter smile and sharper eyes. He nodded for Theresa to continue. She looked distracted, momentarily frozen, but the rest of the words came out all the same.

"…Gavin implied that you kept them on Earth to train them yourself, to prepare them for something."

Richard nodded. "I did. They needed to be ready for colony life, for apprenticeship here. Also, your ship was broken and they were too small for space travel. How many times do you think I could tell a two-year-old, a five-year-old, a seven-year-old, you can't see your mother yet because you aren't big enough? They needed a focal point, a goal. Work hard and learn what I'm teaching you and, when you're ready, we'll go."

"When was that going to be?" Richard shrugged and spread his hands.

"Soon?"

"Okay."

"Next question?"

Theresa frowned, eyes wary of the flirtatious smile he flashed her. It seemed like he was enjoying this. The next question rose to her lips and she froze up again. *What about Diadonna? She didn't trust you.* Was it a fair question to ask now, so soon after the struggle to get off of Earth? Did it matter what an Earth politician thought of him? Theresa closed her lips before voicing it, tucking the question away, buried for later asking or forgetfulness.

When she didn't speak, Richard groaned and rolled over onto his back, bringing Theresa with him so that she was sitting on top. She pulled in a breath, cheeks flushing and eyes darkening with desire, and then she slid off of him, leaving one hand on his chest to curl fingers in the thick hair that grew there in dark, wiry, curls.

"Answers first, please."

Richard chuckled, eyes sparking with mischief as he stared up at the domed ceiling made of red stone. He was stroking her bare thigh with one hand and she shivered. "You didn't ask anything else. I thought you were done…"

Theresa frowned, searching for the thoughts that tumbled away at his touch. She pulled in a breath, releasing it slowly as she fought to block out his scent. She trapped his roaming hand under her own and moved it from her thigh to the silken bedsheets. She closed her eyes and her head cleared just enough. "I've been distracted, and I guess I take people at face value until I have reason not to." She paused, fighting for the right words as her heart took up a swift gallop in her chest. "I know what I'm going to find if I go and check your genetic code against the children's. It never occurred to me to do that, but now I know I have to. Gavin is practically your clone. I see it in all of them. I just don't know why?"

Richard's face grew serious and he went still. "I'd promised not to share that information, but I guess everyone it matters to is dead. Greg was meant to be the genetic donor for Phase Four with you—"

Theresa wet her lips, finding them suddenly dry and parched as if the morning sunlight from the window was baking them. "He was the donor."

Richard's eyes softened with pity. "He was supposed to be, and then when the two of you got involved he couldn't do it. He asked me to fill in for him because it felt too—intimate to have progeny with you that—"

Theresa's eyes were wide with shock, and she blinked twice as if to clear some encroaching hallucination from her vision. "Are you making this up?"

"No. He asked for a transfer off of the project and begged me to be the donor and not tell you. We'd have both been in trouble with Steiner and the board if it got out. But my genetic contributions were already in stock and available from an earlier phase of the project, so we did it. He switched the gametes and then transferred out."

Theresa's eyes were staring at his chest, through it, instead seeing all of the little pieces that fit together. "Genesis is—"

"She's my daughter. Sibling to our hundred."

"Sure, okay. That makes as much sense as anything." Theresa felt dizzy and a bit sick to her stomach, breath ragged despite efforts to control it. She was silent for several moments before she looked into his eyes, searching for something. "You kept all this from me, but you're telling me now…"

"You asked me, and Greg is dead. There was a time when you were the one keeping secrets, if I recall."

Theresa's voice dropped to a whisper. "That was eleven years ago."

"I'm not keeping score. I'm saying I understand why you lied to me, asking you to understand that I had good reasons to keep some things to myself and we didn't have much—opportunity, or reason, to show all our cards."

He took her hand and she pulled it away, folding it between her thighs, crushed against the other one. Richard sat up now, eyes serious and liquid with remorse that hadn't been there just moments before. He reached over the edge of the bed and collected a white button-up shirt and pulled the sleeves on. "I think we'll both have a lot to share, now that we aren't under threat by Earth establishments or past promises. If we can be patient with each other."

Theresa's eyes warned of a storm and her words came out as a low growl. "I've been patient."

He was dressing now, like in VR Comm dream speak when he was preparing to log out. A sense of loss, panic, welled up unbidden and with greater force than she could have anticipated.

He was pulling on other clothes, shorts and weighted vest.

Her voice, when she found it, came out a whisper. "Where are you going?"

"I promised Abby and Bram they could take me swimming in the caves this morning." He glanced up at the time on the wall and gestured to the glowing numbers. "Eight o'clock on the cliffs—I'll be back and we can continue. Anything you want to ask me. I promise."

Theresa stared after him with a vague feeling of having lost her grip on the direction their exchange took, as if she'd steered the ship and then found that it was heading somewhere else entirely. Richard leaned down to kiss her lips and she let him, kissed him back, watched the door seal closed behind him. The motions were the same, the urge to lean in to the kiss, to taste him more, still there locked behind a growing paralysis. She could feel her heart beating in all of her pulse points, and with each beat the heavy, sick feeling grew until it ran from her eyes. She scrubbed at them and stood up, pulling on her own clothes, blouse, pants, weighted vest, lab coat. She braided and coiled her hair, each step in the process making it easier to breathe, to move. She couldn't tell what the sickness in the pit of her stomach felt more akin to: ice, or heat, or some sort of metal amalgam, heavy and churning like the core of the Earth. Maybe it was all three.

There was work to do: planning, Emily's progeny to monitor, her own needing apprenticeship options, further research on the psilocybin treatments…she sat down hard, feeling her teeth click and blood well up from the side of her tongue where she bit it. Genesis's words echoed in her head…*So, is it your refusal to see a lie that's making you dumb, or what?* The words were so clear now that it felt like an attack instead of a memory. They were all there. The full conversation, but certain parts stuck and repeated.…*Thirty minutes to departure, a month and a half in space, and then the two of you will be free to move ahead with your—whatever is between you…Look, Theresa: love him, fuck him, collaborate. I don't care. Just start paying attention and hold him accountable for his secrets the same way you've done for me…*

She sucked in a breath, blinking back fresh tears. Genesis was suspicious of everyone, her sense of trust warped and unrecognizable by the very definition. Theresa swam through the turbulent, conflicting stream of doubts, searching for some kind of buoy to grab hold of…and found it. It was small compared to the hulking, shadowy fears and hurt feelings surrounding it, but would have to do. *He was honest when I asked. Greg asked him to lie for him, and he protected him. Loyalty was important.*

Her breath out was shaky, more of a shudder than a breath, but it was better than before. *Eleven years spent thirty-three point nine million miles apart and I'm expecting an effortless reunion…* What were they before that other than strangers—coconspirators, maybe…and what now? The thought that came was another memory echo…*I don't make emotional decisions, Theresa, but you've proven you do. Maybe now that you aren't ass-deep in lab equipment, take a minute to hear what I'm saying. Thirty minutes to departure, a month and a half in space, and then the two of you will be free to move ahead with your—whatever is between you.* Genesis's words again, but they were true. Whatever was between them needed figuring out and would take work.

Theresa activated her virtual laboratory and watched the agenda for the day's research fill the many screens, and then turned it off again. She stared for a moment and then removed her lab coat with shaking hands, folding and unfolding it in indecision until she finally left it neatly on the top of the desk.

Abby, Bram, Richard, and who knew how many more of her progeny were swimming in the caves. The other things could wait. Bridging a gap created by years and miles across the solar system couldn't.

EPILOGUE

Red sand whispered against itself, sliding away from Emily's bare feet with a hissing sound until it settled into new wave patterns at the base of the dune. Green and black lichen-covered volcanic rocks jutted out from the sand at sharp angles.

Emily paced the top of the dune, digging her toes in as her balance shifted. The large obelisk-like rock projection provided a sturdy handhold as she passed it. She felt a growing heaviness in her lower abdomen and a feeling of tightening that pulled and lifted the unwieldy bulge of her belly and she paused, keeping her grip on the cool, rough stone and leaning forward to sway her hips there until the surge passed.

They were getting closer now. The walking was good. A small smile curled on her lips as she zig-zagged down the side of the dune. The path to the outdoor amphitheater would have been easier, but the dunes had called and the sand pressed into the soles of her feet, shifting and heating away the ache of months carrying extra weight.

The sky was purpling as twilight darkened. Phobos and Deimos were still visible at the horizon line, their ovoid shapes so unlike Earth's moon, but somehow more of a comfort than that blinding skylight was in her memory, garish and demanding to the eye and dominating a sky meant for stars.

At the base of the dune, she dropped to her knees, a rush of fear as another one came so soon, spiking her adrenaline and allowing the wave to get on top of her, the tightening sensation much more like pain than the one before it.

She rocked on hands and knees, moaning, a plaintive gasping cry escaping, and then it passed. Emily stayed there a moment, afraid to move if another would come before she could top the rise ahead of her, but it seemed there would be a longer rest this time, so she forced herself up and made a snaking path up, digging her toes in to keep her from slipping back with the miniature avalanches of sand that accompanied every step.

She felt another one building, lifting the round, jutting fundus of her uterus up even as the bands of muscle within pulled her cervix open millimeter by millimeter. She could see the top of the dune just ahead and she made for it, powering her steps with what strength she had even as she laughed at the absurdity of climbing a sand dune during a contraction. Didn't she and Kendra and Carla tell the other mothers that walking in early labor would help? *Walking, though, not running up sand...*

She reached the top, out of breath, and dropped into the sand on her hands and knees again, savoring the warmth of it despite the burning ache in her calf muscles and the building intensity of another contraction.

She breathed in, sending her focus low, to her core where a burning pressure was building in her cervix, like the heavy ache of monthly blood flow. But this was much stronger than period cramps. Emily lost track of time and awareness outside of herself at the peak.

She rose to her feet, picking her way through the black and red rocks that were growing more and more frequent until they gave way to mostly stone with scattered pockets of black sand.

Another pause, and another—this wasn't stopping. Emily pressed the emergency call button on her jacket.

"Kendra, he's coming now."

Kendra's tone was calm but delighted, giving it a warm glow of excitement that made electric streamers of anticipation trace from her belly along her nerves. This pain had a purpose and it was close, so close now. "I'll bring your Gran with me, might be headed your way already, you know how she always knows."

Emily smiled, imagining Carla feeling her labor along with her. Swaying her hips to soothe away a borrowed ache. "And can you get Donovan? And—I'm, I'm not…" The next wave crashed and roared, almost overtaking her, but she found an outcropping to hold and moved with it, twisting and swaying and pulling in breaths until it eased again. "Sorry, I'm just almost to the amphitheater. Was walking to bring it on faster."

That made it sound like an accident. Was it an accident or had she known and made a choice?

"You want a drone ride back or—?"

Emily hesitated. Would they discourage her choice? It wasn't their policy, but she was different. They babied her without meaning to, tiptoed around her.

"No, I'll birth in the amphitheater."

"Oh! Got it. We'll drone up there and be ready."

Relief flooded over her and she felt flushed and full of oxytocin. She imagined she could feel it swimming through her veins spreading there like a good wine, smoothing away the rough edges and removing inhibitions.

"Thanks Kendra. I love you, you know."

"Oh, I know it. Love you too, Em."

The tops of the ring of aspens Donovan and David planted there years ago, taller now and thriving, were visible ahead, swaying and shimmering in the wind that wasn't a steady onslaught but kicked up in sudden gusts. Emily grinned as a heavy gust grabbed and whipped at her clothes even as another contraction hit. Even if they weren't working together, the storm and her child, she would make it there together.

The smell of lavender on the wind reached her next, and the rustling sound of aspen leaves like muffled coins on a dancer's belt. And then she topped the final rise and reached the man-made plateau holding the outdoor amphitheater.

She could go inside for the windbreak, but the sand wasn't blasting this high tonight or forming clouds; the gusts weren't sustained enough for that.

Emily pushed her coppery braid and several loose strands back over her shoulder and then turned to survey her surroundings. She could see the lights of the colony winking in the gloom far below and a subtle shimmer of twilight on the ocean beyond that.

The next one built in intensity so quickly that she cried out and turned desperate eyes to the immediate landscape for support. There was a wall, four feet tall, bearing a bas relief of Martian life and history. A broad smile overtook her features even as she felt a new intensity building inside her. The scenes were comforting, familiar. There was Earth, the Pinnacle approaching Mars, Neil leading the colonists over the final rise of a hike, Carla crouching next to Theresa as they birthed Abby from the RPU, and then Genesis holding up the first live human birth on the red planet. There were more, but Emily ran out of focus.

She reached out for the mural, taking hurried steps and then grabbing hold and sinking to her knees in the lavender that was blooming in soft sprays of pale purple and dusty green along its length. The burning Pinnacle and ruined elevator was under her hands, a list of names to the right of that. Emily sucked in a breath and felt the building tremor tighten her throat until it escaped with the next breath out as a sharp cry, and then another, until her hands shook against the wall, Jonathan's name cupped under her right palm, the record of her lost children under her left.

She wept as the contraction receded, no longer holding back, the raw emotion, the loss that was ever-present coalescing into a perfect storm as her body worked.

One wave of bunching, working muscles, pulling, loosening, and opening her came after another until she lost track of how many there had been or how long she'd been crying now. It didn't matter. She could cry if she needed to; it was fine now, it was almost over. She heard the reassurances in Carla's voice, warm and roughened with so many years like the soothing, leathery pages of a well-loved tome pored over and referred back to countless times.

Eventually the weeping tapered off and she became aware of a hand on her back, the warmth and physical presence of another person. She opened her eyes and turned just enough to see who was here and found Donovan kneeling behind her, hand on her back and an encouraging smile ready for her. His brows were pulled together with concern and he glanced over her head and then back to her. "I'm here…um, what can I do? Carla and Kendra too."

Emily's eyes were clouded and distant with pain and a focus turned inward, but they lit up when they met Donovan's. She closed her eyes and leaned back against him, gasping and then pulling in a staccato breath as another wave pulled her under and she struggled to integrate the intensity of it. After what seemed like years inside of the pain, it subsided, and she felt the others there now too, heard their breathing, Their presence was a soothing balm, infused with patient attendance and she melted into Donovan, pulling his arms around her and onto her hips.

"Mmmm…just stay right there…and squeeze like this." She pressed his hands firmly into the curve of her hips on both sides with her hands over his. Her voice was a whisper, and she grimaced as she licked dry lips, noticing how parched her mouth and throat had become.

Kendra stepped closer and held something to her lips, the drinking end of a bottle. Emily pulled in gulps of cold, sweet liquid and then pushed it away with a satisfied sigh. She licked her lips again and they were sweet.

"Better?" Kendra's voice had a smile to it. It was one of the things the women liked her for as their midwife, that warm smile sound that made even hard news or unpleasant truths easier to take. Emily nodded and sighed again, reaching out for Kendra's hand and then reaching her other towards Carla before closing her eyes again and sinking into the next contraction.

At the peak of it her moans deepened and caught in her throat as her body bore down and she dropped to her knees, back arching as she used Kendra and Carla for counterbalance.

Her eyes flew open and searched for Carla. It was dark, but there was a dim glow from Carla's handheld, set to provide firelight. She was right there, holding her hand still, and her lined cheeks were wet with tear tracks that shimmered in the firelight. Her whole face smiled and, to Emily, was a sun in the night. This was how it was supposed to be when she pictured giving birth: Mars, with her Gran there to light her way, not the exact circumstances or the timing—so much was different and unexpected, painfully so—but the feeling of it.

"You're doing it, Em. Just like you knew you could when you left Earth and everyone that told you no. This is all you." Carla gave her hand a squeeze, and she squeezed back and didn't release. The urge to push was building with every moment and the next contraction came on full force, with a pressure that felt like she would peel back and split around a whole new planet, giving birth to it and leaving behind nothing of herself but space. She cried out, uncertain, hands tightening, grasping, closing again, as she searched for an escape and then in her panic found there was none.

Kendra squeezed her hand and her voice held an empathy that came from experience. "No way but through it now…"

Emily felt herself release and sink into the feeling with a roar as her muscles bore down and her body opened and expanded. She felt the head come down with sudden force and stretch her wider. There was no stopping now, no going back. She reached back and pressed Donovan's hands into her hips, frantic for something to shift and end the pain. A deep burning suffused her stretching tissues and she sucked in a breath, remembering. *Easy now...don't want to tear.*

She reached a trembling hand between her thighs and felt herself stretched tight around the baby's head. It was wrinkled and slick from birthing fluids and she felt soft hair. *It's a baby.* The thought seemed absurd and yet she needed to hear it out loud so she said it, quietly at first and then louder, through fresh tears.

The next contraction brought the baby's head and she kept her hand there, feeling the rounded nose and lips, the ridged fontanels, peaked together from molding, as the baby head turned to face her right thigh.

She whispered it again and again, laughing as the next contraction brought shoulders and the rest of her child slid out into her hands. Emily pulled her up to her chest, tugging at the sides of her shirt until her skin was bare.

Carla came closer, unfolding a birthing cloth, absorbent and soft and covering the ground under Emily so she could sit back onto it. She pushed Emily's sweat-damp hair aside and kissed her forehead, peeking down at the child that hadn't cried beyond one wet squeak and was now staring up into Emily's face with swollen eyelids framing dark grey eyes.

Emily sat back on the cloth padding and leaned into Donovan. He had wrapped his arms around her and nuzzled his face into her neck. "You were perfect. She's perfect."

Emily sighed and lowered her face into her daughter's wet scalp, smelling the sweet tang of amniotic fluid, and then reaching for the blanket Kendra held out for her to drape over them both.

"Shoulda known Carla's granddaughter would give birth on a hike." Kendra was laughing under her breath and shaking her head. "I'd have kept my boots on if I'd known."

Emily grimaced, adjusting herself on the ground to tuck more padding under herself and then moved into a squat instead as the afterbirth came. Kendra slipped the clay dish under her to catch it and set it aside as Emily sat back again.

"Okay, now let's get Theresa to help with the next one. I'm ready for them both. I'm not walking back, though." She closed her eyes and leaned back.

Carla chuckled and directed Donovan to lift Emily and carry her over to the drone that was waiting next to the amphitheater. "No, Em, I think hiking up here in labor was enough. You can ride back. And we'll make Theresa do all the work."

The End

ABOUT THE AUTHOR

An artist of multiple mediums with a myriad of interests, CL Fors is a multipotentialite, mother, author, and adventurer. Refusing to take the conventional route after high school, she moved down to Hollywood to act in films and later joined the US Army as a military intelligence linguist. She now spends her days raising three sons and a daughter while practicing to become a voice actress and working on both writing and watercolor. She and her husband, Jason P. Crawford, founded the indie publishing house Epitome Press, and together bring the work of talented authors out of the brambles and into the light of day.

Crowning of Mars is the third installment of the Primogenitor series, preceded by *Cradles of Mars*, *Breach of Mars*, and followed by *Futures of Mars*.

Follow CL Fors on social media and subscribe to her newsletter for updates.

Facebook: CL Fors
Facebook Page: https://www.facebook.com/cl.fors
Twitter: @CLFors
Subscribe to her newsletter: http://eepurl.com/cidcjX